THIRST OF STEEL

## Books by Ronie Kendig

*The Warrior's Seal (A Tox Files Novella)*

*Conspiracy of Silence*

*Crown of Souls*

*Thirst of Steel*

THE TOX FILES
3

# THIRST OF STEEL

RONIE KENDIG

BETHANY HOUSE
*a division of Baker Publishing Group*
Minneapolis, Minnesota

Published by Bethany House Publishers
11400 Hampshire Avenue South
Bloomington, Minnesota 55438
www.bethanyhouse.com

Bethany House Publishers is a division of
Baker Publishing Group, Grand Rapids, Michigan

Printed in the United States of America



Library of Congress Cataloging-in-Publication Data
Names: Kendig, Ronie, author.
Title: Thirst of steel / Ronie Kendig.
Description: Minneapolis, Minnesota : Bethany House, [2018] | Series: The Tox files ; 3
Identifiers: LCCN 2018002367| ISBN 9780764217678 (trade paper) | ISBN 9781493414758 (e-book) | ISBN 9780764231933 (cloth)
Subjects: | GSAFD: Suspense fiction. | Christian fiction.
Classification: LCC PS3611.E5344 T48 2018 | DDC 813/.6—dc23
LC record available at https://lccn.loc.gov/2018002367

Interlude chapter titles taken from the poem "Goliath of Gath" by Phillis Wheatley.



Cover design by Kirk DouPonce, DogEared Design

Author is represented by The Steve Laube Agency.

18 19 20 21 22 23 24 7 6 5 4 3 2 1

# PROLOGUE

**— VALLEY OF ELAH—1025 BC —**

They were a stench in his nostrils. Bile in his throat. With their strange one God and arrogance, the vermin invaded this land, seized it, ruled it. It was time to make the dogs return to their vomit, to Egypt, where they had eked out an existence they deserved—slaves at the heels of Pharaoh.

"How?" Sibbekai bellowed. "How do we wipe out this blight? We have tried, yet they persist."

Yishbi grunted. "They are like sores on my feet. Annoying, and just when you think they are gone—they return."

"Cut off the foot," Gulat said, his gaze lingering on the flickering campfires of the enemy. Of the king, whose tent and guards seemed entirely too merry. He curled his fingers into a fist.

"Gulat, I have an idea," said a newcomer.

A commotion arose with the voice, drawing Gulat's attention to a man half his size who approached with six or seven others. Not dressed as those of Philistia, the man held his head high. Black hair oiled back. Tunic and breeches clean but worn. Shoulders squared. Chin up.

Gulat frowned. "You have the look of the Arabs."

"And you have the look of an overgrown ox."

Stunned at the bravado tossed around so casually by this man, Gulat studied him. Considered laughing, then considered crushing his throat. "Why do you tempt death coming to me, Arab?"

"We have a common enemy."

"I have many." Gulat narrowed his eyes. "Which would that be?"

"The one splayed before you."

Gulat shifted his gaze to the Hebrews. Laughter and merriment—the very fact they yet breathed enraged him. "We have been unable to deal with this rot. What makes you think you can?"

"I am Mansur. My tribe, my position are of no importance."

"We are agreed," Gulat taunted.

"I bring you a gift." Mansur faced one of his men, who produced a length of black cloth. The Arab unfurled the cloth and lifted something that glinted in the firelight. With the help of the other man, he aimed it at Gulat.

"This is the Adama Herev." He waited until Gulat took the blade.

Gulat shifted, feeling the implication tease the edges of his mind. The steel felt . . . significant. "What do you want, Arab?"

"If you please," Mansur said as he settled his hand beneath the bronze scrollwork. He gripped the hilt, twisted, and slid it. With a crack, it came free. He held the gold scrollwork up to the firelight. "This contains a very thin duct that feeds directly"—he traced the center of the sword—"from the blood groove."

Gulat imagined—ached—for the blood of the Hebrews to fill that groove.

"You wish to be rid of the Hebrews, yes?" Mansur hefted the piece, then reassembled it with the steel blade. "This will do that. Kill a Hebrew with this sword, and it will enslave their race for all time. They will die in droves. Those who survive will beg at your heels."

"You cursed the sword?" Yishbi asked, shock in his words.

"Is it so hard to believe?" Mansur asked, challenging Gulat's brother.

Emboldened, Gulat reached again for the sword. Tested its weight. Held it out. Dawn peeked over the hill, spilling its first glint along the edge of the steel. "Good balance, though the scrollwork is lighter and goes unnoticed."

"Once it carries the blood of your enemies, it will not be light."

Gulat admired the steel. The scrollwork. "It would seem that we must slake this sword." He grinned at his brothers. Then laughed. "Bring my armor! The steel thirsts!"

# 1

**— LONDON, ENGLAND —**

*The old man trembled as he heard, but bade his followers yoke the horses, and they made all haste to do so. He mounted the chariot, gathered the reins in his hand, and Antenor took his seat beside him; they then drove through the Scaean gates on to the plain. When they reached the ranks of the Trojans and Achaeans, they left the chariot and with measured pace advanced into the space between the hosts.*

Beside Joseph Cathey, the air stirred, and he released a long, grieved breath. "Could you not come during a less daunting part?" he muttered as he tugged down his reading glasses and looked up at his visitor. "And has anyone mentioned to you that it is impolite to appear twenty years younger than a man you outnumber by centuries?"

Ti Tzaddik grinned. "You are too easily riled, old friend."

"*Old?* Speak for yourself." Joseph tapped his book with a glower. "I should make like the son of Atreus: 'As he spoke he drew his knife across the throats of the victims.'"

"Good thing there are no victims here."

Joseph grumbled, setting aside his tattered copy of the *Iliad*. "Since you are not prone to coincidence . . ." He sighed and looked at the old text. Sensed the heaviness of the one who had joined him without so much as a rap at the door or even opening one. "I guess there is work to be done. The final work."

"Are you ready, Joseph?"

Joseph glanced down at the book. "They 'were too old to fight, but they were fluent orators.'"

"I'm afraid I am neither an orator nor too old. You must go to the Americans. Our enemies have hastened the search for the sword and set your apprentice on its path."

"Tzivia?" Joseph blanched. "How have they . . ." He groaned. "Her father."

"Aye. She must not return it to them, old friend. You know the consequences."

Joseph grunted, looking at the bookshelf. "That I do. But unless you are aware of things I am not, the final piece remains unaccounted for."

"That has not changed, but neither will I discount our enemy's fervency this time. You *know* what hour draws nigh, and the way the air buzzes . . ." Tzaddik shook his head and rubbed the back of his neck. "I have not felt this in a very long time."

"Nor I."

Tzaddik stiffened. "We must meet their efforts head on. Go to them. Have them search for the sword."

"How?" Joseph complained. "They are rigid in their thinking. If there is no crime, if there is no activity—"

"There is. When you go, they will know it."

With a labored sigh, Joseph watched his friend rise, and with him went his blood pressure. "You're not going to tell me more than that, are you? Always with the mysteries."

"I trust you to sort it out. If I show it all to you—"

"Yes, yes." Joseph waved a hand. "Importance is lost and all that." He couldn't believe he was stepping into this again. But what did he expect? "Am I going to survive this one?"

"Were this battle about you, perhaps I would offer assurance, but as the battle is Gulat's blade and ensuring the assassins do not rise again, I can only give one promise."

Eyebrows lifted, Joseph looked at him expectantly. "Not especially reassuring, that. Go on."

"'Death and destruction shall be theirs . . .'"

Joseph laughed. "Idomeneus." He nodded. "You chose well, old friend. He is one of the few alive at the end of the story."

"Why do you think I quoted him?"

* * * *

**— MOSCOW, RUSSIA —**

Deserving to die and wanting to die were two entirely different things. A greater desire—to live!—propelled her down the dirty streets of Moscow. Shoes slapping the pavement, she bolted from an alley into the dark, yawning emptiness of a street. Sprinted toward a narrow passage.

From the shadows, a form coalesced. His shape was distinctive. Though there were no lights, she saw him. Knew him. Remembered his hands around Nadia's neck.

Tzivia Khalon skidded to a stop, her feet sliding out from under her. She fought for purchase, using a wall to shove away from him.

"*Ostanovis*!" he shouted.

Ha. Right. She wasn't stopping. Not for anyone, especially the guy who'd just murdered the only friend she had in this godforsaken country. Tzivia threw herself around and sighted her exit. Lunged.

Three men manifested from the void. Tall buildings on all sides had her surrounded.

Darting right, she pulled in a hard breath. Walls hemmed in her front. Men behind.

Trapped.

She cursed her carelessness, her desperation, as she scanned for an exit. A gutter. Fence. Fire escape. Anything! Yet the night closed in, drawing the men and her death near.

Nerves thrumming, she swung around. Faced the converging four. They arced out in a solid mass of muscle and threat that prevented her from escaping.

It wasn't in her nature to give up. Still, four to one . . . "Not exactly a fair fight," she muttered, gauging her opponents. Three average-sized men. One a little taller than her brother, Ram, but shorter than

Tox Russell. Beefier than both. Beneath his jacket bulged the imprint of a weapon.

Yet he hadn't drawn it.

*So you aren't here to kill me. Good to know.* Their orders must be to leash and retrieve, the way one might a stray dog. Drag her back to their alpha.

The biggest man stalked closer. When he came into the wan light of a streetlamp, he hesitated. Darted a look up, as if the beam seared his dark soul. The illumination had an eerie effect, tracing thick, calloused fingers that danced in his eagerness to kill.

Time to plan. First she had to get the giant to her left talking. Force him to engage his brain by asking him a question, which would give her a one-tenth of a second head start. As soon as his mouth opened to answer, she'd lunge. Wicked-fast kick to the groin.

He'd bend, protecting the family jewels, bringing him down to size. She'd close the distance and drive two sharp elbow strikes to his temple. If that didn't take him down, it would at least stun him. Then she'd use her blade. End him. She hated the thought, but he'd spared no mercy with Nadia, and she could not risk being captured.

During his takedown, a task of two to three seconds, the others would be so stunned at the flurry of violence she unleashed on their leader that it would lengthen their reaction time. Thereby giving her the necessary edge.

The stench of rotting waste swept her nostrils, awakening her. Alerting her to movement. They were advancing.

*Ready or not . . .* Tzivia kept her hands at her side, loose. Comfortable. Trying to give them false confidence, she skated around a nervous look. "What do you want?" she shouted in Russian, making her voice pitch.

The giant drew up his chin. Eyed her lazily. "*Ty malen'kiy—*"

Tzivia surged. Snapped a hard front kick between his legs. The giant doubled and groaned.

Sliding in closer, she twisted her torso. Drew up her left arm. Rammed her elbow into his temple with a shout. "Hiya!" Again. "Hiya!" Her shout was psychological. Her blows physical. Nailing him on two fronts.

Moaning, he stumbled, his faculties compromised.

As the giant wobbled to the ground, another fist flew. The strike collided with her cheekbone.

Jarred, Tzivia grabbed the forearm. Twisted it as she caught the back of the attacker's neck. Hooked him around, forcing him to kneel, spine against her knees. She arched his arm up over his head. Even as he howled at the pain of the maneuver, a third man came out of his stupor. Started at her.

Holding tight to her prisoner, Tzivia drove her heel into Third's face. Knocked him around. He face-planted. She focused on Two, tangled in her firm grasp. He was reaching for something. No doubt a gun.

Hauling his arm higher, Tzivia realized time was her enemy.

The pistol came up.

She whipped out her KA-BAR. Drove it into his neck. In a flash, she sheathed the knife, snatched the gun from his limp hand, and spun to the others—Three and Four were gauging her. Staring down the barrel as the slack-jawed men shook themselves gave her time to gather her own wits. She dared them to come. She'd had enough. All she wanted was to save her father. Was it so much to ask?

Three bolted back down the alley.

Four went right.

Tzivia pivoted. Aimed at Three and fired. The suppressed crack wasn't silent but close enough. He tripped yet struggled on. She sighted lower, where he lay scrambling on the ground, and fired again. He slumped flat.

Feet beat a hard path away from her—to the right. The fourth man. She whirled. Darkness warred with her need to protect herself.

A shape blurred at her. Unprepared, Tzivia took the impact in her side. Pain exploded, but she shoved it away. Focused on her attacker, the giant. Furious, she shifted her stance. Glowered beneath a sweaty brow. Threw a right hook straight into his liver to inflict a shockwave of fiery agony.

A gargled scream preceded his fall. But he staggered back to his feet.

She sliced her knife-hand at his throat. He clutched his neck as he went down, gasping. Dying.

But only as she staggered back did the rage of adrenaline surrender to a searing, unrelenting pain. She glanced at her side. Dark crimson spurted from a wound just above her hip. She flicked her gaze to the giant, to the bloody knife dangling from his hand. Stunned that he had stabbed her when she'd nailed his throat.

Gripping her injury, she stood in the alley, sensing the oncoming adrenaline dump that would weight her body in exhaustion. Her limbs felt rubbery. Shuddering through a breath, Tzivia swiped a hand across her sweaty brow. She needed help. Needed . . .

Omar.

A deep, empty ache rose within her. She closed her eyes. Reached for him, for someone. Anyone. For comfort. Reassurance. But she was alone. As it had been for the past six months. Since she'd forsaken everything to seize a tip breathed in passion.

A scream jolted her back to the present. A woman stumbled toward the man Tzivia had shot first. Fists in the air, she railed at Tzivia.

The distant bells of the Cathedral of Christ the Savior gonged their summons. Signaled that her time was up.

"No," she whispered. Tzivia's heart kick-started. It would take at least ten minutes to reach the cathedral. She'd already missed the appointment. But he'd wait. He had to. Because she had what he wanted.

Tzivia made for the alley Four had fled down. Slipping the gun into her waistband at the small of her back, she shifted into a jog. Pain pinched her side. Each step spilled warmth down her hip, saturating her pants. The alley emptied into a tight passage that skimmed her shoulders and dumped her onto a well-lit road, wet from a fresh rain. A trolley clanged past.

Minarets with white plaster bell towers gleamed over rooftops and served as a beacon. At this late hour, few walked the dark streets. Tzivia hung back, scanning for Four. Heavy air threatened more rain, but she forbade it until she reached the cathedral. She skirted buildings, staying close to walls and shadows, then broke into a run, grimacing at the fresh squeeze of pain. Cursing the man who'd stabbed her, she wondered how she'd missed his knife. Hadn't even seen it coming.

*Curse yourself.* She'd brought it on herself, coming here, believing she could actually do this alone. But she hadn't wanted to hear

Ram's remonstrations. Didn't want him clobbering her ears with his chastisements, telling her to let it go. That they must accept the truth—their father was dead.

That was what everyone had thought of Tox Russell for four years. Turned out he wasn't dead. She was now very close to proving her father wasn't either.

*"Fool's hope," Ram growled.*

*Then I will be a fool!* Because she could not give up on this, not when Omar relinquished the secret of this city's name in his sleep. Even as a girl, she hadn't believed her father was dead. There was no proof, just the ardent—albeit naïve—hope of a daughter to see her father again. Over the years, that hope had bloomed into stubborn determination that he was alive.

The tower grew as she closed the distance, until finally the glittering white cathedral glared at her. The cobbled footbridge summoned her across the Moscow River and into the sanctuary.

With relief, she started forward, aware of her surroundings. Cars and trams added to the noise of the city scampering around the luxurious site. By this time most tourists were gone. Crossing the footbridge with its evenly spaced lamps made Tzivia feel exposed. Surely they wouldn't attack here on the cathedral steps.

Illumination grew, as did her hopes that he still waited. She eyed the two men in long black trench coats waiting just inside the wrought-iron fence—more confirmation that her contact was still here.

It wasn't a sanctuary, not for her. This was where she'd sell her soul to Nur Abidaoud.

Bolstering her courage, she crossed the open courtyard filled with people who'd come for the midnight mass. The guards chatted quietly, each drag of their cigarettes lighting their faces. Fierce. Discerning. Both straightened, locking onto her and dropping their cigarettes. Weapons bulged at their sides, but they didn't reach for them. Or stop her.

Tzivia swallowed as she climbed the steps, the wet squish of her pants seeming to echo in the strangely quiet area.

*Too quiet*. Quickly, she stepped inside. She wobbled, taken aback by the enormity of the cathedral and its lavish, brightly colored stained glass. She might not understand religious fervor, but she could appreciate the beauty of cathedrals. Just as she had reveled in the beauty of archaeological finds. Like the one she'd hidden before this fateful errand.

The ominous drone of voices filtered from the main altar, where—like cultists chanting in unison—the churchgoers offered prayers to the white arches, gilt ceilings, and massive murals.

She walked the corridor to the cordoned-off area where worshipers peered over their shoulders at her, brows knotting. What were they looking at?

A fresh squish of her pants made her check the wound. She was relieved to find the black tactical pants concealed the blood sliding down her leg, but she was probably leaving a trail. *Smart, Tzi. So smart.*

Curling her elbow over the stab wound, she kept her gaze low, searching for Nur. There, on the far right. Moving toward her target, she continued down the next aisle, then shimmied to his side, gaze on the priest directing young men in robes. With a breath, she clasped her hands.

"You are late."

Teeth clenched, she kept her face impassive. "I'm here."

"You have it?" he asked as the believers chanted in Latin.

"Would I be here if I didn't?" she hissed, cringing as she thought of the man she toyed with.

"Where is it?"

"You will not get it until I get what I want—my father. Alive."

# 2

— MOSCOW, RUSSIA —

Needle in the proverbial haystack.

With a huff, Ram Khalon slumped back and stared at the papers littering his desk. His gaze tracked the makeshift data wall, notes, and pages to an oversized map of the Tverskoy District. Blurry images of possible sightings, intel reports, HUMINT provided by assets on the ground.

Moscow was home to over twelve million people all trying to eke out an existence, trying to survive. And he had to find one person. One who didn't want to be found. One who had as much training as he did in evasive tactics.

*Where are you, Tzi?*

A beep from the smaller computer yanked him forward. The system culled images from local surveillance cameras he'd piggybacked, then processed them through facial recognition software to narrow the possibilities. When a potential match for Tzivia registered, the system sent him a copy while analyzing build, weight, and height to determine the probability it was her. He stared at the blinking icon, awaiting the result.

A telltale thump at this temples made him aware of the time. He glanced at his watch. *Not yet. Another hour.* Pinching the bridge of his nose, Ram wished to rid himself of the headache. Both the one stemming from finding his sister and the one that had encompassed his life since she went rogue.

The computer dinged again, and a grainy image appeared. He groaned at the poor quality, annoyed that Russia could be so advanced in covert operations but so desperately lacking in many other respects, including the safety of its citizens. He traced the outline of the face—maybe. A little narrower than Tzivia's oval shape. Nose seemed right, though.

A grid appeared over the image, measuring as the computer cleaned up the pixels. Lines flashed red. Words appeared: *Match improbable. Subject height off by 3.5 inches.*

Ram cursed. Ripped off his beanie and pitched it across the flat. He shoved up from the table and paced before the floor-to-ceiling window. She'd always trusted him—until he'd joined Tox's team more than two years ago. Trouble was, she'd been smitten with Tox, and perhaps his friend's disregard for her and subsequent falling in love with Haven Cortes had pushed Tzivia over the edge.

No. Ram wouldn't lay that blame at Tox's feet. The war, the storm within Tzivia, had been brewing longer than that. Much longer. And Tox was one of the truest, most loyal friends he'd ever had. Ram trusted him with this mission. A risk that put Tox in danger. A problem Ram hated himself for.

But Tzivia had never gone completely dark like this before. No word. Not even on their encrypted chat room she'd set up nearly a decade past, when her journey into paranoia grew to a fevered pitch. She'd abandoned it years later but never took it down. Now Ram monitored it closely. Anything—a word, a hint.

It was too familiar. Too painful. So much like the day his father walked out the door and never returned. The whispered words of a phone call. "It was worth the cost. They don't need to know." The conviction that had, over the years, festered into a deep-rooted belief that his father was not dead, though his mother had him declared as such. That his father had left them. Abandoned his family. Children. Why? Ram couldn't fathom. But the belief felt more like fact than theory to him now. And he hated his father for it.

Ram refused to go down that path with his sister. He'd find her. Stop her.

He stalked to the kitchenette and poured a glass of water. Glanced back at the litter across his desk. Sipped water as he skimmed the data wall again. She was in there. Somewhere. He slammed the glass down and went to the window, skin crawling with the futility of this hunt.

*Where the devil are you?*

Russia's largest cities afforded plenty of anonymity for her to move about undetected, and this residential building provided him the best view, though he wasn't fooling himself. No flat had a big enough view.

His phone rang. Ram picked it up and checked the screen, then tensed. Tightening his thin hold on his temper, he answered. "What?"

"Is that how you greet—"

"I'm late, Kastan. What do you want?"

"You are not late," the intelligence agent spat. "And you would do well to remember who your superiors are, Ram."

"I'll remember that, *sir*, along with the reason my sister is missing and who is responsible." Ram's pulse thumped angrily through his veins. "As well as a certain man's inability to protect government secrets when he shares a woman's bed."

"I have something you need to see," Omar Kastan said, ignoring the chastisement. "After the meeting with your asset."

The call ended just as Ram was ready to crawl through the connection and punch Omar. He fisted a hand. It was Omar who'd slipped the name Moscow to Tzivia. The intelligence director had taken advantage of her vulnerability, her desperation to learn more about their father's death, and turned it against her, thinking he had it under control.

Any man who thought he had Tzivia under control deserved whatever happened.

Ram grabbed his coat and beanie, then left after programming the exit protocols. The twenty-minute drive put enough distance between him and the flat for protection. Today it served to calm him down.

It wasn't like him to be this angry, this quick. That was more like Tox. But knowing Tzivia was out there, tangling with the wrong people . . . Every day felt too late to save her.

He pulled into a parking spot and climbed out. Ram set a brisk pace through the plaza, taking in the fountain, the shops. The flower vendor. A family of tourists taking selfies by the dancing water. He shook his head and entered the coffee shop.

"The usual?" the male barista asked as Ram approached the counter.

"*Pozhaluysta*," Ram said with a nod. The Russian variant of *please* expressed both the request and gratitude. He grabbed his wallet and handed over some colorful notes. "*Spasibo*." After his thanks, he took a table at the back of the café and waited for his drink.

His thoughts rammed each other, still angry over Kastan's call. The way that man ordered Ram around without an ounce of penitence or apology. Did he have no care or concern for Tzivia? For what his mistake could cost her?

Once his coffee and sandwich arrived, Ram checked his watch. Scanned the café. The crowded location accommodated a covert meeting. Couples occupied window tables, peering out at the fountain. Other patrons were oblivious to anything but their smartphones. Business professionals huddled in the middle with terse conversations and laptops. A woman sat hugging herself, watching children splash in the fountain. She seemed sad, contemplative. At the table ahead, a man in a trench coat sipped black coffee. His crooked nose hooked the cup as he read a book. Beyond him, an American family had pulled together two tables, the parents replete with dark circles under their eyes and frazzled hair.

Ram scanned the newspaper, then gave his watch one final glance. With an annoyed huff, he picked up the paper and made his way across the café. The man in the trench coat was on his phone now, arguing with someone. His deep voice thickened the Russian spewing out of his mouth.

Stopping by the table, Ram offered the paper. "A waste if I toss it," he said, his Russian perfect.

The man scowled. His gaze snapped back to the table as he stabbed a finger against its surface, growling, "*Nyet, nyet! Poslushay menya—*"

Ram shook the paper. "Want it?"

Attention divided, the man snatched the newspaper as he shoved to his feet. "*Poslushay menya*," he repeated, towering several inches over Ram. He swept around him without a word. "*Vy pozhaleyete ob etom*," he growled, promising whomever he was talking to that they would regret something.

With a smirk, Ram shook his head. "*Proschay*," he muttered in farewell, watching the man stalk across the courtyard, narrowly avoiding a collision with a toddler. He snapped open the paper, still barking into the phone. He straightened at something the person on the other end of the call said, then flung the paper in a trash bin.

"Some people are so ungrateful," the lone woman said to Ram.

"Indeed." He shrugged and left the café.

* * * *

Kazimir Rybakov stalked into Mattin Worldwide, annoyed. He provided his badge for the security station, emptied his pockets, and passed through the scanner.

"Welcome back, Mr. Rybakov," the security officer said. "Feeling better?"

"*Da*," Kazimir grunted as he lifted his things from the small tray.

"That accident," the officer said with a shake of his head. "We thought you were dead."

"*Ty ne yedinstvennyy*." In fact, the officer wasn't the only one—even the doctors had given up on Kazimir Rybakov, declared him dead.

"Miraculous recovery," the guard said.

"Except the scars."

Though the officer grimaced at the telltale pink ridges marring Kazimir's face and neck, he shrugged. "You are alive."

"So I am," Kazimir agreed. "But now if I am late, perhaps I will not be."

The officer nodded. "True."

"*Spasibo*." After taking back his badge, Kazimir entered the private elevator and rode to the fifteenth floor. There, he hurried to the door at the end of the hall. One more swipe of his badge ushered him into the security center.

"You're late," Yefim Popov groused, twisting his chair around. He had never been a fan of Kazimir.

"I had fifteen minutes left—"

"You have *nothing* when Mr. Abidaoud demands you."

Demands? There had been no demands. Slowing, Kazimir let his gaze drift to Yefim. "Mr.—"

"*Da*." Yefim gave a long sigh. "Why he would want you, I do not know. Do not be thinking they are moving you to the twenty-seventh floor. You are mine, Rybakov."

Gaze rising to the ceiling, Kazimir imagined the penthouse level that held both the founder's office and his private residence. The infamous twenty-seventh floor housed the board of directors and the upper echelon of security officers, including their boss, Igor.

Not good. "Why? Is he angry over the time I have missed in recovery? I have not missed a day since I returned." Kazimir touched the scars. "Do you think it is because . . ."

Another shrug. "Maybe this is a free ride down the Yauza."

A chorus of dark laughter filtered through the security center. A ride down the Yauza was a reference to killings where bodies were dumped in the river. It hadn't taken him long, immersed in this office and working security for one of the largest corporations in the world, to discover what that code meant.

"Here." The burly man held out a secure-access card. The golden ticket to the penthouse. He flicked his fingers at Kazimir. "Now go. You *are* late. And he will be angry."

Nervous, Kazimir clipped his badge to his lapel and accessed the private elevator. The mirrored doors slid closed, revealing a man even he barely recognized. Sandy-blond hair curled along his collar. He might need to see a barber. The scars were unsightly, but what could be expected when a car accident rearranged your face and left you for dead?

The elevator slowed, then hesitated.

Kazimir skated a look around the box. Numbers above. Camera in the corner. *C'mon, Yefim. Don't be a jerk.* The security chief was no doubt monitoring his progress all the way to the private offices, where the feed would give way to seclusion. Seconds fell off the clock. Kazimir rejected the jitters demanding attention. This was it. This summons could decide his future.

The doors glided open. Marble gleamed its welcome as he stepped out and took in the area, which felt more like the grand entrance of a hotel than an office. Luxurious furnishings lined the ten-by-thirty foyer. Chandeliers glittered at ten-foot intervals. Four sets of heavy oak doors broke up Venetian plastered walls. An enormous painting hung over an ornate fireplace.

Rich, velvety curtains framed the dark painting, luring Kazimir closer to admire the piece. The terse brow of the central figure grabbed his attention, with its reddish-gold hair and large conflicted eyes. The near-black background forced the eye to the two soldiers flanking the young man at the front—and gradually allowed Kazimir's focus to drift to the decapitated head on the table. Despite the conquistador garb the two soldiers wore, the scene could be none other than the biblical story of Goliath slain by David, who held a sword in his left hand. The gold plate mounted on the wall read: *David with the Head of Goliath—Valentin de Boulogne*. The world over knew that story, yet it seemed out of place here in a shipping conglomerate's private offices. What a macabre—

Terse, frantic words drifted from the corner office.

"You are sure?" one man said in a thick German accent.

"Most certain," said another.

"Then do we confront her?"

Angling his ear that way, Kazimir drew closer, listening. Feigning interest in another art piece, this one smaller and less significant, if placement in the grand hall was any indication. His mind caught up with what he was looking at, and his gut tightened. Another painting of David with the head of the Philistine and the sword. And on a nearby pedestal, a bronze sculpture of David thrusting the sword into a cowering Goliath. Strange obsession.

Adjusting position slightly, Kazimir caught sight of his boss, Igor Polzin, facing a massive dark-wood desk as he conversed with someone. Though only his shoulder could be seen from the door, the other man must be Nur Abidaoud, CEO of Mattin. Who was the third person?

"No, we still need too much," Abidaoud said. "Keep your eye on this. Make sure there are no more missteps. We can't keep cleaning up dead bodies in alleys."

"Of course," Polzin said with a curt nod. His boss had never looked so disheveled or . . . submissive. Interesting.

"If you will trust us with this, we can resolve the problem." The third voice again. One Kazimir did not recognize. "Come with me. A short trip, but I can give you the proof you seek."

Needing a better view, Kazimir shifted his gaze—and struck intense eyes.

The penetrating gaze focused on Kaz. Nur Abidaoud had a powerful presence that commanded submission. "You are finally here."

Snapping straight, Kazimir inclined his head. "Sir."

Eyes dark and forbidding belied the smile on Nur's weathered face. Black hair combed back from the brow and stabbed through with silver. With a flick of his hand, Abidaoud motioned Kazimir into the private office.

As Kazimir eased through the door, he spotted the third man standing to the side, hands threaded before him.

"This is Frans Stroebel," Abidaoud informed Kaz.

Kazimir gave no reply and wasn't really even sure why his employer had bothered to introduce him.

"You know him?" Abidaoud asked.

Kazimir glanced at the German again. "No, sir."

Moving around his desk, Abidaoud rubbed his neatly trimmed beard and hiked up a leg as he leaned against the desk. "Your accident, Mr. Rybakov," he began, homing those probing eyes in on Kazimir. "You nearly died."

Here it was, then. Kazimir nodded.

"Tell me of it."

Confusion poked at his confidence. He dared not question why this was important. "On my way home from dinner with my family, I was broadsided. My car flipped several times."

Abidaoud narrowed his eyes. "The police report said you were thrown from your vehicle and through a plate-glass window."

"Yes, sir."

"And you lived."

"Guess the demons weren't finished yet."

"But your family . . ."

Kazimir twitched. Steeled himself. "Being ejected saved me from the explosion that killed them."

"Indeed," Abidaoud said somberly. "And your skills as a security specialist, they are preserved?"

"They are."

"Prove it."

A test. Warm dread slid through Kazimir. If he failed, he would die. It would not be the first time Abidaoud had shot down a security officer in this suite.

"I have made you nervous," Abidaoud muttered, disappointment shadowing his expression. He returned to the other side of his desk. "I have no need for damaged employees. While you have my sympathies for the loss of your wife and daughter, if you are too affected by the accident to perform—"

"I would caution you against going with Stroebel . . . anywhere." Kazimir kept his gaze impassive. "Sir."

Abidaoud frowned. Glanced at the German. "What do you mean?"

"How dare you!" Stroebel growled, hands coming from his pockets.

"Explain yourself," Abidaoud demanded. "How did you know I—"

"Observation." Kazimir steeled his spine. He had to establish himself as an asset. "A security officer must be aware of what happens, of minute details that betray what is out of sight."

"Rybakov, do you realize what you are saying? Absurd!" Polzin growled.

"Quiet, Igor." Abidaoud's features calmed, but a dangerous glint lingered. "Go on, Rybakov. You don't seem the careless type, so explain."

Rolling his shoulders, Kazimir knew he'd either walk out of this office or get carried out—in a body bag. "Mr. Stroebel's suit is exquisite. In fact, I believe it's your preferred designer, Mr. Abidaoud."

"What does it matter that we have the same taste in fashion?" The German blanched. "Why would I—"

Rybakov spared him a glance, then turned back to Abidaoud, who slid a long look over what Stroebel wore. "It's to distract you, sir."

Abidaoud's lips parted beneath his beard. Wariness crept into his face. "From what?"

"From the fact that it hangs loose on bony shoulders and a half inch too low on his shoes. But the greater task of the ill-fitting suit is to conceal the bulge beneath his left arm."

The German shifted, came alive.

Kazimir slid in, catching the German's wrist, twisting it up and back. Slipped his hand down the man's wrist and covered the finger in the trigger well. Drove the weapon back to the man's stomach. Squeezed.

*Thwat!*

# 3

## — FAIRFAX COUNTY, VIRGINIA —

Exiting the 267 tollway and heading west on Route 7 relieved none of the traffic congestion, yet it was the quickest route to suburban Wolf Trap, Virginia.

Assistant Special Agent in Charge Levi Wallace spent another ten minutes navigating the cramped but beautiful suburb of Northern Virginia roughly thirty minutes outside DC. When he arrived at his destination, six or seven agency vehicles already crowded the small street that boasted homes in the million-plus range. He climbed out and strode down the tree-lined sidewalk, wishing he could afford a place here.

"'Bout time you showed up to do some work." Santi Greco fell into step with him.

Levi passed the cluster of reporters without acknowledging them. "If they'd do something about the traffic . . ."

"That's like expecting another virgin birth," Santi said.

Flowers and perfectly trimmed hedges lined the path to the front entrance. Double doors of wood and glass with an inlaid star sparkled with early afternoon light. Sunlight threw a glare across the marble floor, despite the law enforcement officers huddled there.

Levi nodded to the LEOs and agents at the door.

"ASAC Wallace," one greeted. "SAC Parker is waiting in the living room."

"Thanks."

The air-conditioned home cooled Levi as he let his gaze skim the interior. Marble went eight to ten feet in before crashing into carpet. Furniture in various neutral shades amplified the spacious feel of the front room. Through a molded arch stood more suits and LEOs in a back room with a large, ceiling-to-floor stone fireplace.

Lee Parker lifted his gaze and a hand to Levi, then met him halfway.

"What do we know?" Levi asked.

Parker tugged him toward a folding table, where a woman stood switching camera lenses. Dark hair hung in a loose braid around her shoulder, and for some reason, she seemed oddly out of place.

Levi shifted back to his boss. "Is it—"

"If you'll excuse us," Parker said to the woman, then waited for her to leave. He turned to Levi. "It's bloody. Gruesome. Never seen anything like it. There are chemical burns throughout—well, whatever wasn't liquefied."

"*Liquefied?*" Levi nearly choked, his gaze traveling to the garage. "How?"

"All we have are guesses right now. There's no apparent weapon, just a large puncture wound in the chest."

Crazy. "Let me check the scene, then we can talk."

"Hey." Lee jutted his jaw. "How's Cortes doing?"

"Fine." Levi started toward the four-bay garage. Of course, for him to know for sure, he would've had to talk to her recently. But he hadn't. He'd taken the hint to move on when she showed up wearing Tox's engagement ring. In fact, he'd severed ties with the special activities team as well. No need to be involved in their crazy stuff.

The acrid odor of burnt hair and flesh seared his nostrils as Levi skirted the crowd of uniforms and suits. It took him a second to spot Santi, who squatted beside the crime scene photographer. There was something distracting about her.

She turned brown eyes to Levi, which drew him across the room. Her smile hesitated, then slipped as she considered her camera, then snapped a photo of the body.

The victim lay sprawled on the floor. Extremities were . . . melted. Eyes gone. Earlobes missing.

Disgust tightened Levi's chest. *Millionaire bites the dust in a seriously heinous murder.* But why?

Santi ambled up with a folder. "George Schenck. Fifty-three. Married five years to second wife, Lucille. Two adult kids from first marriage. None living in the area." He sighed and flipped a page. "Came home before a flight out of Dulles to New York for a client meeting."

"What about the neighbors?"

"Thirty-eight-year-old woman walking her dog saw Schenck come home but nothing else."

Levi's gaze struck the small black dome mounted in the corner by the door to the house. "Security company?"

"Crenshaw's on the phone with them now," Santi said, nodding to a bald guy in the dining room. "Thinking we should head over there."

"Agreed." But Levi's mind had collapsed on the ground by the victim. That was a vicious way to die.

"You okay?" a concerned voice asked from behind. Levi turned.

An agent touched the shoulder of the crime scene photographer, who looked up, revealing an unnatural pallor to her face. "Just need some air."

Santi moved to her side. "C'mon. I'll walk you out."

Levi eyed them as they left the garage, then turned back to the body. To the—

A shadow swept over the garage, him, and the body—the sun had been blocked. Levi saw something in the dimness. His heart skipped a beat. He glanced back to the driveway, where LEOs hovered as the crime scene team worked.

Levi stared at the body. "Son of . . ." Couldn't be.

"What?" Parker was there, anticipation in his voice and eyes.

"There's . . . something." Levi pointed to the guys near the control panel. "Hey, hit the button to close the garage door." When the suit straightened and looked at him, hand hovering over the panel, Levi nodded. "Yeah."

"Back up, everyone," Parker said. "Clear for the door."

As darkness descended, leaving only the wan light of the control mechanism, a hue emanated around the corpse. Dread churned in Levi's gut.

"What the . . ." Parker crouched, squinting at the body.

"Is it *glowing*?" Santi asked.

"Yeah." Levi didn't want to admit that. Didn't want to go where his brain was dragging him. Right into the past. Into a fight with a lethal organization. It meant he'd have to make a call. Violate his vow to move on and not work with them.

But why wasn't there an arrow?

"You have an idea?" Parker eyed him over the necrotic body.

"Yeah." If Levi was right, there should be an arrow. So maybe he was wrong. He'd happily be wrong this time. "I need to make some calls."

"SAARC?"

"Afraid so."

* * * *

**— WASHINGTON, DC —**

"Well, that was a bust." Shoving her hair from her face, Haven Cortes slumped behind the steering wheel of her Audi Q7 and glanced at Chijioke Okorie in the passenger seat.

Reassurance covered Chiji's consistently calm demeanor. "We will find the answers."

"I hope you're right. I can't let go of what Tzaddik said on that moun—"

VVolt thrust his head up between the two seats, swiping his slick tongue along her face.

"Ugh," she said with a laughing groan as the Belgian Malinois panted excitedly and laid another wet one on her jaw this time.

VVolt loved visiting new places and sniffing every nook and cranny. She'd gone to great lengths training with him so he could retain his working-dog certification. Of course, it helped that her brother-in-law was the president of the United States, but she hated pulling those strings.

Today they'd ventured to the historical society to research Cole's genealogy. After that bizarre yet amazing encounter with Tzaddik on Catoctin Mountain, she'd been anxious to get answers, especially since Cole was off saving the world again.

"We are looking," Chiji said with a firm nod. "That is the best place to begin."

"I suppose." Haven wrinkled her nose as she pulled into traffic. "But I prefer starting with answers."

Chiji laughed, a nice deep rumble that made her relax.

Her phone rang, and she grabbed it, grateful for the red light so she wasn't a distracted driver. "Levi. Long time since we talked."

"Yeah. Sorry. Been busy."

Which sounded a lot like *I'm avoiding you.*

"Listen," he said, his voice weighted, "I think you should see something."

Haven frowned, glancing at the still-red light. "Okay."

"You busy?"

"Just left a museum. Going to grab lunch, and later we have a training session with a handler to help me with VVolt." When she said his name, the telltale squeak of his nails on the leather seat caught her ear.

"I could use your help. Have a minute?"

"Um, sure. You want me there now?"

"It's . . . yeah, you should come now."

She glanced at the six-five Nigerian beside her. "Chiji's with me."

"Not a problem," Levi said. "Just let the officer on scene know I called you in."

Haven started. "A *crime* scene?"

"You'll understand when you get here. Got a pen?"

"I'm driving. No." She eyed Chiji, who nodded his understanding. "Give it to Chiji. Here."

Once he'd recorded the address, Chiji hung up and returned her phone. "This does not sound good. Are you up to this? I thought you were tired."

For years Chiji had been Cole's conscience, and with Cole gone, he'd become hers. Or perhaps *bodyguard* was more accurate, in her case. It was a sweet, if unnecessary, gesture, considering VVolt's protective instincts and thousand-pound-per-square-inch bite, but she enjoyed Chiji's company.

"If you need to rest—"

"I do. I feel like I could sleep for a month!" She took the Route 7 exit. "But Levi has avoided me since Cole and I got engaged, so whatever this is about, it's big."

"Ndidi would not like you going to this man now, while he is gone."

The innuendo about appearances was clear. And she appreciated that. "Cole trusts me. Besides," Haven said with a smile, "I have you and a working dog with aggression training, and I'm not sure which of you has the worse bite when it comes to protecting those in your charge."

Chiji didn't smile.

It took them twenty-two minutes to arrive at the address of the crime scene. They couldn't get any closer with her crossover, so they climbed out. Since the temperature was edging to the upper seventies, they brought VVolt rather than leaving him in the vehicle where he could overheat.

An officer approached with an upheld hand.

Haven pulled out her credentials. "Assistant Special Agent in Charge Wallace asked me to come, and this is my partner Chijioke Okorie."

"Just a minute." The officer keyed his mic, repeating the information. When his radio squawked, he motioned her through. Strolling down the street, she couldn't help but notice the general mood—heavy. An ominous silence hung over the crowded area. Officers leaned against vehicles. Those talking did so in quiet tones.

Levi's distinctive frame emerged from a huddle of suits. He met her gaze but didn't smile, which made her tense as he stalked toward them. "Thanks for coming." After shaking hands with Chiji, he gave VVolt a glance and swallowed. Hands on his belt and sleeves rolled up, he had clearly been working this scene for a while.

Haven shifted. "You okay, Levi?"

Somber blue eyes met hers. "It's not pretty." He looked at Chiji. "Stay close."

What did that mean? She glanced between the men as she tightened her hold on VVolt's lead. A double-click of her tongue had the six-year-old Belgian Malinois shouldering into her leg, a sign of both situational awareness—*I'm here*—and obedience.

Down the driveway, they ducked under the yellow tape. At the demarcation line in the cement that signaled where the driveway ended and the garage started, Haven recoiled at the hideous odor. Obviously coming from where the man in a navy jacket crouched with a pad.

VVolt whimpered.

Levi pointed to the body, where the crime scene photographer huddled. "Smell familiar?"

She twitched. "I don't often encounter decomposing bodies. Dead leads, yes. Dead bodies, no." When VVolt tugged hard, going in a circle, Haven shifted the lead to her other hand to give him more room.

"Not just decomposing," Levi said. "This was done very quickly. Weapon is missing, but"—his gaze struck Chiji, worrying her again—"the body was burned. Melted. From the inside out."

"I don't und—" She gasped. "Wait." Hauling in a panicked breath didn't help. VVolt jerked at the lead again. Hard. He nearly pulled her off her feet, but she couldn't stop gaping at Levi. "AFO?"

He gave a grim nod. "That's what I'm thinking. There's no arrow, but . . . it's the same."

The Arrow & Flame Order. "How?" She indicated around them. "But here? They . . ." Her mind whirled. Why here? This wasn't their normal grounds. The biggest question found voice. "Who is he, the man who died?"

"From all appearances, just an average Joe. Wealthy, but not filthy rich." Levi shrugged and glanced at VVolt, who now strained toward the driveway, his nails scratching against the cement.

Chiji motioned to the lead. "I think I am with VVolt and do not like this place. I will walk him."

"Thanks," Haven said, distracted by the keen possibility the AFO had killed a man, right here. So close to her home. But as she handed off the lead, somehow it slipped between their fingers.

VVolt seized the chance and bolted away, nose to the ground as he hauled in big draughts of air. Chiji ran after him and caught the lead.

Haven shook her head, refocusing on Levi. "So . . . why am I here? How can I help?"

Levi squinted his left eye. "Think you could talk to Tox or SAARC? Give them a call and see if they know anything about AFO activity in the area? Maybe a plot I should know about?"

Haven let his suggestion catch up with her, recalling his all-too-insistent demand to be released from working with them. "I . . . yeah. But so could you."

He looked away. "Robbie wasn't too happy with me."

*She isn't the only one.* Haven had expected more out of the man she considered a friend. When he finally accepted she was going to marry Cole, he cut ties. Said it was better that way.

Haven glanced at VVolt, who was now on a rise across the small cul-de-sac, snout riffling through the leaves. Back and forth. Pacing. Weird. He took a few paces to the right, then zipped again left. And dropped his rear end onto the grass as he peered up at Chiji.

Haven's heart thudded. "Uh, Levi . . ." she said, recognizing the retired MWD's cue for telling the handler he'd gotten a hit.

"I see it," he said, touching her arm as he stalked away, calling to one of the LEOs.

She followed them, armed with the excuse of collecting her dog to answer her curiosity over what VVolt had discovered. The K9's actions, coupled with the reaction of Levi and the other LEO, created a wake of awareness over the crime scene, pulling more than a dozen officers to the hillside.

"Cordon it off," Levi ordered. "We have evidence here!"

A wall of officers formed in front of Haven, and one turned, holding out a palm. "Sorry, ma'am."

"My dog—" She didn't want to argue. Didn't want to disturb the scene. But she also didn't want to be left out. "Assistant Special Agent in Charge Wallace asked me to come." But even as she said it, Haven made eye contact with Levi, who was escorting Chiji and VVolt back to her. "What is it?"

"A plastic cap of some kind. Maybe for the arrow tips."

Remembering the night in Spain when Barclay Purcell caught an arrow whose tip failed to activate, Haven gulped. The tips injected the phosphorous. "So someone stood there and shot that arrow into the victim . . ."

"There's an access road on the other side. Guessing they shot from there into the garage."

Haven assessed the angle between the hill and the garage. The distance. "Homes and trees would shield the assailant pretty well."

"He or she knew what they were doing. Scouted this. Picked the best time." Levi sighed. "And here I thought my days with SAARC were over."

"Working with the team isn't so bad, is it?" She squinted up at him. "I'm on that team, so be careful how you answer."

He huffed. "It's fine if you like danger served up with a gallon of psycho-doused-death."

"And how is that different from FBI cases?"

"Cases like this aren't the norm," he argued. "And if it's what I'm thinking, this is straight-up crazy SAARC stuff."

"See? You made my point."

He snorted. "Look, we have a lot of work here, now that our crime scene has expanded to the road. I'll give you a call later. Let me know what you find out from SAARC, okay?"

*Nice way to brush me off*. "Will do. Do the same if you find anything else here."

Clicking her tongue to VVolt, she started back to her vehicle and fished out her phone to start that call now. When she woke the phone, she stopped short. "No." Her screen warned that she'd missed two calls. From Cole. "No!" She stomped her feet. "I missed him."

For most people, missing a call from a loved one wasn't a big deal. But Cole had only rare occasions to call, so she might not hear from him again for weeks.

# 4

**— MOSCOW, RUSSIA —**

**LION:** You are in over your head.

**LAMB:** Nothing new. But I'm close.

**LION:** Remember, they will tell you whatever it takes to buy your loyalty.

**LAMB:** They will never have that. Only my able-bodied action to get what I want.

**LION:** Don't fool yourself, little lamb.

**LAMB:** He is alive.

**LION:** So the Christians said, and the Romans slaughtered them.

**LAMB:** Their own people slaughtered them. Are you saying you're going to betray me?

**LION:** Not what I meant. Come back. At least give me your location.

**LAMB:** Can't. Gotta go. Talk later.

**LION:** Wait!

Tzivia logged out, wiped her history, and powered down the computer. On her feet, she strode through the towering shelves of books and encyclopedic references, aiming toward the main doors. Cold nipped her as she crossed the Moscow State University campus. She stuffed her hands in her hoodie pocket and hurried to her flat. As she crossed the Moscow River bridge, she cracked the memory stick in half and tossed the pieces into the churning, icy waters.

At the cathedral last night, Nur had promised her father in exchange for the sword piece. But she'd refused to leave with him or betray where she'd hidden the first half. To continue this daunting quest for the ancient sword, she required proof that her father was alive.

She rounded the corner to her flat and slowed at the sight of three men on her stoop. Tzivia backed up but heard the squelch of tires on the wet road. Behind her, two more cars appeared, blocking her. She drew her hands from her pocket, shifted her stance.

"He said you would come—in peace," the approaching man growled. "You wanted proof of life." He indicated the car.

Swinging her gaze around again gave her little confidence. But she only needed a little to fight.

*Bad idea, Tzi. Bad idea.* Yet her feet carried her to the vehicle. A blond man opened the door, and she bent inside, gaze connecting with that of Igor, Nur's head goon. She hesitated.

"Get in," he barked. "I have a schedule to keep."

Tzivia slumped against the leather seat, mentally tapping the knife in her boot as the car pulled into traffic. She paid attention to roads and buildings to better remember the route, in case they tried to make her disappear. When the gleaming white structure of the cathedral came into view, she slid Igor a look, but he only smirked. The car glided up to the rear of the building.

Men flanking him, Igor started for an entrance to the cathedral. She wasn't surprised when his thugs surrounded her. Hands cuffed the soft flesh of her upper arms, pinching.

She gritted her teeth as they dragged her through a heavy door carved in religious reliefs. Stone steps delivered them to a dark, dank passage where moisture clung to whitewashed walls. She could only guess the Moscow River must be on the other side.

Sconces lit the way every twenty paces, the descent nauseating and frightening. The deeper they went, the harder it would be to escape. They banked right, and she glanced back. How many steps had it been before they turned? Twenty?

They yanked her on.

Tzivia stumbled. Hit the next step wrong. Lurched forward. Hands grabbed her. "Get off me!" She threw off their assistance. Gained her feet. Squared her shoulders. And found Igor waiting on a mosaic floor. Flanked by his thugs, he watched her impassively.

When she finally reached the bottom, he pivoted and continued down the cold stone passage. Only as she closed the gap between them did shadows surrender to light, revealing alcoves hewn into the walls. Crudely made, they concealed their contents until the last second, when light exposed their bounty—skulls. Skeletons. Cracked coffins.

Catacombs. Worse than tunnels.

Skin crawling, Tzivia drew in her arms. Held a breath she was afraid to release, in case she touched the dead. A chill scampered up her spine and wrapped around her throat, choking her. Moving quicker did little to relieve the dread pimpling her flesh.

"Is this a game?" Even as her voice reached out to Igor and his men, they vanished. Emptiness echoed back to her.

"Move," groused a guard nearby.

She stiffened but complied, anxious to be among the living once more. The darkness grew heavier. Air thinner. Strangling a cry did nothing to bolster her courage. Sensing her surroundings closing in, she thrust out a hand as a glimmer of light snuck into her periphery. She spied another passage to the left. Partially lit. As they emerged into a large, cavernous area, she expelled a captive breath.

Igor waited, bemused at her desperation. "Very good, Miss Khalon."

The men circled up on her.

Vision adjusted, she noticed the bars jammed into the hewn rock. "Do you intend to make me a prisoner?"

Igor flicked a hand, and one of his guards tapped a switch in the wall.

Light flared to her left, spilling over the rock and past the bars. Dirt and rags had been discarded in the unkempt space. "What is th—"

The rags shifted. Eyes squinted beneath wiry, dirty hair. The man had a thick, gnarled beard.

Tzivia hauled in a breath. She'd know those eyes anywhere. Anger thrummed, her reaction strangled in the horrified truth that her father had been kept here. A prisoner of darkness and death.

"*Abba!*" She rushed to the cell, grabbing the rusted bars. "Abba, it's me! Tzivia."

He peeled himself from the ground, his hand shaking. "My Tzi—can . . . not be." He struggled to his knees. Tried to stand, but his legs buckled. He dragged himself the last few inches to her.

Tears blurring her vision, Tzivia gripped his hands. Kissed his knuckles. "Abba! Abba, I found you."

"What are you doing here, Tzi?" he said, his voice gravelly. Angry. "Go! Get out while you can."

"Not without you, Abba!"

"Tzivia," said Igor, his voice intrusive and cold, "we had a bargain."

She spun at him. "What have you done to my father? This was not part of the bargain."

Igor displayed his palms with a lazy shrug. "Our treatment of him was never mentioned. Only the exchange."

"Release him!"

"That will not happen," Igor argued. "Not yet."

As her gaze tracked over the fresh cut splicing her father's cheekbone, fury unfurled through her, igniting, searing, screaming. Tzivia lunged at the closest man, not caring who he was. What he did. They would pay. They would all pay for what they'd done.

Pain pinched her back—the telltale prick of a dart thumping into her muscle. Shock froze her, then a river of ice coursed through her veins, dropping her to the ground. Hands pawed at her. Hauled her upright, rough fingers digging into her hair and tearing it from her scalp.

"This is what happens for disobedience," Igor growled, pointing to his second thug, who gripped a lever and tilted it up.

"*Nooo*," her father howled as electricity surged through his body.

* * * *

"Sir, he's returning." Kazimir Rybakov held his hands behind his back as he stood before Nur Abidaoud, the man whose safety he was personally responsible for now.

"About time." Nur slammed down a pen and looked toward the doors.

The private elevator intoned its arrival. The doors slid open. Igor emerged with three men. They wrangled a limp body between them.

"I expected you last night!" Nur growled.

"She did not return to her flat until this morning," Igor complained.

Kazimir angled, trying to see the face dangling beneath a tangle of black hair. "Who is she?"

As the men lowered her to the ground, she moaned and curled away.

"A deadly siren who would have her way and not yield an agreed-upon bounty." Nur pivoted and looked at Igor. "She saw him?"

Igor nodded. "None too happy either."

Nur smiled, then returned to his desk. "Good. Leave us."

Hesitating, Igor glanced at Kazimir, then the girl, and finally at his boss. "I'm not sure that's wise."

"You question me?"

"She's lethal, sir. Killed two men. Her brother has trained her well. Too well, perhaps."

"You don't think Kazimir"—Nur indicated him—"can handle this spirited woman?"

After a long, uncertain gaze, Igor still hesitated.

"I trust my safety to him," Nur said with a shrug. "Have I erred in that judgment?"

"Want to test me and relieve yourself of this worry?" Kazimir offered, trying to hide his smirk.

"Tell you what," slurred a woman's voice, "why don't I kill you both and settle this testosterone war."

Nur chuckled. "Miss Khalon, welcome back." Though he laughed, he moved behind his desk and sat in the high-backed leather chair. Was it for power or protection?

Warily, Kazimir watched as the woman sat up, pressing a hand to her temple.

"Welcome?" she murmured. "Strange way to show it." She staggered to her feet, wavered slightly, then straightened. "Give me my father."

"That wasn't the arrangement."

She drew in a heavy breath, her chest heaving. Then another. "It was. My father for the artifact."

Nur held out both hands. "I have no artifact, not even a third of it, which you promised to secure, so why would I give you anything, let alone your father?" His brow knotted, a darkness hovering there. "Where is the piece, Tzivia? You're playing with your father's life."

"He's dying down in that dungeon," she said. She took a step closer. "Let him go." She bent sideways.

Kazimir knew those moves. He'd seen them time and again. Her bargaining served as distraction.

After sliding a look to Kazimir—*he anticipates her attack*—Nur focused on the girl with a sad smile. "Now that, I'm afraid, I cannot do."

She growled, her hands twitching. Kazimir inched behind her, grateful her attention and hatred were on his employer. Just a little closer . . .

Fiery brown eyes snapped to his. She bared her teeth. "Try me."

Surprised and impressed, Kazimir froze. Though he stopped, he didn't remove himself. He would not give her that satisfaction.

"The artifact," Nur said. "Bring it, and I will consider releasing your father."

"Consider—"

"You're failing. Why would I keep my end when you do not?"

"Why do you care about this sword?" she demanded. "It's just a sword. It might not even be—"

"No!" Nur punched to his feet. "It is the Philistine sword. It's imperative that I find it. Time is not on your side, Miss Khalon." He rounded the desk, apparently recovering his confidence. "Bring the first piece, and perhaps we can continue, despite your less-than-peaceful approach to these negotiations."

"Negotiations? You're *selling* his life!"

"I am," Nur said, unrepentant. "But what price will you pay?

And maybe I should sweeten the pot?" He fastened his suit jacket and lifted his chin, appearing magnanimous. "Let me show you how generous I am." He nodded to Igor, who left the room, then returned with a young girl in a hijab. "This is Aisha. She is an archaeologist, just like you."

Tzivia stepped back, and though Kazimir wanted to do the same, since he knew what was coming, he could not. If he showed himself weak, he'd be kneeling on the floor next.

Tzivia jerked. "No, stop this!"

"She's been searching longer than you. I gave her everything she asked for, believing her lies, but she failed." He retrieved a weapon from a cabinet, then a smaller piece—a silencer—and strolled toward the girl, who was sobbing violently now. "She knew she could not locate the sword, so she helped her family escape. But we will find them." He smirked at Tzivia. "Sadly, they will not find her. Ever"—he aimed and fired, a sound that defied the silencer and cracked through the room—"again."

Tzivia whipped aside. Then spun back and threw herself at Nur.

Kazimir intercepted and wrestled Tzivia away from Nur. Away from the body and blood.

Behind them came the *thunk* of the cabinet door closing.

"Now," Nur said with a huff, "for the first piece delivered, perhaps I can increase our care of your father. Perhaps even allow *you* to care for him."

"Care?" Tzivia scoffed. "You have him locked in the catacombs. In a filthy stone cell with soiled clothes. No running water. No food. No respect!" She shoved Kazimir off of her and slapped his chest, to which he cocked his head in warning.

"Then change his fate and situation: find the first piece of the sword." Nur's words were a slick, well-oiled mechanism controlling her. "Timing is critical, would you not agree?"

Tzivia didn't move. But her fingers coiled into tight balls, knuckles white beneath the effort, which made Kazimir hold his close proximity. "If he dies—"

"Then you wavered too long." Nur reclined against the desk.

"Augh!" Tzivia lunged again.

Kazimir caught her. Hooked her throat and pressed her head forward, cutting off her air supply.

"The air you are losing," Nur said, "is the same air your father loses each day you linger. Bring the first piece, or he may find himself unable to breathe."

# 5

**— MOSCOW, RUSSIA —**

"We have a problem," Robbie Almstedt insisted.

Hands tucked in his armpits, Ram stared into the camera, the dot on his laptop. By keeping his eyes there, he didn't have to see her tiny pupils that spoke her anger. "We all do."

"You've been gone nearly a month. Tox longer. *What* is going on?"

He bit his tongue. The authorization from General Rodriguez and SAARC for Tox to do this, to help him—it had been costly. Dangerous. "It's nearly over." He had become a practiced, skilled liar in his years of cooperation with the Mossad. "Then I will give a full debrief."

"Debrief? You'll be locked away at this rate! Look, things are happening here. We had a man show up dead, his insides boiled out."

"Sounds terrible."

"It *sounds*," Robbie growled, "like the AFO is active, killing people on American soil."

Ram grunted, his curiosity admittedly piqued. "How do you know? An arrow?"

"Negative," barked Rodriguez.

With a sigh, Robbie dropped her gaze. "There was no arrow, and we aren't sure why, because it was definitely the work of those accursed phosphorous arrows. But I've done some digging. Killings like this have happened in other countries, too—random deaths. Those all have arrows to link back to the AFO—"

"But you don't." He squinted, the monitor straining his eyes. "That's what you said, right? You don't have the arrow or proof."

"So help me—*do you* know anything about AFO attacks?"

"Possible escalations in their strategy?" Rodriguez asked.

Was the whole world falling apart? "No, but I'll ask around. What else?" Ram had angles to probe, actions to take after that note drop from his source.

"You're putting us in a terrible spot," she said. "We can't keep stalling the brass, the government, or the president!"

"Khalon," General Rodriguez barked through the line, "we gave you six months with this little venture. Time's up."

"It's only been five," Ram argued.

"Five months, two weeks, three days," Rodriguez countered.

"And you, better than anyone, should know that when an operation is going well, you don't arbitrarily yank and tank. It's important to assess and reevaluate. We need him on this op, as you both said, to find names and help us dismantle the AFO from within."

"Do you think they're retaliating?" Robbie asked, her voice hesitant.

They were worse than conspiracy theorists. "Against what?"

"Us. For digging."

"Digging is one thing," Ram rebuffed. "Have you carried out an op against them that would draw their fire? I don't think you have. At least the guys haven't mentioned it."

Rodriguez tensed. "That's need to know."

"Ram, listen," Robbie said, "if we get axed, your mission collapses—that could be dangerous for Tox. For you. Funding. Support. And I am two years shy of retiring."

Ah, plying him by insinuating Tox was in danger, which she couldn't know. The crux was Robbie's fear for her job. Herself.

"So what does he have?" Rodriguez demanded. "We need to know who's in the upper echelon of that danged corporation. They've hidden too long and done too much damage!"

Robbie leaned in. "Give us something—*anything*—to show the brass this money is well spent and this mission worth continuing."

Ram couldn't win. Not yet. He held too few cards right now. "I'll get back to you." Without waiting for a response, he disconnected and buried his face in his hands. Threaded fingers through his hair and stared at the blank monitor. Finally, he lifted his phone. Dialed.

"We found her."

Ram stilled at that revelation. Then breathed, "Where?"

"There in Moscow."

"Where in—"

"We weren't able to isolate it. This is the closest we've come."

"Get it isolated. We need to find her." Ram stood, lifting papers and stuffing them in boxes. "Look, I need a distraction."

"I never thought you needed help with women—"

"A name to give SAARC," Ram bit out.

Omar Kastan snorted. "Americans applying pressure again, huh?"

"I warned you this would be tricky. Tox means too much, and he's been gone longer than expected—"

"These wars aren't won overnight."

"Agreed, but I need them off my back now that we're closing in on her. And if I can't give them something soon, they'll come looking for him."

"If they're not already."

True. Ram knew they wouldn't wholly let go of Tox. Not after all he'd done and risked. "Which is why I need rocks to throw and distract them."

"Give me—"

"Eight minutes." It was an exaggeration, but he had to keep himself alive and safe.

Kastan cursed. "I'm not a vending machine!" Keys clacked behind his grunt along with the general chatter and noises of a busy command center. Finally, "Check your access portal."

When Ram glanced at the file that landed in his inbox, he grunted. How long had they had this name and withheld it? Why play games? Why not just deal with it? "Thanks. Later." Ram ended the call—his second hang-up on superiors in one day. Man, what was wrong with him? He'd never been short-tempered, especially not with superiors.

The dossier was on a Congolese male, nineteen, Didier Makanda.

Awful young to be AFO. Might not be legit, but Ram needed SAARC off his back.

Fed up, he shoved away from the workstation. They were so close. Tzivia was out there, neck-deep in a big pile of dung that reeked around the world. Following three months of training, Tox had been in play for two months and still hadn't found her or infiltrated the AFO as hoped.

The intricate plan included excruciating preparations—more so for Tox than for Ram, yet painful all around. Pacing, Ram yawned and caught sight of the clock. So late? No wonder he couldn't think straight. He dropped onto the bed and stared at the data wall, thinking. Plotting. It was quiet, and he was glad he'd rented the flat that abutted his three-story base of operations. Both in different names. For privacy and security.

He woke to an annoying buzz and spotted the telltale glow of his secure phone. His heart slammed into his throat as he catapulted off the bed. Snatched the device and scanned the text. He grabbed his beanie and jacket, then rushed out.

Across town, he shoved his way through a raucous, throbbing nightclub. Bodies pressed on every side, all but carrying him to the bar. He planted himself on a stool and ordered a vodka and tonic. He wasn't a drinker, but coming into the bar and not ordering would mark him as trouble.

A scream shot up from the right. Ram glanced over his shoulder, eyeing the men fighting over a scantily clad woman. He shook his head and turned back to his glass.

A new napkin rested beneath the snifter. Black ink read: *She's alive. Eyes on her. Contact soon.*

Ram skated a look around but knew better than to expect anything. The contact had a way with disappearing. Had a way with finding people and staying out of the grave. Yet . . . couldn't he have given more explanation? "Alive" simply meant breath pushed through her lungs and her brain still worked—maybe. Was she okay? In danger? Where?

It was worth it, even though this trip could expose him. But it also fed Ram's futility. How hard was it to provide details?

*Details that could get her killed?*

The cryptic message prevented Ram from rushing into the fray. Going after his little sister. Doing whatever it took to bring her back alive. All his life, he'd worked to find the truth about their father. There had never been ironclad proof that their father was alive, but enough clues added up to hard-to-ignore possibilities. Tzivia's belief was a naïve hope. His grew on the clues—the phone call, seeing his father leave without a suitcase. They never got more than that. But Tzi didn't let that stop her, so he'd done his best to keep an eye on her. To protect Tzivia from those who wanted her to bleed.

Hands stuffed in his jacket pockets, chin to his chest, he trudged back to his flat. Nearly at the steps, he stopped short, some awareness, some dread buzzing his nape. He lifted his head from the stupor of frustration and scanned the street. Quiet. Cars. Homes. Lights in flats. Dogs—

"Lights," he murmured, gaze striking his place. Lit up. Shapes moved through the rooms. Who knew what they'd discovered, relayed back to their home office. Crap. He had only one choice now: those intruders couldn't leave alive.

He pivoted. Pulling out his phone, he cursed himself, his carelessness. As he entered the code that would detonate the well-hidden charges throughout the flat, he started the walk back to anonymity.

Bright white cracked the void of night. The concussion punched him forward a step. Rustled his hair into his face. He glanced back. A cloud of smoke and fire engulfed the building. Destroyed his work. Eliminated the enemy.

* * * *

*He's alive. Abba is alive!*

Gear in her satchel, Tzivia trudged down the alley behind the restaurant, taking solace in the clanking boat masts nearby. At the door, she gripped a new stainless steel lock. What the—where had this come from? She jangled it. Grunted and glanced around. Someone had apparently discovered her last trespass and tried to prevent another.

With a snort, she rammed her booted heel against the jamb. It rattled but held. Another kick freed it from the lock and splintered the jamb. No time to mourn the damage. She pushed through the long passage to the kitchen, where she lifted a grate from the middle of the floor, then dropped into the old tunnel. She hurried through its rank innards toward the lapping of water. There, she knelt and dropped her waterproof pack.

Shouts gave chase.

Tzivia peered toward the voices, surprised to see flashlight beams sweeping the darkness. With a grunt, she continued her course, faster now. Grateful for the neoprene that coated her body against the frigid water temperature, she slipped on her mask and rebreather. She stepped off the cement floor and into the hole, sinking into the shallow waters. Swam a meter out to a small shelf in the river wall. There, she retrieved a plastic-wrapped object.

Beams of light probed the dark waters.

Tzivia surged aside, taking shelter behind a pier post. Frantic, she searched for safety, but there was no choice except to swim through the boat-laden canal. Away from the obscurity of the restaurant and wall. After tucking the piece into her sack, she swam out farther, aiming toward the nearest dock. It took her longer than expected, her limbs growing rubbery, her legs cramped. Once she broke the surface, she tugged out the rebreather and hauled in a greedy draught of air.

Cement scraped her fingers as she traced the dock's shape to a steel rail. Gripping it, she hauled herself up—and lost her footing. She splashed back into the water. Nearly swallowing a mouthful, she clamped her lips tight. Pushed herself back to the dock. Demanded her weary limbs cooperate instead of working against her like everything else in life.

Cement scored her knees as she scrabbled over the incline. Water puddled beneath her as she hung her dripping head and steadied her ragged breathing. Closed her eyes. Fought the urge to lay there. It was too cold. She was too wet.

"You have it?"

Tzivia jerked straight, snatching her knife from its leg sheath—and found herself staring at the barrel of a gun. A tall man, the one who'd secured her when she'd stupidly tried to go after Nur in his office, stared her down.

Defiance flared within her. "What if I do?"

"You don't value your father's life?"

Swimming a freezing river proved she did. But she hated this man and his confidence. And . . . "Your English is too good."

"And your Russian is bad," he countered, shaking his head. "Artifact."

"I'll only give it to Nur."

Eyebrow arcing and impatience marking his response, he extended a hand toward a waiting car.

Tzivia stomped up the steps. Passing him, she thought about stepping back with her right foot and throwing—

"Keep moving," he growled, relieving her of the sodden satchel . . . and the artifact.

She whipped around, but he cocked his head, sending a warning. A strangely familiar one. "Give it back," she said.

He didn't comply.

"Give it back or we have fun . . . in reverse."

He started walking. Not guiding her. Not manhandling her. He just walked to the car. "In."

Tzivia hesitated, confused. Concerned.

He opened the rear passenger door. "I thought you wanted to see your father."

Hope threw her into the armored vehicle.

# 6

**— CAPITOL HILL, DC —**

Though the historic landmark was rife with senators, staffers, Supreme Court justices, and law clerks involved in the negotiation of bills, Capitol Hill was also home to nineteenth-century row houses and tightly packed neighborhoods.

Levi skirted the residential areas, his destination the domed and columned Capitol, though he wished it wasn't. "*You're sure?*" he'd asked at least a dozen times, unwilling to believe the murderer would strike at the heart of the nation's capital. Where security was the highest imaginable. Where surveillance cameras proved innumerable.

This might just be the break the Bureau needed. *He* needed.

He produced his credentials for a Capitol Hill police officer, who granted him access to the crime scene, a parking lot along Southwest Drive. He strode beneath a sun that did little to subdue the early spring chill.

"Wallace!"

At Santi's voice, Levi searched for his partner, who stood amid a cluster of suits and uniforms. Levi joined them.

"This is some seriously messed-up stuff."

Levi wasn't surprised, but he still had to ask. "Same as last time?"

As Santi nodded, a woman rose from a squatting position, camera angled as she thumbed one of the controls. The same woman from the Schenck crime scene? What were the chances? She lifted brown eyes, which widened as they met his. "ASAC Wallace."

He wouldn't correct her that they didn't pronounce it as *ay-sack* anymore. Really didn't matter. "Hi . . ." Levi hesitated, flicking confusion into his face in the hope she'd offer her name, since he didn't recall catching it previously.

She extended her hand. "Maggie Lefever."

He definitely would've remembered that. "Surprised you're here."

"I'd say the same," she said, squinting one eye, "but it'd just come off as lame and flirtatious."

He started to laugh. Wait, was she accusing him of flirting? "I—"

"Greco!" someone shouted.

After a pat on Levi's shoulder, Santi started away. "Be right back."

"I was kidding. I contract with the Bureau." Maggie motioned around. "This was in close enough proximity for me to get called in again." She gave Levi a coy nod before glancing at her camera. "Guess I'd better get to work."

And he'd better start.

Levi walked the scene. The victim lay partially caught on his car door, body at a weird angle. Sagging between two vehicles as if his spine was missing. Levi shifted around and stopped short. His breath crammed into his throat. He swallowed a curse.

An arrow protruded from the victim's back. There could be no doubt this time.

"His name is Travis Seaton."

Turning toward the soft voice, he couldn't hide his surprise at the news Maggie dropped. "*Congressman* Seaton?"

"The one and only."

The congressman had been in the news a lot lately, both sides hating him for one thing, loving him for another. Recently, there'd been a big falling-out over a piece of legislation he'd championed in conjunction with the Justice Department: the Twice As Fast Fingerprint Identification Protocol.

"It's strange," she said. "You'd expect one of his political enemies to be the culprit, but with the tie-in to the Soup Maker, you can't really—"

"Soup Maker?"

Maggie paused. "That's the nickname LEOs are giving the killer."

He snorted. "Great."

"You know, because he makes soup out of their—"

"I get it," Levi grumbled, shaking his head at the macabre humor. Was it humor, or a way to cope? He nodded to the scene. "Anything unusual?"

"Besides the deflated corpse and the arrow sticking out of his back?"

Why her sarcasm bothered him, he didn't know. Maybe because he couldn't run from the truth that this was AFO handiwork. "Excuse me. I need to check some things."

Anger trailed him to the other side of the car, where he spent too long looking for evidence. He couldn't help but feel close to this one. Congressman Seaton had worked with his field office to tailor TAFFIP into an effective, efficient system. Now the FBI used it to quickly identify suspects across a uniform, national database. It'd given them an edge in tracking down criminals and had increased productivity 28 percent.

Besides the arrow and the body, nothing else pointed to the AFO. Most likely the perpetrator had stood at a distance. Levi straightened and scanned the area, searching for shooting spots. It could've even been a drive-by.

But this was Seaton! Grimly, Levi glanced down at what was left of the man. *What did you do to draw the AFO's eye?*

"Hey!" Santi jogged over. "What's that look for?"

"I can't believe this is Seaton."

"I know. Sick, right?" Santi tapped Levi's arm. "But good news."

That'd be a change. "What's that?" His gaze surfed the crowd, knowing some killers liked to watch the crime scene get worked. His gaze bounced to Maggie, snapping photos of the gathered people, many using smartphones to video and snap pictures. Reporters were clustered to the far side.

"Security footage—which is crazy thorough around here, of course—

caught something." Santi thumbed over his shoulder. "Parker's talking to Capitol Hill police to get the footage. Rumor is it captured the killer."

And nobody said anything to him? Levi stalked toward the SAC.

Parker caught sight of Levi and smiled. "This might be our lucky day," he said. "Waiting on final approval, then we'll see it."

"Okay, gentlemen," said a uniform, who motioned them to follow.

They made their way up the side entrance of the Capitol. Inside, they were led to a security office where one uniform ordered another to play the video feed. The screen was crisp and clear. A silver van slid up behind the sedan. A midthirties man emerged, aimed a crossbow as the congressman opened his car door.

"Insane," someone muttered.

"He didn't care about being identified," Levi noted.

"We'll need a copy of that, and print off a still," Parker said. "Sooner we get this out there, the sooner we can bring in this psycho."

They were so brazen. As if they thought themselves above the law. Disbelief cinched Levi's throat as he warred with the truth. Truth he'd hoped never to face again. Sickening, disgusting minds that dreamed up heinous methods of killing their victims. If there was even a scrap of doubt that this wasn't them, he'd seize it. But the method was too unique.

Parker indicated the monitor. "Run it again." After watching it a few more times, they found nothing new. No anger on the killer's face. No apparent motive. Just sheer determination. He knew who he wanted to kill and carried it out in broad daylight. That alone told them a lot.

They excused themselves after getting a USB copy of the video. Parker tapped the drive against his palm as they stepped back into the chaotic crime scene. "What was that in there?"

Levi stopped, looking out toward the chaos that was Washington. He expelled a heavy breath. "Just reminds me . . ."

"Of?"

Opening this can of worms could be more trouble than Levi wanted. "My time with SAARC and an organization they came up against repeatedly called the Arrow & Flame Order." He exhaled deeply. "I would've taken on the Crown of Souls psycho again over this group."

"They're that bad, huh?" Parker eyed him. "What makes you think it's them?"

"The phosphorous arrow." He shook his head. They walked a dozen more feet, silence thick between them. Levi wanted to leave. But he wasn't finished here. They weren't.

"So this is SAARC territory."

"It just won't leave me alone." Levi shook his head.

Parker squinted against the sun just over Levi's shoulder. "Why don't you contact them?"

"Already asked Haven to do that."

"Well, follow up. You have connections there, so give that woman, the chief there, what's her name—"

"Almstedt."

"That's the one. Give her a call. Find out what they have."

Levi felt the growl in his throat and swallowed it. "Just once, I want to do our job the way we're supposed to and solve the case. Like old times."

"You're up for my position, remember?" Parker wagged his gray-blond eyebrows. "Solve this, and you move into the big office." He smiled, but then it slipped away as he eyeballed the crime scene and the chaos engulfing it, the media swarming the street. "What's got you scared, Wallace?"

"Like I said, not scared, just—"

Parker scowled. "Lie to someone else. I've worked with you too long to believe the crap you're shoveling out. You're running scared."

Levi shouldered up to his boss, dropping his chin for emphasis. "I've got my life back. I'm focusing on my career. I don't want to go backward or deal with those people again."

"You mean Cortes?"

"No," he growled. "Yes. But only because she's tied to that team. They're . . ."

"Bad?"

Levi snorted. "No, they're the best. But they're . . . military. Different breed. I don't fit there. And what they track, what they hunt?

I don't want to do that anymore. I want"—he couldn't believe he was going to say this—"normal neuroses and psychosis."

Parker barked a laugh.

Levi drew in a measuring breath. "Let's just catch this guy. Plain and simple."

"Simple it isn't." Parker glanced off to the side, his eye catching on something, and clicked his tongue. "Let me know what SAARC knows."

# 7

## — MOSCOW, RUSSIA —

"I already told you—I haven't heard anything about AFO killings," Ram said across the live feed from Russia as he teleconferenced with SAARC and Levi Wallace.

"It's the second death by phosphorous arrow here in the U.S. within the last month," Wallace said. "That's notable."

"Noted," Ram replied, unable to avoid being sarcastic with him.

"Look," Robbie said, "we're not alone in these attacks. I've been in contact with the Netherlands' Special Interventions Division because they had an arrow death three weeks ago that got swept under the carpet as an unsolved murder. They're forwarding the files on the victim, Jens Abrams, who is influential among the Dutch."

"Again, this is great, but all you have is unsubstantiated proof of AFO involvement." Ram held up a hand when they both started arguing. "I get it. This isn't a coincidence. Still, there's no artifact. No reason to engage SAARC." He touched his temple. "Or am I missing something?"

"You're missing the fact that we are involved because this organization has been the bane of our existence. They've killed our people and a lot of innocents," Almstedt said. "Not to mention, you've got Tox out there doing who-knows-what to find the top-tier leaders.

That connects this, regardless of an artifact. We need to end this organization."

"Any move that endangers Tox will be met with resistance."

Almstedt narrowed her eyes. "Is that a threat?"

"It's a promise," Ram said. "Mossad has invested a lot in this mission, and we aren't going to rush things to satisfy some agenda you have with the brass."

"Understood." Wallace had terminated his involvement with SAARC, but now that he wanted help, he came back. The agent needed to feel the repercussions of bailing on the team. Besides, he had taken too long to surrender his feelings for Haven and for a while actively sought to draw her back to himself. He lost points for that in Ram's book. "They told me to ask, so I said I would."

"Special Activities *Artifact* Recovery and Containment. No artifact?" Ram shrugged. "No SAARC."

Levi gave a nod. "Figured you'd say that."

"He's not calling the shots," Robbie countered, "but he's right. We're stretched thin at the moment. Levi, you're dealing with some awful murders, and we don't take that lightly. So we'll keep our ears open. Should anything come up, we'll notify you."

"I appreciate it. Thanks." Wallace terminated his feed.

Almstedt waited, eyeing something—probably verifying that Wallace was gone—then shifted. "The AFO is stepping things up, Ram. Killing people in broad daylight with those vicious arrows. *What* is going on?"

"If I knew, I doubt I'd be sitting in a flat, staring at a data wall." He shrugged, recalling the heinous mission eight months ago that had them chasing a crown-wearing madman on a killing spree that could, technically, have been considered a serial killer case.

"So," she said with a sigh, "they found you."

What he'd lost in that explosion still ticked him off. "I took care of it." Authorities had recovered two bodies from his flat. No other casualities or injuries.

"Are you compromised? You sanitized the apartment, but—not to sound like a broken record—they found you, Ram."

"They found the flat. There's a difference." He hoped. Finding the flat could just be logistics. Knowing who owned it and lived there—that could be a problem.

"Timing is all that separated you from being exposed."

He folded his arms and stared back.

"We're looking into official reports, watching underground chat rooms to see why they were there, who they were, what they wanted."

As he had been and would keep doing until he knew who he'd killed in that explosion.

"Could've been innocent—"

"They weren't," he said.

"Then you slipped up." Robbie clicked her tongue. "You can't afford another mistake like that."

There was no argument, no defense. *Had* a mistake been made? Maybe. He wasn't sure at this point.

"And your sister—is she really MIA still?"

Almstedt was probing too much. She knew better than to ask these things. But this one wouldn't hurt. And he'd respect the fact that she'd worked with Tzivia, too, so she might legitimately care. But . . . "Are you asking if I lied?"

"You're playing incognito, and you've taken one of our best assets—"

"Borrowed."

"—but you can't just string us along. You cannot expect us—"

"Didier Makanda."

Robbie blinked. "I . . . what?"

"It's a gift." This probably wouldn't go over well. "I do not know what or who he is. Only that Mossad said to pass the name on." He shrugged. "I would look into it if I were you." He paused as she wrote it down, then abandoned note-taking for a keyboard.

After a moment, Robbie glared into the camera. Silence hung rank and rotten between them. "You're sure?"

"As I said, a gift."

"Why?"

This was where things got a little hairy, fudging the truth in a way that wouldn't set off her alarms. "You've allowed them to borrow your operator and made it clear that SAARC has one goal: taking down the AFO."

"This man is connected to that?" she asked, typing. "What am I supposed to do?"

Ram smirked. "Director, if I have to tell you that, then maybe I should be sitting in your chair."

"Don't get smart with me, Mr. Khalon." She caught her mouse, clicked around, her face awash in monitor light. "Where are they getting this information? What are they basing this intel off of?"

"As soon as you're ready to share *your* methods, assets on the ground, and intel gathered, maybe they'll reciprocate."

"You know very well we can't do that."

In silence, Ram waited.

Almstedt let out a long sigh. Her hazel eyes peered long into the camera, and the length of time that stretched, the way she stared, made it creepy. "How is he? Can you tell me that?"

Ram considered answering. Weighed the pros and cons. The latter greatly outweighed the former. An enormous amount of trust—not just political, but tangible, real lives—had been placed in his hands. He wasn't going to make careless mistakes now and screw up everything. "Good night, Director."

* * * *

Creaking and groaning surrendered to an explosion of light. Tzivia winced away from the glare, then peered at the large shape that loomed. At the rock walls. Bars. A prison? Were they kidding? Something about that form tugged at her brain. Or maybe that was the knot they'd put on the back of her head when she'd climbed into the car. How long had she been out?

She hopped to her feet. "Why are you holding me?"

"For being out for two days, she's pretty feisty," a voice growled.

*Two days?!*

Keys jangled, but the door wasn't unlocked. The man who'd found her on the dock tucked his chin and eyed her. "Hands," he said, motioning her forward.

What she'd heard wasn't keys, but the metal cuffs he held. "You're kidding right? I did what—"

"Would you like to stay, then?" The tall oaf indicated the exit.

"Because I can leave." He shrugged. "Who knows what will happen to your old man, left to rot because you didn't want to come for him."

Glowering and fingers laced, she shoved her arms between two bars so he could secure them.

"I've heard these hands are lethal." He strapped on the cuffs. "Killed two men in an alley."

She threw as much threat as she could into her response as she drew back. "Those are only the two they found."

He snorted. "Tough talk."

"Not tough. True."

He moved to the lock and freed it. "I know cuffs won't inhibit you, but since you're so desperate to see your father—and to have him remain alive—I know you will not try any more stunts."

Futility roiled as he took her arm and led her from the cage. Her muscles tremored, aching to deliver a lethal strike to this arrogant jerk's face. But he was right—she wouldn't. Because she *did* want her father alive.

"What did you do with the sword piece?" she asked as they climbed stone steps toward an ever-expanding speck of light. She squinted against the glare cast by sconce embrasures in the narrow passage.

He gave her a sidelong glance. "You think I would keep it?"

"You could've lied and said I hadn't brought it."

"Then Mr. Abidaoud would not only be angry with you, but also with me for failing him."

"And you like living too much."

Something glimmered in his eyes—again, familiar somehow—that allowed a trickle of hope into her desperate world.

He caught the cuffs and tugged her forward, pain chomping her flesh as he led her down a series of passages. Distracted by the familiarity ringing this man, she quickly lost her mental map. Maybe because he had the same nose as Omar.

Her chest squeezed at the thought of him, but she shoved it back into the past. She couldn't think of Omar. Couldn't think of the hurt she'd caused.

Emerging into the thick, damp evening, they passed through a barred entrance and descended a flight of steps, unusual tapestries lining the walls. Gruesome, bloody depictions of beheadings. Only as they reached the final step did it dawn on Tzivia that it wasn't several killings. Each was a different portrayal of the victory of the Hebrew king, David, who'd slain Goliath.

A shudder traced her spine. She shouldn't be surprised. They were forcing her to track down the sword that delivered victory to the Hebrews.

*But Abidaoud is Muslim.*

After a corner, they stopped short before steel doors to an elevator. She frowned. "I thought we were in the cathedral's catacombs, or whatever you people call it."

"Why would we be there?" He pressed a button, and a panel slid back, revealing a slick black surface. After palming that, he entered a code—too fast for her to catch.

"Because my father is there, and I was promised—"Air gusted with the swift *whoosh* of the opening doors. She drew in a breath and eyed the interior.

He motioned her in.

"No. I gave you the piece—"

"Your arrangement is not with me. Now." He nodded again to the yawning elevator. "Please."

Tzivia curled her fingers into a fist, deliberating. If it weren't for her father . . .

"He holds something over your head . . ."

"I don't need the reminder." She pushed herself inside, feeling his presence behind her, sealing her into the contraption. Immediately, her mind went into fight mode. The box was small. Confined. That could work for her or against her. She wasn't inclined to let it be the latter.

He was tall—probably six three or four. A bit taller than Tox. Lankier build. But there was nothing lanky or lazy about this man. He held his arms loose at the side. Ready. But was his left arm held a little higher? Maybe an old injury?

"Considering options?" He chuckled. Shook his head.

"What? You don't think I could—"

"No." His expression turned hard. Angry.

"Why?"

He angled to her, his gray eyes odd but fierce. "You're too ticked at me. You're assessing me, weighing whether you can take me. But you won't do it."

"Think you know me that well?"

"You love your father, Miss Khalon, and that will keep you in check."

But her fist struck out.

Lightning fast, he caught her hand. Gripped it in a vise and twisted it—and her—around. Slammed her into the mirrored walls. "*Think*," he growled, "of what he holds over your head."

The words were hissed right in her ear. Into her soul, which breathed, *Abba*. Grimacing against his pinch hold, she pushed her gaze to his. A wealth of meaning piped through his strange eyes. To behave. To guarantee her father stayed alive.

"Understood?" His voice was a growl again.

Anger, confusion, desperation coiled around her throat, allowing the merest of nods.

After giving her a small shove into the reflective glass, he stepped back.

Tzivia lowered her head, gathered her senses and pride as the elevator climbed. With a quiet tone, the doors glided open.

Scowling, he nodded her out.

Irritated, feeling powerless and out of control, Tzivia removed herself and wished she could be removed from this man's all-too-perceptive eyes. And why? Why was he helping her, unlike the other bloodthirsty thugs ready to put her down?

Marble spread out in luxury and extravagance. Yet where she expected to find van Gogh or similar paintings, the walls were once more adorned with the same dark theme of David slaying Goliath.

Making their way to a set of double doors, the lanky guard kept pace with her. Slowed when she did. Resumed course at the same time. The doors swung open, and Tzivia slowed.

Nur Abidaoud sat in a high-backed leather chair like a king on a throne. Too bad he didn't have the Crown of Souls on his head—but only at the moment it had melted the brain of its wearer. Which made her wish for Barclay Purcell and his genius tech mind to help her find a way out of this mess. *It's your own fault.*

The guard cuffed her arm, forcing her to continue. The move invigorated her courage. She stepped forward, sneering. "Where is my father?"

Wood scraped gently against wood as Nur, mocking eyes on her, reached to a side buffet and lifted a long, thin box. He set it on the desk. Opened it.

Carved steel sat in black velvet. Tzivia stiffened. Hating that he had it. Hating that she had only found half of the famed blade.

Nur sat back, the leather chair hissing like an elongated sigh. "I will choose to believe you were bringing this to me. Not escaping with it."

"Had your men"—she glowered at the thug beside her—"given me the chance, I would have come directly here with it."

He sniffed a laugh. "Since we are all versed in your attempts to evade and escape, I thought it best to send Mr. Rybakov to . . . motivate you to keep our agreement."

"Does that include holding me hostage for two days?"

His shoulders bounced in a lazy shrug. "I was out of the country. You were drugged."

"Well, you have half of the blade now," she said. "I want my father. You promised I could take him."

Abidaoud sneered. "Nice try, Miss Khalon. I said you could see him, care for him."

Tzivia pinched her lips, nostrils flaring under the very strained, toxic breath she pushed out. "What good is he to you? I've cooperated—got you the piece."

"And you have two more to acquire, as agreed."

She tightened her fists.

"Oh." He looked at her hands. "Have you changed your mind? Would you like an incentive?" He lifted a remote and aimed it at the wall.

Rybakov moved closer to Tzivia, making her frown.

The upper portion of the wall above the fireplace slid away, revealing a screen, which sprang to life with video footage. A barking dog snapped through the feed, then the camera zoomed in on a shape—her father.

"Abba!"

Tzivia realized it wasn't a dog barking. Her father was coughing. She lunged—only to be restrained by Rybakov. "Release me, you ape!"

"The second piece, Tzivia," Nur crooned.

She wrested free. Glared at Nur. "Take me to him now. Before I do anything else."

Smirking, Nur kept his eyes on her. "What do you think, Kazimir? I mean," he said with a laugh, "she tried to *attack* you in the elevator, right on my doorstep!"

Ice filled Tzivia, realizing how much this murderous filth had seen. Why had she thought he couldn't? His reach seemed to extend to the heavens.

"She *tried*," Rybakov said.

"So punish her?"

Chest tightening at the way they toyed not only with her, but also with Abba's life, she grew infuriated. But her anger, her propensity to attack first and think later wasn't working so well for her this time.

*"You have a good mind, Tzi. I just wish you'd use it first."* Omar hadn't meant the words to be mean, but they'd cut. Deep.

"I think she's punishing herself enough," Rybakov said.

"Perhaps." Nur stood and gave her a smile that felt as slick as the oil beneath her car. "If it takes her as long to find the remaining two pieces, the next time she comes, he may not be alive."

# 8

## — WASHINGTON, DC —

They climbed the thousand steps to her front door. Okay, so maybe not a thousand. But it felt that way. Haven groaned. "Really, Chiji, if you're going to help me, you need to buy me an elevator or something."

"Perhaps a membership to a gym?"

"Oh, ouch," Haven laughed, digging in her purse for the key as VVolt sniffed the door, pushing against it with his snout, anxious to be inside. Anxious for another bully stick. "Hang on, boy. We'll—"

"Excuse me."

VVolt whipped around her with a barrage of barking and rippling muscles that immediately morphed into a smidgen of a whimper as he rubbed his snout and neck along the thigh of a man Haven hadn't seen two seconds ago.

"Mr. Tzaddik."

He smiled, smoothing a hand along VVolt's broad skull and dense fur.

"Checking up on me?" she asked as she tugged at the Malinois, muttering, "Traitor."

Tzaddik and Chiji shook hands. "I've come to hear what you have learned of Cole's lineage."

She grunted and let VVolt into the townhome. "Aren't you omniscient or something?"

He joined her inside with a smile that wasn't a smile. "I am not all-knowing. Merely . . . timeless."

"Timeless." She squinted at him. "What exactly does that mean?"

"My existence is not of importance here."

"Well, it kind of is because you, Timeless One, are putting demands on me to find information that is impossible to find. Besides, if you're timeless but not all-knowing, you got ripped off." She removed VVolt's harness, and the eighty-two-pound hero wandered over to his water bowl. "As for what I've found about Cole's family—a big fat nothing. We went to the historical society, and they didn't have anything on him."

"What about his mother?"

"Cruising around Italy on vacation. When she gets back, I'll ask."

"You must understand the urgency."

Haven considered him, glancing for a moment at Chiji, who seemed as enamored by Tzaddik as she was confused. "Well, I don't. And honestly, with Cole on mission—gone—I'm struggling."

"Which is why I am here. Start with his father's line."

Haven dropped her head with a huff. "Fine. They return Sunday, and I'm going over for dinner. I'll ask then." She propped her hip against the kitchen counter. "What exactly are we looking for, anyway? A wealthy cousin?"

"Just follow the line. Find the missing piece."

"Missing piece of what?"

"Follow the line."

"Must you always be so cryptic?"

"I apologize. If I had more information, I would give it." Earnestness marked eyes lined with years, but not enough to measure this man's existence. "As I said, I'm not all-knowing. What I know is limited. Find the missing piece, Haven."

And he was gone.

Haven twitched, swallowing hard at the sudden chill that came with his absence. She lifted her chin and met Chiji's wide-eyed gaze. When he didn't say anything, she couldn't help but ask, "What? No perfectly placed proverb?"

"I am sure I can think of one, if you would give me a moment to recover from the shock of seeing a man disappear before my eyes."

* * * *

## — EN ROUTE TO THE CONGO —

"What in the usurper is this?" Cell rested his hands on his tactical vest as the team grouped up inside the hangar.

Leif "Runt" Metcalfe bobbed his head. "I'd feel the same way if our roles were reversed—"

"But they ain't," Cell groused. "You're new, and now you're taking the lead?"

"Hey," Maangi said calmly. "We're a team. First, second, last. No numbers."

Cell lifted his hands. "*You* should be annoyed the most, since you should be leading when Tox and Ram aren't here."

Shrugging, Maangi didn't seem to mind. "I don't have the experience or connections in this region, so explain how that makes sense."

"Because when Runt screws up and takes a bullet," Thor sniggered, "Maangi needs to save his butt."

"Or not," Cell grumbled.

"I hear you," Leif said, placating. "I'm the new guy. But I'm also the one who knows the team coming to help us, and I do have general experience in this region. So while your loyalty to Tox is appreciated, let's get our heads in the game. You have the dossier on this guy, Didier Makanda. Mossad dropped his name, and now we drop in on him and let him explain why."

Thor nodded to the tarmac. "Welcome party has arrived."

In the early morning light stood a half dozen men, booted feet shoulder-width apart, hands dangling casually at their sides. Most had on ball caps, and one had flipped his backward. While they wore tactical pants and long-sleeved shirts, their bearing betrayed them. They might try to look like civvies, but they reeked of experience behind scopes and under brain bowls.

"Squids," Thor said with a sneer.

"Tasty with butter," Cell snarked.

"I'll make sure they serve you up cold," Leif said, slapping Cell's arm as he strolled out to the meet the men who wore the same Trident he'd earned. "Riordan!"

Dark hair, dark eyes—some even said a dark heart—Riordan was one of the best SEALs Leif had ever worked with. They clasped hands and pulled into a shoulder hug. "Glad you're still sunny-side up, Runt."

"Hold up," Cell said. "You're the dudes we worked Kafr al-Ayn with," Cell said.

"I lost some good men there." Riordan puffed out his barrel chest and adjusted his backward ball cap.

"We all did," Maangi said.

"Let's not repeat that." The SEAL extended a hand, smile stretching his thick beard. "Special Warfare Operator Riordan. Runt, you remember"—he indicated to his nine, then clocked around—"Trigger, Grease, Hyde, and Jekyll."

"Wait, what? Seriously?" Cell snickered again. "Jekyll and Hyde?"

"Brothers," Riordan said. "They aren't much alike, but they're both deadly." He didn't crack a smile, but it was clear he loved that line.

"Heck yeah." Leif grinned hard. "This is my new team. Big guy's Thor. That's Maangi and Cell."

Riordan squinted at Thor. "God of thunder, eh?"

"Loud and proud." Thor threw out the comeback he'd always used when people questioned his call sign or assumed he had a god complex.

Amusement sparked, then Riordan pivoted. "Let's gear up and head out." He drove them across the airstrip to a small warehouse, then unlocked and shoved back the sliding door. Three beat-up Jeeps waited.

Thor drew back. Frowned. "Last time we were given junk like that, a kid was killed right in front of me."

"Don't worry," Riordan said, a bit of twang in his words, "they look old, but they're not. Came to us this summer. And"—he swung open the rear door, pointing to the inches-thick width—"armor-plated."

"Expecting trouble?" Maangi asked.

"Every day of the year," Leif and Riordan said around a laugh.

"Trigger, Jekyll, get 'em geared up," Riordan ordered his men, who moved to the remaining vehicles and dug out the weapons.

Leif took a sniper rifle, an M4, and a Glock. He broke them down, checked the magazines, then chambered a round into the handgun and strapped it into a leg holster.

Maangi sidled up, threading the strap of a leg holster. "Lot of hardware," he muttered as reached for an M4.

"The more the merrier," Leif said.

The mission should be simple—in and out, grab the guy and leave. But nothing was ever simple. Few missions went perfectly. Preparing for the unknown gave them a better chance of coming out alive. Leif looked past Cell, who was laughing and nearly got punched by Riordan, no doubt for a smart-mouthed comment.

Maangi dropped a magazine and checked the count. "Something seem off to you about this, or is it just me?"

"Not just you." Leif had a twitchy feeling about this mission, but he couldn't believe his SEAL brother would knowingly walk him into trouble. He slung a weapon over his shoulder as he worked his way closer. "It's not the company, though. These men are some of the best I've ever worked with. Villages out here are tricky, but thankfully Trigger has a way with the language."

"And the people," one of the SEALs muttered.

"Because he's black?" Cell said.

"Because he knows their customs." Riordan held his gaze for several long seconds before he turned to the others. "Pack it up, ladies. Time to move out." He slapped Leif's shoulder. "Forty-minute trip to the village, then the fun of finding the needle in the haystack. We need to be back before nightfall with our 'plus one.'"

Vehicle One carried Thor, Leif, and Riordan, who climbed behind the wheel, then pulled out of the bay. Beyond the windows, the lush Congo blurred. Predominantly jungle, the Republic of the Congo had finally entered its dry season, where rainfall would be rare and the sun warm. At least it wasn't summer. Even still, the air hung heavy amid the thick trees lining the great Congo River.

"Greener than I thought," Thor said.

"The Congo or your team?" Riordan taunted.

Leif snorted.

Set along a dull sloping hill and hugging the river, the village had rammed mud-and-thatched-roof homes into the hillside, then spread out in an ever-widening arc like the ripples of water on a still pond. Disturbed but not chaotic.

Their caravan jounced along the hard-packed dirt road that carved a stark line through the village teeming with people. Children swam along the shore of the river, which looked muddy but offered relief from the eighty-something-degree heat and the boredom of village life.

"Education is standardized in the cities. In some villages like this one, which isn't as far out, the kids will walk three or four klicks to get to the nearest primary school." Riordan snorted. "Kids back home complain about walking down the block to the bus stop."

They pulled up to a large round structure whose roof draped in an elegant sort of way. Branches stitched together with twine and vine were topped with leaves and fronds. Two men emerged from the structure and waited at the top of four steps. Though one had scraggly gray-white hair, he stood as tall and strong as the younger man to his right.

"This is what you might call the town hall," Riordan said.

The opening of the rear passenger door and the subsequent *thunk* of it closing snapped Leif's gaze around. He spotted Trigger striding toward the structure.

As Trigger climbed the steps casually and respectfully, Leif exited the vehicle and trailed him slowly, sensing Maangi and Cell with him. A stream of words flew off Trigger's tongue and were received by the two men, who returned a volley of dialogue.

"Dude." Cell edged closer. "That's French."

"No duh, genius," Leif snarked as Riordan joined them. "The Congo is part of *French* Equatorial Africa. Primary language is French, with Lingala and Mbosi second- and third-most common."

Trigger inclined his head to the apparent elders, then returned to the team. "He says we can come in."

"Come in?" Leif frowned, eyeing the reed-like walls. "We need—"

"There is a custom," Trigger said, a ferocity bleeding into his dark eyes. "Respect first. Once we earn it, we can ask what we want." He motioned up the wood steps.

"So much for in and out." Noting the quickly gathering crowd, Leif entered the structure.

"Won't take long," Riordan reassured him as they sat cross-legged on the wood floor. "Eyes out. Makanda may be among those watching."

Seated on the outer perimeter of the group, which held the two elders and Trigger, Leif glanced around the thickening crowd of mahogany faces etched with curiosity and perhaps even annoyance. But curiosity about the visitors proved too much for them to stay away.

"What's he saying?" Cell whispered to Leif.

Head angled to hear better, Leif said, "Trigger asked about their health. The older complained about his knees hurting."

"Arthritis is a b—"

"*And*," Leif continued, cutting off one of Riordan's men, "the younger said they are glad the plague is gone."

"Dude. Am I going to get sick?" Cell hissed.

"Can't handle it, get out," one of the SEALs shot back.

"Now he's asking about his family," Leif continued.

"Since when do you speak French?"

Leif looked over his shoulder to silence Cell—but his gaze hit a face. The person shifted and slid behind a woman, but something about him started a buzzing in Leif's brain.

He waited for the man to slip back into view. But he didn't. In fact, Leif couldn't find him now. He skimmed the rest of the nearby faces, but the dialogue was shifting into the purpose of their presence and returned Leif's attention to the elders.

Trigger spoke fluently and calmly, then pointed to Leif—who acknowledged them with a nod—saying it was very important they locate a young man who could help resolve some problems.

*Diplomatic way of putting it.*

Leif monitored the mood of the crowd. They'd all been taught to stay eyes and ears out, even when engaging locals. Especially locals. It was too easy for a situation to go sideways in a blink.

That face. The eyes.

Leif jolted out of his musings, brain whiplashing. Where had he just seen that person again? He reeled back through the crowd—there. To his three, where an opening led to a path that wound up the hillside before it spliced in opposite directions. The man had large eyes beneath a thick, bushy brow and hair twisted in knots all over his head, which he bent toward another man—thinner, with hair closely shorn. The two whispered, and the thinner man's face darkened. His gaze shot straight to Leif.

Knot Head slapped his friend, yanking his attention back.

There were times during a mission when a soldier got that gnawing in his gut that told him to pay attention. Be smart. Be ready. Or they'd put him six feet under. And this was one of those times.

"Something wrong?" Riordan asked.

Leif flinched, meeting Riordan's gray eyes. "No." But that person . . . What was Knot Head up to? He retracked the guy and found the thinner man had left. His instincts blazed. Leif searched the crowd. Spotted the thinner man weaving through the throng, straight toward Cell.

"You sure?" Riordan was persistent.

"Well, see . . . there's this story . . ." Leif muttered.

"Aw, man. He's always telling stories," Thor groused. "Don't get him started."

It was the perfect distraction, allowing Leif to monitor the thinner man, who'd made a circuit and was coming up alongside the team to Leif's seven. He tracked Thinner, turning his head to alert the guy that he had his number.

But Thinner was oblivious, intent on whatever he was doing. Scowling. Hands in front of his face. Hiding something. Fingers tapping. Brow sweaty.

"No."

Thinner reached between two people who stood directly behind Cell. Reached . . .

Leif came to his feet, rotating to face the guy and going for his weapon because training and habit told him he'd need it.

*It's a diversion!* From what? The other guy—Knot Head. Where had he gone?

"I see him." Riordan stepped to the right.

Thinner reached . . . right for Cell's holstered Sig.

# 9

## — MOSCOW, RUSSIA —

Walking through a field of knee-high manure wouldn't have smelled this bad. Stomach roiling, arms full of a jug, soap, and cloths, Tzivia cursed herself when she hesitated just inside the cell.

Rybakov jangled the keys as he secured the lock. "Twenty minutes." He gave the door one final tug before retreating to the shadows. Probably to get away from the smell.

She stabbed a glower at her jailer, willing it into barbs as sharp and fiery as the ones searing her heart. She hated them—Rybakov, Nur, the Arrow & Flame . . . herself.

Mostly herself. Because she hadn't looked for Abba sooner. She hadn't believed the lies that he was dead, so why she took so long to find him . . . And now she couldn't bring herself to turn and face what they'd done to her father.

Tzivia mechanically forced herself around. For courage, she breathed in—a mistake. The stench coated her tongue. She coughed, eyes watering, and resisted the urged to spin away. Shield her eyes from the horrific reality.

*He's your father, for pity's sake!*

Bracing herself, she squared her shoulders. Clutched the towels and jug of water they'd provided to clean him. Would it hurt the billionaire to give her father a bath?

No, Nur knew this would hurt *her*. And that was his point.

Tears stung as she knelt beside his huddled body, a gnarled hand clutching a torn, threadbare sheet over his shoulder. "A—" His name caught in her throat. She swallowed, told herself to gut it up. "Abba," she said, firming her greeting. "Abba, it's me—it's Tzivia."

He grunted, rocked away from her.

She reached for his shoulder, only then noting the brown stains on his hands and arms. Wiry gray hair, dirty and grimy. Unkempt beard. So unlike him. So not him. Her fingers trembled as she reached again toward him, toward the man who'd been a lecturer, a politician, a proud abba and husband, revered across the Levant in his day. The man she knew him to be, not the creature before her.

"Abba." Tzivia clasped his shoulder and tugged. "It's me, Tzivia. I'm here."

"No," he moaned, again rocking away. "No, leave me alone. I didn't do anything!"

Tzivia moved to the other side to face him. "Abba, it's me. See? Your Tzi."

Gray-green eyes fluttered beneath short lashes as he peered up at her. Confusion creased his brow. "Tzi . . . ?"

Tears blurred as she nodded. "I'm here. To help you." By all that was holy, she would not let this go unpunished.

He scowled, his beard rippling as his lips moved. "No. *No!* It's not. You trick me again. Play with my mind. Tzivia thinks I'm dead!" He waved her away. "Leave me. Do not torment an old man any more."

"No, Abba." She caught his hand and pressed it to her cheek. "See? Real."

His eyes brightened, widened. "Is it . . . really . . ." He lifted his head. "My Tzivia?"

"Yes! Yes, Abba. It's me."

He pushed up from the floor. "Oh, Tzi—God hears the prayers of His—" A coughing fit seized him, and he grabbed his chest.

Tzivia curled closer, bracing him as he struggled to remain upright. Nur would pay. They would all pay for this cruelty. This inhumanity.

But for now, she'd roll that anger aside. "I . . . I have water. To"—how did one tell their abba they would give them a sponge bath?—"help you."

Grief weighted his features. "Bathe me," he grunted with a shake of his head. "Is there no shame they cannot imagine?" His growl bounced off the stone ceilings.

"Shh," Tzivia said, turning a glower to her jailer. "At least we are together. And you will be cleaner." She splashed water onto the towel and wiped it along his face. "I swear to you—"

"Tzivia," he said, voice filled with chastisement for her swearing.

"I care not, Abba. I swear on my life they will pay."

* * * *

*No one ever told me grief felt so like fear.*

Kazimir Rybakov was sure the British author C. S. Lewis was referencing the physical response of the body to fear—flutterings, imaginings. While Kazimir was not *fluttering*, he did have a gnawing in his gut, because the Tzivia Khalon who'd first clung to the bars was not the same woman who walked out thirty minutes later, spine straight, chin up.

Seated in the darkness of the strange flat, he bent forward and roughed his palms together, mind snagged on the expression that had been on her face. He knew it. Knew what it meant. Knew there would be a lot of trouble if something—*someone*—didn't intervene.

But he couldn't. Nur had her neck in a noose. Kazimir should tell the billionaire, warn him that Khalon had left in a different state of mind. To which the AFO leader would laugh, say it was good she had changed.

Kazimir could simply sit on his thoughts. Monitor her closer than before. Pace her. Track her. He grunted, glancing around the darkened flat, the sun having long ago set. Tracking didn't guarantee anything, but he'd done that regardless. It wasn't really something that could protect her. At least not to the level she'd need in the days ahead with that dangerous glint in her eyes. No, Tzivia Khalon needed armor-plated protection.

Which was how Kazimir found himself in this flat, waiting in the dark hours past sunset. Alone. Cold. Afraid. It was the right thing, to come. To reveal what he knew. But doing so could wreck . . . everything.

He threaded his fingers and pressed his knuckles to his forehead, appreciating the counterpressure to the dull throb that had grown with each passing tick of the clock.

A noise in the alley drew his attention. He checked it, seeing nothing of interest.

He'd been integral in creating this mess, on the heels of another made by the one and only Tzivia Khalon. Middle name: Trouble.

And yet doing anything about Tzivia could compromise her, him, and the mission. He couldn't risk that. Couldn't let it happen. Not yet. Too many pieces were still in play. A dozen others hinging on the continuation. Pawns to maneuver. Traps to align.

Finding her had been a mission objective. But if Mossad learned he'd located her . . . she might not live to see the sunrise. They'd made it clear she was a national threat.

She had no idea the mess she'd stepped into. No, that wasn't true. She did know. And worse—she didn't care. She had a singular focus. Unfortunately, she didn't know the entirety of it. When a person grasped too tightly to only one idea, one way of doing things, they missed the ability to see alternatives. Smarter, stronger alternatives. She'd rushed headlong into his nightmare, convinced she knew right from wrong. And not caring if anyone agreed.

How did he make her care? How could he get Tzivia to pay attention to what was going on?

There was only one option. And it put him in the crosshairs.

Metal scraped metal, the grind of a lock being freed.

Kazimir lowered his hands, gaze sliding to the door at the far end of the darkened hall. From here, he was but one of many shadows in the unlit flat. The security panel blinked frantically as the door swung open. No beeping. No alarm. Silence. A shape filled the entry, backlit by the corridor of the residential building. Ram Khalon glanced around the darkened flat—waiting, listening—as he reached for the keypad, entered a code, and kicked the door shut. He'd done it many times. Rehearsed and regardless of visitors or trouble.

Tonight, the Mossad asset had both.

Curling his fingers into fists, Kazimir watched Khalon stroll down the hall, toss his keys on the kitchen counter, and lift a pile of envelopes. Mail. Bills. Normalcy.

Tensed, Kazimir thought of the weapon at the small of his back. Wondered if Khalon had one, too. Probably did. If not at his back, then around the apartment. Kazimir had to make sure he didn't reach one before they could have a talk.

Ram kept moving, rifling through the stack. He was within a half dozen paces.

Heart thudding, Kazimir readied himself. He'd only have one chance before Ram reacted. Activated an alarm.

Four paces.

Kazimir punched upward. His right leg shot out simultaneously with his right arm, effectively scissoring Khalon's body.

But Ram ducked and slid sideways.

Kazimir closed the gap.

Khalon was a blur of movement, plowing into Kazimir. Registering the move a second too late resulted in an agonizing blow to his gut. Thrust him backward. His legs clipped a small table. He hooked an arm around the back of Khalon's neck, bringing him down in a crescendo of shattering glass and cracking wood. Fire lanced his side, but he ignored the signal.

Pain exploded through his other side—a blow to the kidney. Agony nearly crippled him, but he knew Khalon was a master at Krav Maga and could deliver.

Still holding Khalon's head, Kazimir swung his legs and torso away, rolling and pulling Khalon with him. But Ram was faster. Stronger. More experienced. He shoved upward, slamming his head into Kaz's nose. Kazimir's vision blurred. Somehow disentangled, he hopped to his feet. Held his hands near his face, feeling the warmth sliding over his lip and mouth.

"Did I break it?" Khalon bounced a foot back. Waiting.

Kaz readied himself, mentally probing the injury to his nose. "No."

Khalon nodded. "You have two minutes."

Oh crap. "You hit a panic code."

"I could feel someone inside. You shouldn't be here." He stomped into the kitchen, grabbed a towel and some ice from the freezer, and tossed the makeshift ice pack to Kaz. "What're you doing here? You know the—"

"They have her."

Though Khalon was an expert at covert ops, at blending seamlessly into a situation, he could not hide the reaction that created a three-second hesitation. He nodded, but this time there was less confidence. Less authority. "You said you had eyes on her."

"And your father."

Ram jerked, eyes widening for a second before he steeled it. "So he's *not* dead."

"No, but if they keep him much longer . . . They're using him against her. They—"

"This!" Spinning away, Ram shook his head. Sighed and made a circuit around the flat. He paused at a bookcase. Faced Kaz. "This was stupid." His expression shifted from washed-out adrenaline slump to annoyance. Then anger. He shook his head again. "You've blown me. Blown yourself."

Kaz fisted a hand. "I know what coming here means. Don't think I didn't put a lot of thought into it. After what I went through, the months I spent preparing, leaving the woman I love . . ."

Ram's gaze hit the floor.

"It was a risk, I know, but we can make this look like I tracked down the devoted brother searching for his sister."

"The best lie is baked in truth."

"I confronted the famed Mossad asset, and we fought. I held my own."

"Not by my account."

"I'm still alive." Kaz smirked. "And though you tried, you didn't break my nose."

"Uncle Sam will thank me for not ruining that million-dollar job."

"Doubtful," Kaz said. "Then you gave me a message for Nur."

Ram sighed. "Might work." He snatched off his beanie and scratched the back of his head. "Why'd you come? Surely not just about Tzi." He eyed Kaz. "If Mossad loses confidence in me, they will deactivate me."

Which was code for *kill him*.

Kaz checked his watch, realizing he'd lost more than half his time already. "This whole thing with her is about a sword broken into three pieces. The adam-something or other." He noted Ram stiffen. "She already delivered the first piece."

Ram swore. Turned another circle. "Why didn't you tell me this sooner?"

That was a lot more reaction than he'd expected. "They're watching me—close. I might be his personal guard, but I won't mistake that for trust. I had to do a lot of switchbacks to make it here undetected." He frowned. "What do you know about this sword?"

"Later. We don't have—"

"No." He wasn't walking out of here empty-handed. "Give me something. I'm flying blind. What do I need to know?"

"Too much. We'll meet again, talk more."

"The sword?" Kaz reiterated.

"The Adama Herev—the sword of the mercenary Goliath."

Kazimir thought of the paintings in the penthouse. "He's jumping through a lot of hoops—using your sister, holding your father. Why is this sword so important?"

"It breaks a curse."

After his career in relic hunting, Kaz shouldn't be surprised, but the idea struck him wrong. "A curse?"

Resignation sagged against Ram's shoulders. "So they believe." He nodded to the door. "You have to go."

They didn't have any more time. "Eyes out, Ram. Something is off about this. Tzivia is *killing* to get this done. It worries me what she'll sacrifice to save your father—"

"Has she figured you out?"

Kaz shook his head. "I can see hesitation and curiosity when she looks at me, but she's too focused on the sword and your father." He extended a hand. "Stay strong."

Ram pulled him into a shoulder-patting hug. "And alive."

Though Kaz knew he shouldn't ask, though his training and wisdom told him to walk out the door, he glanced back. Their eyes locked. Meaning swirled. His thoughts on one person . . .

"She's fine," Ram said.

A thousand-pound weight lifted from his chest. But it didn't leave him. Wouldn't until he was back home with her. For now, that cinder block sat on his shoulders, a burden and responsibility, an obligation to keep the vow he'd made by the Sea of Galilee six months ago. "Thanks." Relieved, he started for the door.

"Wait." Ram was watching a security feed on his phone, face awash in the glow of the screen. "They're coming up the stairs," he finally said, then met Kaz's gaze. "The roof. There's another building to the north. Easy jump."

With a nod, Kaz twisted the knob.

"Hey."

He glanced back.

"Be careful. Nur isn't known to be forgiving."

"No kidding."

"Watch yourself, Tox."

"Will do."

# 10

## — REPUBLIC OF THE CONGO —

A shout went up—Riordan—commanding the attention of everyone in the hut at the exact same time Cell's hand latched onto Thinner's wrist.

Leif pivoted as screams rent the air. Shouts. Wails and cries. *Where's Knot Head?* The sea of bodies rose into churning chaos. He glanced toward the rear opening of the hut.

Streaks of tan shot through the dense jungle foliage beyond the hut. Leif surged, convinced it was Knot Head. When he reached the hut's first step, he spotted the lanky form bounding up the hillside, his tan shirt glaring against the green foliage and deep brown dirt.

Over his shoulder, Leif checked the team. "Cell! Maangi! On me!" He burst after the escapee. The guy looked like Makanda, but they hadn't been close enough to verify. But why would he need to set up a diversion and escape? Why had he been so nervous during the meeting?

Leif threw himself up the hillside, using a side-to-side motion to gain momentum. Leaves thwapped his face, but he locked onto the frantic pace of Knot Head.

"Runt! What?" Cell shouted, his voice growing closer.

They gained a road, and the terrain leveled out enough that Leif's speed was no longer impeded. And that gave him the advantage. "Stop!" he shouted as he lifted his Sig and aimed. "Stop or I will shoot!"

The guy either wasn't listening, didn't speak English, or didn't care. But the sound of a gunshot was a language everyone understood. Leif aimed carefully at a tree just over the guy's shoulder and fired. Bark erupted. Just as fast, the guy banked right—as anticipated. Leif fired again.

Ricochet effect. Like a ping-pong ball, the guy went left.

Leif aimed at Knot Head's feet and fired a round into the ground. Rock and dirt exploded, forcing the guy to skid to a stop. He lifted his hands.

Sig trained on him, Leif closed the gap. "Do you speak English?"

The man's eyes rammed into his. His lips tightened.

"Makanda." When he still didn't respond, Leif tested a theory. "Speak, or I shoot."

Eyes widened. Hands shifted. "Little."

"Are you Didier Makanda?" Leif asked, reaching for his printed copy of the photo—he never trusted technology to work in the field. "Didier Makanda." He held up the photo. Matched the eyes. "Why aren't you talking?" They needed him to verify his identity.

"Scared."

"Of what?"

A moment later, somone emerged from the jungle with long, purposeful strides. Brow creased, lips tight, Trigger stalked toward them, followed by Riordan. "Guys, what's going on?" he demanded. "The uncle is—"

"What's your name?" Leif demanded again.

The man's eyes widened as the team closed in, weapons up, tensions high. "Mani—Mani Ilunga."

Like a bolt of lightning, Trigger blurred into action. A strike to the back of the man's legs delivered a resounding *thwack* that brought Mani to his knees. Another to the back of his head pitched him forward. The hits were hard enough to nearly face-plant him but not enough to knock him out.

Leif started. "What the—"

"Stop!"

"Hey!"

Leif lunged between them, holding Trigger off. "Stop, stop!" He looked between Trigger and the man he'd literally just brought to his knees.

"Dude. What the *crack*?" Cell asked, his voice a mixture of fright and disbelief.

Trigger lifted hooded, annoyed eyes to them. "*This* is not Mani Ilunga." He pointed to the hut. "Mani is the one who tried to steal the gun."

"You sure?" Leif asked, wary.

"I wouldn't have humbled him if I wasn't," Trigger said. "Uncle called Mani by name inside."

Weapon down but still ready, Leif edged closer to the villager. "What is your name?"

The man slumped lower but didn't answer.

"Name. Now."

Unyielding.

Trigger crouched and slid a hand toward the man's throat, a move that worried the man into lifting his head and leaning away. A stream of French flew from Trigger's lips with no effect.

"Just kill him and move on?" Cell said, in threat only, to get the man to talk. It had worked before.

"His eyes are empty of hope," Trigger said as he straightened.

"What if he's not Makanda?" Maangi walked a perimeter around them. "We're wasting time."

"But if he is, then we're right where we need to be," Riordan said as he gave Runt a nod. "I'm with you on this one."

"Are you Didier Makanda?" Leif repeated.

The guy didn't budge.

Leaves rustled, and movement came from Leif's three. In his periphery, he caught sight of Grease hurrying toward them. The SEAL closed the space between them and pressed his chest to Riordan's shoulder, whispering, before heading back toward the village.

"Might have trouble." Riordan shifted. "Jekyll sighted two SUVs entering the village, hot and fast."

Their attempted escapee shot upward, which made gazes and weapons snap at him.

"Stop!" Leif stared down the muzzle of his Sig with fierce warning.

The man lifted his hands. "You come with me." He slapped a palm against his chest. "Hurry. Hurry."

When he started backing up, Leif tensed his arms. "Stay there! Stay!"

Shifting, still inching backward, the man rattled in French, his expression packed with panic. But there was one word—a name—that came out clear.

"Wait. Dude—did he just say Makanda?"

Trigger twitched. "He says that Labaka is coming. That he doesn't talk with words but bullets. If we go with him, he will take us to Makanda."

Leif's hesitation vanished, then was replaced by a completely new one. "A bit handy that he's suddenly cooperative."

"Or that he suddenly knows the guy we're after," said Riordan, touching his comms piece and glancing back. "Copy that," he said into his mic. "Negative. Clear out and head north two klicks." He met Leif's gaze. "Newcomers are paying a lot of attention to our vehicles. Whether or not this guy knows Makanda, it won't hurt to put some ground between us and the newcomers."

"Agreed."

*Crack! Pop!*

A chorus of shouts and cries went up from the hut. Villagers spilled onto the hillside, screaming and crying. Mayhem ensued.

"Move, move!" Leif ordered.

Knot Head flung himself into the foliage, hands slicing the air as he sped around fronds and trees like nobody's business. Was the guy trying to lose them?

The team sprinted after him. Hopping over logs and avoiding the sting of swaying fronds, Leif hustled. He considered himself in pretty good shape, but moving ninety to nothing uphill through jungle cover slowed him enough that the newcomers could catch up.

They rounded a tall tree, and realization hit Leif with a baseball bat—Knot Head was gone. He slowed to a stop, weapon up as he turned a circle but only saw foliage—fronds, plants, flowers, trees.

"Where'd he go?" Riordan growled, doing the same, as the rest of the guys caught up.

Panting, Cell brought up the rear and muttered an oath. "You have *got* to be kidding!"

"Think he wanted to lose us?"

Leif nodded. "Probably his one goal. I knew he was moving too fast."

Cell growled. "Going to hurt this guy when—"

"Here. Here." Unbelievably, not three yards to their twelve, a massive frond shifted aside and revealed the bright, amused expression of their runner. "Come. Come. Good hide, yes?"

Leif eyed the team, then caught a glower from Riordan. Knot Head had played them. Deliberately used the distance he'd gained to hide himself. With caution, they realized he was in a type of hideout. Walled in with bamboo that left gaps to watch through, the space was contained. Hidden. In plain sight.

They entered, and the guy secured a makeshift door. "We can stay here until they leave. It is safe."

Leif snapped up his weapon and noticed Riordan and Cell had done the same, forcing the guy to take a step back and lift his hands again. "Where is Makanda?"

"Worry about the men who came. They are sent by Herve Labaka."

Riordan snorted. "Herve Labaka is the prime minister. He's revered for the change and stability he's brought to the region."

"Only to his own pocketbook." Lips tight, the man scowled. "Labaka is not good man. He has an angel face but heart of a devil."

"Why would Labaka care about a village like this?" Leif asked.

The guy lifted his chin, but there was something broken, something grieved in his expression. "He does not care about village. Or my people—my friends or family. Or my uncle."

"Dude. Your uncle?" Cell sniggered.

"Fan out. Take cover," Riordan ordered. They took up positions to watch for trouble.

"Out here, the eldest uncle is the tribal leader," Trigger explained. "Essentially, their chief."

Family. Friends. People. The wording bounced back to Leif, snagged on one thing he hadn't said. "What about you?"

"Me?" Black eyes challenged—no, dared Leif to make the connection.

"You said Labaka didn't care about *this* village, your people, your friends, or your family. You never said he cared about 'our' village, 'our families.'" Was he out of his gourd to think this? "This isn't your village, is it?"

The guy swallowed.

"So Labaka is here because of you." Leif nodded. "You're Didier Makanda."

The man sighed. "I am."

"What does he want with you?"

Makanda tapped his temple. "I know something he not want anyone to know. The code to *Blood Genesis*."

Maangi barked a laugh. "To what?"

"It is a game," Makanda explained. "I was attending university—"

"Never mind," Leif said, feeling too closed in, too trapped. Too far from safe ground. "You're Makanda?" he asked, merely to reaffirm.

"I am."

"Then let's go." Leif pointed toward the makeshift door. "We clear out before—"

"No, no. We stay until they leave. A friend tell us when it safe."

"It's safe—"

*Boom! Boom-boom! Boom!*

Vibrations wormed through his boots as Leif's gaze lifted to the canopy. Heard the rustling of limbs shaken by a concussion. What had just been blown?

"What was that?" Cell muttered, then whistled.

"Big explosions," Trigger noted.

"Huts wouldn't blow like that, not on their own," Leif said.

"That was mechanical," Riordan suggested.

"And you know that how?" Maangi groused.

"Bamboo doesn't have an ignition source that would create a secondary explosion."

"Maybe they have fertilizer." Cell clicked his tongue. "We need—"

Riordan yanked his gaze away, angled his head as he pressed his comms piece. "Go ahead, Jekyll." He listened, then shifted back to them, locked on Leif. "Copy that. Hold position." He released the mic, his beard and the muscle below his left eye twitching. "Those were our vehicles they just blew."

Understanding dawned on Leif. "Making sure we can't get away easily."

"Or alive," Riordan said. "Jekyll says they blew two, left one—but they messed with it. He couldn't see for sure, but he thinks they planted pressure plates."

Leif ran a hand down his face.

"We stay until dark," Makanda said, "then I take you back."

Leif didn't like the idea, but they had little choice. "A'right. While we wait—tell us about this *Blood Genesis*."

# TILL CONQ'RING DAVID O'ER THE GIANT STRODE

For years he had fought with him. For years he had warred at his side, their long blades clashing time and again with the Saracens. Defending our Lord Jesus Christ. Defending the faith. The Church. Christians.

But this day, this battle, the impact of a sword unseated him. Knocked Giraude Roussel to the ground. Pain sluiced through his side as disbelief colored his world. Shame wrapped him in its heavy cloak and he cradled his wound, struggling to his feet on the rain-drenched hillside. He felt the way his leathered gloves stuck to the blood pulsing from him. Stumbled to a knee. Took a measuring breath.

This battle Giraude was not sure he would survive. The heady thought held him to the ground, his gaze tracking the brutality with which his brother-knights fought. The fury leaching blood from their enemies.

With a roar, Thefarie dug his heels into his destrier. The beast reared before pitching itself down the body-strewn field.

*All this for a sword.*

Bereft of willpower to climb to his feet, Giraude braced himself there. His destrier stomped closer with a nervous nicker, and though he caught the reins, the strength he would need to pull into the saddle spilled from his side onto the bloody field.

An arm came around his. Tight yet frail. It hauled him upright. He met a pair of brown eyes with surprise. Flicked a frown. "Get to safety."

But the diminutive man nodded to the horse, indicating Giraude should mount up. His gaze shot to Thefarie, as relentless as the dawn. Had he the same mettle, Giraude would be there, protecting his brother-knight's back rather than being coddled by a servant.

The thought pushed him to his feet. Giraude reached for the reins and accidentally knocked the man in the head. Something fell loose, and he frowned as he caught sight of a length of hair hanging over the man's shoulder.

Not a man.

Her eyes widened. She tucked the long queue beneath her mantle.

"Why are you here, girl?" he growled, casting a glance about, fearing she might be seen and taken, then ravaged by the Saracens.

"Your injury," she said nodding to his side. "When the battle is ended, Yitshak the healer will tend you. Find the three oaks on the hillside. He's there." She shot away, her movements agile and quick.

Swords sang through the air, yanking him back to the battle. Steel clanged against steel as a Saracen met him on the ground, shrieking as he threw his full weight at Giraude. Though injured, Giraude still had his wits. Using the Saracen's momentum against him, he swung around. Swept a foot out and caught his leg.

The Saracen's face plowed the muddy and blood-drenched ground. He flopped like a fish out of water, struggling for solid footing.

Giraude would give him no time to find it. With his solemn oath thudding against his heart, he hefted his sword and drove it into him, simultaneously stepping in and removing the Saracen's long blade before it could be turned against him.

The Saracen stiffened as Giraude twisted the sword, being sure to inflict the most damage for a swift, clean death. After extracting it and watching the Saracen fall to his death, he considered the battle. His vision blurred, the loss of blood evident. A great shape beat a hard path to him.

"Brother!" Thefarie.

Giraude felt a smile crease his lips. "It is done?"

"The sword is not found, but the battle is over." With a flourish, Thefarie dismounted and stormed to his side. "You need a healer."

Shifting on the mud-slicked ground, Giraude looked to the hillside where the girl had run. "There. A healer is there."

Thefarie assisted him back to his destrier. Regrouping with their sergeants and the other brother-knights, they rode through the rain to the cluster of oak and fig trees. Relief warmed him when the three oaks finally took shape.

Giraude dismounted, his legs going limp beneath him. Thefarie was at his side before he even realized what had happened.

"You'll soil your mantle, brother," Thefarie warned, his tone light, deflecting any humiliation as he drew Giraude to his feet. "Here, boy!"

No. Not a boy. It was her. She glanced over her shoulder, a worried expression stealing into her face. "In here," she said.

"You're a girl."

She skewered both of them with a glare, then vanished beneath the flap of the tent. Thefarie chuckled as he helped Giraude through the entrance.

Giraude smelled it. Metallic. Foul. Blood. His eyes hit the body laid out in the tent. He brandished his sword, an angry growl climbing his throat at the sight of the Saracen.

"No!" she shouted, hands out in a placating manner. "He is not an enemy."

"He is a Saracen," Giraude barked.

"He is wounded, and my abba is a healer. Please," she implored. "No violence." Her eyes. Those eyes. They pierced the veil around his heart. "He says he knows what you want. That he can take you to it, if you will let him be healed."

# 11

## — MOSCOW, RUSSIA —

"Ram, you live?"

"Roger," Ram said, adjusting his laptop in front of him. He angled into the feed, gazing behind Almstedt and the team to the dark-skinned youth handcuffed at the far end of the table. Beside him sat the lanky form of Chijioke Okorie, and near him, Haven. The former was there for translating language, the latter would translate body language, if needed. Two Marines were within reach of the boy, their hands clasped, gazes zeroing in on nothing yet everything.

Wraith had made quick work of locating and extracting the Congolese boy. Didier Makanda had the wide-eyed stare of a kid caught in the middle of an adult argument.

"Okay, Mr. Makanda," Robbie said, turning her chair to face the boy. "I know you explained some things to the soldiers here, but this meeting is to be thorough and explore all possible questions. Understood?"

Makanda eyed Chiji but nodded before the Igbo native responded.

"Okay, good." Robbie smiled. "Why don't we start at the top? When the men arrived on site, you fled. Tell us why."

Threading his fingers, the boy leaned closer to the table, skating a quick look at Chiji again. "I thought Labaka's men had found me."

"You refer to Herve Labaka?"

"Yes. He is a bad man." He sliced his hands over the table. "People think he is this great leader, but he makes us do things."

Nodding, Almstedt jotted notes, and Ram noted Rodriguez squaring into the feed on the lower half.

"Why would Mr. Labaka come after you?" the general asked.

"It started as a game," Makanda said. "Something I do in my time when not studying at university. My friends and I work hard on this game."

"Wait," Ram said, his brain catching up. "You mean a real game?"

Makanda looked to Chiji, who spoke quickly and quietly to the boy in French.

"Yes," Makanda said. "A game on the computer. I have brain for that thing. How I get to university. But *Blood Genesis*—my game—"

"Dude." Cell leaned forward, his eyebrows raised. "*Blood Genesis* is yours?"

Makanda nodded.

"*Blood Genesis*?" Thor asked.

"Just one of biggest viral hit games of the year."

"What's it do?"

"It's a game. It entertains," Cell snarked.

"The game is based on interacting with a procedurally generated world with procedurally generated creatures," Makanda said.

"Yeah, but it's legit. Not boring the way he makes it sound." Cell shook his head.

"How did that draw Labaka's attention?" Ram asked.

"I do not know. We make the talisman program, and the game does really well. Then they come to me and say they hire me. Give me a million dollars if I change the program to help him. So I did. One week after I turn it over to them, they try to kill me. So I hide."

After an hour of similar questions and more frustration, Thor tossed a pen on the table. "What am I missing? Why is Labaka interested in this? Why did we pull this kid—for a freakin' game?"

Ram ran his knuckles over his mouth, studying the boy. "Cell, talk to him and see if you can find a connection."

"Whoa, dude. This is like apples and oranges. The kid's a genius with coding, but I'm not. That's like asking Maangi to do neurosurgery."

"A body is made of hands and feet, Mr. Purcell," Almstedt said, her voice thick with frustration. "Each one has its purpose, which in turn cooperates with other parts to serve the whole."

Cell glanced at her. "That was a bad analogy, ma'am. Especially if you're saying we're the feet."

"Or armpits," Thor muttered, eliciting snickers from Maangi and Runt.

She turned back to Makanda. "Thank you. The Marines will take you back now." Once he was gone, she said to the others, "A ten-minute break. Dr. Cathey's on his way up."

Haven stood. "Sorry, I would love to stay and help, but I have an appointment, so I need to go as well."

"What did you think about the boy?" Robbie asked.

"Scared but honest," Haven said. "I could watch the video, but this time I think what we see is real."

"Thank you."

Haven glanced at the camera, at Ram, telegraphing her ache for Cole. "If you see him . . ."

"Will do," Ram said, not wanting more to be said or to be dragged into a conversation that couldn't be finished for security reasons.

* * * *

**— WASHINGTON, DC —**

Haven waited in the secure passage as Chiji whispered with the young Congolese man, who looked concerned.

Ram had deflected her question, which she'd expected, but she didn't like what she saw in his eyes. Where was Cole? Was he okay? Why wouldn't Ram give her some reassurance? Did he know their secret? Was he annoyed?

"No," she whispered to herself as voices swirled through the cold, cement bunker. She smiled, her spirit lightening at the arrival of three men who had impacted her life in one way or another. "Levi."

"Kasey." He nodded. "I didn't realize you were still consulting."

"Mostly not, but I came with Chiji, whose language skills were handy." She embraced Dr. Cathey with a laugh. "Very good to see you again, professor. How are you?"

"Never better, and I see"—he clasped her shoulders and peered over his readers at her—"the same is true for you. My dear, you look radiant!"

Haven laughed. "I'm sure that's exaggeration, but I won't correct you." She took a breath to bolster her courage and meet the last set of eyes. "Mr. Tzaddik." She never could bring herself to call him by the other name, which was probably his true name.

The Timeless One drifted closer and pressed a kiss to both of her cheeks. "Have you found anything yet?"

"No—"

"But Sunday was days ago." His brow knotted.

"It was." Haven hated herself for cringing. "But Charlotte returned ill and postponed the dinner. I'm on my way there now."

The dark clouds parted, and he eased back. "Good." He touched her shoulder. "Forgive my urgency, but it is . . . I cannot express the importance."

She arched an eyebrow. "I think you've done that quite well."

After a nod to him, then Dr. Cathey, she started for the stairs, hoping Chiji would follow soon. It simply took too much out of her to remain with Tzaddik. He both emboldened and sapped her. By the time she reached the top step, Haven heard the approach of Chiji and the *whoosh* of the security hub below that swallowed the three men.

The trip out to the Russell estate took twenty-five minutes, a short commute by DC metro standards. The last ten unwound the tension knots that seemed to leach the strength from her limbs.

They approached the front door, which swung open.

"Ah, Haven, darling. Come in. I'm terribly sorry I had to cancel on you last week." Charlotte led them into the family room. "Haven's here, Eric."

Mr. Russell came up out of his recliner and muted the news glowering from the large entertainment wall. "Haven. Good to see you."

She returned the greeting, unable to miss how much Eric's sons resembled him—Galen in the swagger and debonair looks, and Cole in the powerful presence and natural authority.

"What do you think of that one?" he grunted, waving at the screen, where journalists were interviewing a woman. "Charlie and I don't agree."

"Not true," Charlotte countered. "You said she's too young to know anything, and I said you can't discount her on age alone."

"Well, it's hard to tell with no sound," Haven said, "but her posture seems defensive or concealing."

"Ha!" Mr. Russell said, pointing at his wife. "See? What'd I tell you, Charlie? That woman's hiding something!" He pounced in his recliner and jammed the remote. Dialogue blew through the room, both on the television and with Chiji, who positioned himself on the loveseat near their host.

"Aren't we all?" Charlotte said with a laugh. "Everyone has a secret."

Haven started. Felt a trill of warmth. Cole's mom couldn't possibly know. Could she?

Charlotte motioned to the kitchen. "So, you said something about genealogy."

"Yes." Haven slid into a padded shield chair at the dinette. "Cole was looking into it before he left, but he didn't get to the French side."

"French?" Charlotte sat back as the butler brought over steaming tea and scones. "There isn't a drop of French blood in Cole's veins. My family was from Scotland and England. Eric's is almost entirely from London. The Russells had a barony and quite a large estate there going back centuries."

Confused, Haven hesitated, recalling with perfect clarity the name Tzaddik had given—Giraude Roussel. French. Definitely French. "Knights."

"What—knights?" Charlotte laughed. "Oh yes. There were knights among Eric's family. It was an arduous process to become a knight, to prove oneself to the crown."

"And Templars?"

"Why on earth would you ask that?"

Haven smiled. "I guess the last mission, with the historical elements and that knight who tried to find the crown, got me thinking . . ."

"Show her the journal," Eric said, walking through the dining area into the kitchen, where he poured a glass of water.

"The journal!" Charlotte shoved up from her seat. "Of course. I haven't thought of that old thing in ages." She bustled through the halls.

Eric gulped some water, then glanced at the glass, standing still and distracted. Completely unlike Eric Russell.

"Is everything okay?" Haven asked.

His gray-blue eyes came to her. "How is he?"

Her heart melted, surprised at the undercurrent of sentimentality in that simple question. Haven smiled. "Fine. Last I heard."

"You brought him back once. I know you'll do it this time." He winked. "You want to get married, so pray him home. Charlotte can't handle losing him again. None of us can."

"He knows I'd chase him to the grave," Haven said with a grim smile. "He doesn't take this new lease on life lightly. He's determined to make the best of it."

"Then why'd he leave us again?" Without another word, Cole's dad strode out of the kitchen.

Deflating at both the hurt and anger she heard in his voice, Haven turned back to the table. To her untouched scone. To the glint of sapphire on her left ring finger. She thought of the gold band at home in the safe. Of the commitment made with it. Of the secret they could not share . . . until he returned. *Yes, you'd better come back to me, Cole Russell.*

"I cannot believe I forgot about this." Charlotte's lighthearted voice drifted from the hall, preceding her by seconds. As she rounded the corner, she was brushing her fingers over aged leather. She passed it to Haven. "I imagine this will be a nice read for you until Cole returns."

The large journal had a thong wrapped twice around its width, tethered to a gorgeous green stone. Stamped into the walnut-colored leather was an emblem of an *R*, but behind it—"The Templar cross."

Charlotte drew back with an "Oh!" She huffed. "So it is. I don't recall that being there. It could be a normal cross, you know." Was she justifying? "English nobility were expected to patronize the king, who was the head of the church."

When the butler removed her scone and cold tea, Haven thanked him, then set down the journal and opened it. The press of years released, fanning the air with the indelible scent of ink, history, and a long legacy.

The stiff, brittle pages seemed to resist her intrusion. What a marvel! Peering into Cole's ancestry. Into men who had taken wives, who had borne children. Time blurred the inked years and names. Sketched on random pages were emblems, renderings of homes, faces. Which would soon surrender their secrets.

# 12

## — MOSCOW, RUSSIA —

After a two-hour delay, Ram watched the feed as Levi Wallace stepped through the door and held it for Dr. Cathey, who glanced back out into the hallway, then again to the command center. He shook his head, elevating the tension and buzzing of nerves in the room and feeds.

"Where'd Tzaddik go?" Levi asked, shuffling to check outside.

"He had other errands, apparently," Dr. Cathey said.

"Looks like things are about to get downright historical," Thor said as he returned from the break room with a cup of black coffee.

"Let's get started." Deputy Director of the Central Intelligence Agency Dru Iliescu never wasted words or time. "We have a lot of irons in the fire and need to pull things together. Ram, you have information?"

Ram sat forward. "I have it on good authority that the AFO might be a little distracted right now. They're apparently on a search-and-destroy mission for an ancient sword." He let his gaze hit Cathey.

"Boom!" Cell said with a puff of his cheeks. "Missing artifact. Here we go, boys!"

Ram continued. "My asset said the sword is in three pieces, but one has been found." They all had to know what artifact it was. There could be no guessing. Not among those on this team.

A chair groaned, drawing his gaze to Dr. Cathey's haunted expression. "Ram." His tone seemed burdened. "You are sure that's what he said, that they are searching for it—a piece has been found?"

Irritation scraped raw the wound that had festered in Ram for most of his life. "I wouldn't mention it otherwise."

"No. No, of course not." Dr. Cathey sounded hollow.

"You look like you've seen a ghost, professor," Maangi noted.

"A very large one, I'm afraid," Dr. Cathey replied. "I heard from Mr. Tzaddik that, aside from strategic maneuvering on a global scale with governments and world powers, the Arrow & Flame Order has always had one goal."

"Wait." Cell held up a hand, glancing around. "How'd we drop-kick this from a three-piece sword to the AFO?" he asked, rubbing his chest. "Not exactly fond of those arrow-shooting vermin."

Dr. Cathey inclined his head. "Mr. Tzaddik often goes on about the AFO and the one mission they always fail. One they have pursued at great cost and with much bloodshed."

Ram took a measuring breath as he stared at Dr. Cathey, whose forlorn expression mirrored his own. "To locate and control the sword of Goliath of Gath."

"We're talking fee-fi-fo-fum Goliath? The giant?"

"Cell," Thor said. "That's an English rhyme."

"About a giant. I'm just saying." Undeterred, Cell dragged a tablet closer and started tapping away. "David and Goliath. Like from the Bible." He stifled a smile. "This is right up our alley."

"You mentioned artifacts," Robbie cut in, "so you've got my attention. Fill us in—what's special about that sword?"

Why did answering her questions feel like stepping off a cliff into a churning, boulder-strewn river? "It's been the AFO's veritable Holy Grail for centuries," Ram said.

"The AFO and this sword . . ." Almstedt leaned in, arms on the table as she narrowed her gaze. "Is that"—she shook her head, squinting—"somehow connected to the arrow serial killings? Because I'm not seeing it."

"The only connection is the AFO," Dr. Cathey said.

"That's a phosphorous-big connection," Cell muttered, his gaze on the tablet, intensely focused.

"He's right," Robbie said. "And I'll be hanged if I'm going to stand idly by while they strike at us again. Wallace, what have your people found out about the murders here?"

Wallace shrugged. "Little. Congressman Seaton had a dozen different programs in the pike and many more he'd championed, including the FBI's TAFFIP."

"Then what are you saying?" Robbie hesitated. "That the AFO isn't behind the killings?"

"Considering the means of the murders, I don't think anyone would be foolish enough to say that," Levi said. "But the death of George Schenck has no apparent connection to the congressman or the killings in other countries. The only similarity is means of death. We can't find a link between the victims."

"I noticed that, but I think there's something we're not seeing." Almstedt slumped back in her creaky chair.

"Agreed," Iliescu said with a slow nod that built to a fervent one. "There's a connection between the killings and Makanda's work with the game—*Blood Genesis.* They are both singularly unique, both arising now." His gaze hit Almstedt again. "You're right. They're connected. We just have to find out how."

Almstedt sighed, seemingly half-relieved, half-overwhelmed. "Okay, you heard the deputy director, Wallace—keep digging. If you find anything, keep us posted." She turned and glanced down the command table. "Moving on. Mr. Tzaddik said the AFO's long-range goal has always been this sword. What accelerated their timeline?"

"I believe," Dr. Cathey said finally, shifting, "this hunt for the Adama Herev—"

"The what?" Cell propped his ankle on his knee.

"The name of the sword the AFO is after," Dr. Cathey explained.

"It has a name?"

"All great swords have a name," Runt retorted.

"The meaning"—Dr. Cathey slid his readers up onto his head to peer at them better—"loosely translated, is the 'thirst for the blood,' or 'the thirst of steel.'"

"So," Thor muttered, "sword. We are talking about the one David used to kill Goliath, right?"

Eyes on his tablet, Cell raised a hand. "Didn't I already ask that?" Then he yanked his gaze up. "But wait. David used a slingshot to slay the giant. Didn't he?"

Dr. Cathey nodded. "Yes, David used his slingshot to fell Gulat, but then lifted the sword—which would've been a feat in and of itself, as the sword was purposed for Gulat, who is said to have been a giant, descended from or one of the Nephilim. Legends differ. He was to wield the Adama Herev against the Hebrews." He lifted a finger. "Homer recorded a similar story about the battle of champions in the *Iliad*."

"Back that truck up," Cell said, setting the tablet on the table. "I think . . . I think I might see a connection." Sliding his thumb along the screen, he pointed down range to Wallace. "That senator who was killed . . ."

"Seaton."

"Yeah." Cell snapped his fingers. "Him. You said he was behind that fingerprint system."

"He sponsored it but didn't create it."

"Yeah, yeah." Cell wagged his hand in a circle. "But you see—that. I need to talk to Makanda again, but . . ." He drummed his thumb on the screen. "I think I might know why the AFO wanted his program."

"You have the floor, Mr. Purcell," Robbie said.

He looked at her, distracted, then glanced back at his tablet. "I mean—yeah, I need to look into this more, but the basis of Makanda's game is these generated creatures." He touched his fingertips together. "But when creatures meet and interact, the computer is detecting similarities between the two totally random creatures and then deciding a course of action based off that data." He looked at them, a grin stuck on his face.

"I'm sure that means something," Thor grunted.

"English," Ram muttered. "We need that translated."

"The program aggregates data . . ." Cell's smile fell. He narrowed his eyes. "Hm, maybe not." He shifted and bent over the tablet. "I need to talk to Makanda."

Robbie nodded. "Work on it, Mr. Purcell."

"Wallace, how many stateside murders so far?" Ram shifted.

Wallace's jaw muscle popped a few times before he answered. "To date, two."

"And as mentioned before, there have been a smattering of them around the globe," Robbie said. "I had another two tracked down in Europe, and I think we've found at least three more in Asia."

"Yeah," Cell said, squinting, "and the most recent got splattered all over the news because it was that senator."

"Congressman."

"Right. Whatever. Politician. Same meat. He helped the FBI—" Hauling in a sharp breath, Cell jerked straight. Animated. "Wait-no-what!" He snatched up the tablet. "That program y'all use for fingerprinting, what is it? Tepid something."

"TAFFIP."

"Right!" Cell snapped his fingers again. "Twice As Fast or some bull."

"No bull." Wallace seemed more annoyed than ever. "The program works."

Cell's face was tied in knots of consternation. "How's it work?"

Wallace shrugged. "I'm an assistant special agent, not IT."

"Right." Cell turned to Ram. "What if they're using that to track down people and kill them?"

With a barked laugh, Wallace shook his head. "How did you connect those dots?"

Cell rubbed his chin. "Just seems interesting—Makanda's got this program. The congressman that got killed championed a program—"

"Along with umpteen dozen other bills," Wallace challenged. "There are no connections between the victims, save that they are all male." He shook his head, dripping disdain. "They didn't know each other. Different appearances, ages, body types."

"Blood types," Cell suggested.

Shaking his head again, Wallace huffed. "TAFFIP doesn't take blood. Only fingerprints."

But Cell had chomped onto this flank steak of an idea and wasn't letting go. "This is connected. Soup Maker and the AFO sword hunt are linked. I can feel it." His fingers danced over the tablet again. "It's here somewhere. I need a full system."

"Reel it in, Purcell," Almstedt ordered. "Let's get back on track."

"Ram, professor," Rodriguez said with a long-suffering sigh, "why does the AFO want this sword? And why the push? They seem to have a fire under them now."

Ram didn't want to voice the truth, the reality of why the AFO was so obsessed with that sword. A truth that affected—*infected*—him.

"There is a curse," Dr. Cathey rejoined the conversation, "at least in Judaic tradition. Though the Bible mentions Goliath's sword, it does not delve into the dark history of that sword, where it came from, as it doesn't for many things."

"Fill us in, professor," Runt said.

"To explain the curse, we must step back to the origination of the sword." Dr. Cathey glanced at a tablet. "While you were chatting, I scanned some articles. The very simplified version is this: During the time of wars between the Philistines and the Hebrews, a band arose that eventually gave rise to or were re-created as—there is debate over which—the Hashashin, the first assassins. Originally they were called the Niph'al. It is believed by some that the Philistines—of whom Goliath was descended—were essentially mercenaries. The Philistines were long at war with the Hebrews and could not wipe them out. So some of their sect colluded with the Niph'al to end what they saw as the Hebrew blight."

Dr. Cathey took a long, heavy breath, then let it out slowly before continuing. "The Niph'al were eventually absorbed into the Nizari Ismailis. Today, the Nizari are a branch of Shi'a Muslims who broke from the main line on the issue of succession. However, in their origin days, they developed a form of defense that led to their being known as the Hashashin—or assassins. Today, there are many of them in the Arrow & Flame." He cocked his head in a crooked nod. "At least, that is the tale. There is an ongoing argument among scholars and clergy about whether Gulat was one of the Fallen, or if he was but a half-breed, a descendant." He pursed his lips in another shrug. "Or perhaps he was simply a man grown too tall."

"The Fallen?" Thor barked a laugh. "Now it's angels and demons?"

Dr. Cathey considered them. "I was not there, so I cannot guarantee it, Mr. Thorsen, but I am sharing what the legends say. It's lore. For you to hear and decide. But if these interruptions persist, you will not hear and cannot decide. Now, do I have your ears?"

"Pretty sure you have your own," Thor taunted. He fist-bumped Maangi.

"The sword, Dr. Cathey," Rodriguez said as he shot the guys a glare. "Why now? Why . . . at all?"

This was where things got tricky, and Ram wasn't sure he wanted this information divulged. It was like filleting his own flesh.

"Of course." Dr. Cathey paused to take a sip from a water bottle. "As the Bible relates, the angels were cast down to Earth for their rebellion and attempt to seize power for themselves. Though running rampant and set violently against God's greatest creation—mankind—the Fallen were still tethered to the will of God, which, for example, is why Lucifer needed God's permission to test, or sift, His servant Job. It's why the demons possessing the boy obeyed Jesus's command to go into the herd of pigs, then ran them off the cliff. The Fallen have long sought to usurp authority here on Earth. Despite many attempts to wipe out God's chosen, they have failed. So they devised a plan with the sword to enslave the Hebrews for all time.

"Fast forward to the time of David and Goliath. The great irony is that nobody expected Goliath to be defeated, certainly not by a smelly shepherd boy. It's said the early sect that would become the Nizari Ismailis made the sword for Goliath to use and enslave the Hebrews, but it backfired. He was such a formidable warrior, so they chose him to wield the Adama Herev. Some have speculated it was a battle of champions—Goliath versus David—a little-used form of battle to decide the victor." He smiled and snickered. "Imagine the great shock when David felled the Philistine, then used the Adama Herev, which was meant to enslave David's people, but instead—"

"Enslaved the Philistines," Runt finished.

"Indeed. And some suggest the sect was placed under a curse as well for conspiring against God's people by producing the sword."

"So," Thor said, sitting straighter, elbows on the table, "why does the AFO want the sword? To . . . what? Free them from this"—he swung his hand in a circle—"curse?"

"What exactly is the curse? What's it do?" Maangi asked. "How can finding it free them? Because why else would they want it, right?"

Slipping off his glasses, Dr. Cathey shook his head. "Unfortunately, I do not have the details. The information is terribly hard to come by. I would"—he shook his head—"I urge you to seek out Tzaddik. He will have your answers. I would also recommend talking to a metallurgist. Zoryana Skoryk is a brilliant metallurgist and the foremost collector of metalwork in the world. But I would not advise sending any of the men in this room."

"Are you asking me to go?" Robbie asked in a near growl.

"I would not dream of it," the professor said.

"Good, because I don't do the field anymore," Robbie explained.

"Forgive me," Dr. Cathey said, "I meant that Zoryana will not welcome soldiers into her home. *I* should go. And I need Ms. Cortes with me, because while Zoryana has a thing against soldiers, she also has a thing for lying. She does it very well."

"You're not going after the sword without me," Ram stated firmly. "Haven's off the books. Not happening."

"I agree with Khalon," Rodriguez added.

"Very well," the professor said with a sigh. "I will concede to Ram's presence with one of my own concessions: Miss Cortes *does* come." He chuckled. "Yes, perhaps you can distract Zoryana into giving us the information."

# 13

## — NORTHERN VIRGINIA —

Back at home, Haven curled up on the sofa beneath a blanket, Edward Russell's leather-bound journal from 1803 on the arm of the chair and her computer whirring quietly on her lap. VVolt sailed effortlessly onto the cushion, pressing his spine against her legs with a satisfied moan. She ran her hand along his dense, burnt-toast coat and thanked him for the company.

With a smile, Chiji looked up from his chair in the corner, where he sat reading the Bible. "I think when Ndidi returns home, those two will have strong words about who sits next to you, Ngozi."

At the endearment he'd bestowed on her after Israel, which meant "blessing," Haven grinned and tugged her laptop closer. "Two alphas vying for my attention. Kind of nice."

"I am sure I know who would win," Chiji said with a wry smile. "Ndidi has waited a long time for you."

*A long time* . . . The words pushed her attention back to the journal. To the lives and events recorded there. She continued transcribing, taking the handwritten dates and entering them into the genealogy software program. Incredible, seeing the many different styles of handwriting as the journal passed through the generations after Edward had started it.

She turned the page and froze, hand hovering over the rhythmic scrawl, over a name in elegant black ink. Elisabeth Linwood. "What a . . ." The word refused to leave her mouth. She knew it wasn't a coincidence.

Haven grabbed her cell phone and dialed her mom.

"What's wrong?" her mother gasped. "What is it?"

Blinking, Haven lifted her head, the darkness registering. The fact that at some point Chiji had gone to bed and she hadn't noticed. "I . . . I'm okay. Sorry."

Her mother released a weary, staggering breath. "Do you know what time it is?"

A glance at the time in the upper left corner of her laptop made Haven wince. "I—sorry. I didn't realize." Push on? Or stop while she was still alive for waking her mother at one in the morning? "I'll let you get back to sleep."

"That's not going to happen until I know what's worrying you."

"Not worrying, exactly." The names called to her again. The handwriting. "Does Dad have an ancestor named Elisabeth—with an *s*—Linwood in his line?"

"What?" her mother balked. "Are you—"

"I know this sounds crazy, but I'm looking through Cole's genealogy and found where a Raphael Russell married an Elisabeth Linwood. Their son, Edward, wrote this journal that Charlotte gave me." She toyed with a length of her hair. "Is this Elisabeth connected to our line?"

"Haven, honestly." Exasperation was a sound her mother did well. Of course, with two daughters, she had a lot of practice. "How would I know?"

"Is there any way you could check?" Haven chewed her bottom lip. "Please?"

"Heaven help me," her mom muttered. "You know I'd go to the ends of the earth for you. And now that I'm more awake, it seems your father's great-aunt Agatha had a cousin named Elisabeth. The girls were more sisters than cousins. Very close."

Haven stared at the chart created by the genealogy program. Incredible. The Russells and Linwoods looked to be connected not just by marriage, but by blood! She turned the page and scanned the information. "These entries record that Elisabeth and Raphael had a half dozen children, and Raphael had ten siblings."

Paper crinkled as she pushed back another generation and stilled. This time the drawing of a woman stared back. Beneath her picture: Adaline. She was beautiful, with a riot of curls around her face and seemingly pinned up. A necklace hung on her bosom. Her features were delicate but strong. And there was love in the sketch.

"Dear, I'm going back to bed. Maybe we could ask Aunt Agatha."

"Sure. I'll arrange to see her. Thanks. 'Night, Mom."

Haven fought the greedy maw of sleep and dragged her laptop from the coffee table. She logged in, using the secure protocols Cole had given her, and opened the email server. Excitement pinged through her as she waited for it to connect. When the screen finally changed, her hopes plummeted at the blank screen.

No message.

Tears burned her eyes, blurring them with exhaustion and depression at not hearing from him. Not hearing his voice. Not seeing the intensity that defined Cole Russell.

Aching just for a glimpse that he was okay, she typed into the box: *Sunshine needs rain to be appreciated.*

Hmm, maybe that was too corny. But what could she say? What metaphor for how empty her life felt without him, that just a jot would do?

"Please," she whispered, her eyelids growing heavy. She scooted down, resting her head against the arm of the sofa. Settled the laptop in the bend of her waist. Yawned. Deleted what she'd written, then typed in: *A* T *without a crossbar is just an* I.

Ugh. "You suck at metaphors," she groused to herself, yawning again. She backspaced, erasing the line. Closed her eyes to think, to figure out something smart and clever that would let him know she missed him terribly.

Missed his kisses. She sighed and settled deeper against the cushions, allowing herself to relive the memory of their first kiss—on the plane. He'd pinned her against the wall. It had been startling, sweet. Yet urgent. As if he was afraid she'd disappear. No, he'd been afraid she'd reject him.

"Once you know me, you won't want to be here," he'd admitted later.

"But I do know you." She had always seen his heart, the goodness, the hero, the strength that defied logic and trials.

*Water lapped her ankles, teasingly cool yet warm, too. His arm encircled her waist, tugging her up against his chest. Her hand landed on his pectoral, right over the spot he'd been shot that terrifying Fourth of July. But she didn't feel the marred, rough skin. She felt his thundering heart.*

*"I do," Cole murmured as he claimed a kiss. "Mrs. Russell."*

*Haven laughed against his mouth. "I like the sound of that."*

*A gull squawked.*

*The squawking turned shrill—*

*The doorbell!*

*The beach didn't have a doorbell.*

Snapped awake, Haven flung herself upright, hearing the *thud-clunk-thunk* of her laptop as it hit the floor. She glanced at it and groaned, holding her head, which felt like it had been dunked. The poke of morning light through the curtains made her skull throb.

Ocean. Cole. That dream!

She drew in a shaky breath, but the bell rang again—and with it an internal alarm pierced her. She set her laptop on the table and started for the door. No. Not the door. Her phone. Where was it?

She found it stuffed beneath the cushion and VVolt's flank. She retrieved it and glanced at the caller ID, deflating when she saw the SAARC code.

Why would they be calling? She squinted at the time on her phone and couldn't believe she'd crashed the whole night on the couch. But it was still early, so this couldn't be good. But they wouldn't call if something happened to him. They'd be on her front porch, ringing the doorbell.

She answered. "Hello?"

"Ms. Cortes, this is Dru."

"Hi. How are you?" she said around a yawn.

"Good. Listen, we have a situation here"—his words made her heart stumble—"and Dr. Cathey is heading to the Ukraine. He has requested your help and expertise."

Her mind struggled to make sense of what he'd said. "Oh." Definitely not what she'd been expecting. "What for?"

"He's meeting a metallurgist who seems quite good at carrying on a charade. He wants your help reading the situation and the expert."

"Oh. Okay."

"Is that a yes? You'll go?"

She glanced around, knowing Cole wouldn't want her to go. He'd asked SAARC to leave her alone while he was in the field. "Do you know how long I'll be gone?" Why was she even considering this?

*Because I'm bored!*

"A few days at most."

That couldn't hurt, right? "Okay, sure. I can do that."

"Great. We'll send your packet over."

* * * *

**— MOSCOW, RUSSIA —**

Ram folded his arms over his chest as he stared at Cell through the uplink. "Look, in that meeting, I saw it on your face—you had an idea."

"Yeah, but what you saw on my face and what's happening in my head?" Cell grunted. "I can't get them to gel."

"It's okay. That's why we're a team."

"A team that's on different continents." Cell raised his eyebrows. "Am I right?"

Ram jutted his jaw toward the camera. "Tell me what's brewing in your head."

Cell scratched the side of his face. "Right. I'm not a prodigy the way Makanda is, and I could work for years and *maybe* understand what he's done here. Just remember—there's no solidity. I mean, we're talking soupy water."

"Soupy water. Go."

"So, being a gamer, I've been inside Makanda's game. Played it. Aware of it. Impressed—majorly, ya know, because of its ability to branch and grow?" Cell pointed to another screen, where he had the game open. "*Blood Genesis* uses what's called procedural generation.

There are a lot of reasons why it's used, but mostly because of its ability to randomize the game for less predictability."

"And that's good."

"Absolutely. Who wants to play the same, predictable game? You can come back to it, upload a different identity, and get a completely different game. As more people play, the game grows, constantly aggregates and sorts data. Gives a new experience. Creates new creatures, just as DNA has done through generations, but maintaining the same lettering." He snorted. "I mean, the kid's a freakin' genius—and how he did this at nineteen is a little frustrating, since it takes most gamers years to develop something this sophisticated."

"A million dollars to a Congolese kid is a lifetime of provision and then some," Ram noted. "You said 'DNA.' Explain that."

"Yeah. Sure." Cell snatched something from a square box and stuffed it in his mouth—a breadstick. Probably last night's dinner. "The kid based his algorithm off a genetic model, so these people, creatures, whatever you are in the game—the artificial intelligence all have unique DNA-like structures for information." He chewed the breadstick slowly, staring at the screen. He left the wad of bread sticking out of his mouth as he started typing. Clicking. Mousing around. Shaking his head. "What?" He drew back with a scowl that had him jotting notes. Soon, keys were clicking again.

Ram was sure he'd been forgotten. "Cell?"

"But how . . ." Cell flicked on another monitor.

Although the feed was a bit grainy, Ram had no trouble making out the lettering. "Cell!"

He jerked. Looked at the camera. "Oh." Cell shot Ram a sheepish grin. "Sorry." His arm slid to the monitor with the FBI logo on it, and he turned it off.

Hacking. Ram didn't want to ask. "The connection?"

"I . . . I can't get into the FBI program—that would be illegal, of course."

"Of course."

"But I just . . . it'd make sense—a *lot* of sense—to take Makanda's program, which is based off genetic models, and have him tailor that."

"To what end?"

Cell shrugged. "I . . . I don't know. It's a leap, I admit, but it wouldn't be that hard to use his model to trace some genetic marker or bloodline or something. The more data inputted, the more the AI has to work with." His face enlivened. "*That* is why I think this TAFFIP program Congressman What's-his-name sponsored could somehow be connected."

"But TAFFIP is American."

"Maybe." Cell cocked his head and stretched his jaw, squinting. "I mean, that's some genius coding. I'm not skilled enough. I'd have to work on this more." His shoulders bounced. "Look, I'm a comms specialist, not an investigator, but this"—he wagged his hand at the monitors—"I think there's something there. I haven't drawn the big black line between the dots yet, but with Labaka suddenly wanting to shut Makanda down, it makes me wonder why they don't want witnesses."

"Maybe they don't want to pay him."

Cell grunted.

But even Ram was starting to see an opaque connection. "Well, keep me posted. Might stay quiet about this."

Snorting, Cell bobbed his head. "No kidding. They aren't the most receptive to creative ideas."

"Get the information and they'll listen. But, Cell?"

"Yeah?"

"Come to me with it first."

* * * *

When immersed in a covert operation, the operator had to fully assume the false identity. No, they had to do more than assume it. They had to believe it. Live it. Breathe it. Tox had become Kaz. The similarity of names was enough for him to feel as if he maintained some of his true identity.

And yet, he still had to do things Tox would do, like rummage through digital files looking for breadcrumbs to pass along. As he was doing now. Alone in Nur's personal library, he sat at a computer, his legs stretched out and ankles crossed as he leaned back in the chair. One hand on the mouse that played solitaire. His other hand slipped in a USB that would allow Ram and the Mossad to rifle through the files. Because this computer was in the company's personal library, they were hoping it would give them access to what they hadn't been able to get into through the Mattin Worldwide internal network.

"Kazimir! Have you located the spy?"

Tox tensed at the question and probing of Nur Abidaoud. "Not since that altercation."

Nur sauntered in and lifted a decanter from the crystal tray. "Your nose doesn't look like it's healing well."

With a flick of his thumb, Tox extracted the drive and returned it to his phone, molding it to his case, which would prevent it from emitting a signal or drawing attention. Unlike his still-bruised nose. "Hairline fractures take longer."

Nur eyed him as he recapped the decanter. He stood the same height as Tox, and broad shoulders warned he could handle his own, even if he easily had twenty years on Kazimir. Eighteen on Tox. But the reconstructive surgery and artistic rendering of scars purported to be from the accident that had killed the real Kazimir Rybakov had the desired effect. Nobody wanted to look too close, stare too hard. It'd be impolite.

Thereby providing the perfect opportunity for Mossad to replace the man who'd died that rainy night. In his place, Tox had lain on a hospital bed while his surgical scars and body healed.

Nur sipped his drink, squinting over the crystal snifter. "Should I be worried this man bested you?" He tossed back the drink, then motioned for Tox to follow him into the office.

Tox had rehearsed this lie. Walked through the scenarios. Played them out to their full extent. "I made a mistake." Let the boss know you'd messed up. "Got a little cocky because I'd gotten into his place without him knowing."

At his desk, Nur lifted a cigar, sliced off the tip, then lit it. He took several long puffs before thick smoke snaked into the air. "That's how he got the upper hand?"

"Upper *cut*," Tox replied, using humor to deflect, but he saw the way Nur scowled, so he shed the smile. "Won't happen again."

"You get arrogant, you get sloppy." Nur poked the cigar at him.

"Do not make that mistake again—it could be *my* life next time. If you do and I live, you won't."

Tox hesitated. Shifted back and lowered his head. Contrition worked well with the power hungry. "Yes, sir."

"Igor," Nur barked. "What of the girl? What progress has she made with the next piece?"

"None that I know of, sir."

Nur grunted as he paced behind his desk, puffing on his cigar. "I think she needs to talk to her father again." He pointed at the two guards hovering near the doors. "Get her and take her to him." Then to Igor. "Ready Mr. Khalon for visitors."

Tox hated the sound of that. It gutted him for Tzivia to see her father in that prison. Gutted him to see anyone living in those conditions. But he had a job to do. He'd been recruited because his build and height similarity to the dead Rybakov could get him into Mattin Worldwide headquarters. The bonus of becoming Nur's personal guard should've given him the perfect opportunity to complete his mission—put names to faces and cut off the head of the giant. Return to the States. To Haven.

But the discovery and capture of Tzivia butchered those plans. Yet it had also put Tox in the most precarious situation, a brutal one—watching her. Protecting Nur from her—which was really him protecting Tzivia from herself. Keeping her alive. But both missions seemed destined for failure. He'd yet to see or identify official visitors that could be tied to the AFO.

"Remind her what she's fighting for, Igor," Nur said.

"Would you like me to go, sir?" Tox offered. "I can be persuasive."

"No." Nur nodded to Igor and the lesser guards, then pulled his attention back to Tox. "I have a breakfast meeting."

Tox nodded but winced internally. He followed the AFO commander out of the penthouse, hating how those thugs would treat Tzivia.

# 14

## — MOSCOW, RUSSIA —

"Abba! Abba, I'm here." Tzivia rushed into the cell, grateful they had allowed her inside again.

A barking cough rattled her father's frail form.

She went to her knees beside him. "Abba," she whispered, catching his shoulders. Heat radiated from him. She gasped and leaned over to see his face. His eyes were closed, and he looked flushed. "He's feverish," she shouted to the guards, who stood motionless outside the cell. "He's sick. He needs a doctor." She carefully turned him onto his back.

He broke into a coughing fit, his shoulders hunching. Slowly, his eyes flitted open. "Tzi . . ."

"Yes, Abba. I'm here."

"Go," he growled. "You should not be here. I am old and useless."

"Not true! You are important to me."

He groaned, and she removed the jacket she'd intentionally worn to give to him. She cocooned him in the warmth. "It's not much, but"—she glanced at the guards, who scowled back—"they won't let me bring anything to help you."

He patted her hand, grunting. "You are good to me, Tzivia."

She leaned closer. "There's a knife in the pocket. If you can get close, maybe you can pick the lock or force the guard to free you."

"No, no. They will beat me if they find it." His trembling fingers reached toward the pockets. "Take it back."

Tzivia took his hands in hers. Held them to her face. Kissed his dirtied knuckles. "Keep it. It might help."

"You are . . . thickheaded."

Surprise held her fast, then a laugh bubbled up. He'd always complained about her stubbornness. "As an oak."

A crooked smile worked its way onto his face, though his eyes were closed, and she could see him—see the abba she'd loved and cherished as a girl. The abba who admonished her, chastised her. Over and over. Threatened to beat the wildness from her. What she would not do to hear him rail again. To hear him strong and confident.

"The sword, Tzivia," he murmured.

"I know. I might have another lead."

"No," he groaned. "You must not give it to them. Must not do this."

"If I do not, they will kill you, Abba."

"Then let an old man die in peace."

"No!" Tzivia threw herself at him, hugging him tight. "I won't. Mama is gone. I will not lose you, too."

Coughing choked off his words, rattling his entire body. "Tzivia, the Valley of Elah celebration—"

"It's in two months."

"Yes. They want the sword for that. It would be"—more coughing—"catastrophic."

"Shh, Abba. Do not worry about the sword."

"I am an old dying man. Let me be done with it and—"

"You will get better. I am doing this for you, for me. For Ram." She held his hands again. "We will be a family again."

He shook his head, but then he grew still. "Your brother is here?" His gaze was on the ceiling.

"I don't know where he is."

The guard rattled the door. "Time's up."

"I barely had ten minutes!" Tzivia snapped.

"Let's go. Out."

She glared. Fisted her hands. "I will not. I want—"

"Out, or I will drag you out."

Defiance flared. "I'd like to see you try."

He hoisted a gun, aimed it, and fired.

Something struck her leg. Startled, she glanced down to once again find a dart sticking out of her thigh. The feeling in her body faded with her vision. "Coward."

* * * *

When they arrived at the restaurant, Tox climbed out of the armored Rolls Royce and paused in front of the door, scanning the plaza. Satisfied there were no threats, he moved aside, signaling to Nur that it was safe. The door opened, and his employer emerged. Tox escorted him into the restaurant. His job was to remain innocuous while Nur had lunch with an Asian businessman.

As he stood guard, Tox tracked every person and vehicle that passed the restaurant or the table. The woman with a little girl. The Sikh man with a white turban. Teens, noses stuck in their smartphones, hung out in sharp contrast to the elderly man shuffling by on his cane and accompanied by what must've been his wife in an electric scooter.

Tox wanted to smile, wondering if that might be him and Haven in fifty or sixty years. *If I survive that long.*

Behind him, Mr. Abidaoud said his good-byes.

Tox keyed his mic. "Exiting now," he alerted the driver, who'd bring the car to the curb.

As they strode through the plaza to the armored vehicle, a white van slid by. Tox's pulse jacked when something registered. Snagged his brain. Made it buzz. On the other side of the street, he spotted two men hovering near a car, smoking.

A cyclist circled round, riding past a small candy vendor where a woman waited. Staring. With something in her hand.

The car that slid by—turban.

The people across the street, by the vendor, the cyclist—all Middle Eastern.

Things out of the norm. Too perfectly placed. An ambush!

Tox stepped back. Flashed out his hand, pushing his boss behind him. "Down!" He snapped up his gun even as the first man dove for cover. Urging Nur to the safety of shelter, Tox fired, noting the woman producing a gun of her own, then taking cover.

Tox grabbed Nur by the collar, half dragging him to a waist-high wall. "Ambush! Under attack," he said into the comms even as cracked wall spit at them.

This was it. This could be the end. He could let Nur die, and the head would be cut off of the serpent. But Mossad would not have the other names. And he had to locate them first. Killing the head would drive the others deep underground. They needed a coordinated attack to take down the entire beast.

He glanced at Nur, who held a gun. Where had he gotten that? Tox shouldn't be surprised, after seeing him shoot the failed archaeologist.

The thudding of approaching feet stilled Tox. In the reflection of the restaurant window, he saw a man sprinting toward them. Tox watched, waited.

"What are—"

Tox held up a finger, eyes on the ghostlike figure closing in on them. He eyed angles. Obstacles. Clear.

In three . . . two . . . He threw himself to the side, shoulder colliding with the paving stones, weapon aimed up at their attacker. He fired. Once, twice. Three times.

The man pitched forward, face thudding against the cement as he dropped hard.

Tox searched for more contacts.

Screams rent the afternoon, pulling his attention to where their armored vehicle barreled over the plaza's curb and shot toward them.

Tox grabbed his boss's jacket again. "To the car," he ordered.

Nur scrambled to his feet, stumbling before he found traction. He raced toward the SUV that torpedoed through the vendor carts, sending candy and magazines flying. Tox sprinted to the vehicle with Nur and yanked open the door.

Sparks zinged off the armor plating.

Tox pivoted and sighted the Sikh he'd first noticed outside the restaurant. The attacker hurtled at him. Slammed Tox into the car. But he caught the man's shoulders. Flipped their stances. Drove a fist hard into the man's nose.

The Sikh punched, but Tox deflected, twisting him and ramming his head into the limo. Tox hauled him up and did it again, this time also nailing the back of the guy's neck with his elbow. A sickening crunch told him he'd at best paralyzed the man, at worst killed him.

A weight plowed into Tox. He grunted, pinned between the body of the dead Sikh and a new attacker, who hooked an arm around Tox's neck. Stupid.

Tox clamped onto the man's arm and dropped his weight dead, slipping under the hold, then stepping back, twisting the man's arm down, back, and then up.

*Pop!* The man howled.

Tox wasn't up to killing this one, too. He pitched the guy onto the ground, then lurched at the car door. Dove into the rear.

"Go, go!" Nur shouted.

The car surged, bucking and jouncing away from the plaza ambush.

Tox peeled himself off the floorboard and climbed onto the seat, rubbing his jaw and then his knuckles.

"I'm impressed," Nur said.

"I should've picked up on it sooner," Tox muttered, annoyed he hadn't paid more attention when he'd noticed the Sikh earlier.

"This morning I was concerned that you might need to be . . . retired."

That pulled Tox's gaze to his boss. Retired meant dead.

"But after that"—Nur shook his head and laughed—"I would be a fool to retire you." He huffed. "Those were Stroebel's men."

"Retaliatory strike." Tox silently thanked God he was still alive.

"Now, we plan one of our own. They must understand that what I do is for the ultimate good."

The driver returned them to Mattin headquarters. Tox followed Nur up the private elevator to the penthouse offices. Palming his weapon, anticipating trouble as they entered the office. But it was untouched and unoccupied.

"Maybe you even need a raise," Nur suggested.

"I make enough already, sir." Tox inclined his head. "But thank you."

"You are a hero."

"No, sir. Just doing my job."

"To me," Nur said, wrapping an arm around his shoulders, "you are a hero—you saved my life. They would have killed me had it not been for you."

"That's why you have me there, sir."

Nur laughed, then pointed to Tox's hands. "Go get some ice for that. And clean yourself up."

Tox glanced down at his bloodied suit. "Yes—"

A shadow moved where one shouldn't have. Shouldering in, Tox snapped his gun toward the intruder.

Shorter than Tox by a head, the man had brown eyes that were dark. Not just in color.

"No!" Nur shouted, slapping down the weapon. He patted Tox's shoulder. "Go—clean up, get something to eat, then come back. I don't want you gone too long."

Tox eyed the man who stood near Nur's private office, uninvited yet there. "Of course, sir," he said, then turned away, discreetly lifting his phone and snapping a picture.

"That man just saved my life," Nur informed the uninvited guest.

"Fortunate."

"Indeed. So." Nur's tone changed. "What do you think? Is it working?"

Tox slowed, wiping at something on his pant leg as he stood a few feet from the door.

"Like a charm. Our American counterparts will be pleased, too."

# 15

— NSA, MARYLAND —

Diana Prince had her Steve Trevor. Superman had his Lois Lane. Bruce Banner had his Betty Ross.

Mercy Maddox had her . . .

"Nobody." She slumped against her chair, staring at her ringless left hand and a picture of her pet ferret, which had recently been euthanized. With a sigh, she peered around her cubicle peppered with comic book paraphernalia and stubby plastic figures of her favorite TV and movie characters. "Surrounded by heroes . . ."

When the company phone rang, she wiped away her sadness and pressed the button. "Maruta Takeri's office. How may I help you?"

"Sure are moving up, aren't you?"

Breath stolen by that voice, a blast from the past, Mercy leaned into the phone. "Barclay?"

He chuckled. "Very good."

She skated a glance around the office maze. "What're you doing, calling me here? I can't take personal calls."

"Well, good. Because this isn't personal."

It had always been personal with Barc and his never-ending attempts to weasel a date out of her. "It's not?"

"Okay," he said in his awkwardly adorable voice, "maybe it is. I need help. Professional help."

"You need the counseling hotline again?"

"No," he growled. "And I told you that was just a joke."

She remembered, but taunting him never got old. "Suicide isn't a joke."

He growled again. "For someone named Mercy, you don't give much."

Definitely true. *Hurt me once, shame on you. Hurt me twice, shame on me.* These days she skipped the first one in exchange for preventative maintenance and upkeep of her mental state. "Did you need something, Barc?"

"Can we meet? I want you to look at something."

From the corner of her eye, Mercy saw the perfectly coiffed hair of Ms. Takeri bobbing across the office. "Gotta go."

"*Meet?*"

"The Rave. Same table. Ten o'clock." She disconnected and looked up with a smile. "Ms. Takeri, how can I help you?"

"Did we get that packet from Langley yet?"

"No, ma'am." A tone sounded in her headset, and Mercy checked her monitor, which logged calls inbound and outbound, as well as messages within the NSA building. "Though I did just receive a ping from the front desk that we have a package. I'll go down right now and check."

"No, no," Ms. Takeri said, her blood-red manicured nails raking the air. She touched her dyed-black hair. "I'm on my way out. I'll pick it up."

"Very good." Though Mercy noticed her boss's strange expression, she said nothing.

Ms. Takeri's eyes scrunched and shifted to something on Mercy's desk. With a grimace, she demanded, "*Why* do you have a picture of a rat?"

"Not a rat," Mercy replied without anger or annoyance. "He was a ferret. My dad gave him to me, and he was euthanized last night."

"Ugh. Good riddance." Ms. Takeri shuddered. "You had that thing in an apartment?" She shuddered again. "I can't imagine living somewhere people can keep rodents."

*Smile before you say something ugly or kill her.* "Have a good evening, Ms. Takeri. I hope your dinner with Senjen is pleasant." Redirection was better than explaining a body.

Her boss's face pinked at the mention of the Indian businessman. "Make sure your work is done before you leave," she said, sauntering off.

"Of course." Why did that woman always look down on Mercy? Treat her like she was second-class or something? Maybe it was time for a little payback.

Watching Ms. Takeri wait for, then step into, the elevator, Mercy silently plotted how to frustrate her opinionated, mean-spirited boss, who had known about Clark because Mercy left work early yesterday for the euthanasia appointment. She also knew Mercy loved that ferret the way normal people loved children.

An idea struck her. "Hmm, going to a restaurant, are we?" She turned to her keyboard and let her fingers roam. Ms. Takeri might find her credit card didn't work. Wouldn't that be embarrassing when she insisted, as she always did, on paying for Senjen's meal? Or maybe she'd find her employee ID failed in the morning. Again.

"Silly woman," Mercy murmured as she worked the system, bypassing protocols, diving deep so they couldn't backtrace her cyber trail. "Don't you know leather purses deactivate cards?" She gave a dramatic gasp, then mimicked her boss's voice. "Do they? But it's a Torry!"

She wrinkled her nose and rolled her eyes, executing her revenge. "I'm so sorry you're foolish enough to pay a thousand dollars for a purse but can't remember it makes your security access card for the NSA dead in the water.

"Of course," Mercy said with a jut of her chin, chuckling to herself, "that *could* be the case, but we all know it was really the brilliant computer hacker of an assistant who wrecked your day. Again." She lifted her fingers and wiggled them over the keyboard. "Boom!"

"Uh-oh."

Mercy jumped, letting out a small yelp as she glanced up at Henry, an analyst who'd given her a lot of attention and leniency.

Handsome as far as nerds went with his brown hair and brown eyes, Henry had a little too much slick-business-professional about him for her taste. "How'd she tick you off this time?"

Mercy lifted her photo. "She called Clark a rodent. *Again!*"

"Oh, ouch. For an NSA director, she's not real quick. I'm sorry about Clark."

Mercy sighed. "Thanks. I miss him."

He nodded to her terminal. "So she still hasn't figured out you're the phantom behind her troubles."

She flashed him a devious grin, then returned to her cyber warfare. "I'm not mean to her. Just . . ."

"Wearing her down."

She smiled, disappointed at having her surly side revealed. She should be ashamed of herself, but when someone went out of their way to run over others, to berate and belittle them—well, Mercy had no mercy. Like someone else she'd known once.

"Heading home?" she asked.

Henry shook his head. "Out for drinks." He waggled his eyebrows. "Want to come?"

Anything to get out of here and unwind. "Sounds wonderful." Wait. Barclay. "Shoot. No, I'm meeting someone later."

"Oh." Henry frowned. "A date."

"Not like that." Mercy snorted. "I mean, Barc's nice and a nerd—which means he's good people—but he's . . ." She pursed her lips. "Not right for me." Instead, a pair of hazel-green eyes invaded her mind. She swiped away the image as easily as if it had been on the screen of her phone.

"Who is he?" Too much legitimate interest and offense sat in Henry's question.

"Well, Bruce has a lot going for him—smart, kindhearted—but he gets a little green sometimes." She snorted, avoiding a real answer with a playful one. "But his anger—woofta!"

"Ha. At least I can control my temper." Henry leaned on the wall of her cubicle and peered down at her. "What do I need to win you? Four legs and a long, segmented tail?"

"Ferrets have furry tails. They're not rats, Henry. You lost major points there." At the embarrassment reddening his face, she added, "But maybe a pink button nose could salvage you."

He rolled his eyes. "You're hopeless."

She shrugged. "This is true."

"Okay," he said, hooking his arms over the divider as he homed in on her. "Seriously. Give it to me straight. Why won't you go out with me?"

She held up her pointer finger. "One, never date a co-worker. Things go bad, then they make your life and job unbearable." She held up her second finger. "And two—well, nothing personal, Henry, but you guys are way too much work. And I'm not into becoming a breeding farm."

He nearly choked. "Breeding farm? It'd be one date!"

"That's what y'all always say. But then it's two, then you start applying tags—*girlfriend, mine, taken, hands-off*. From there, life gets dull, and guys get fat."

"Good grief, Mercy! Who jaded you toward males?"

Though her heart skipped a beat, remembering those green eyes, she ignored it. "All of you." There'd been exactly one guy. He'd tilted her world's axis.

Henry shook his head. "Brilliant and beautiful, but hopeless."

"So they say."

"Want me to walk you out?"

"Sweet, but no thanks." She bobbed her head toward the computer. "Going to get caught up, now that the shrew is gone."

"Your loss."

"You tried to save me," she sighed dramatically.

"That I did."

She waved. "'Night, Henry."

* * * *

**— VIRGINIA —**

"Aunt Agatha?" Haven crouched at her great-aunt's wheelchair and touched her parchment-thin skin.

"She is not asleep," the maid said, clucking her tongue. "That's her wanting attention again."

"Oh, shush, Marguerite," came Aunt Agatha's creaky, amused voice. Bright eyes like Haven's green ones shone as she opened them.

They crinkled beneath years of laugh lines as she placed her other hand on Haven's. "How are you, dear?"

What a character. "I'm fine. How are you doing? Is Marguerite being good to you?"

"Good? That woman wouldn't—"

"Don't be telling lies now, Mrs. Agatha."

"I thought you had work to do," her aunt said, laughing. Then she patted Haven's hand. "Now, what did you need, dear? I know you aren't here just to hear an old woman scold her maid."

Haven breathed a laugh. "I'm ashamed. It's been too long since I visited."

Bony shoulders lifted beneath a cream cardigan. "Don't do that."

"Do what?"

"Guilt. Too many people fling it around as if it were maple syrup." She stabbed a gnarled hand at Haven. "Some might say cream, but I like maple syrup better. Do you like maple syrup?"

"One of my favorites."

"Now." Aunt Agatha leaned to the side as her gaze took in Chiji's very long frame. "Heavens, you are tall, young man."

"God knew someone needed to reach the top shelves," Chiji said with a smile.

"That's what my Reggie always used to say," her aunt said, beaming. "He was six one, you know. Handsome as the day was long. Much like your friend there." Quick eyes fastened on Haven. "Is he your fella?"

Haven shook her head. "No, Chiji's a very good friend."

"Well, he could be your fella. Is it because you're different colors? I know some people have a problem with that, but I'd be gravely disappointed in you, if—"

"No," Haven said. "I have a fella. He's . . . working right now. Chiji is like a brother to him. We're looking into some things for Cole."

"Cole. Is that your fella's name? That's nice." Aunt Agatha tilted her head. "But I like Reggie better."

"I'm sure you do." Haven had to bite back another laugh. "Aunt Agatha, Mom told me that you had a cousin named Elisabeth. Is that right?"

"Cousin? Oh lands, no."

Haven frowned. Felt her heart trip over that declaration. She pulled the journal from her tote bag and unraveled the leather thong.

"Elisabeth was my *aunt*. But we were very nearly the same age. We were like cousins—no, like sisters." Aunt Agatha seemed to glow with the words, touching her necklace. "Very close. We did everything together."

"Elisabeth Linwood," Haven said as she flipped through the pages to find the sketch.

"Well, of course, dear. What other last name would she have?" Aunt Agatha shifted in her chair again, then primped her hair.

"I have a journal . . . that lists Elisabeth." Haven angled it for her great-aunt to see. "But she married a Russell—a Raphael Russell."

Lifting her readers from the chain around her neck, Aunt Agatha craned her neck to see. "Oh, that's not my Elisabeth."

"It's not?"

"No, it's her great-aunt. Elisabeth was named after her. Everyone talked about Lady Elisa," she said, pronouncing the name with great reverence and pomp. "Lady Elisa was a baroness, you know. So pretty and elegant, just as you can see in that picture. They said that when she died, the estate died with her. She died very young. Too young. I think that's why Raphael took Edward and came to America with Lady Elisa's brother, Anthony." She smiled conspiratorially. "That's how I met Reggie. We were new in the city, and he was so smart and fast. He was a runner, you know."

Haven urged the journal sketch back into her great-aunt's view. "Do you know anything else about the Elisabeth who married Raphael Russell?"

"Now, what would I know about them?" She straightened and her eyes widened, smoothing out her wrinkles. "Oh. The bust."

"Bust?"

"Yes, yes," Agatha said, wagging her hand. "My picture book. Young man," she said to Chiji, who stood near the wall-to-ceiling bookshelf, "be a dear and bring it to me." She pointed to a black leather album on a bookshelf.

Haven waited as Chiji lifted it, then he handed it to her. Surprise rippled through her as she eyed it. "This is a photo album."

"Of course it is. That's what I said—a picture book. Bring it here, dear."

Haven delivered it as ordered.

Agatha wrangled the book onto her lap and turned the pages with shaking hands. "Here." She tapped it twice. "The bust. Made of marble. And just glorious." She turned the picture toward Haven. "See? That was Elisabeth's great-aunt."

"And your great-great-aunt." Haven admired the picture, an old tintype of a man beside an exquisite sculpture. She noted the familiar background in the picture. The man stood with the bust before the grand staircase of this very home.

"Yes. Which makes her your great-great-great . . ."

"Something like that, yes. Who's with the bust? He was here."

"That's Edward, Lady Elisa's son. Raphael Russell and Anthony Linwood were thick as thieves and came to America together. Edward spent a lot of time here. This was Anthony's home, which passed to my father, Charles. My brother Albert owned it, then willed it to me upon his death. When Reggie died, it seemed only right I return to the home I was all but raised in with Elisabeth." Her smile faded as she recounted less-happy times. "Anthony had to sell his sister's bust when the family fell on hard times. They came to America, where Edward eventually made his fortune in banking. He returned to England and located the bust, bought it, and brought it back for Charles."

"Where is the bust now?"

"Sold again, I'm afraid," Aunt Agatha said gravely, trembling fingers again going to her throat. "My father said something about how that piece haunted him. He always hated it. During the Depression, Uncle Philip—my father's oldest brother—sold several family heirlooms through his friend's auction house in order to keep the estate in the family. Emerson and Hyatt handled the entire transaction with the utmost integrity and respect."

"Emerson?" Haven asked, glancing at Chiji, who shrugged.

"Oh, that's the auction house—Clarence Hyatt was Philip's friend. He came for the bust himself. I remember that statue." Her teeth clacked. "I nearly toppled it over a couple of times myself, chasing Rupert, the dog."

Haven deflated. "So you don't know where it is now?" she asked, staring at the bust in the photograph. The eyes and nose had transcended time, coming to rest on her own face. It was mildly creepy.

"I've told you what I know, dear. I'm not as young as I used to be—and neither is my mind!"

"And the bust is lost?"

"As is every Elisabeth named after her since."

# 16

— MARYLAND —

After finishing a few things, tying up loose ends, and stuffing some letters to send out in the morning, Mercy grabbed her crossbody bag and the photo of Clark, then went down to her Kia Soul. She got tacos from Bueno Nacho and ate in her car, refusing to face her empty apartment. For fun, she surfed the net on her tablet and did some random digging around, trolling security cameras at the Rave to get a feel for what was happening, then headed there.

She had *her spot* on the upper balcony. A two-seater against the wall that afforded a great view of the entire dance floor and bar. But mostly, the corner padded her from the noise and kept her back safe.

Safe. She snorted as she planted herself at the table and ordered a Killer Whale cocktail. Tablet out, she wormed into the security feeds again.

"Easy breezy, HackerGirl," she whispered as she loaded her favorite gaming site and settled in for some postapocalyptic survival hunting. Sipping her drink, killing zombies, and saving the world. "What's not to love?" She'd leveled up twice and defeated a major boss before she sensed him.

With a rush of crisp cologne and a bucket of good looks, Barclay Purcell slid into the booth to her right.

"How's it going, Dog?" Mercy kept her eyes on the game, guiding her character across a night-riddled sky.

"*Sheep*dog, Mercy. I'm a *sheepdog*," Barc said as if he'd said it a thousand times. He probably had over the years they'd known each other.

"All Barc and no bite," she teased.

"Baby, I got bite."

She laughed and looked up into his brown eyes. "Hello, Barclay."

Nodding, he studied her. "Hello, DreamGirl."

Lifting the fourteen-inch fluted glass that held her bubbling, pale blue drink, she took a sip. She set it down. "So, what's got your tactical briefs in a knot?"

Concern creased his brow, and he looked at her laptop. "We shielded?"

As if she'd leave herself unprotected. "Always."

Hands lifted in surrender, he shrank back. "Just making sure. Don't get all offended."

He read her decently for a grunt, though no one had done that as well as Mr. Green Eyes. Which was why she'd cut Barc off. There was nothing between them except a hefty dose of respect and camaraderie. With his job in the Army and hers in hacking, it seemed best to keep their paths separate, lest they combust. "I'm waiting."

Arms folded on the table, he hunched closer. "You ever gone through a back door"—he hesitated, not for emphasis but for . . . fear—"into the FBI?"

She widened her eyes a little. FBI. An Army grunt wanted into the FBI computers. That was interesting. "D'you expect a girl to kiss and tell?"

He huffed. At least, she thought he did. The throbbing music in the club made it hard to tell. "So you can—do it, I mean?"

Mercy rolled her eyes. Sipped her drink. "Would you be here"—she motioned to the chaotic din—"if I couldn't?"

The first hint of a smile crossed his lips. He'd kissed her once. It wasn't very good. But he was nice. Protective. Like a big brother—*little* big brother, since they were the same height. Which was why he fit so perfectly into the *Friend* category.

"Good. I need you to do that," he said.

Break into the FBI servers. Nothing like a little challenge to brighten her day. Breaking in was the easy part. Getting out, tricky. Not being backtraced later, the least likely part. The FBI might be slow, but they weren't inept.

Well, not all of them.

"What would I be looking for?" She took another swig of her drink and set it aside. Lifted herself and tucked a leg beneath her, adjusting closer to the laptop. Her fingers were alive and her heart thumping.

"Whoa. Wait." Cell closed her laptop. "Not here. Not now. Not with me."

She curled her fingers over his, squeezing, glaring, digging her nails into his flesh. When he got the message and removed his hand, she murmured, "Chicken."

"They find out I asked you to do this—"

"That would imply that, one—they caught me. Which they won't. And two—that I'd rat you out. Which I won't." She squinted and scrunched her nose. "So I'm not seeing the problem."

"I need to get into TAFFIP."

"The fingerprint thing?"

He nodded. "I don't know how, but I think it's connected to something bigger. I need you to look at the coding. Compare algorithms with me."

"Why?"

"I think it's somehow collecting DNA."

"A fingerprint system? Collecting DNA?"

"I know." He raised a hand again and tucked his chin. "I know my theory's out there. But I can't let go of this buzzing at the back of my brain."

"You think the FBI is collecting DNA samples?"

"I'm not convinced it's the FBI."

She screwed up her face tight, then freed it in a breath of shock. "You think they're being hacked?"

"Yeah." He darted a glance around the club. Rubbed his jaw. "Maybe. I don't know. Now that you say it like that . . ."

Mercy crossed her arms and sat back. Defiant. "*What* is going on, Barc?"

"What do you mean?"

She narrowed her eyes. "Doing this—you're asking for my high game. Even with as good as I am, they could catch me, and then I get locked away. They take away Sunshine." She nodded to her laptop.

"What happened to Moonbeam?"

"Died. Big ugly crash, brought on by violating visiting hours at the Pentagon."

Barclay hissed. Ran a palm over his head. "Maybe this was a bad idea. You're probably on a million watch lists."

"And a million *call* lists. What I do, people pay big money—"

"Which you know I don't have."

"Good thing you're almost as cute as Bruce."

Barc snorted. "Banner again?"

Bunching her shoulders, she drew in a dreamy breath. "Always Banner. Brilliant scientist. Passionately compassionate."

"But it's the temper that'll kill you."

"Not for Betsy. She was his Calgon."

Barc shook his head, shifting his gaze to the crowds pulsating to the music. He looked back. "Can you do this?"

"Why?"

Reluctance held him hostage, but she saw it in his eyes—he'd surrender. They always did. She had a pretty face and prettier skills. How the mighty crumbled! "I think someone's using TAFFIP to track down certain people. Then they're killing them."

She drew in a long, hard breath, her mind processing faster than an Intel chip. "The Soup Maker."

He frowned, obviously wondering how she'd guessed that.

"It's all over the news."

He scooted closer. "Listen, the congressman who died last was the sponsor of the bill that got TAFFIP approved and implemented."

Mercy wet her lips. Finished off her drink, thinking, anticipating. "I see where you're going with this . . ." Unable to resist the lure of danger and subsequent victory, she started walking through what root she'd need to dig her way into that program. "It probably has all kinds of safety protocols. Trip wires." They'd naturally expect someone—lots of someones—would want to get in and clean up their records, which were being used unilaterally across government agencies like the TSA, FBI, CIA, ICE. Which meant she'd need to watch for those traps. Could be tricky. Which meant it was deliciously primed for her skills.

"Mercy?"

She lifted her gaze to Barc. "High risk. This'll cost you, Dog."

He winced. "*Shee*—" He paused. Then grinned. "So you'll do it?"

She gave a reluctant-but-excited dip of her head.

"If you get in and we prove my theory," Cell said, "I'm pretty sure you could name your price."

Name her price? That penthouse overlooking Central Park . . . But she shoved aside her dream, because deals like that were too good to be true. Made to entice the gullible guppy into cooperating. She'd been that victim once. Not again.

She sat back, concerned for the first time. "Why me? Don't you work with powerful three-letter agencies, Mr. Black Ops?"

"I do." His brown eyes caught the club lights as he skidded a gaze around once more. "But they won't listen. Dudes blew me off." He tapped the table. "You know me, Mercy. I wouldn't be here if I didn't have a solid instinct on this."

She did know him. It was the only reason she was still listening. But . . . "Why *me*?"

"I trust you. Proving that a system is vulnerable is important to you, so I know you'll dig until you're convinced. *That* will convince me, regardless of the outcome." He smirked. "And you won't leave a trail of your adventures in cyberspace to bring this back on me."

"Well, a trail most don't know how to find," she clarified, "but when you violate sacred cyberocity, it *always* leaves something behind." It was her turn to smirk. "If this flatlines, you just don't want anyone knowing Barclay Purcell didn't listen to his elders. Again. You've always had a problem with authority."

"Says the pot to the kettle." He grinned. "So yeah?"

Mercy bounced a shoulder in a lazy, near-petulant shrug. "You dangled the forbidden fruit." She sighed. "I am a weak woman when it comes to slipping beneath silky codes."

He snorted, scooting to the edge of the leather seat. "Thanks. Keep in touch."

"Oh, I will. But, Barc?"

Glancing over his shoulder, he quirked his eyebrows in question.

"I need guarantees."

Standing at the edge of the table, he studied her. "You mean promises."

"Promises are broken." Mr. Green Eyes invaded her thoughts again. "I need a guarantee that even if I don't find what you want, I get paid."

He hesitated before nodding. "Don't worry. I'm pretty sure you'll find it."

"A girl has to make a living, Barc." She had to make sure he understood what she'd do to protect herself. "With my skills, you don't want to betray me or let me down."

# 17

**— MOSCOW, RUSSIA —**

Strange to be living someone else's life, taking the furnishings and clothes that had belonged to the late Kazimir Rybakov. One might think becoming another person was a matter of simply donning clothes and appearance, but it was more. So very much more. Clothes did not a man make. It was the little things—the mannerisms. Choosing one creamer over another. One blend of coffee. Wearing certain clothes, notably without tags. Which had hinted to Tox that perhaps Rybakov had some sensory issues.

Tox wiped his hand over the fogged bathroom mirror and stared back at the reflection. It wasn't him. Hadn't been for months. He heaved a sigh. There were days he felt Cole Russell slipping further from his grasp, from his conscious mind.

But that had been key, pushing Cole to the back of his consciousness and fueling all things Russian, all things Kazimir Rybakov. He'd had this man's identity and existence beaten into him during a grueling training by the Mossad.

*You're Cole Russell. Tox to your friends. Cole to Haven. You love her. She loves you. She's the reason you're fighting to get back. To finish this. Empty your life of the AFO so you can live in peace, maybe have a kid or two. Wake up next to her beautiful face. Taste those sweet lips again. Hear her gentle voice. That laugh . . .*

He hung his head, gripping the edge of the sink as the water swirled away the grime. He ached for her. Ached to talk to her. To reassure himself that he was Cole. That he wasn't Kazimir, loyal to the very enemy Cole sought to destroy.

He pressed his chin to his shoulder and clenched his eyes. Blotted out the way he'd fought to save Nur. Killed people who were—he snorted—trying to fulfill Wraith's primary objective.

How would the guys feel, knowing he'd protected their enemy rather than killed him? How many times had the opportunity presented itself? And yet—again—Mossad had tied his hands.

Tzivia.

He wanted to curse her, but after seeing her father in that dungeon, smelling him, he understood why she fought. He'd do the same for his mom, for any of those he loved. Even Galen. The violence he'd do for Haven . . .

He balled a hand into a fist, shoving that ache deep down so Kazimir Rybakov surfaced again.

After his shave, he slipped into a stiff dress shirt, resenting the starched collar. What he wouldn't give for a tactical shirt. He powered up the computer, checked email as any normal person would do, but then he bounced to the private email server. Logged in with the same information Haven would use. His heart rapid-fired at the words sitting in the unsent message.

*Flowers only bloom with sunshine.*

Though she left him messages that said she missed him, loved him, he always kept his response the same because he feared making a mistake and jeopardizing the mission or—worse—her life.

*Weather is fine. Ready for some more beach time.*

He didn't hit enter nor send the message. Just left it there so that when she logged in, she'd find it. Delete it, then enter her own.

But as he stared at the words, he hated himself. Hated that this organization had to be dealt with. That he'd volunteered for it—desperate to end their reach, their control over his life and so many innocents. If he was going to have a future with Haven, the AFO could not exist, because he would be tracking artifacts for all time and continually putting his life on the line.

When he got back, he'd take a desk job.

He breathed a laugh and leaned against the sofa. Three years ago, he wouldn't have been caught dead taking a desk job. But now? It was all he wanted.

No. He wanted Haven. The job was a means to an end.

He'd given Uncle Sam fifteen years of his life. That was enough. Of course, that meant he'd have to put up with his brother more often. But maybe it was time to heal old wounds.

Another snort. *What* was happening to him?

The phone rang. "*Privyet*," he answered, speaking in Russian as naturally as he'd done English back in the States.

"Rybakov, come in now."

Was he late? He glanced at his watch. He still had forty minutes. "On my way."

"And bring a suitcase. Ten minutes."

A suitcase? The line went dead, and unease settled into his gut. Where was Abidaoud headed that he wanted Kazimir to travel with him? Should he alert Ram? Not with only ten minutes to pack and get to HQ. Tox stalked down the hall and packed. He hurried to the living room, checked the laptop to verify the browser history had cleared. He'd set it to automatically do that, but he'd been trained to remove the litter from the hard drive that most people didn't know how to access. He wouldn't leave even a character for someone to find that would blow his cover or trace back to Haven.

En route, he navigated the streets like a kamikaze, constantly glancing at his watch, wondering how he could notify Ram that he'd be out of pocket. He whipped into the parking garage beneath HQ and sprinted for the private elevator. When he reached the penthouse, he slowed his breathing, smoothed his suit, and was able to draw an even breath by the time the doors slid open.

He strode to the grand foyer.

"Ah, about time," Igor said, emerging from Abidaoud's office. He swiped a card in the access panel that opened the door to the private residences where Nur and Igor slept, ate, and lounged.

Okay, this was weird.

But Tox followed dutifully down the classy hall with several doors branching off of it. Two waist-high tables sported elaborate floral arrangements beneath impressive six-foot chandeliers.

Igor handed Tox a card as he reached the second door on the left and opened it. He nodded Tox inside.

Shifting the bag to his left hand, Tox freed his ability to reach for his weapon as he stepped into the room, which turned out to be a suite—small kitchen, sofa, table, bathroom, and tucked against the right wall, a bed, desk, and dresser. Tox opened the closet to check it, then glanced back at Igor. "Someone coming to stay?"

"I have decided"—Nur's voice preceded his entry to the room and the conversation—"after the most recent attempt on my life, that it is of great benefit and importance to have you here with me. All your needs are cared for. This apartment is yours."

"Mine?" Panic spilled through Tox. How would he communicate with Ram? How would he sneak messages to Haven?

"Yes. You'll live here so that you are able to be with me at all times, go where I go. We will not have to wait for you to drive across town." Nur brightened. "It is a promotion. You are not pleased?"

"Stunned," Tox said with a nod, glancing around. This was good. Better. He could snoop more easily. But . . . "I had not expected this." He should appear grateful. "Thank you, sir."

"No, it is I who should thank you. Because of you, I can live and breathe another day!"

"Just doing my job, sir." Tox took in his new home. Not as big as the flat the real Kazimir Rybakov had, but much nicer. And probably no rodent problems either.

With a final nod, Nur left, and Igor got down to business. "Dinner is served each evening at seven. Breakfast and lunch, when you are here, will be delivered at six and one, respectively."

Overwhelmed, scrambling for purchase in this new hiccup in the plan, Tox nodded. "Understood."

"Food allergies?"

He had to find a way to notify Ram. "No."

Igor shifted. "I thought you were allergic to tree nuts?"

Tox blinked. "Right. Sorry." He rubbed his forehead. "I'm . . . this has thrown me. I wasn't expecting it. It's too generous, sir."

Igor's suspicious expression flicked away. "You earned it. At least, he thinks so."

There. That was the old Igor.

He came forward and held out his hand. "Phones or laptops?"

Tox hesitated.

"They'll be replaced."

This felt a lot more like them *controlling* him and his movements, rather than a promotion. But since Kazimir had no legitimate reason for withholding his phone and computer, Tox turned them over. Igor left the room, and with him went any semblance of security Tox had in this operation. Which he'd been foolish to allow into his mind in the first place. The truth was painful—there existed no safety net.

But he should look on the bright side. This might provide the perfect opportunity for him to take out the AFO head. He could simply slip into Nur's room and kill him in his sleep. But the greatest irony was the two-edged sword—they could more easily kill him.

# 18

**— ODESSA, UKRAINE —**

"Eccentricity has marked the life and home of Zoryana Skoryk for decades," Dr. Cathey said as the hired cab navigated the winding streets to her home. "Her lavish lifestyle is well-known, but how she has funded it is another question. Metallurgy is not exactly a lucrative field. Unless one does like Zoryana and makes millions off the trade and procurement of ancient artifacts. Collectors and museums alike have paid her in whatever currency she demands, but her preference is usually gold bullion."

The car pulled to a stop on a cobbled drive. They were quickly escorted through so much lush vegetation that the home was not visible until they cleared a set of double glass doors covered by exquisite ironwork.

"From a dig in Istanbul," Dr. Cathey explained as they entered the sprawling villa, welcomed by a humble seventy-year-old butler who had a wary smile, crooked back, and shuffled across the black-and-white marble floor. With a reaffirming nod to Ram—they had paid extra to convince Zoryana to allow his presence—Dr. Cathey followed the butler. Haven walked confidently beside him. And from what the professor said, she would need that confidence with this woman.

Ram let out a low whistle as they passed marble columns. A massive balcony that hung over the Black Sea threw glittering sunlight across the foyer. In truth, the balcony was not directly over the water, but instead stretched over a hidden quarter-mile of property that led to the waves crashing against boulders below. All belonged to the metallurgist.

"Remember," Dr. Cathey said as he relied more on Haven's arm support, "let *me* do the talking."

"You old fool," a melodic voice called before a woman glided from a hallway whose plate-glass wall afforded a brilliant view of the ocean.

"Zoryana," Dr. Cathey said, moving toward her.

Their host wore a vibrant dress that hugged her waist and billowed out like clouds. Jewels sparkled around her neck and on her ears and fingers. A silk turban wrapped her head, its coral fabric setting off her rich complexion and bright yellow-green eyes. "What *are* you doing in my country, Yusuf?" She held out her hands.

Dr. Cathey clasped her fingers, lifted them to his lips, and kissed her knuckles. He swung out her arms to appraise her. "You are as beautiful as ever."

Haven didn't need deception skills to know that was a lie.

"Of course, I am," Zoryana said with a trifling laugh and then waved him off, her glittering eyes landing on Ram. A hungry gleam slid into her expression. "And who is this gorgeous specimen you've brought into my home, Yusuf?"

Ram shifted uneasily, a flush rising through his olive skin.

She extended a hand to him.

Dr. Cathey sighed. "He is my friend, Zoryana, not a flank steak. This is Ram."

"I think he is much more than your friend, Yusuf." Her eyes were globbed with makeup and meaning.

The other warning Dr. Cathey had given them—never underestimate Zoryana—hung in Haven's mind at the way the woman seemed to be dissecting Ram. Alarm tremored through Haven, though she could not say why.

"And this lovely?" Zoryana asked, trailing manicured fingers along Haven's cheek. The feeling of being inspected felt as pleasant as if those nails were scalpels. Haven braced herself against the woman's glare, which had turned icy. "My, my." Her eyes latched on to Ram again. "Is she your woman? Your pet?"

Heat shot through Haven, both indignation and outrage clamoring for a voice. She pushed away the woman's hands.

Ram scowled. "Neither."

"Zoryana." Dr. Cathey moved in between them. "Our time is short—as you insisted."

"Yes, yes, Yusuf. You can be so droll." She huffed and started down a long hall lit with antique sconces from the Roman era. She waved a hand over her turbaned head for them to follow. "Come along, darlings."

After a withering look from Ram, the professor took Haven's arm for assistance, and they started after Zoryana. They followed her through one hall, into another, then down a flight of steps.

"You trust her?" Ram muttered as they hesitated.

"No," Haven injected. "They don't trust each other at all."

"True," Dr. Cathey whispered. "At best I would call it tolerating one another. She is too eccentric and rude. And for her, I am too conservative and old-fashioned."

"Sounds a lot like you and Tzi," Ram said. "You have your type, don't you?"

Reaching what appeared to be a new foyer, Haven saw doors still in motion from having been flung open.

"You've come to talk steel," Zoryana called from the darkness of the room.

"Why are we here if you don't trust her?" Ram hissed.

As they entered, Dr. Cathey squinted at the light splashing across the room, and Haven did the same. The space held little furniture, save a leather tufted bench surrounding a display case in the middle. The walls, however, were lined with glass cases that held an array of weapons—daggers, scythes, lances, knives, swords. Hermetically sealed, she guessed, to protect the artifacts. She could feel the professor's awe through his grip on her hand at the sight of so many of history's pieces collected beneath this roof.

"Regardless of my trust, she is the best in her field," Dr. Cathey said. "If we want answers about this sword, Zoryana has them."

"What sword would that be, dear Yusuf?" Zoryana swung around a door and sauntered toward them.

"As I told you—"

"The Adama Herev." She clasped her hands, as if he were a naughty child and she the schoolmarm.

Dr. Cathey sighed. "You will tell me it doesn't exist."

Her silence was as chilled as the temperature-controlled room and seemed to indicate she intended exactly that. "I think not." She finally sighed. "I will not toy with you, because you are old and frail."

"I am losing my patience," he bit out.

She motioned to the wall where embrasures supported long and short blades. "As you can see, I am fond of swords. There is as much life to them as the breath in us. They speak of culture, of customs. The metal to the era, to the progression of time and ferocity. It was not until the Iron Age—"

"Forgive me, but we have no time for history lessons." Dr. Cathey snorted a laugh, catching Haven's eye. "Sorry," he whispered, apparently realizing, as she had, that he'd quoted one of Cole's favorite arguments about historical backdrops.

"Come." Zoryana whirled and vanished through the door she'd just emerged from. It was part of the wall, and the display case hanging effortlessly from its front panel held a massive sickle dangling in midair, as if suspended by some invisible hand. The door nudged outward to grant them entrance.

Inside waited a long table and a wall of scrolls and books. Tomes hugged all sides. The dank, musty texts sucked moisture from the air. Dimly lit, it felt more like a dungeon than a library. Zoryana went to a high shelf at the far wall, climbed a three-step ladder, and retrieved a cylinder from the top shelf.

"This," she said as she descended, holding her long dress with one hand and the cylinder with the other, "contains all the notes, drawings, depictions—whatever—of the sword." She passed it to Ram.

He took the cylinder, uncapped it, and slid out a bundle of vellum, which Zoryana intercepted. She unrolled it, her palm splayed over one side, her nails reminding Haven of talons, and revealed a depiction of a sword. With Ram's help, she placed ornamental weights at the corners, then hit a switch. Light bloomed beneath the glass table, illuminating the drawing and instantly brightening the room.

"This is from a depiction given to me from"—Zoryana swirled her bejeweled fingers—"some society. I remember not the name."

That was a lie. Zoryana's eyes didn't convey the forgetfulness. In fact, they seemed to home in on something familiar.

Dr. Cathey leaned over and stared at the rendering. "Simple, but perhaps effective."

"It is dull. Boring in the way of ancient swords," Zoryana complained. "But then, I know what brilliance can be wrought of steel and iron, so to see one so blasé hurts the soul." She laughed, then released one side of the vellum, allowing it to roll back up before she spread out a second. "This one is a twelfth-century design."

"Who drew these?" Haven asked, glancing at the sketch.

"I did, of course," Zoryana snarked. "Who do you think? A twelfth-century knight?"

She clearly hadn't met Tzaddik.

"Be nice," Dr. Cathey said, then looked to Haven. "She has long had a fascination with the Adama Herev, which is why I wanted to come. Her collection of drawings and anecdotes is unparalleled, as is her knowledge of it."

"You're such a dear," Zoryana said, but her tone betrayed nothing of whether she meant that sincerely or sarcastically. Probably the latter. "Yes, most I drew from other etchings, paintings, or portraits. My goal is simple: to have every possible semblance of the sword here"—she nodded to the room—"and someday, perhaps, the collection will be complete." She plucked out another drawing. "This I sketched from the painting by Anton Robert Leinweber." She laid out a third. "And this from Peter Paul Rubens's work of the slaying of Goliath."

"Both artists painted the sword?" Haven asked.

Holding up a long, gnarled nail, Zoryana smiled. "They painted the beheading of Goliath. But since I have no need for brutality or violence"—she trilled her fingers at the drawing—"I 'extracted' the sword from their renderings. Let the vicious have the paintings. My concern is steel." She scrunched her shoulders as she considered the image. "But both are unrealistic—the size of it alone would have toppled the shepherd boy. Had he lifted it above his head, he would never have exerted enough force to sever a man's head."

"People also say David could not have killed him with a slingshot or stone to the head," Haven said with a rueful smile.

"Yet *you* believe he did." Zoryana gave a mocking laugh. "But that, too, is part of the fun, is it not? The low probability that this actually happened." She arched an eyebrow at Dr. Cathey. "But your dear professor there believes anything the Bible says."

"I believe in the inerrancy of God's Word, yes."

"Despite all the inconsistencies and—"

"I am not here to debate."

"All's the pity," she said.

Haven glanced over the renderings, tucking her hair back. "Which do you believe is the most accurate representation of the sword?"

"What does it matter?" Zoryana scoffed. "It will not be found. Men have searched for centuries—and who is to say it even exists or ever did?"

"Men also searched for centuries for the Crown of Souls, and it dropped into our laps," Dr. Cathey said. "Please indulge us."

Rolling her eyes, Zoryana sighed. "Yes, I heard about your little adventure in Qal'at Sherqat." Her gaze popped to Haven. "You survived nearly drowning!"

Startled Zoyrana knew about that part of that terrible mission, Haven tried to restrict her response. "Something I won't soon forget," she whispered.

Zoryana considered the professor. "Do you think it's your job to find all the treasures? Why is this so important to you?"

If they told her why, would she try to seize the sword herself? Sell it? She certainly seemed the type to profit off a powerful artifact.

"Perhaps," Dr. Cathey said, "because it might have been found."

"Impossible!" Zoryana hissed, but there was a light in her eyes, a hope. "I would know if that were the case. Besides, the Adama Herev is in pieces, scattered across the world. No one knows where they all are."

"Who broke it into pieces?" Haven asked.

"After the sword was used *against* the Philistines instead of *for* them, David took it. Kept it. Then it vanished from lore. Some say it was melted down. But it was too late. The bloodline had been contaminated."

"Contaminated? You mean cursed," Ram asked.

Surprise leapt through Haven as Ram entered the conversation. He wasn't one to engage, especially not a woman like Zoryana Skoryk.

Her smile turned sultry. "You are the handsomest devil, with those hazel-green eyes and that dark curly hair. Why *do* you hide it under that ridiculous hat?" She reached those blood-red nails toward his beanie.

Ram veered away. "Why do you hide beneath that oversized towel?"

She sucked in a breath—then laughed. Shocked and yet entertained. "I *like* you."

"Then tell me what we need to know, as a favor," he replied, apparently using her attention and distraction to their benefit.

"*Need* to know?" Though Zoryana looked surprised, there was a knowing in her eyes. "I thought this was research."

Dr. Cathey shifted at the way Ram held her gaze, defiant, strong. Though Haven didn't know this woman, she had a bad feeling about the black widow Ram was staring down.

"Why do you play with us?" Ram demanded. "You know we aren't treasure hunters. If you are so much the expert, then you, too, have heard the sword is being hunted and a piece located."

Zoryana squinted. "It is *always* being hunted, darling." Something filtered through her expertly applied face, eyes sparking at Ram. "One member or another of the Niph'al always wants that curse lifted. They want their line cleansed." She leaned in closer to Ram, then planted a hand on his chest. "Don't you, little Hashashin?"

At the ancient name for the assassins, Ram grew visibly tense. A dangerous glint grew in his expression. His fists balled.

Haven looked to the professor for help, afraid to step into the land mine of their confrontation.

"Zoryana, the curse," Dr. Cathey prompted. "Tell me what you know, and we will be on our way."

Sneering, Zoryana pushed Ram back a step. "When the sword was used to slay Goliath, it drank his blood."

"Zoryana!"

"Do not speak to me in such a decibel, old man!" Ms. Skoryk shook her head and looked at Haven. "Men can be so difficult." Angling her attention back to the men, she continued. "It is said the Niph'al created a bronze guard around the hilt to draw the blood from the blade's groove and encase it, thereby enslaving the slain people for all time."

"That sounds outrageous," Haven said. "A sword that drinks blood . . ."

"It gets better, lovely," Zoryana said with a smirk. "It is said because of the curse of the Adama Herev, the entire bloodline—those of the Philistines and those of the assassins—also have the thirst of steel."

"The what?" Haven glanced at the others in confusion, disliking how Ram turned away and started studying the renderings.

"The sword—the steel," Ms. Skoryk said, "it *thirsts* for the blood of those who enslaved it. It calls to the mercenaries, demands they release the blood trapped in its steel."

"Dramatic," Haven said.

"Perhaps," Zoryana said with a lazy shrug. "But it *is* true thousands of Philistines dropped dead in the days following the battle in the Valley of Elah."

Haven blinked, then looked to Dr. Cathey and Ram. "So some survived?" She folded her arms, rubbing her shoulder as she shivered.

"That is the trick of it." Zoryana's eyebrow winged up, as did the corner of her mouth. "Only males died."

"But," Haven said, not meaning to state the obvious or be argumentative, "clearly some survived to manhood, right? Or there wouldn't be any here trying to break the curse."

"Yes, yes." Zoryana sighed. "You are not so much fun, Ms. Cortes. The Niph'al marry their sons off as soon as they reach adulthood so they can father children. There. Are we happy now?"

"How does finding the sword—"

"Its *pieces*," Zoryana corrected.

"—break the curse?" Haven asked. "If it 'drank' the blood of the Philistines . . . how do they free themselves?"

"Truly!" Zoryana glowered at Dr. Cathey but pointed to Haven. "This one is exhausting!"

This woman infuriated Haven. But perhaps that was her game. Distract with insults. Did that mean Haven was hitting a nerve?

"Her question is sound," Dr. Cathey said, stroking his beard. "How *is* the curse broken?"

"It is broken only by the blood of David, who wielded the sword."

"The blood of David?" Haven's frown was severe. "King David? He's been dead since—"

"His *blood*—kin, heirs, progeny!" Zoryana shouted, flinging her hands in the air. "Merciful, you are a—"

"How does the blood break the curse?" It was Ram this time, his voice steady. Electricity zapped through his question, his stance.

It drew Zoryana like an assassin to the kill. She slid closer, placing her hand on his shoulder. "I would tell you anything, darling."

At the less-than-coy declaration, Dr. Cathey tensed. "I—"

Ram held up a hand, his glinting gaze on the metallurgist. "So someone born of David's bloodline . . ."

"The blood groove of the Adama Herev holds Philistine blood, which enslaved the mercenaries. David's blood will cleanse that, neutralizing it, as it were."

Haven nodded. "If they have the thirst of steel and crave the blood of their enemies, why do they not simply wipe out the line?"

"Oh my dear, some are trying, very vainly," Zoryana said. "But you can imagine their plight—have you any idea how large the line of David is? He had dozens of wives and concubines. Solomon, his son, hundreds beyond that! Where does it start? Where does it end?" She stabbed a finger in the air. "But do not think they have not tried. Time and again. But without the sword brought back together, they cannot find freedom, no matter how great the thirst."

# 19

— MOSCOW, RUSSIA —

**LION**: You must stop.

Tzivia's heart pounded against his words. Against him insisting on what he knew very well she would never do. Her fingers shook as she typed a reply.

**LAMB**: Stopping means giving up on him. Would you do that? To your family?

**LION**: It is too dangerous. Angering powerful enemies is not smart.

**LAMB**: Neither is letting them win.

**LION**: This isn't about winning. It's about living—surviving!

Anger tumbled and crashed through her as she stared at the monitor. How could he do this? Why was he turning against her? Omar had been her one true supporter, even with all she'd done to him. The way she had betrayed him. Perhaps this was payback.

**LAMB:** Survival means nothing if you betray those you care about. If surviving means leaving loved ones to their graves, what is that but the worst betrayal? I will not be that person.

**LION:** Anger is natural, but be cautious. They are watching. Very closely.

Her heart spasmed. *Watching* her? How? How had they found her? Though she didn't want to believe it, didn't want to search her surroundings, she allowed her gaze to skim the monitors for green "active" lights, the ceilings for black nubs, the light fixtures and electrical outlets. Surely not.

**LAMB:** How do they know where I am? Is it you? Have you betrayed me?

**LION:** You know I would never do such a thing. I am not the only asset they have. I've given everything to protect you, but your own foolishness, your own carelessness has put them on to you.

Anger writhed as she read his admonishment. She could hear him. See those dark eyes ablaze over her impetuousness. It would not be the first time. Why he put up with her, she did not know. And why she tolerated his tongue-lashings was as much a mystery.

**LION:** If you persist, they will intervene. I do not want to see that happen.

*Intervene.* Stop her. Kill her.

She cradled her head in her hands. Dug her fingers into her scalp and fought back the scream welling within. She was violating so much of her own code. Her own rules. But it had to be done—to save her father.

**LAMB:** If you had seen him . . . It's horrendous. They are brutalizing him. Beating him. Starving him. All to force my hand.

**LION:** . . .

**LAMB:** I cannot live with myself if he dies because I did not try. He would do this for me. I can do no less for my father. Tox did it for his girl. Would you do this for me?

The question was bold. But she feared she already knew the answer. Omar was a warrior. However, his loyalty was not to a person, but a country. He would die for Israel. He would not die for her.

**LION:** He is one man, Lamb. You risk an entire nation!

Throat thick with raw emotion, she covered her mouth. Only then realizing how much she'd hoped, with a wild, crazy, desperate hope, that he'd sacrifice everything for *her*. Nobody had ever been willing to do that.

So she must rely on herself. As she always did. It was what had gotten her to this point.

**LAMB:** Must go. Have a new lead that needs my attention.

**LION:** I beg you.

**LAMB:** Begging looks good on you.

She ended the transmission, cleared the history, and strolled out of the Moscow State University library, aware of her surroundings and weakness. Weakness for Omar. For the yearning to talk with someone. Ram was out of the question—one call, and he'd track her down, destroy what little progress she'd made. There was a time she might have wanted to talk to Tox, but she didn't want to create trouble for him and Haven.

As she made her way off campus, Tzivia couldn't believe the idea that came to her. She knew better. But the one person whose brain she wanted to pick was Dr. Cathey. She didn't need his religious ramblings, but she could no more separate Dr. C's faith from the other side of him—the logic, the intellect—than she could make a whole sword from one piece.

He'd know. Dr. Cathey would know where to look for the next piece. She had ideas and had pursued them. For the first piece, dumb luck had let her stumble on a link in a scholarly article that led her to a recent gallery at the State Archive. It had been mislabeled as Roman era, when the work and weight convinced her it was Iron Age. And that the edges were so straight and grooved. Nur's expert said it would take time to verify, but Tzivia was convinced of its authenticity.

As if she would risk her father's life with a fake!

She'd been irresponsible in her legwork once before, and the professor had raked her over the coals. He'd demanded hard work and superior character from his students. Of course, he wouldn't be happy that she'd stolen the piece from the Archive, but then, he probably wouldn't approve of her working for the AFO either.

*She* didn't approve.

"*You are better than this, Tzivia!*" His words sailed from the past, four years ago as she stood in Dr. Cathey's office at Oxford, where he was an adjunct professor and she a lowly graduate student, desperate to finish her degree. Desperate for recognition. But she'd cut a few corners. And inadvertently cut off another doctoral student, leaving her . . .

*"You are too bright for this, too promising!" he barked, slamming her file on the table. "And to do this to Margaret when you have every opportunity before you—"*

*"I only have what* I *have seized," Tzivia bit back.*

*"But that is just it!" he growled as he stepped closer and caught her arms. "You are a natural, Tzivia. Brilliant, passionate. There is no need to usurp your colleagues, to* compete *with them. We, each of us, are working toward the same goal: revealing history! Work* with *them. Support them. Champion them, and you will find that you rise* with *them, not against them!"*

She'd stood there in his office that night, so hurt and angry that he'd called her on something she'd known better than to do. But desperation to have that recognition, to be plucked from her sad, nondescript scrape of a life, had driven her to stoop low. So very low. Grieved that she'd disappointed him, she couldn't face him. Hated that roiling emotion in his eyes. Instead, she'd bored holes into the framed picture on the shelf behind him.

Back then, she couldn't understand why it angered her so much. But she could still hear his anger, though his voice never rose. Could still see the disbelief and something far worse—disappointment—in his gray eyes. A pang over her petulance then thumped in her breast.

She stuffed her hands in the pockets of her hoodie as she walked back to the flat. If only she could say she'd been young and inexperienced. But that had only been a few years ago. Just before Kafr al-Ayn and Tox Russell.

What would Dr. Cathey say now?

She snorted. She didn't want to know.

Tzivia stopped. *Wait.* Her heart skipped a beat, mind vaulting back to that memory. Not his reprimand.

*Wait wait wait.*

She shoved her hand into her hair and turned a slow circle, thinking. What . . . *That photograph!* Dr. Cathey and an old friend of his. But it wasn't the two friends laughing, arms around each other as they posed for a picture, that snagged her thoughts. It was what sat behind them. On a glass stand on a bookshelf.

She hauled in a hard breath. Snapped up her head. With a gasp, she pivoted on her heel and sprinted back to her flat. There, she shoved the key into the lock, flung open the door, and dove for her laptop. In the split second between her entry and the door shutting, she realized her mistake.

The alarm hadn't gone off.

As she registered this, panic erupted. Adrenaline shot through her veins. In the space of a heartbeat, she saw the man coming at her.

# 20

**— MOSCOW, RUSSIA —**

Crash-course lessons in surveilling and recon came with being an operator, teaching the soldier to read a situation in order to stay alive. Two minutes ago, Tox thought for sure Tzivia had eyeballed him when she'd pivoted right in front of him. He'd shoved himself back into an alcove but noted she had a skip in her step. She'd figured something out. But she was distracted, and that planted him the shadows as she sprinted up the stairs and aimed for her apartment. It told him to watch.

That and the vibrating along his nape that warned of trouble.

Tox heard a confrontation. Punches. Breaking furniture. Shattering glass. Heavy thuds. A scream. It wasn't Tzivia. She wouldn't scream.

He took the steps two at a time, sometimes three, and vaulted through the narrow stairwell. Barreled down the hall. He drove his heel into the door. It flung inward, splintered. Smacked a wall and flapped back. He shrugged it aside, weapon drawn as he pushed into the small flat, nearly tripping over a body.

A man. Sprawled between the small three-foot hall and the twenty-square-foot living room.

The shrill sound of glass raining down came from his right. Tox twitched that way and started for the bedroom, where shadows leapt and dodged across the wall. He pushed on, staring down the sights of his gun.

Edging into the room stalled his mind.

Tzivia was fighting two men—both nearly twice her size. She was a blur of strikes, kicks, punches, and blocks. He knew that about her. Knew her lethality.

A knife-hand to her side nailed her hard. She groaned and kept fighting, but she was slowing. Wouldn't last much longer.

Tox aimed at the closest man. Eased back the trigger.

The loud crack of the weapon shoved Tzivia and the other man apart. Both took cover.

Tox stepped back, reminding himself that Tzivia wouldn't recognize him, but she'd recognize Kazimir. And she wouldn't know if he was there to end her, the attacker, or both of them. He shouldered the wall but kept a line of sight on the man cowering on the other side of the bed. Tox had to let her know he was there to protect her. She'd think that an interesting twist.

"Don't move or you'll end up like your buddies," Tox warned in Russian.

But when the man looked over the mattress, Tox understood what—*who*—he faced. And that he could not let this man leave alive. Then again, if he killed him, a boatload of heat would come down on his neck. What the heck was he supposed to do?

Tzivia scrambled toward him.

The man rose, producing a weapon. Made the decision for Tox.

Tox fired again. The man shifted, stunned as Tox placed another bullet in his chest. His eyes registered shock, then went vacant as he slumped across the bed.

Frustration coated Tox's muscles as he slipped farther into the room. Waited a second, then edged closer. Pressed two fingers to the man's carotid. Nothing.

He turned—and a black blur sailed at him. Flinging his hand out, he blocked. Pain rattled up his arm and into his neck. He stumbled from the momentum of the strike. Nearly cursed, realizing his attacker was Tzivia. "Stop!"

Her fury continued, unrelenting. She punched. Jabbed. Tox deflected but pushed in closer, forcing her backward, exposing her exhaustion. Tzivia would otherwise never have surrendered ground. He moved in again. And again, until she thumped against the wall, pinned. Startled.

He flipped her around. Smashed her cheek into the plaster and pressed his chest to her spine so he could manacle her hands. "*Stop*," he hissed in Russian. "I'm not here to hurt you, but if necessary, I will."

"Why are you following me?" she growled, bucking beneath his bulk, which only cracked her head against the wall again.

"Mr. Abidaoud has trust issues," Tox grunted. "He doesn't *trust* you." Time to figure out a plan, get himself together. Wailing sirens gave him the ammo necessary to force her cooperation. "The authorities are coming. Do I need to hold you until they arrive?"

"They can't arrest me," she breathed. "If they take me in, I can't find the sword."

"Then we have a problem. You are bent on snapping my neck, but I'm not inclined to lose my head, so . . . will you behave?" Though she glowered, he saw her surrender, and stepped back. "Get your things."

After another glare, she stalked from the room.

Tox hurried to the window and peered out, gauging their opposition. Police racing up the street. He checked the other end of the road. Nothing tha—

A cruiser catapulted around a corner two blocks down.

"We have to go. Now." He hurried to the living room, where she was sliding a laptop into her pack. She slung it over her shoulder with a curt nod.

That was all she needed? He shouldn't be surprised. She'd been on the run for a long time. Having a go-bag was part and parcel of life on the lam.

"The street is littered with cops," he said.

She hopped over the dead agent in the foyer and shoved around Tox. "This way." Halfway down the hall, she picked a lock. The door opened into a maintenance room with a boiler, a pipe, and a washbasin.

"This is a coffin," he spat.

She knelt by a shelf, reached under it. Wood scraped, and next thing he knew, she vanished. He squatted and eyed the darkness.

A tunnel. Tox nearly cursed. Always had to be tunnels.

With no choice but to follow, he hauled himself into the dank, dark passage and low-crawled, chasing her boots. She moved as fast as the rat scurrying past him.

A few minutes later, she turned into a tight room with an iron spiral staircase that pushed through the floor. Tzivia was scurrying down it by the time he extricated himself and shut the panel. He hustled but could tell she was trying to lose him. He would not let that happen and endure explaining to Nur why he'd been too slow. Instead of coiling the last dozen steps, he hoisted himself over the rail. Dropped down.

She crashed into him with a yelp, and they fell into the wall.

Tox used his weight to hold her. "Going somewhere?"

That fire again flashed into her eyes. Her lips tightened. But something twitched in her gaze. A change. Her brows tugged down and together.

Recognition.

Not good.

She blinked. "I—"

"Let's go." Distract and deter. "Mr. Abidaoud will want to know what happened." He yanked her toward the door, then out into the night.

"It'll attract attention if you're dragging me away from the building," she said, her voice way too calm.

"Only if someone sees us."

"You seem familiar."

He scowled. "Don't flirt with me."

Her expression morphed into shock, then anger. She tried to wrest free. "As if I'd want anything from a dog like you."

As long as she kept thinking that, they'd be okay. He sneered, opening his car door and pushing her inside. Behind the wheel, he ferried them away from the apartment. Too bad she couldn't blow her place the way Ram had with his compromised flat. Erase any evidence. Like those bodies.

"Want to tell me why the Mossad were after you?" he asked.

She shifted as they wove down streets lit only by city lamps. "How would I know?"

"I'm sure it's no coincidence that your father is Jewish and the

Israelis are hiding in your apartment. And I noticed you were in a terrible hurry to get there." He arched an eyebrow. "Were you taking information to them?"

This time she twisted to face him, sitting cockeyed. "Did the dead guys *look* like I gave them information?"

"Maybe that was for my benefit, to throw me off—"

"Why would I do that? *You* have my father!"

"Not me," he corrected.

"To placate your boss, I have bent over backward and violated my conscience more times in the last few months than in my entire life!" The veins at her temple throbbed beneath the occasional street lamp. "I have no pretense, no intention other than doing *whatever* it takes to get my father back!"

Glad to have her riled so she'd be less likely to see the man behind the face, he nodded. "Explain why you were in a hurry to return to your flat."

"Why were you following me?"

"Fine. Keep your answers and see how your father fares when Nur finds out."

Dark, furious eyes stabbed him as he made the final turn toward Mattin Worldwide. No doubt she wanted to argue, to ask if he was threatening her. But that dialogue would only get her father deeper in trouble. Her struggle was real, and he didn't like threatening her father to influence Tzivia.

"I have to go to London," she finally said.

Relief and victory churned inside him. "What's in London?"

"A lead on the next piece, what else?" She sneered. "A vacation? A lover?"

No, she'd left him in Israel. But saying that would betray his identity.

"Withdraw your claws," he said. "You told me because you need help getting there. That means convincing Nur to send you. So what's there?"

Though Tzivia said nothing, her posture revealed plenty. Why did she have to make everything so difficult? He longed for the simplicity of honest, caring Haven. Then again, to Tzivia, he was a stranger. "You don't have to tell me—"

"There's a photograph," she said with a huff as they entered the parking garage. "In the home of a . . . friend."

"Dr. Cathey."

She drew in a breath. "How—"

"You two have a strong connection. He lives in London and worked at Oxford."

Silence rang through the car as he pulled into his reserved spot by the elevators. No doubt she probed his answers, wondering if it was commonly known that she and Dr. Cathey were connected.

"Why can't you email him about this photo?" He gave her a warning look, one he didn't really feel. "Is there a reason you need to see him?"

"I don't need to see him to see the photo."

Tox hesitated, realizing what she intended. "You'd break into the flat of a friend to steal a picture?"

"It'll be easier," she said. "He's a nosy old man. This way he's not in danger. And I have no intention of stealing it. I just need to see it again, maybe take a picture of it."

"What's it of?"

She snorted. "You must really think me stupid." She shook her head. "I tell you that, and there's no reason to keep me around."

"You tell me and we find it—that's still only two pieces."

"Yeah, and what if the third magically appears?"

"Now you must think *I'm* stupid." When she opened her mouth with a comeback, he motioned her inside the elevator. "I get it. You want to keep your father alive."

"And myself."

They rode the elevator in silence, and he escorted her to the foyer. Leaving her with the hall guard, he made his way toward Nur's office. No longer a mere bodyguard, Tox had free access to the inner passage. As he neared the office door, he heard the rumble of conversation and slowed. Always good to seize chances to overhear a nugget or two. But the voices were too low.

Laughter barreled out, and Tox eased open the door. Late for a bender, wasn't it? Or a mixer? No, they would have told him about that so he could be here to protect Nur.

The man he'd seen briefly in the private residence hall sat with a brandy snifter in hand, laughing and shaking his head. Eyes crinkled under years of experience flicked to Tox. His smile changed—as if someone had caught him doing something wrong—but then just as swiftly, it returned. "Ah well," the man muttered. "Good times, good times."

Nur set aside his glass. "What is it, Mr. Rybakov?"

"Excuse me, sir, but I have Ms. Khalon."

"Tzivia?" Nur's eyebrows winged up as his guest stiffened, though he tried to hide that, too. "At this late hour?" He angled his wrist and checked his watch.

"I have an early meeting," the guest said. "I'll check with you in the morning."

Nur inclined his head and came to his feet.

And though Tox was sure he misunderstood, it seemed Nur offered deference to the other man. Nur Abidaoud gave that to no one. He was head of the AFO. Head of Mattin Worldwide, and in essence, the world itself.

But he stood there, watching as the older gentleman in his slick Italian suit ambled out without ever acknowledging Tox. Though why would he? Tox was merely a hired gun. And why was he leaving via the inner passage? It would take him the long route to the private residence. All he had to do was exit the main doors and cross the foyer . . .

"Why is she here?" Nur asked once they were alone.

"She was ambushed in her flat." Though Tox didn't want to admit he knew the nationality of her attackers, he'd shown that hand with Tzivia, and it could come back to bite him if he didn't mention it.

"By whom?"

"No IDs, but I believe Mossad."

As Nur absorbed this news, his eyes widened a fraction. He rubbed his jaw. "What did they want?"

"Her dead, I think."

Nur slid his hands into his pockets and drew in a measuring breath, then slowly started nodding. "They know what she's doing."

Tox paused to give his answer a more thoughtful appearance. "That'd be my guess."

"You brought her here—why?" Nur was swiftly connecting dots.

"She wants to go to London to find a clue to the next piece."

"But not the next piece itself?"

Wishing she had been more forthcoming, Tox hesitated. "I'm not sure. She wouldn't tell me—she's withholding exactly what it is as insurance against her life and her father's."

Nur smirked. "Smart girl." He jutted his jaw. "Take her."

Tox started. "Sir? Me? Who will protect you, then?" *Who will break into Mattin's system and find the names of the top-tier AFO operators?*

"Igor does quite well. Besides, if she finds it and manages to escape, then my life is forfeit anyway. No," Nur said with a nod, "you must take her. Ensure she returns with the piece or a certainty of its location."

# GOLIATH'S SWORD THEN LAID ITS MASTER DEAD

When Thefarie lost his Miryam, the time seemed right to Giraude to vow that he would never make the mistake of bending his heart to a woman. Delivering Thefarie's child to a family in the Golan Heights sealed that choice. Seeing the babe scream and wail, begging for her father and mother, 'twas too high a price. One Giraude's heart could not afford.

And yet, how easily an ache welled within him beneath a pair of pretty brown eyes, demanding he toss aside those vows.

"She is young."

The deep warning from Thefarie pulled Giraude's gaze from Shatira, daughter of Yitshak, the Hebrew healer. True. She *was* young. But of age.

The thought shamed Giraude. "My oath is to the Order."

Thefarie's laugh taunted him. "Have you yet convinced yourself, brother?"

Giraude gritted his teeth, his betraying eyes landing once more on the comely girl. "She harbored the enemy."

"Aye," Thefarie said, tossing a pack over his supply horse, "and neither of us have ended him because he holds information we seek."

*Focus on the enemy*—a better place to set his thoughts. "He toys with us."

"Aye."

"Must you be so agreeable?" Irritation had been Giraude's constant companion since the injury left him nearly bedridden. Fever set in after the healer stitched his flesh. Admittedly, he did not complain. It allowed him to be near Shatira longer. But now the wound was an encumbrance, restraining him in convalescence instead of allowing him to return to battle.

Thefarie chuckled. "Aye." He nodded, then stepped away from his destrier and slapped Giraude's shoulder. "Ask for her, brother. She is pleasant, and her eyes seek you as much as yours prowl for her."

Giraude lifted his head, surprise tingeing his face with warmth. "Do they?"

Thefarie laughed harder. "Do it. Her father is amenable, I venture."

"I have naught—"

"Then you are well-matched," Thefarie grunted, tossing another bundle onto his destrier. "She offers no dowry other than her beauty, both that within and that without."

"Shall we ride, brother?" Ameus stalked from the others. "The sun rises."

"Aye." Thefarie pivoted and made his way to Yitshak. He shook the healer's hand and exchanged words.

Giraude envied the ease with which Thefarie conversed with others, the respect he commanded. As he watched his brother-knight say his farewells, Giraude tensed when the Saracen emerged from the inner tent.

Shatira went rigid, a posture that trapped Giraude's breath. He locked onto her, noting how she peered between her father and Thefarie, then to Giraude, her cheeks flushed.

Nervous dread wormed through Giraude as Thefarie, smirk firmly affixed to his features, came to him. Slapped his shoulder again. "It is done." He stood by his horse. "I expect to see a babe in her arms when I return."

Breath stolen, Giraude stared at Shatira. Then her father. "Brother," he pleaded, turning to his brother-knight, who'd just violated every semblance of decency and respect. "Pray, tell me you have not—"

"Aye," Thefarie said with a cheeky grin. "Heal well, brother. We shall return."

The strangeness of being left behind, of his brother-knight's imminent departure, opened a chasm in Giraude he had not imagined could exist. "Brother—"

"*Dawiyya*," called the gravelly, alarmed voice of the one called Matin.

Giraude spun to the Saracen, but Matin looked south. Giraude followed his gaze to the horizon, where a band of ten or twelve Saracens rode hard, stirring dust. "They are yours?" he demanded.

"No," said Matin. "They want the sword."

Giraude tensed. It had been weeks since the great battle. Weeks of recovery and trying to pry from the Saracen the location of the Adama Herev. "Where have you hidden it? We've toyed with this long enough."

"If they find me here," Matin said in warning, "they will slaughter all of you."

"Then let your blood be the first that is spilled," Ameus growled.

"Wait." Matin held out a staying hand. "I will hide. Tell them I escaped." His eyes sparked with excitement. "In the night. And stole a horse."

"Easier to tell us where you've hidden the sword," Giraude said.

Grief creased the Saracen's brow. "That I cannot do. I am sorry."

In a flash, he was gone, leaving Giraude confused. Stunned. Why would the Saracen not return to his own? Why would he hide? Unease settled in his gut as he turned with his brother-knights, who were readying themselves to confront the band of marauders.

A feather-light touch came to his hand. Giraude glanced down, surprised to find Shatira at his side. Fear marred her beautiful face and gold-flecked eyes that met his.

Something deep and powerful rose in him. "Go to my tent," he said.

Pulling in a sharp breath, she stared.

The meaning of what he'd ordered—by sending her to his tent, he claimed her as his own to provide for and protect, as a husband—could not be discounted. Sending her to his tent would also keep her safe from Matin, who he yet feared they could not trust.

She squeezed his hand, then rushed into his tent. Accepting, he realized, what he offered.

When he faced the others, Giraude detected her father's gaze.

"I am a healer. We have no bride price," Yitshak whispered.

"She is enough," Giraude muttered as he unsheathed his sword. He stalked forward to meet the enemy, yet remained close enough to protect what was worth protecting.

A shadowy form rushed at him, a blur of black and steel.

Giraude met the onslaught with his brother-knights. Vibrations rattled through his sword, but he gave it no thought. He instead focused on pushing back the Saracens. Pushing them down.

A scream from behind spun him toward his tent. Toward Shatira. He threw himself at the flap, not caring what he might face. Darkness engulfed him, but he adjusted quickly, sighting the Saracen who'd slipped inside.

Their swords clashed in a song of rage. He arced. Parried a blow. Lunged in.

Light came from behind him. Giraude knew he was trapped—a Saracen behind and in front. He must focus.

Shatira gasped.

Giraude stiffened as the sound of metal grating bone brought him around. There, Matin drove his blade through a newcomer. With no time to process, Giraude pivoted in time to see the first Saracen scrambling out of the tent. The meaty thud of a body hitting the dirt told him another brother-knight had likely felled him.

Warm softness flew against Giraude's chest. He curled an arm around Shatira, shifting to lock gazes with Matin, who breathed heavily, then gave a nod of uneasy alliance.

# 21

— MOSCOW, RUSSIA —

Weakness. Aches. He'd been plagued with both all his life. Hidden them from everyone imaginable.

Yet here he sat on the bathroom floor. With practiced precision, Ram slid the needle into the fatty tissue of his thigh and pressed the plunger, forcing the milky white substance into his system. He sat on the tiled floor and waited. Tilted his head back against the cabinet, expecting the violent reaction of his body to the drugs. As he waited, he thought, as he always did, about the legacy his father had left him.

His father. He rammed his head against the bathroom wall with a growl. He'd suspected his father was still alive, but finding out it was true intensified the fires burning through his chest.

Tzivia might have assigned noble aspirations to their father's actions, but Ram held no pretenses. What father abandoned his children when he still lived and breathed? Now, knowing his father was alive, held captive by the most notorious man in the world . . . rage tore through Ram. He rammed his elbows back. Heard the crack of weak plaster.

Weak. Everything was weak. He was weak. His father was weak.

Bile surged up his esophagus. Burned his throat. Ram threw himself to the side and hugged the toilet as his body warred with the drug he'd just injected. He'd lose some but not all. And what remained would be enough.

Spitting caused him to vomit again. He coughed. Choked. Wiped the tears from his eyes as his system slowly quieted.

The tone for a text message hit his sat phone. Limbs trembling, he hauled himself off the floor. At the sink, he washed his face and brushed his teeth. As he rinsed the acidic taste from his tongue, he grabbed his phone. Glanced at the message.

T2K threading needle for the queen.

Ram hesitated for a moment. The words were hints. T2K—Tox and Tzivia. Needle—London had the Eye. You could thread the eye of needle. And London had a queen.

Why was Tox going to London? Ram texted back.

Sightseeing?

Babysitting. She was attacked.

By whom?

Israeli friends.

Not possible.

Tell that to the dead rats.

Ram hesitated, staring in disbelief at the words.

I'll look into it. KMP.

Pot is boiling. Dangerous to touch.

KMP—keep me posted—wasn't a request, no matter the danger. Ram was typing a reply when an incoming call took over the device. He swiped to answer. "Hello."

A long pause. Then, "You should be retired."

Ram tensed at Omar's voice, thinking of the dead operatives. Of them attacking his sister. Mossad had provided the funding for the mission to send Tox in undercover, but the mission should be more covert, less . . . discussed. Especially by Omar, whom Ram had yet to forgive for taking advantage of his sister. "Is there a problem?"

"She has given them the first piece."

"I just found out." A while ago, but he wasn't ready to send the wolves after her, and he wouldn't tell them she was in London now.

"You spoke to her? What did she say?"

Ram gritted his teeth at the hope in Omar's voice. "What I have is from the asset." He hated that this man felt invested in her life.

"Does she know where the other pieces are?"

Ram snorted. "Nobody who knows would tell anyone else, so I do not expect her to tell." But if Tzi knew where the pieces were, she wouldn't be hanging around her flat to get clobbered by Mossad agents. Which was probably why they were headed to London.

"We are concerned."

We. The IDF—Mossad. Revelation pulled Ram up straight. "Why?"

"She killed three operatives. Threatened me."

It took Ram a minute to process those two pieces of information, to merge them with what Tox had just said. What he knew of Tzivia and Omar. They'd dated and lived together for months before she vanished with a piece of intel Omar inadvertently divulged one night. Yet for all her bravado, for all her sharp words, Tzivia had been unable to hide that she had real, deep feelings for the Mossad director. And while she was trained to protect herself, she wasn't bloodthirsty. "What'd you do to tick her off?"

"We didn't do anything to—"

"Tzivia would only fight to the death if she felt threatened," Ram countered. "*What* did you do?"

Omar sighed. "She's getting too close to putting the Adama Herev back together. I tried to stop what Mossad had planned, but it—" There was a long pause. "They went over my head. She has been deemed a threat. They sent messengers."

Ram's eyes slid shut as he pinched the bridge of his nose, still feeling the tumultuous effects of the drugs. "Is the order STK?"

"I'm losing traction with my superiors, Ram."

"Is the order STK?" he repeated.

"Not yet, but soon. If she persists, they *will* shoot to kill on sight."

If she really found the remaining pieces, would it be over? The curse lifted?

He snorted. *Curse*. It was a curse—riddling males of the mercenary line with a debilitating disorder that afflicted them with a hybridization of hemophilia and muscular dystrophy. Combined and untreated, the Matin Strain plagued them with rapid degeneration of muscle tissue and progressed to the point of paralysis. A simple fall during that stage could result in massive internal bleeding, eventually leading to death. It had killed many boys for centuries, nearly wiping out their line. Today it could be managed with injections, which he'd hidden from all his records—military and otherwise.

His mind swam back to the caller. To the reason. The real reason. Omar wanted Ram to warn her. "Understood," he muttered into the phone.

"Do you?" Omar's voice pitched. "Because I cannot shield her anymore."

Ram mashed the END button and trudged into the kitchen, rubbing his eyes. His leg caught the edge of the counter hard. Pain thudded to the bone. "Augh!" He held it, feeling the double header of the injury and the injection site.

His phone rang again.

With a growl of frustration, he answered. "Khalon."

"I need you in Virginia. Now."

Iliescu. Argument leapt to the tip of Ram's tongue, but he had to make it sound good. Legit.

"Don't even think about arguing," Iliescu barked. "You need to be here."

As the tone buzzed in his ear, he noted an ache worming through his thigh. He lifted the hem of his shorts and saw a swirl of red and blue swimming to the upper layer of his dermis. It would be big and ugly soon. Had he waited too long for the injection this time?

* * * *

**— SAARC HEADQUARTERS, VIRGINIA —**

"What is this, a rite of passage? Y'all tricking me into making an idiot of myself and betraying a fundamental trust?" Leif stared back at Thor and Maangi with a mixture of disbelief and amusement.

"Hey," Thor said with a mock grin, "you brought it up."

"You say that like this is my fault. Like I made up what I heard."

"What you heard," Maangi said, "and what you think you heard could be two different things."

"You're trapping me." Leif nodded, then shook his head. "Beautiful." He hadn't expected integration to be easy, but he also hadn't expected to run afoul of their team loyalties. "You really think I'll go to the general and rat him out?"

"What else are you going to do with this nugget of information?" Thor slapped Leif's chest with the back of his hand. "Why did you bring it to us?"

"Because we're a team"—he tossed up his hands—"I thought. I have a concern, so I bring it to you. I don't run it up the flagpole. We deal with it. Between us."

"And how do we deal with this?" Maangi asked, his dark skin seemingly darker as he stared back. "You come to us, suggesting Ram is doing something underhanded, bringing Cell into it as well. So far you've implicated half the team."

Thor's blue eyes sparked. "Makes me wonder what you're accusing me of behind my back."

"If I were out there and got into trouble, if someone suspected that, I'd want them to do something. Talk to someone." Because that *had* happened before, and nobody did a thing. And he had the scars to remember it by. But these guys were more about making him an outsider than watching his six.

"You know what?" Leif huffed. "Forget it. But if things go south, if Ram gets ensnared in something he can't handle—"

"He's team leader for a reason. So's Tox. You might have led the Congo mission, but that's a whole separate thing," Thor said. "Let's let them do their jobs."

"Fine." He'd tried to take the high road, but he'd known they wouldn't be receptive. Somehow, he had to find a way—

"Hey!" Cell burst out of the elevator, rushing at them, face a mixture of worry and urgency.

They all turned to him, tension thickening more than it already had.

Thor came to his feet. "What's up, Cell?"

His brown eyes surfed the command hub. "Iliescu here?"

"Negative."

Maangi started over. "Why?"

And that drew Leif, too.

"I . . ." Cell tapped his thumb against his thigh. Then checked Almstedt's office. "I have a friend I'm worried about."

Thor lifted his hands. "We all have people we're worried about."

"Nah, I mean—"

The secure elevator intoned another arrival.

When Iliescu emerged, Cell all but threw himself at the doors. "Sir!"

The deputy director paused, ignoring Cell, who was a flurry of movement, and looked to the team. "Ram here yet?"

Thor slid a glowering look at Leif. "Negative, sir. We expecting him?"

"An hour ago."

"Listen," Cell broke in. "I have to talk to you."

Iliescu's expression pinched. "Slow down, Mr. Purcell."

"I have this friend," Cell said, then cleared his throat. "I'm worried—I think something happened to her. She's not answering my calls or—"

"That sounds like a law enforcement problem." Iliescu kept moving toward his office.

"Or a girlfriend problem. Get a clue," Thor grunted. "She grew a brain and dumped you. Moved on."

"No, no. She and I weren't like that. I mean"—he gave a one-shouldered shrug—"she's gorgeous, but you see . . ." His gaze bounced around the room, meeting everyone's expectant stares. "I might have—no, I *did* . . ."

"Did what, Purcell?" Iliescu growled as he reached his desk at the hub and tossed his briefcase onto it. Tucking aside his expensive suit jacket, he planted his hands on his belt.

Cell had a whole lot of guilty going on. "That line you established? The one we weren't to cross . . . ya know, when you said to keep things here between us." He nodded around the hub. "Well, I crossed it." Guilt hung on him like sodden blanket. "I have a friend. She's really good at finding stuff on the internet that people don't want found. I mean, crazy-good."

"This going somewhere?" Iliescu demanded.

Holding up a finger, Cell nodded. "You know how Wallace was all tough and macho, blowing off my suggestion about this thing being related to TAFFIP. Well, after our last meeting, Ram and I were talking . . ."

Again, Leif felt Thor's probing gaze, but he ignored it. Focused on the jabbering comms specialist and the deputy director.

Iliescu's dark brows dove toward his nose. "*What* did you do?"

"Nothing. Really." Cell swiped a finger across his upper lip. "I mean—okay, I asked her to look into this, check to see if she could find anything in there—"

"In *where*?" Iliescu demanded.

"The FBI servers."

Iliescu cursed. Then huffed. Swallowed what looked like a grenade ready to detonate.

Cell had violated a dozen codes and laws. But they couldn't change what he'd done now.

"Did she find anything?" Leif asked.

Eyes wide, Cell pointed at him. "That's just it—I don't know, because she's missing now. I tried to call her. I went to her place, and she never came home. She hasn't responded to my texts." He seemed ready to toss his cookies. "I'm telling you, something happened to her. Honestly, I'm worried."

"Did you get dumped again?" Ram Khalon's voice carried through the command center as he emerged from the elevator.

Leif stiffened, feeling as if his words and conversation with the team could be replayed verbatim. And it probably would be. Then he'd have Ram breathing down his neck.

Thor grabbed Ram's hand, then shoulder-bumped him.

Cell stabbed a finger at him. "Don't get me started, man. You told me to do this, and now I have an asset who's gone missing."

"An asset?" Ram snorted.

Cell's brows furrowed. "I ain't messing with you, man. This is—"

"Calm down, Purcell." Scratching the side of his face, Iliescu sighed.

"Do *not* tell me to chill out. When Palchinski died, you went ballistic. Then when Haven was in trouble, you were all over it." Angry Cell looked like a squirrel on crack. "But now I have a friend who's like the closest thing I've got to family in trouble, and you're blowing me off?"

Iliescu straightened. "Like family?"

Cell shuffled his feet, a frown flickering through his expression. "Yeah."

The noticeable difference in Cell's vehemence made Thor chuckle. He'd clearly been caught in a lie.

"You don't know her or me like that, so don't go making assumptions." Cell touched his fingers to his temples, then snapped his hands away, palms flat. "And can we just get past this to the fact that she's been taken? If she's not already dead, your jacked response might get her killed. And that—that I won't let lie."

"Wow, Barc, sounds like you really care for me."

# 22

## — SAARC HEADQUARTERS, VIRGINIA —

Life seemed to have a vendetta against him. Or maybe it was the curse come to roost in the insanity of an existence that filled his days with cruel pain and opposition. Ram stared at the athletic woman with more punch in the tips of her fingers than her fist and realized he had two options right now: pretend he didn't know her, or call her out. Since she had that look in her gold-flecked eyes that warned she wouldn't go unnamed, the choice had been made for him. But first, he needed to address something that bugged him.

He homed in on Cell. "How do you know her?"

Cell's mouth opened, hesitation guarding his lips. He bounced a nervous gaze around. "*You* know Mercy?" Disbelief colored his words. "How? When?"

"Mercy." Ram flicked his gaze to her. "Interesting choice."

She gave him a lazy shrug with a sly smile, her eyes lit with the same attraction he'd seen before. "I became what you never gave."

Oof. She'd nailed that one—and the coffin lid on their relationship. Or maybe he'd done that when he walked away.

He had to admit, she still looked good. Really good. But then, she'd always had what it took to bring him to his knees. In his occupation, that could be deadly. And it had nearly killed them both. Thus, the leaving.

"Dude." Cell huffed. "What is this? And what do you mean 'interesting choice'?" He pivoted to Mercy. "Wait—what the fluff are you even doing here? Deputy Director?"

"Okay," Iliescu said, stepping forward. He leveled a gaze at Ram, delivering a stiff warning to drop this and leave Lara Milton—or whoever she was these days—alone.

Mercy. That name would take some getting used to. She'd always been easy to read, at least for him, especially her intent. She'd want to talk. Pick up where they'd left off. But Iliescu wanted this buried. Probably to protect her. Or whatever mission had landed her in the SAARC command hub.

Interesting. Ram had always wondered who she reported to. Ironic that they were connected to the same man. But it was the worst possible scenario. Especially now. He couldn't afford divided attention or loyalties, and that was the only thing she came with. Her amber gaze drew him into a line of questions, forced him to erect defensive barriers. She was too good at undoing him. *Why are you here? What are you after? Are you going to be a problem?*

Iliescu shouldered in, breaking Ram's visual interrogation with a stiff warning in his expression. A warning that said, as an operator, Ram should know better than to get in the middle of another operator's mission. He needed to yield before Iliescu made him.

Ram lowered his gaze. Took a step back.

"Okay," the deputy director began. "Mr.—"

"Wait. *I* want to know what's going on," Thor said with a chuckle. "I've never seen Ram stand down like that."

"I'm with Thor," Runt said. "Some serious stuff just happened without a single word being spoken."

Ram tightened his jaw. His hands were tied—but that was an excuse he allowed. He wouldn't tell the guys they had a mission, a reason for gathering, and to focus on that. Nor would he verbally disrespect them, though his actions would do that very thing.

"I want to know what's going on, too," Cell insisted. "Mercy went missing, but now she's here, and you're all acting like high schoolers with some secret."

"She didn't go missing," Iliescu said. "She was right where we put her."

Brows rising, Cell repeated, "Where *you* put her?"

"Come on, Barc," Mercy said, splashing that million-dollar charm at him. "You have a brain in there somewhere."

Mouth agape, Cell blinked. Looked at her. Iliescu. Ram. Then back to Mercy. "You . . . you're a freakin' *spy*?"

She shrugged, her auburn hair bouncing. "I prefer the term *agent provocateur*"—she wrinkled her nose—"though you can call me an 'operative' for short."

"What needs to be said"—Iliescu took control, his tone grating against his need to preserve a delicate situation—"is that Miss Maddox is a contract analyst for the Central Intelligence Agency. And Mr. Purcell violated mission parameters when he read her in on a situation outside her clearance level." The deputy director glared at Cell, who was anything but repentant. "Fortunately, his egregious breach of protocol worked in our favor."

"Dude. What?" Cell squared his shoulders. His gaze hit Mercy. "You found something? Why didn't you call me?"

"You said I could name my price, Barc." Annoyance played along her very full lips. "You never said he"—she thumbed toward Iliescu—"was your boss."

"He's not," Cell said. "I report to the DOD."

"Yeah, well, then you owe me a penthouse overlooking Central Park, Dog."

"*Sheep*dog. I live to protect the flock and confront the wolf."

"Dogs are dogs, no matter the breed. They're smelly and flea-bitten." She had the guys sniggering now. That was her way. She won hearts and minds without even trying, including Ram's.

Once. A long time ago.

His gut tightened as he watched the flirting between "Mercy" and Cell. What did she see in him? He wasn't her type. Ram was. He clenched his jaw, teeth grinding so hard that an ache pulsed through his neck.

"Okay, let's dig into this." Iliescu pointed to the conference table.

Ram turned and pulled out a chair.

"Not even a hello, Ram?" Her voice was as smooth as a silk cord forming a noose around his mind.

He allowed his gaze to meet hers for a heartbeat. "That would open the door I shut years ago."

"Then used a rivet gun to make airtight?" she taunted.

He planted himself on the chair and adjusted his beanie. But he nearly cursed when she sat next to him. He slid her a look.

"You can hide, but you can't run."

"I think you have that backward," Maangi said quietly.

"Do I?" Smiling, Mercy shrugged.

She didn't have it backward. She'd said that to him when he'd broken things off with her. She'd said he could hide from her, but couldn't run from himself. Somehow, back then, she'd known. Known there was more to his decision than being compromised.

Once Almstedt joined them, Iliescu lifted a small remote to activate the wall screen. "Mr. Purcell asked Miss Maddox to dig into the FBI-sponsored, interagency TAFFIP program." He nodded to Mercy.

She leaned forward in her seat, elbows on the table. "As we all know, the Twice As Fast Fingerprint Identification Protocol was championed through Congress and put into operation a little over a year ago. It's designed to compile data across agencies. From the Department of Motor Vehicles, collecting prints from those applying for driver's licenses or state-issued identification cards, the Department of Defense—our soldiers and their families—and other entities like banks, corporations who use fingerprints to secure entry and data access, et cetera."

"I think we've all heard about this monster," Thor said. "Some people decried it as a violation of privacy. Conspiracy nuts said they were scanning us and getting biometric data."

Mercy nodded. "Well, I can't speak to whether or not *that*'s happening, but I did find some interesting trails."

"Define *interesting*," Cell said.

"This program wasn't built in or designed by the U.S." Mercy's face flushed, the excitement of the cyberchase always her thing. "Being immersed in that world once, I recognized the coding and pursued the microscopic trail."

Quiet blanketed the room.

"It took some digging, narrowly avoiding some vicious counter-attacks, but I identified its origin. The foundation of the program was built by the Russians." She didn't blink when curses seared the air. "And I'm not sure what's worse—that it was built by the Russians or that our government knew and ignored that juicy nugget."

"Russia? Are you freakin' kidding me?" Cell sat forward. "The *Russians* have our data. And we *knew*?"

Russians. Phosphorous arrows. Goliath's sword. Mattin Worldwide. AFO. It was connected. Had to be. Ram shot a look at Iliescu and found the deputy director eyeballing him. So he'd been thinking the same thing.

Almstedt lifted a placating hand. "The FBI insists the Russians have no access to the program now that we've implemented it across the country."

"True," Mercy said, her hands doing as much talking as she did. "To protect the program, our coders heavily padded and stripped it of some obvious back doors."

"But you got in," Ram ventured.

She hunched against the table, folded her arms, and propped her chin on her shoulder as she coyly met his gaze. "I did."

"Through their back door."

Pride rippled through her ivory features. She was good at that, even with people. Finding a way into their lives and embedding herself.

"So the Russians are spying on us," Cell said.

"Russia is always spying on us," Runt grumbled.

"It's worse than that," Ram cut in.

Mercy touched his arm, excitement thrumming through her contact. "Yes, far worse." She looked at the team. "Not only did the Russians hand us this program, but we've used it, *expanded* on it to include all agencies—which, by nature, weakens it—and in doing so, we've essentially been delivering the identities of every American entered into the system to the Russians on a silver platter."

As she talked, Ram eyed her, traced the coils of her auburn hair, the curve of her cheek and neck. He remembered . . . *too* much.

"That is some seriously messed-up stuff," Cell said as he moved to the edge of his seat. "But how does this play into the Soup Maker? Wait." He tensed. "Isn't the AFO HQ at Mattin Worldwide in Russia?"

He huffed in disbelief. "I was right. This *is* how they're picking their targets!"

"We don't know that," Mercy argued. "But I can say that the TAFFIP artificial intelligence is super complex, and"—she bobbed her head—"it seems to make decisions similar to the way Makanda's *Blood Genesis* program does. It isn't immediately crazy for the two to be similar, but the AI for TAFFIP seems to be based off genetic algorithms, which is *very* similar. But are they the same? I'd need more time and better access. Hacking gives you a limited view."

"You think a closer look is warranted?" Iliescu asked.

"Definitely," Mercy said, nodding.

A closer look meant Mattin Worldwide. Which meant Russia—Moscow. Which meant Tox and Tzivia could be compromised. Ram needed to tell them. Come clean with what was going on. But doing that could get Tox and Tzivia killed. He wouldn't go there.

"Is it really possible this is tied to the AFO killings?" Maangi asked.

Mercy shifted in her seat. Her tell that she hadn't sorted that yet. If Ram read this right, she had an inkling that, given time, would be proven correct. She was an artist with coding. She could tell something wasn't right with code the way writers knew something was wrong with a scene but hadn't yet figured out exactly what. Or the way a painter knew something wasn't right, that it would take more experimenting with pigmentation to find that revelation.

Poising her hands as if holding apples, Mercy looked at her palms. "We have the data coming from TAFFIP. It's aggregated and organized, but I haven't yet determined its sort command or what the sorted piles are. Right now, they're just gobbledygook."

"So, Russia," Runt offered. "Doesn't that sort of reel in every line we've got out there? Wallace's cases are all phophorous arrows—that's AFO. Mercy finds this code, created in Russia. The AFO is headquartered there at Mattin Worldwide. So what I'm seeing," he said, glancing around the room and getting only stares, "is that they're all connected."

"Possibly," Robbie said. "But we need a lot more than speculation to go up the chain with our efforts against the AFO."

"Exactly," Iliescu agreed. "We walk very lightly over this minefield so it doesn't blow up in our faces. I've tasked Mercy with digging further. She has some leads, which she'll work on and we'll monitor."

"Have you shared the intel beyond this room?" Robbie asked the deputy director. "We need to pull in—"

"Negative," Iliescu said. "This stays here. We go live with this, the vault opens, and we won't get squat." His tight lips and furrowed brow warned there'd be no negotiating. "Mercy will keep hunting. Ram will stay on mission, and the rest of you keep training. Be ready. We're closing in on another name." The meaning he sent through those words was received loud and clear.

"So is Mercy working with us now?" Cell asked.

"Don't get excited, Mr. Purcell."

"Wrong angle, dude," Cell said, straight-faced. "But seriously, we need to talk. She doesn't want pay, she wants a penthouse overlooking Central Park. And I don't want her trying to take that out of my retirement fund—which she could do in a blink, in case you were wondering."

"Why, *Dog*, are you worried about me again?"

Cell scowled. "I'm not kidding, Mercy. Stay out of my wallet."

The flirting grated on Ram. He nodded at Iliescu and pushed back his chair. "Keep us posted on what she finds."

"She?" Mercy lifted her eyebrows. "I do have a name, you know."

"You have many." Ram stood. "I need to check on my asset."

"Yo," Cell called. "When will we see him again?"

"When he's done." Ram started out of the hub.

"Done with what, exactly?" Runt called.

Ram aimed for his assigned ten-by-twenty quarters that felt more like a prison cell. He stood just outside the door and ran a hand over his head, dragging off the beanie. He closed his eyes and pinched the bridge of his nose.

"I see you still have it."

His hand curled reflexively around the beanie, a gift from her. She'd made it.

"I didn't know you worked with Barc." Her soft words held an apology.

He opened his eyes and slid a gaze to the left, where he found the toe of her shoe. Sneaker-like flats with polka dots. "We had a deal."

She came around in front of him, tipping her head to look up at him. "No probing," she said with a nod.

"No probing," he affirmed.

They'd crossed some lines on a mission that started in Kirkuk and ended in Greece, but there'd been one guiding rule: They didn't probe into why the other was in-country. They were both operatives. Both had a mission. They'd teamed up for efficiency . . . and other things. But he'd fallen down a chasm of bad judgment and almost couldn't claw his way back up. Breaking things off hadn't been personal. It had been desperation.

Eyes still locked with his, she touched his forearm. Tendrils of electricity leapt from her fingertips, crackling and popping up his elbow, over his bicep, and into his shoulders to create a trill at the back of his head. "You're bruising," she whispered.

His heart crashed against the secret. He glanced at his arm, surprised to find a bruise. He had no idea where it had come from or when, but the medication should've stopped such easy bruising. Imprisoned behind his unwillingness to betray himself, Ram said nothing.

"Taking too long with your medication again?"

He shifted around her. "No probing."

"So that's it. No, 'It's been a while. Great to see you. Sorry for shattering your heart in a million pieces'?"

Clenching his teeth, he skated her a glance. "You don't seem shattered."

"That's because I've had a few years to superglue the pieces back together. Ya know, I kintsugi'd myself. Reassembled the broken pieces with gold—better, stronger, more value now."

"Then it paid off." He pivoted to her. "I told you—"

"Yeah, you did. With your mouth," Mercy said, "but your eyes told a very different story, Ram. You wanted to stay as much I wanted you to."

"Yes." He stomped a step forward. "I told you it *had* to be done. Leaving wasn't something I *wanted*. It was *necessary*." What would it take for her to get it, to understand? "To protect you, to protect me—the missions." He moved another step closer. "I'm not going to let you screw things up here. What we did, what we had? It's not happening again, Lara." He flinched, cursing himself for using that name. "Whoever you are."

Hurt flickered through her face, brightened by a flush in her cheeks. His fingers itched to touch the lazy curls around her temples and neck.

"Names are just masks, Ram, the same way you wear that beanie or take the medication." There was a childlike innocence wreathing her eyes, which had seen more than most people did in a lifetime. "At the core, it doesn't change who you are. I'm still me, the girl you talked to, shared your secrets with. Secrets I still haven't told anyone else." Her gaze drifted to his arm.

Despite his determination to be unmoved by her, Ram glanced at the spot. The yellow-green bruise had faded some. Fist balled, he lifted his gaze—and fell right into hers.

*There.* A weight tugged at him, pulling him from his resolve. Flashes of the past shuddered through his mind like pieces of broken glass. He saw their first kiss. Her laughter as they rode a water taxi. The two of them holed up in a dusty shelter, sweaty and exhausted but . . . happy. The moment he'd been paying more attention to her and missed the shooter stalking them. Nearly ended her life. Left her with a permanent reminder. His thumb traced the scar across her cheek. She'd been lucky, the medic said, and warned her to be more careful next time.

Mercy's lips parted. Her eyes fluttered as she drew in a breath.

They had been good together. No, great.

But they were better apart. *He* was better apart.

Ram lowered his hand. Backed to the door and caught the knob. "Good-bye, Mercy."

She sauntered toward him, and in that maddening, adorable way of hers, she smirked. "You can hide, but you can't run, Ram. The truth will always find you and knock you upside that gorgeous, thick skull of yours."

"I'll be waiting."

"Ram!"

He glanced down the grate-floor hall to where Thor stood.

"We got news—Tzaddik's in trouble. We're heading out to extract him."

# 23

## — FBI RESIDENCE AGENCY, MANASSAS, VIRGINIA —

"So . . . nothing?" Levi straddled a chair and faced her.

"Sorry," Haven said around a yawn. "I'd say this one is legit as well."

Discouragement weighted his shoulders as he folded his arms and sighed. His expression betrayed his desperate hope that this witness would break open the case. "This investigation is killing me." He glanced at his desk, piled with files, organizers full of papers, and more files. "I'm convinced the killer is in there somewhere. I'm just missing it."

Haven touched his arm. "You'll find it. You always do."

Weariness scratched lines around his eyes. "When you were working here, we made a great team."

She smiled. "We did. Well"—she shrugged—"except when D'Angelo tied up my time vetting girlfriends."

Levi laughed. It was good to see the darkness chased from his countenance. "Speaking of significant others," he said, nodding to her left hand, which sported the engagement ring. "How's that going?"

She couldn't help the grin that stole across her face. "If by *that* you mean our engagement, it's wonderful. Never been happier." *Except when I was in his arms.* Or when she actually heard from him. It had been a couple weeks again.

"Have you set a date yet?"

"March. Maybe." At least, that was the plan for the formal celebration.

Levi nodded but said nothing. Then his gaze hit hers. "He'd better take care of you."

"As you can see"—she nodded to Chiji, who sat in a nearby conference room—"he takes care of me just fine."

"By giving you a babysitter?"

"You know Chiji and Cole better than that. Don't you dare make this into something negative." She shifted to the edge of her chair. "I'd better get going. Charlotte wants me over for some charity work." She stood, yawning again.

"You okay?"

She scrunched her nose, noting Chiji quietly joining them. "Long nights working on the big celebration for Evie's Sour Fifteen."

"Her what?"

Haven laughed. "Since next year is her Sweet Sixteen, we're calling this one her Sour Fifteen." She bounced her shoulders. "Fitting, with the attitude she's grown this last year." She shrugged. "Teens."

"Have pity on her—her dad's the president."

"She's spent nearly half her life in the limelight." And had been shot with an arrow, which put her out of school for part of her freshman year in London. "But you're right—it's a lot to deal with, especially when you're still figuring out who you are as a person."

He escorted her to the hall. "Take care, Kase."

"Do me a favor?" She squinted up at him. "Call me Haven. Please." Once she'd committed her heart to Cole last year, she'd abandoned the "Kasey" nickname that had been bestowed by her late husband, Duarte.

"Right. Of course."

She gave him a good-bye hug.

A gasp sounded behind them.

Haven looked over her shoulder to where a dark-haired woman stood with two bags of Chinese takeout from Levi's favorite dive, Kwon's. Hurt massaged her pretty features as she stared at them.

"Maggie," Levi said, moving toward the newcomer.

*Well, that's interesting.*

"I . . ." Maggie hoisted the bags, her gaze bouncing nervously around the hall, over the offices, deftly avoiding eye contact. "I brought photos from the crime scenes. Like you asked." Her face went crimson. "And takeout. You said you like Chinese, but I didn't—" She looked at Haven finally. "I didn't realize you were . . ."

"Haven was just leaving."

Wow. Cue taken. "Yep, I was. And for the record, I'm happily marr—engaged," Haven said, wagging her ring as she scooted past the woman and prayed nobody caught that slip. "Levi and I worked together for a couple of years. He's a friend, like a brother." She winked at Levi, then hurried out of the building, aching more than ever to hear from Cole.

She wasn't sure why, but by the time she and Chiji reached her SUV—a trade-up Cole had insisted upon for her safety—tears blurred her vision. Leaning into the headrest, she closed her eyes.

"Seeing Wallace makes you miss him," Chiji said calmly.

"Very much," Haven admitted. "I just need to hear his voice."

"It pains you to have me here," he said. "It, too, reminds you he is not."

The tears rushed down her cheeks, but she took a measuring breath. "I'm so grateful for you, Chiji."

"He will contact you soon."

It had been longer than normal. Of course, every day felt longer than the normal twenty-fours hours when he was gone. She nodded, drying the tears with her sleeve as she eased into traffic.

She took the Beltway, heading toward the Russell estate. Driving through the countryside, she came to a small town with a lone stoplight. There were a lot of one-light towns on this route.

Her phone pinged, signaling an email. She grunted, not really wanting to read the message. Not caring if someone wanted her attention. Life was too hard right now, being away from Cole. Pretending on so many levels that she was okay.

She lifted her phone from the console and glanced at it. Her heart climbed into her throat at the dialogue box that floated on the lock screen. Then, frantically, she swiped and accessed her email.

*Regarding Order LUMU1983757—Delivery beginner professional club water.*

The words were intentionally random and meant nothing. It was the letters. The first four of the order number that meant: *love you, miss you.* The clue was basic and the information nonexistent, save that he was alive and he missed her. It was all he could risk.

"It's him." She began crying again. Told herself to stop. But that made her cry more.

Why was she so doggone emotional?

* * * *

**— NSA, MARYLAND —**

Why didn't you tell me you had a thing with Ram?

Mercy rolled her eyes and set aside her phone. But seriously? What was Barc doing, being so needy and girly, pouting that she'd dated Ram? She grabbed her phone and texted back.

Jealous much?

The guy wears a beanie. What's there to be jealous about?

He had me, remember?

What do you mean HAD?

Get your mind out of the gutter, Barc. Gotta go.

Be nice. I meant—is it past tense? Didn't seem like you were over him the other day.

Not your biz. GTG.

She stuffed away her phone and situated herself at the monitor, her mind playing the very question Barc had asked—was it over? Would

Ram ever . . . ? The sting of how easily he'd walked away would never end. He was a master at executing missions—and his feelings. Right on the chopping block of civility and so-called common sense.

She groaned. Falling in love defied common sense. But he'd never understood that. The only thing that spoke to Ram Khalon was the protection and defense of Israel.

She got it—she really did. The Bible even said to pray for the peace of Jerusalem. It was an obligation, she was convinced, to look out for God's people. But . . . to the brutal excise of anyone else?

She chewed her lower lip, lost in those green eyes once more. In the huskiness of his words after his kisses. Which were amazing. Tender. Urgent. Passionate.

Giddiness swirled through her stomach at the memory. Ram might seem like the most dispassionate man in the universe . . . until his lips caught hers. Then—Armageddon.

"What's his name?"

Mercy jumped. Turned to find Ms. Takeri standing behind her with a latte in one hand and her purse in the other. "Sorry?" The heat climbing into her cheeks warned she couldn't lie her way out of this one.

"His name," her boss insisted, arching an eyebrow. "I've never seen you mooning."

"I wasn't mooning. Besides—he dumped me."

"Ha. So I was right. And yet you still daydream about him?" Ms. Takeri snorted and spun on her heels before stomping to her office. "I'll get you hooked up, if you're so desperate you reach into the past for a date." A hand lifted in the air. "Come along. We have the benefit tonight. Need to plan."

Cursing herself for losing her thoughts and edge because of Ram Khalon, Mercy snatched up her legal pad and hurried after her employer. Then scrambled back to grab her phone and tablet. She scurried into the office. Normally the bumbling ditziness was a role she played. Today it felt too real.

Settled in a chair across the desk from Ms. Takeri, Mercy organized her notes and her mind. "Okay, Major Ibarra called and said he—"

"No, no." Ms. Takeri lowered herself onto the throne of her office chair and bestowed a condescending look on Mercy. "Name." She lifted a glass of water and took a drink.

Mercy frowned. Checked her notes. "Major Ibarra—"

"No." The word was spoken with razor-sharp severity, silencing Mercy. "I want the name of the man who has your head in the clouds."

"Why, so you can have him killed?"

Laughing, Takeri arched an eyebrow. "If only that's what our department did, life would be so much easier." She adjusted in her chair. "So. This guy. Does he *need* killing?"

"On most days."

The gleam of gossip widened Ms. Takeri's eyes as she peered over the water glass again. "Did he love you, then leave you?"

"You could put it that way," Mercy conceded, though the truth was far more complicated.

"Pfft." Ms. Takeri took another sip of water then set aside the glass. "Then he's not worth your time or thoughts. Move on, girl. I need your mind here."

Though the words stung, they delivered her from the bloodbath of trying to lie her way around naming Ram. "Speaking of here—Major Ibarra wants to meet with you tonight. He swears it'll only be a few minutes."

"All that man does is swear," Ms. Takeri said, but she sighed and nodded. "Make sure it happens."

Mercy jotted a note in her tablet, then glanced back at the messages she'd taken. For the next hour, they went over plans for the evening's event—which Mercy would attend as well—then reviewed reports for the Pentagon and FBI regarding recent cyber attacks.

By four o'clock, Ms. Takeri left for her private apartment—a thousand-square-foot space in the office building with shower, closet, kitchenette, and bed—to freshen up for the event to be held at a hotel down the street. Mercy packed up her attaché case with reports, aggregated dates, notes, and files from Ms. Takeri's desk, then reached for the dirty glass. As she did, the files in her arms slid free. Thudded onto the desk, nailing the keyboard.

The inadvertent attack woke the computer and opened a document.

Mercy growled at the files and scooped them back up, then grabbed the mouse, eyeing the *X* to close out the program, but four letters at the top of the document snagged her attention.

"What're you doing?"

Mercy twitched. "Sorry. The files slipped. Hit your keyboard." She righted the glass. "You're back. Did you need something?"

"My keys." Ms. Takeri stomped around the desk as Mercy closed the file.

"The water didn't spill—I saved it just in time," Mercy said. "Phew."

Suspicion crowded her boss's face as she plucked her keys from the desk. "What opened?"

"Some document," Mercy admitted. "I didn't look—it's none of my business, so I *X*'ed out." She started for the door, glancing at the clock. "Oh. Dinner starts in thirty." Over her shoulder, she surveyed her boss's attire. "I see you're ready. I'll get this packed up and meet you downstairs in fifteen."

Walking out exerted her authority, her naturalness that nothing untoward had happened. That she hadn't seen the file on Takeri's computer labeled *TAFF*.

Her heart thudded, then slowed. Had her years at the NSA finally paid off? Would she find out who'd been the leak, who'd fed their secrets internationally? Iliescu had been convinced it was high-tier. The nauseating thought struck Mercy that she might just be working for the traitor. More determined than ever, she knew she had to survive the hours-long dinner and avoid her boss's probing gaze. Then . . . hack Takeri's files.

# 24

## — NEAR MASADA, ISRAEL —

"Intel states Tzaddik was holed up, his books and scrolls secured offsite. AFO showed up, and when he wouldn't tell them where his library was, they hauled him out here for some desert torture." Ram turned to the team and the map pinned to the wall. "Mossad doesn't know we're here. And if they find out—" He grunted, then refocused on the paperwork. "We just have to make sure that doesn't happen. We get in, grab Tzaddik, and get out."

"What about his stuff?" Cell asked. "I mean, is he any good without those scrolls and books?"

"First, the Keeper," Dr. Cathey suggested. "There is no finding that collection without him anyway, so we start by securing him."

"Professor, you'll wait here at the base." Ram gave a curt nod. "Wraith will chopper in, then we'll fast-rope down and make it to the southern base of the fortress. Split into two teams. Cell and Maangi take the eastern side—that'll bring you to the back of the reconstructed area. Stay there until we have Tzaddik. Runt and I will take western. Thor, I want you on this hill for overwatch."

Bobbing his head in agreement, Thor shifted around to stare at the map, then pulled out his phone, checking wind and temperature variables.

"Stay off the main trails, but wait for line of sight once topside before approaching." Ram again tapped the paper laid out on the beat-up table. "Source onsite reports Tzaddik's being held underground."

"Fish in a barrel," Runt said, tracing a finger along the rendering of Masada, the ancient fortress in the Judean desert. "These openings lead to passages—tunnels. One way in. One way out."

"Unfortunately." Ram slid black-and-white satellite photos onto the table. "Aerial shots of the last three nights." He stabbed one with his fingertip. "Eight sentries each night. Same position. They're not expecting trouble—lazy, chatting, sleeping. Shift change at twenty-three hundred. That's when we hit. Infil here," he said, pointing to the nearest entry point. "Two lefts, stairs, a right, and a left." He flicked another image out for them to see—a far wall with four doors. "Second from the right is where they have him."

* * * *

**— NORTHERN VIRGINIA —**

She awoke to a buzzing. Three buzzes, then a pause. Three buzzes.

Haven pried herself off the bed and squinted around the room. Phone! She grabbed it from the nightstand and growled at a missed call from a number she didn't recognize. It had to be Cole. She wouldn't miss the next one. They'd agreed that if a call went unanswered, he'd try again seven minutes later.

She laid out a pair of jeans and a black shirt to wear after her shower, which she'd take once she'd talked to Cole, then plucked her electric toothbrush from the charger. The whole time, the box under the cabinet nagged at her awareness. Her good senses.

She rinsed her mouth and stared at herself in the mirror, as if *that* would give her courage, then—with a huff—retrieved the box. Held it for several long seconds that pounded through her veins.

*Truth or dare, Haven.* She had to face the music eventually, right? People would think the worst of them, if this was true, because they didn't know what had happened in Israel. Didn't know the promises they'd made. The vows . . .

Chewing her lip, she pushed to her feet. Shoved back her hair and ripped open the box. She withdrew the wand, then sat on the toilet and relieved herself. *This is stupid. This is stupid.* It couldn't be. She refused to believe it. Didn't want it to be—well, she did, but not without Cole here.

Nerves thrummed as she washed her hands. A buzzing summoned from the bedroom again. She abandoned the stick and lunged out of the bathroom. She snatched up her phone and answered. "Hello."

"I thought you weren't going to answer again."

His voice warmed her. Threw her mentally back to Israel. To their time alone. She wanted to breathe his name, but that wasn't allowed. "Hey," she said, melting onto the bed. "Sorry about missing your first call."

"Wish you were here."

She closed her eyes, aching. "Me too."

"No. I wish I were *there*. That this was over."

Something . . . something sounded off. "Is there a problem—with the order?"

"No."

That was quick. Defensive.

"Yes. I . . . I just need—"

She pushed off the bed and paced, distressed at what she heard in his voice. "Should I be concerned—"

"No." He cleared his throat. "Not at all."

She heard the lie. But also the firmness that told her not to push. "I don't like this . . ."

"Neither do I. None of it."

Arm wrapped around her stomach, Haven leaned against her bedroom door, dropping her head back and closing her eyes. Talking proved difficult, because the likelihood of it being traced or monitored was enormous.

"Listen. Money's tight. I might not place an order for a while."

She straightened, frowning, and caught her reflection in the mirror. The messy bun atop her head. The circles under her eyes from worrying over him. And now he was saying he might not call for a while. "We had an arrangement." She moved to the bathroom and propped her hip against the counter, fear tearing the giddiness that had moments earlier soaked her at the sound of his voice. "Please—"

"I should go."

Her gaze hit the wand. Two blue lines. *Two!* Her pulse sped up. Skipped a beat. Tripped and fell over the realization of those precious two lines.

"Pleasure doing business with you."

In disbelief, she snatched up the wand from the counter as his words registered. "No, wait!"

The tone buzzed in her ear. Tears spilling down her cheeks, she stared at the wand, trembling, wrecked.

* * * *

**— NEAR MASADA, ISRAEL —**

"Eyes out." It felt good to don a brain bowl instead of a beanie. To hold an M4 instead of a mouse. To stare at a blanket of stars rather than moldy ceilings in a rented flat. Ram had missed the action and cadence of being downrange with the guys.

Being away from Tox posed a risk, but sitting in that flat for one more day was a greater one to Ram's sanity. Besides, Omar was there. In control. Monitoring.

"This dude's like a hermit or something," Cell said through the comms as they hiked, scattered along the ridge at the base of the ancient fortress. They had fast-roped in, dropping every five seconds and scurrying for cover, the chopper on silent to cover their insertion.

"Seriously?" Runt asked.

"Every time we need him, we have to go to a new place. First Aleppo, then the Old City, now"—Cell nodded toward the looming plateau—"Masada."

"Whatever he is, I need to thank him," Runt said. "I love this place."

"Been here before?" Ram eyed him, still unsure what to make of the kid they'd first met on a mission in Egypt.

Runt grinned, pale eyes glowing in the moonlight. "Only as a tourist with a church group ten years ago. My parents were into that kind of thing. Wanted to be sure I didn't turn out like my brother."

Annoyance crept along the edges of Ram's nerves like thousands of tiny fire ants, biting him, stinging him. Leaving welts desperate to be scratched. He curled his fingers into a fist and closed his eyes. Worked his jaw muscle. Told himself it was in his head. There was no curse. At least not a supernatural one.

"Heads up," Thor said through the comms. "Tangos are switching early."

Ram nearly cursed. With a nod to Runt, he jogged up the fortress's eastern side.

"Three in position," Cell announced.

"Four in position," Maangi reported. "No joy on objective or Alpha."

"One and Five fifty meters and closing," Ram subvocalized as he bounded from shrub to shrub, monitoring the landscape and the guards.

"Down down down," Thor growled through the comms. "Five, sentinels grouping up on your three, eyes on you."

Ram threw himself behind a boulder and pressed his shoulder to the still-warm rock of the Judean desert. Peering down the length of his body, he stared across the incline to the road below, then again up to the fortress, easing out to get a better line of sight. He whipped back to the road. A speck of light snagged his attention. He keyed his comms. "Two. The road."

"Copy that," Thor said. "Incoming vehicle, two klicks and closing fast."

This time, Ram did curse. He shifted. Looked up. "Four and Three—can you get in?"

"Maybe," Cell reported. "Guards are distracted by the car, moving away from checkpoint."

"Means whoever's coming is expected, important," Runt said.

"And the reason they're coming this late?" Ram struggled not to curse again. "They're here for one person."

"Our objective."

"Roger that. Which means our window is closing," Ram bit back. "Four and Three, move in."

Runt shimmied closer, rocks and dust dribbling down the rugged terrain as he slid into place beside Ram. "What's the call?"

"Four and Three moving in," Maangi informed.

At this hour and considering the anticipation of those in the fortress, whoever was in that car had one of two missions: kill Tzaddik or take him. Ram couldn't let either happen.

With Cell and Maangi advancing, Ram's options were limited. He met Runt's pale gaze, white against the moonlight. But there was no panic in his eyes. Just a calm focus. Resolution to get the mission done. "Force that car to turn around."

Runt nodded. "Split up. You take high. I'll go low. Draw them out of the nest."

"Less chance of both getting caught." And a greater chance of mission success. But at least one of them could get caught or killed. Ram hit his comms. "Two, I need you to shoot at that car."

Silence gaped. "Repeat, Actual."

"Fire! Do it now!" Ram rolled to his left and came up in a crouch, jogging away from Runt. "Keep shooting till they turn around." He found a spot, wedged in, and started firing at the sentries. He picked off the first two without engagement.

Shouts and the report of weapons rent the air.

"Time to wake up, boys," Runt said calmly through the comms. "So, a major was assigned to a new office on base," he started, telling a joke. "While he was setting things up, a private knocked on the door—"

Rock spit at Ram, chunks peppering his face. He ducked and rolled again, taking shelter in a better position. When he reacquired the target, he was surprised to find two men rushing down the steps from the fortress.

"Look at that, boys," Runt muttered, his voice still creepily calm, "they're coming to us. Fresh meat delivery."

*Crack-crack!*

The second man on the stairs pitched forward into the first. They both tumbled into the darkness.

"Car's turning around," Thor intoned.

Relief chugged through Ram. "Three and Four, get our objective and get out. We'll have company soon."

"Two, can you help us with a little headache?" Runt asked.

"Roger that." Thor's sniper rifle finished his answer, pitching a guy off the wall. Ram cringed as the shadowy form hit the ground with a soft thump.

"Where're they coming from?" Runt asked.

Up top rushed another half dozen guards. Dread churned and knotted in Ram's gut. "Move move move!"

In a bound-and-cover manner, he and Runt threw themselves up the hill. Bullets cracked and rocks spit at them.

"Crap!" Thor groused. "I'm hit."

The knot tightened. Ram dropped to a knee. Without cover fire, the odds fell against them. "Two, start toward rendezvous."

"Roger," their sniper grunted. "Moving out."

Climbing the side of the mountain, Ram eyed Runt sprinting for the terraced part of the fortress. He leaped over a wall. Skidded up against the cliff face, making those directly above him blind to his location. Smart. He'd made the most progress.

Hope clawed back to the surface. They might actually be able to do this still. Ram hit his comms. "One, keep moving."

"Roger." Runt flew into motion, lightning fast as he scaled the steps.

Ram provided suppressive fire as he navigated the terrain, angry. Furious. This mission had gone south in a dozen different ways. All for Tzaddik. Logic told him Tzaddik was a threat to the AFO because he had answers. But that threat often seemed to work against Wraith. Ram dove over a rock, landed hard and twisted his knee. Felt a jarring pain but didn't stop.

"We have the objective," Cell reported amid gunfire. "But we're trapped. Taking fire."

Ram made for the fortress wall. Sprinted, his weapon cradled in both hands. He took the steps, realizing they weren't level or even completely intact. They made for tricky navigating, but he wasn't leaving his guys there. Their rendezvous point for an evac was two klicks out. With Thor shot and their objective in tow . . . could they make that?

Fire punched his arm.

Ram dropped against the wall, eyes swinging upward to the shooter. He glanced at his upper arm, where a dark line split open his tactical sleeve. Weapon tucked to his right pec, he peered down the stock and sighted the top of the wall.

A head moved into view. Ram eased the trigger back. A short burst delivered a heavy thud—the shooter—to the stairs a dozen feet away. Ram started forward, only to have a spray of bullets force him down. He grunted. Lifted his weapon and edged—

*Crack! Pop!*

A trail seared his cheek. Lips pinched, he harnessed the fury roiling through him. "They're ticking me off," he subvocalized. Took a step out. Only to again be forced to the ground amid a hail of rocks, plaster, and bullets pinging off his weapon and helmet, jerking his head back.

Ram cursed. "I'm pinned down."

*Crack!*

A few feet away, around the switchback of the stairs, came another thud. Then another. Seizing the quiet, Ram shoved himself into the open, hooked the switch, and propelled himself up the next ramp, staying close. At the next switchback, he crouched at the last ramp before the terraced top. He'd be in the open. He'd either make it or he wouldn't.

"Five!"

Ram jarred himself. "Five. Go ahead."

"We're out. But there's a buttload of 'em in the passage. We can't get past."

Slingshotting around the corner, Ram tore up the incline, then dropped to a knee at a half-wall. Scanned with his weapon. Keyed his comms again. "One, report."

"In the passage." Runt's calm voice defied the severity of their situation.

*Crack! Crack!*

A deafening cacophony of shots and shouts reached Ram. He stilled but realized he wasn't taking fire. In fact, he hadn't for several seconds. Shoving himself forward, he crouch-ran along the wall to the last corner. On a knee, he carefully tested the angle. No shots. He eased forward.

They were running. Four guards raced toward the passage.

Ram took aim and fired. Fired. Fired. "One, target them! Don't let them enter."

"Three and Four—take cover," Runt called. "Frag out!"

With that, Ram punched to his feet. Shoulders forward, eyes on the targets, he advanced, firing. Neutralizing. He hustled up to a waist-high reconstructed wall and went to a knee again. Aimed at the mouth of the passage.

*Boom!*

The ground shook. Dust and dirt dribbled from the mantel of the opening. Shots pursued the concussion. Haze drifted out, delivering with it four more guards.

With tight, controlled bursts, Ram dropped them in their tracks.

"Friendly! Coming out!" came Cell's gruff voice. A second later, he appeared in the smoke cloud with Maangi, supporting between them a battered Ti Tzaddik.

# 25

**— MOSCOW, RUSSIA —**

Tox had to own up to his failure. He wanted to get home to Haven. Home to the life they'd promised to build together. But he was stuck in this cold, dirty, godforsaken country. To go home, he had to complete this mission, discover the names at the top of the AFO's org chart. But he'd found exactly zero.

Not acceptable. Which was why he was sitting in a pew at the rear of the cathedral's smaller chapel. He lowered his head, whispered the last of his prayers that God would help him get it done and get back to Haven, then stood. He rounded the row and collided with a man.

"*Prosti*," the man apologized.

Tox muttered, "*Izvinite.*" *Excuse me*.

A small object dropped into his palm, an exchange. As Tox pushed out the rear door of the cathedral, he shoved his hands and the small piece into the pocket of his heavy wool coat. Shoulders hunched against the cold, he trudged back to Mattin Worldwide, formulating his plan and cracking the protective plastic case around the tiny object.

Since Nur had assigned him work detail with Tzivia, that meant less time in-house. Less time to compromise the system and get those names. He had one last shot to access the system, and to facilitate that, he'd just been given a spy camera no bigger than a grain of sand. It had a six-hour shelf life from the time he activated it, which would take some planning to figure out when Igor was most often at his desk. The short lifespan and its size limited the camera's abilities, so it would only send a single burst with the gathered intel to Tox's phone, then the battery and all electronic circuitry would fry.

It was a big risk. If they caught him, there'd be no explaining why he had such advanced technology. Its size and sophistication, however, made it less likely he'd get caught. It also increased the chance this could be for nothing if the camera somehow failed.

Getting into Nur's locked office was out of the question. If he tried, a dozen different alarms would trigger. Kaz was just a hired gun. He wasn't trusted beyond his ability to detect and neutralize a threat. But someone had to make flight arrangements for Nur, right? Probably Igor. Beneath that bald head lay a lot of secrets. At least, that was Tox's guess.

At Mattin Worldwide, he pushed through the bulletproof glass doors. As he neared the security hub, he lifted a hand in greeting, cupping the small grain between his palm and the phone, using the phone to shield any electronic signal emitted by the camera.

"Grigor," he said with a nod to the security guard.

Tox strode toward the elevators, head up, pace brisk. When he stepped into the metal coffins without an alarm or shout being raised, he felt hope. The door slid shut, and he staggered out a breath, slowly, carefully—because even the elevators had cameras.

He pressed his hand against the scanner and selected the twenty-seventh floor. With a deceptively quiet thrum, the elevator lifted and quickly delivered him to the senior floor. No sooner had he stepped through the doors than he felt the steely gaze of Igor.

Silently pleading with his boss not to call him in just yet, Tox stalked to his cubicle and powered up his computer. Once the boss left his office, Tox would need a reason to stop by and plant the grain—and there it was. An email from Igor with details for the trip in which Kazimir would escort Tzivia to London.

After he printed the itinerary, Tox slid it into a manila file folder, but his heart slowed as he scanned the information. He was to leave with Tzivia shortly after midnight for a red-eye. But the grain needed six hours before it would transmit, and Tox had to be nearby to receive it. Otherwise the information would be lost, along with the tech. He'd planned to show up early tomorrow morning to receive the data drop. But now he'd be in London.

Crap.

"Rybakov!"

He jerked his head up and saw Igor holding a phone to his ear, beckoning Tox into his office.

Could he plant the grain now? Without Igor noticing?

He was about to find out.

After grabbing his phone, the grain, and the manila file folder, he headed to the office. Rapped on the jamb and entered. "You wanted me?"

Face alive with irritation, Igor talked quickly in Russian. There was a furor over someone named Raison, it seemed.

Glancing at the computer monitor, Tox guessed the best placement of the grain would be on the credenz—

No. With Igor sitting there, it'd only get his broad back. The grain would have to be on the desk. A stack of books and ledgers sat on the corner, along with a bottle of vodka, an ashtray, and a snifter. With all that on the pile, the books were unlikely to be moved any time soon.

"Da. I will tell him." Igor hung up and cursed. Then cursed again. "You leave tomorrow with the girl."

Tox nodded. "I got the itinerary." He set down the folder, flipped it open, hiding his left hand as it positioned the grain between the pages of the top book. "But I don't understand why we're on different flights."

"What?" Igor balked. "That's not what—" He peered at the printed page, effectively giving Tox time to make sure the grain was firmly embedded. "What are you talking about? It's the same flight." He stabbed his finger at the info. "Look!"

Tox blinked. Frowned. "I . . . I swore it—Sorry. Must be tired."

Igor scowled up at him, his burly face a knot of frustration. "Nightmares still?"

Relief teased Tox's nerves. "It was worse at home in bed without her every night. Here, not so much, but on occasion."

"See? And you thought moving you here was just for control." Igor's menacing laughter didn't help. "London will do you good, no?"

Tox arched his eyebrow. "With that woman?"

Igor barked a laugh. "We must go up." He stood and grabbed his phone from the desk, pushing around Kazimir. "Still a full day for you, regardless of the flight."

A full day, indeed. He rode with Abidaoud to a cocktail meeting at a restaurant, then a brief dinner engagement that ended quickly and poorly with a perceived slight. By the time they returned to headquarters, Tox barely had twenty minutes before the grain sent its burst of information. If he wasn't within range, this would all be for naught.

He delivered Nur to the penthouse, then started for the elevators again.

"Where are you going?" Nur asked, hesitating at the residence foyer.

"My cubicle," Tox reported. "I left my itinerary down there."

He told himself to keep moving, act natural. Besides, he was the only one who knew something was up. Lose his mind, and he'd betray himself. He pushed into the stairwell, skipping the wait of the elevator, and hustled down the steps, drawing out his phone. Thumbing it, he unlocked it, then tugged open the door of the twenty-seventh floor. He emerged and rounded the corner, and despite his training that said to keep moving, his body faltered. Hesitated for a fraction.

Igor was still at his desk.

*The phone still works. Keep moving.*

Tox dropped his gaze. Realized he shouldn't put his attention on the device. He strode to his cubicle and glanced around, searching for the file.

"Rybakov!"

Panic drilled through him, but he crushed it. He pivoted. "Sir?" He fisted a hand.

"Long day?"

He exhaled. "Yes." He glanced around his desk.

"Looking for this?"

Tox looked back at Igor, who held up the file. "What . . . ?"

"Must've left it in here earlier."

Tox walked toward him, feeling his phone vibrate in his pocket, signaling the burst from the grain. But even as he closed in, the security chief turned back into his office.

*Just has to get more difficult . . .*

Entering the office felt like entering a minefield. "Sorry. Didn't realize I'd left it here."

Igor sat behind his desk and grunted. "Right there," he said. "We were in a rush to get topside." He laughed, swiping at something on his desk.

The grain dropped from the stack of books, and with it went Tox's heart. But it had transmitted, so it was dead.

He held up the file. "Thanks. I'll report in."

"Do that." Igor went back to his work, and Tox left the office, glancing at his phone.

He saw the file and initial drop of information, but even as he did, the phone glimmered and glitched. Then went black. He pressed the home key. Held the three buttons at the same time. Nothing. "What . . . ?"

"Something wrong?"

Tox jumped. Turned to find Igor glowering.

"Yeah," Tox muttered. "I think my phone just died."

Did that mean the burst was lost? That the entire attempt to ghost the system had failed?

* * * *

**— VIRGINIA —**

Her morning had gone wrong—with the exception of discovering she carried Cole's child—and now the genealogy hunt was going down the same path. She couldn't help but marvel that there would be another name added to the Russell lineage now. It was hard not to be distracted, to focus on hunting down a marble bust and more names.

"You would think," Haven muttered as she turned another page, inhaling the sinus-drying mustiness that came from being among books, "that they would have caught up with the times and digitized this information."

Chiji smiled at her over another large black binder.

She glanced at the light fixture, which was just as antiquated. "An auction house that specializes in antiques. I guess they want to make sure there's plenty of ambiance." Cheekbone pressed to her knuckles, Haven scanned another page. Four hours and nothing to show for it save an ache in her neck and a throb in her temples.

Aunt Agatha's information had led them to the Emerson & Hyatt Auction House in downtown Washington. As an auction house that dealt with wealthy clients and near-priceless pieces, E&H stunned Haven when the director said they were simply too busy to go back more than ten years in the files and update.

So here she sat. Stifling a yawn, scanning a ledger that recorded sales. From there, once they found the right entry, they'd need to pull the file. That wouldn't take nearly as long, the curator, Ellen, had reassured them.

Her stomach rumbled, protesting that she'd skipped breakfast. "I'm not even sure why we're doing this," she admitted with a sigh as her finger skimmed line after line of entries. "Except that Tzaddik said we needed to." They should just go home. They could look for days and probably not find the listing.

"And we trust him," Chiji put in. The scrape of another page turning finished his sentence.

Haven met Chiji's probing gaze. She sighed again. "We do." She shook her head. "I'm not sure why, but yes, we trust—"

"Good to know."

Haven whipped around, her heart in her throat. Tzaddik stood behind her. "Where did you come from?"

His eyebrow arched. "Do you really want to know?"

He looked terrible, bruised and battered, and she decided she probably didn't want to know.

"Wait a second. If you can appear and disappear anywhere, why have Cole and his team *ever* assisted you?"

His eyebrow arched. "Even I am tethered to His will. I can go but where He allows." He indicated the stacks of paper. "How are you doing?"

She grunted. "It's entirely unfair that you can appear out of nowhere, yet you can't tell me what page I'm supposed to be looking for—or better yet, tell me *what* we're looking for, so I don't have to keep digging through these dirty, musty ledgers. They stink of cigarettes and cigars." She huffed.

"The desire for more power was the reason Lucifer led the Fallen." Tzaddik gave a grim nod. "I will never again wish for more." He inclined his head to the book. "You have what you need. Though time is short, it will be accomplished."

Her mind took a whirlwind trip through the Bible, following the tale of Lucifer and a third of the angels who revolted. "You're one of the Fallen?" She laughed, more at herself and the ludicrousness of her question.

A tangle of emotions twisted through his features. "Waste not time, Haven. Cole's life depends on you finding the answer."

She frowned, not surprised he wouldn't answer her query, but . . . "How does genealogy impact his life?" Why was he besieging her with idle searches?

Tzaddik tapped the ledger. "It is there." His eyes, fathomless and calm, stirring both fear and awe in her being, held hers.

"Why are you even here?" she asked.

"Because I felt you surrender to the doubt of success. And despite my beginning, I am tethered to the will of God. Where He sends me, I go."

She eyed him skeptically.

"You believe in an all-powerful, all-knowing God, yet you find it too hard to believe that a realm exists outside this one. A realm where angels and demons war for the hearts and minds of His creation. Have you, like the angels who fell, grown so prideful that you exalt your belief, your will over what is written?" Tzaddik's eyes blazed. "You decide it is too fantastical for one like me to exist outside of time, yet is it not God who created angels? Is it not God who is the same yesterday, today, and forever? You accept that He cursed man, that He wrought great miracles—water turning to blood, snakes to staffs, dead brought back to life. What were those miracles, but demonstrations of His power to turn hearts back toward their Creator? How then is this any different? You may understand that I have asked you to do this, but not the why. But trust . . . as Chiji has said. Trust me in this. Trust me that it must be done. Trust me that you are"—he nodded at the book beneath her hand—"on the right path. And give care to the secrets you hold. If anyone learns you are married to him and carry his progeny, they will use you and the child."

Haven drew up sharply. Out of the corner of her eye, she noted Chiji straighten. "Nobody knows that."

Tzaddik smiled. "Keep it that way."

"Are you doing okay?" a soft voice from behind drew Haven around. It was Ellen.

"Yes," she said. "Thank you."

"We close in an hour," Ellen said.

"Of course." When Haven turned back, she wasn't surprised to find Tzaddik gone again. "I will never get used to that." Still stinging from the chastisement, she slumped. "He's right," she admitted. "I believe in the Bible, in God's Word, but to think of such incredible things happening today . . . I guess we've rationalized it away."

"And that is what the Dark One wishes. For us to be caught up in the belief that we are so much more advanced now, so much more intelligent, that we desperately search for justifications to drag God to our level where we can see Him. Where we can control what He does and does not do." Chiji swung his head back and forth, long and slow. "That is not a God I can serve. Mine is mighty. Powerful!"

"He is," Haven said with a smile, feeling the truth of that infuse her limbs. When she glanced down at her hand, to the last place she'd read before Tzaddik showed up, she hit a familiar name. And gasped. "Here." A giddy trill ran through her. "I found it!" The entry simply read: *January 1972—Linwood Estate—20 items 72.13.01. E.C. Fellowes.*

"Looks like we might just beat the bell," she said, copying the information as Chiji gathered the most recent ledgers they'd been through. Collecting her coat and purse, Haven hefted the book.

They hurried down the all-too-quiet passage, and something skated heebie-jeebies up her neck. Grateful when they emerged into a well-lit reception area, Haven smiled at the curator. "We found it!"

Ellen lifted her coiffed head, hesitated, then peered at the clock.

Haven's tension rose. "You said once we found the listing, it'd go quick," she reminded her.

"So I did," Ellen said with a smile as she took the slip of paper with the information. "Wow, that was ages ago. Carson hasn't worked here in decades."

Haven glanced at Chiji as Ellen came around the desk with a ring of keys in hand.

"He was brother-in-law to Mr. Hyatt—very good friends, those two." She led them down another dim hall, all the way to the end. Shoes clopping out each step, Haven ignored the chill scampering up her spine but couldn't help glancing over her shoulder.

"Here we are," Ellen said, unlocking the door and flipping a switch.

Flickering lights sprang to life, cascading down a very long, narrow corridor lined floor to ceiling with shelves.

"This is our document storage—the walls are reinforced concrete, and there are multiple redundancies to protect against fire." Ellen wandered about halfway down the aisle, glanced at the paper, then at the labels on the end of the rows. "Ah, this should be . . ."

Haven followed her around the corner. A crooked file box caught her shoulder. She stumbled, bumping her other shoulder into the opposite shelving unit.

"It's tight in here," Ellen said. "Be careful." Tilting her head back, she pointed to a box on the second to the top shelf. "I think that's the one."

Chiji was there, his presence eerily quiet and stealthy as he reached without effort and caught the edge of the box. He lowered it, backing up as he did to give them room.

Ellen verified it was the right one, then walked them over to the sorting table along the wall, free of the claustrophobically placed shelves. She removed the lid and set it aside. Hands poised on both sides of the box, Ellen crawled her fingers over the tabbed tops, muttering dates as she went. "Seventy-one . . . seventy-one . . . two! January."

Haven's heart beat a little faster, and she felt Chiji's presence close in.

"Here!" Ellen snatched out a file folder, reread the tabbed header, then handed it to Haven.

When she opened the leaf, she found all the pages were held together by a giant bracket at the top. Haven laid the folder on the table and fanned the pages, grateful to see a series of old color photographs on each item of record. "Ah!" she yelped, seeing the bust slide by. She flipped back two pages to the record of the bust. "How do I know who bought this piece?"

"On the back," Ellen said. "They record the purchase, and the buyer signs and dates it."

Haven turned the page over and skimmed the information, but her gaze dropped to the signature line. She sucked in a breath. Her gaze popped to Chiji, who looked just as shocked.

"This can't be right," Haven said. She stared at the buyer's name.

*Joseph Cathey.*

# 26

— FBI RESIDENCE AGENCY, MANASSAS, VIRGINIA —

Four bodies now, and the heat of every politician breathing down his neck. And what did he have? Bubkes.

"We need answers, Wallace."

Tapping the folder against his palm, Levi nodded, unable to meet Special Agent Parker's gaze. "There are no matches on facial recognition across any database from the Seaton murder. Wolf Trap is just as blank—worse, because three people saw the same person, but they can't agree on a description."

"You realize if you don't solve this, they'll never advance you," Parker said in warning. "This case is too high-profile now. You fail, your career goes down with it."

Levi clenched his teeth. "I don't care about a promotion—I care about stopping this. These are especially cruel killings. We can't let it happen again, but to prevent it, we need a suspect. SAARC has a plausible organization connection, but it's like going after an entire government." He shook his head. "We need a person in our sights. I want this solved, not because of a promotion, but because it's my job."

"Understand, I'm not threatening you."

"Right," Levi breathed as he came to his feet. "Just telling it like it is." He turned toward the door, hating this case with every ounce of guts he had left.

"Maybe if you paid as much attention to this case as you do that photographer . . ."

Levi stopped. Glanced back. Pulled himself around. "Come again?"

"Larsen saw you with that crime scene photographer in the conference room, eating Chinese food and laughing." Annoyance played over the SAC's face. "Having a real good time, he said."

"Larsen should mind his own business," Levi bit out. "Ms. Lefever was here with crime scene *photographs* from the Capitol Hill murder." He pointed to the updated report he'd handed Parker. "We worked until ten that night, so yeah—we ate dinner."

"Well," Parker said, shaking a finger at him, "keep your nose clean, Wallace. They're all watching you."

"Maybe they should start doing their jobs instead of watching mine." Levi pivoted and left, throwing over his shoulder, "I've got work to do."

Stalking down the hall, he bit back his anger. He'd lost Kasey by not making a move, by respecting boundaries and not crossing lines. But he'd be hanged if he was going to lose Maggie, too.

Back at his office, Levi pitched the file on his desk. Stared at it. Wiped a hand over his mouth, then stalked to the blinds that shielded his office from the afternoon sun. He opened them and squinted out. Sighed heavily. What was he missing? What clue, what nugget was staring him in the face, mocking him?

*"What if they're using that program to track down people and kill them?"*

TAFFIP.

As Barclay Purcell's words played in his head, Levi glanced again at the file. Was it possible? But fingerprints tracking down people connected to the AFO . . . how? He moved to his desk and flipped it open. Rifled the pages. Slid out the profile sheet he'd put together on the initial list of victims. There appeared to be hundreds across the globe, entirely too many for them to sort through in a limited time, so he had started with American cases, including the newest one in

Queens that had been sent from New York, and the first two Robbie had confirmed internationally.

Travis Seaton—45, congressman, divorced, Washington

George Schenck—53, married twice, Wolf Trap, two adult children

Bernard Kline—35, butcher, Queens, married, four kids

Paul Toledano—67, screenwriter, St. Petersburg, Russia

Jens Abrams—58, politician, Netherlands

Only two common denominators—males and MO. Age, marital status, occupation, number of children—all different.

"Hey."

Levi snapped his gaze up to the door. "Maggie." Relief chugged sweet and strong through his chest at the sight of her.

Black hair swirled around her elegant neck, accenting the blue shirt that clung to her waist and curves. "Still no closer?" She came to his side, nodding at the file.

He moved around the desk and closed the door. Tweaked the blinds to afford them a modicum of privacy. "Hey, um . . ." Parker's words gonged in his head, planting his feet by the door. He wanted to go to her but instead scratched his jaw, knowing he was giving tells and not really caring. "I think you should steer clear for a while."

"Steer clear of what?" She frowned and closed the distance. "What happened?"

When she touched his face, he felt a bolt of electrical surprise. Which wouldn't help things. He caught her fingers. "Things are . . . this case . . ."

Hurt surrendered to sincerity as she smiled. "I want to help, Levi. In fact, I noticed something in one of the photos that we missed."

Hesitancy guarded him, anxious—desperate—for a lead to chase.

"You have that photo from Toledano's living room?"

Scowling, Levi returned to his desk and fished out the photo. "What about it?"

She took it and shifted in the light so her back was to him, then lifted it. Pointed. "Look."

He craned closer, keenly aware of her bare neck. Her floral perfume. His hand somehow found its way to her waist and rested there. "What am I looking at?"

"The family photo on the wall."

He squinted and angled in even more. "What?"

"Paul Toledano is wearing a *kippah*."

Levi's thoughts slowed, processing the information. "Jewish." He snatched up his list and glanced at the names.

Maggie wedged in closer. "Abrams and Schenck are German-Jewish."

"So, anti-Semitic?" That would fit with the AFO, who seemed to be on an annihilation mission against the Jews. "I . . . I think you're onto something."

She was near again. Smiling. Thickening the air and his ability to think. He looked at her, noticed she was chewing the corner of her lip. Full lips. It wasn't the first time he'd thought of kissing her. What would she do? Was he really interested in her like that?

He wasn't sure. But he wanted to find out.

"Levi?"

Only then did he realize she was staring back. She took a step in, and he accepted the invitation. Lowered his head to hers, homing in on her mouth. Her arm came around his neck. Hand at the small of her back, he tugged her against himself. She was warm and willing, and it spurred him to deepen the kiss. Pressure against his chest snapped some sense back into him.

When he eased off, she smiled, her breathing as ragged as his own. "Whoa," she murmured.

A crooked smile slid onto his face. "I'm sure my boss won't like that."

"Um, hello." A strange voice joined the conversation—from behind him.

Levi spun. Found a woman in one of the chairs to the side of his desk. "Who—"

"Yeah, you're asking that two minutes too late," the woman said with a wry grin.

Levi went for his weapon.

"Whoa, easy there, Clark." Palms lifted, she came to her feet. "I'm here with full autonomy, immunity—whatever you want." She nodded to the desk, where a white card had appeared. "My Get Out of Jail Free card."

When had she put that there? Weapon in hand, he lifted the small card from his desk and cursed when he saw the name on it.

"Boom," she said.

His gaze snapped to her. Then awareness ignited. He sighed in defeat at Maggie. "Sorry . . ."

Maggie eyed the intruder, then nodded, cheeks flushed with embarrassment and maybe a little leftover passion as she started for the door. "Call me."

"I will." Levi let her out, then turned. "Why are you here? How'd you get in?"

"Sorry, but I don't kiss and tell." His visitor scowled. "Wait. I don't kiss—at least, not the way you were working her."

What little he'd relaxed vanished, his weapon shifting.

"Whoa whoa whoa," she said with a backward hop. "Okay, bad joke."

"What're you doing here?" he growled, rumbling with anger. "What do you want?"

She smiled. "Now you're asking the right questions."

* * * *

Mercy had to hand it to him—she wasn't surprised he'd pulled a weapon, but she had been to find him lip-locked with a woman in his office.

"Why'd Iliescu send you?" Levi Wallace demanded.

"I can talk a lot better without that in my face," Mercy said, nodding to his agency-issued weapon. When he didn't lower it, she gave him a sardonic look. "I can disarm you, if that'd make it easier for your ego."

Challenge hit his blue eyes, but he finally holstered the gun. "Start talking."

"Mercy Maddox at your service," she introduced herself.

"And Iliescu—"

"Didn't exactly send me." When the Glock started coming up again, she huffed. "Like I said, I work autonomously, but . . . under his authority."

Wallace holstered his gun. "Try that again. Why are you here?"

"Because my friend had an idea, which you soundly rebuffed." She pinched her lips together and bobbed her head back and forth. "Well, I'm here to give him the benefit of the doubt."

Hands on his hips, he stared at her impatiently. His eyebrow lifted, as if flagging down her intention and ordering it to land.

"I need to see a TAFFIP console," she said.

His eyebrows now dug toward his nose. "Purcell."

"Wow, two points for you, Clark. Kryptonite isn't affecting your brain today."

Impatience scratched at his handsome mug. She could see why they called him Superman, and why that woman had so willingly kissed him. But he was too pretty.

"Look, I really—"

"I want to see the console." She nodded. "Now."

"Why?"

"I thought I explained that—to give Barc's theory some exploration, since it's pretty clear you have no intention of doing that."

"There's no direct or obvious link."

"So you've said." Mercy folded her arms. "Console. Now. Please."

He pointed to the door. "Down the hall."

Mercy followed him to a large area that branched off into a series of conference rooms. He let her into one where an entire wall was lined with consoles. "Just awaiting inspection, are we?" she said with a wry smile. Two white PVC tables huddled off to the side. Her fingers itched to play with the systems. "Do they work?"

He nodded.

"All of them?"

"To my knowledge," he said. "I'm not IT."

Mercy hauled a PVC table closer to the last two waist-high consoles, whose power buttons she pressed. As they powered up, she removed her crossbody satchel and set it on the table. She tugged out her laptop and turned it on as well. A login screen appeared on the TAFFIP.

Pocketing his phone, Levi towered over her, his presence strong and confident, yet . . . not. "Let me ask IT for that."

"No need." She dragged over a chair and settled in it, watching the two screens. Her fingers went to work, easily bypassing the login screen.

Agent Wallace grunted but said nothing as she worked past the security protocols, digging deeper and deeper. Annoyance leached off him. "You do know the agency has double- and triple-checked for back doors, right? They haven't found any."

"I do." Mercy linked the two systems with a cable, then stood and logged in to the second console. "Can you walk me through this?"

Wallace frowned. "What do you mean?"

She flipped her hands at the black box. "How would I register and add my fingerprints?"

Hesitation gripped him.

Mercy glanced up. "What?"

"You work for the CIA. Do you really want your fingerprints in TAFFIP, if you think it's corrupted?"

"One, you're adorable when you're trying to outthink me," she said with a laugh. "Two, you're assuming I'm not already in the system. And three"—she wiggled her fingers at him—"you think my fingerprints will trigger something."

He considered her, as if he wasn't sure what to think.

She nodded to the console again. "Show me."

"It's self-guided," he finally said. "Designed to be user-friendly. Agent types in information from government-issued and -approved documents, then the system instructs the person to place their fingers on the glass plate and press down until the light turns blue."

Mercy nodded, then followed the steps. Fingers on the glass, she did as instructed, watching the red strobing light turn an appealing blue. It registered the print, reported *Successful Capture*, then returned to the start screen.

Curious. She rubbed the glass plate, eyeing it, then shrugged.

"Satisfied?" Levi asked.

Palms on the table, watching the coding bouncing between the first console and her laptop, Mercy lifted her gaze to his. "Not in a long time, Clark."

He huffed. "You calling me that because I look like Superman?"

"No, because my ferret died." She met his gaze, seeing his confusion and uncertainty. "Look, I really could use some alone time with these babies."

His brow rippled.

"I don't have to be babysat."

"I can't leave you in the building unsupervised."

"Nice sentiment, Romeo. So cute, trying to outthink me again. I'm a smart girl with higher clearance than you, though. Besides, I'll be here a while." She lifted her hand, saw a red dot, and swiped at it. Weird. "Can I get a paper towel?"

Annoyance pinched his face as he had an internal debate about leaving. Finally, he left and flipped the bolt on the door. Was he locking her in or others out?

"Whatever," she muttered and drew a toolkit from her satchel. She went to work disassembling the console, starting first with the easiest part—the glass tray and plate for the fingerprint pad. Next, she worked to remove the hull of the console and set that aside. A few keystrokes on her laptop sent different worms and Trojans into the isolated coding. It wouldn't affect the systems out there in the real world, but it would give her a direct response from the program.

Within minutes, she had the frame off, the cooling fan removed, and was working on the motherboard. So far, mostly standard components. The glass plate was a bit weird. Flimsy even.

How could this be used, as Barc suggested, to track down certain bloodlines? They couldn't do that just with prints. So were they gathering DNA? Was the flimsy glass more than just glass? She held it up to the ceiling light and squinted.

"What the heck?" Levi returned, a stack of paper towels in his hand. "You did all this in ten minutes?"

"Unless you hopped a time machine and were gone for hours without my knowing it," Mercy muttered. Something about this glass . . . She glanced up at him. "You hanging around all night?"

"No, and neither are you. I'm leaving in twenty, so that means you are, too."

"Um, no," Mercy said with a snort. "I'm staying till satisfied. Since you already called Iliescu, you know I'm legit and have—"

"Autonomy. Yes, but I have a date."

"Oh, with Hot Lips? Or someone else?" She knelt beside the system, realizing the front of the console held an entirely separate, self-contained box. "That's interesting," she whispered.

Frustration coated the sigh he tossed into the room before lowering himself to a chair.

She lifted the support plate for the fingerprint glass and held them together, again up to the light. "I really didn't figure you for the playboy type, Clark," she muttered as she worked.

"You don't know me."

She clicked her tongue. "I do. It's my job to know people. Read them."

He breathed his amusement.

"My guess is this case you're working is screwing you over. Miss Photographer Hot Lips croons and feeds something that maybe you thought had died."

On her knees, she worked the coding, tracing one rogue program, then another, before settling back into the console disassembly process. The whirring of a vacuum lifted her gaze long enough for her to see the cleaning crew moving through the now-empty cubicles outside the conference room. Her gaze hit the clock. Twenty-two hundred hours. Oops.

Wallace looked worse for the wear, tie loosened and hair disheveled as he fought back a yawn.

"What makes you say those things about me?" Heaviness weighted his expression, and she saw again the "something" hiding behind his confidence.

"Huh?"

"The case *is* screwing me over."

"Oh." She smirked. "I watch the news. They reported just before I showed up that the FBI"—she raised her eyebrows and traced the ceiling of the room—"had no new leads." She plopped on her rear and scooted closer to the console, unscrewing the self-contained unit.

"That's cheating, using the news."

"Is it? Or does it mean I use every resource at my disposal?" She frowned as the case loosened. Lifting it, she felt the weight shift. A second box revealed itself. "What on earth?" She touched it and sucked in a breath. "It's cool—cold, even."

Wallace sat forward, forearms resting on his knees. "Why would it be cold?"

"You tell me. Use that X-ray vision of yours, Clark." She adjusted, planting a hand to brace herself. A prick against her palm surprised her. "Ow!" Scowling, she checked her hand, surprised to find a dot of blood there. What on the floor could have cut her? Her gaze landed on the glass plate. Weird. It was smooth, flat.

"Mercy."

Her gaze snapped up to Wallace, who nodded to the console. There, beneath the second containment unit, was a very small—no bigger than a dessert plate—cylinder.

"What's that?"

Her mind wouldn't wrap around what she saw. "A minicentrifuge."

A heavy *thunk* clapped through the building. The lights winked out.

Mercy's heart climbed into her throat, pulse pounding as she raised her gaze to the ceiling. "Clark, I think it's time to change into your supersuit."

# 27

**— FBI RESIDENCE AGENCY, MANASSAS, VIRGINIA —**

"Get behind me."

*Did he seriously just say that?* "You're adorable."

Levi looked confused.

She nodded to his gun. "Glock 22 in .40 Smith & Wesson, standard issue for the FBI these days—well, that or the Glock 23. Unless you failed your safety course, then it's a lowly Glock 19 to aid qualification."

He hesitated. "No offense meant."

"Plenty taken." She nodded to the door. "Now, let's not be fish in a barrel, okay?"

Crouching, he slipped out of the room. She scrambled across the open stretch between cubicles and shoved herself up against the east wall. Levi came up behind her.

The sound of hurried footsteps made Mercy draw back, her shoulder pressing into Wallace's. Neither moved as the steps grew closer, then slowed. An M4 slid into view as the man approached. Tactical gear. Gas mask.

Gas mask?

Well. That wasn't good. Were they here to poison or disable them? Both? Did it matter? They were going to release a chemical agent for which neither she nor Levi were prepared. She motioned to Wallace to make for the stairs.

He shook his head. Arguing, just like a guy would, to engage the two. Which was stupid. They were outgunned, and the risk of gas—

A muzzle swung toward her. Mercy sucked in a breath.

*Crack!*

The noise was like a punch to her ear—Levi had fired. Right next to her. But there was no time to chew him out. The second tango rushed them.

Mercy launched herself at him. Slammed an uppercut into his jaw. Sent him reeling backward. She kept coming, noting in her periphery that though Levi had shot the first attacker, he hadn't taken him down. Another shot sounded, and the first man stumbled toward the conference room.

Mercy snatched a mechanical pencil from a nearby table and dove for the man, who drew up his weapon.

A shot popped through the air.

Mercy crashed into the man, driving the pencil into his neck. Even as his blood slicked against her palm, she expected to feel the pinch of pain and life slipping away from her. Instead . . . no pain.

She shoved off him, one knee on the ground, the other straddled over him. Shock widened his eyes as he rasped for air. Scanning for more assailants, she let her hands roam the guy for ID. What pockets he had were empty.

With a growl, she punched his chest. He hissed out his last breath.

"Search yours," she barked to Levi. Not that he needed instructions. He was an FBI agent, after all. But they needed to know who'd sent these thugs.

"Find anything?" She removed the dead guy's M4, holstered handgun, and the knife tucked in a leg sheath. "Anything?" When no answer came, she glanced over her shoulder. "Clar—" She pulled in a hard breath.

Wallace lay at an awkward angle against the wall.

Mercy lunged at him. "Wallace! Wallace!" She patted him down for injuries but found no bullet holes. She reached for his throat to check his carotid and spied a tiny ampule lodged in his neck—drugged! An expletive escaped her mouth as she yanked it out. Grabbed her phone. Dialed in. As the call connected, she smacked Wallace's cheeks lightly. Then harder. "C'mon, Wallace, don't leave me hanging like this."

"Go," came Iliescu's bark.

"We were hit," she said, hearing the clack of keys on the other end. "Wallace and I discovered a centrifuge hidden in the TAFFIP console. They drugged Wallace. He's unconscious."

"You have proof about the machine?"

Mercy glanced through the glass door into the litter of parts splayed across the floor. She eyed the glass plate and centrifuge. "Maybe. It's—"

A *ding* from the elevevator alerted her to more trouble.

"I have company." Heart in her throat, she rushed to a cubicle wall to shield herself from view. Then she slid upward until the narrow four-bay elevator foyer came into view. "Two suits just showed up."

"Too late for suits to be there."

"No kidding."

"Get out of there."

"I have to get the pieces."

Mercy thrust herself across the small space. She slipped through the conference room door, which was propped open by the other dead tango. She hauled herself over him, careful not to bump his body and inadvertently move the door, signaling the newcomers. She planted a hand on the carpeted floor, right next to his arrow-tattooed forearm. That explained who these guys were. She lifted the weapon from his hand and kept moving. Scampered across the floor. Retrieved the glass plate and centrifuge. No way could she slip away quietly with these. Or fight those goons and not damage the evidence or herself.

"Wallace is down," one of the suits grumbled. "Took a dart."

Mercy scrambled toward the coffee cart in the corner.

"Where's the girl?"

"I'll check the conference room."

She hid the pieces, then dropped to the ground and feigned dead.

"Here! She's in here." Feet crunched over the machine she'd disassembled, and then came the creak of an arthritic knee close by.

Mercy groaned and pulled herself up, acting disoriented.

"She's waking," the man called.

"Knock her out. She can't—"

She surged upward. Caught him off guard. Drove her heel into his gut, sending him backward. But he righted himself. Bounced back. His fist collided with her cheekbone. Pain radiated through her skull. She lost her balance and tumbled sideways.

He pounced, hands cuffing her neck, strangling.

Panic exploded. *Can't breathe! Can't breathe!*

She hooked her arm over his. Swung both legs far to the side, then used the floor to gain traction and twist her torso sideways, forcing his hold to break.

On all fours, Mercy dragged in several greedy draughts of air.

The man flipped over. Produced a gun and a sneer as he aimed at her. "Should've stayed down."

A shadow loomed over him.

*Crack!*

Mercy flinched at the sound as her attacker tilted away. Then dropped into the coffee stand, his head thunking hard against it.

"You first." She smiled wearily up at Wallace, who clasped his neck. Her gaze whipped to the other dead operative, and she was impressed with Levi for taking him out. She grinned. "Done with your nap?"

* * * *

**— EN ROUTE TO LONDON —**

Tzivia's hands and head still ached from the fight in her apartment two nights ago. Now she sat on a private jet belonging to Mattin Worldwide, headed to London, and she could only hope Dr. Cathey still had what she needed in his flat. He was sentimental to the core and a pack rat. That should work in her favor. She hoped.

In the seat facing Tzivia, her babysitter was scowling at his phone. His legs were stretched out, ankles crossed. He pocketed his device, then folded his arms and closed his eyes. As if he'd done this a thousand times. Minutes fell away into silence.

"You don't have to fake being asleep," she muttered.

The din of the airplane bobbed between them for several long seconds. No answer. *Was* he asleep? She studied his face. Hooked nose with a bony ridge that seemed exaggerated. Strong cheekbones and lips that were neither full nor thin. Unlike Omar's—nice and full, soft and warm. Plus, he had scars. Freaky ridged welts . . .

She turned her gaze to the window, thoughts drifting to the Mossad agent. The man she'd been determined to work over but ended up falling in love with. Had she developed strong feelings for the gregarious, all-too-perceptive, muscular director? Yes. Did she think about him too much? Definitely. But love?

Even as she scoffed internally, she felt a twist and twinge. Something clanging against something else. Her lies and her conscience? Her heart and her fears? There had always been a demon inside her, one she'd worked hard to conceal. She scared away friends and on most days didn't care.

Omar was one of the best men she knew. Only two other men fit that description—Ram and Tox. Her brother and her might-as-well-be brother. Oh, she'd had a thing for Tox once, but . . . Haven got the doe-eyed look when Tox was around. But it wasn't a guppy thing. It was love.

Omar didn't love her. He was using her the same way she'd used him—for business. Her mistake had been letting her guard down. Peering a little too deeply into his brown eyes. Enjoying the domestic bliss as he made omelets in the morning.

Kazimir's phone buzzed, and he drew it out again. Slid his thumb over the screen, eyes absorbing whatever message came through. A moment later, he was working on it. Probably sending reports to Abidaoud about their trip.

The attendant came toward them with a silver tray. "Would you like a snack or something to drink?"

"Water, please," Kazimir said in a clear, firm voice.

"Vodka?" Tzivia asked.

"No," Kazimir barked, pocketing his phone. "Water."

Tzivia bristled. "Excuse me, you're not—"

"We land in two hours. You need to be clearheaded."

Glowering, she tightened her jaw. Then slid her gaze to the attendant. "Vodka."

"Water," Kaz repeated.

"Coca-Cola," Tzivia hissed. "I'll have a Coke."

Her babysitter tossed back the water he'd been handed, then folded his arms, leaned his head back, and resumed his fake sleeping posture.

The attendant passed Tzivia a bottle of Coke. She grunted and turned her anger on the babysitter. "You are here to make sure I don't run off," she hissed. "Not tell me what I can and can't eat or drink."

"I'm here," he said, eyes closed, "because you've shown yourself to be reckless and disloyal."

"Your boss has my father," she growled quietly but loudly enough that he wouldn't miss her words. "The only loyalty I have is to freeing him and seeing your boss go down in flames."

The right side of his mouth quirked.

"In other words, Brainless, I'm getting what I came for and going back. Got it?"

Opening his eyes, he stared at her.

Something sparked at the back of her mind, vibrating down her spine. That move, the angle, the build . . . was so familiar. What was it?

"Something wrong? Annoyed with being caught in a lie?" he asked.

"Something is very wrong." No—if she was wrong, he'd think her crazy. "You're beating my father to force my hand."

* * * *

Tox hated that she thought of him that way—but of course, it was Kazimir Rybakov she aimed that accusation at. "I haven't touched him." He made a stiff expression. "Give a care to what you say in public."

"Why? Afraid your boss will be discovered?"

Was she really so shallow-minded? "You think he has gotten to where he is by being careless, by not having connections and liaisons around the globe to sweep away the dirt?"

Speaking of dirt, he feared the data the grain had captured. When he downloaded it, relief had swept him—until he saw what it transmitted. Especially three words: *Raison*, *Yauza*, and *Camarilla*. It was *Yauza* that alarmed him. He could only guess it meant they intended to kill a person. Sending the information to Ram was risky, but if Raison or Camarilla were assets, then they had a problem. Were they AFO operators? Spies? Maybe someone high enough up to be a threat. If so, could SAARC turn them? Hopefully they weren't too late.

Risk. So much risk. Every step he took to undo the AFO created more distance between him and Haven. Man, he missed her.

"And you take pleasure in this, that your boss—"

He growled. "The only pleasure I take is in hot showers and long meals." *And Haven.*

"What? No woman willing to put up with your beak nose and acidic personality?"

"We all have family, do we not?"

"Then you're married?"

He pointed to the scars. "Do I look married?"

"A lover, then."

He lifted an eyebrow. "What about you? Has this quest for your father turned you sour on men? Or are they too threatened by a woman with years of Krav Maga training?"

Tzivia's chest rose unevenly, lips parting. "How do you know I had years of Krav?"

"I think the dead operative in your flat is proof enough." Tox knew he'd messed up and hoped she bought his explanation.

She hesitated. "Where did you work before you became Nur's personal thug?"

Probing. "Bodyguard," he corrected. "I worked as a Mattin security officer."

"Before that?"

He had to throw her off. "Interrogating me now? Hoping to find a weakness to exploit?"

She lifted a shoulder in a shrug as she eyed him, suspicion crawling through her olive complexion. "Is there a girl?"

"Is there a man?"

"Yes," she said quickly, as if afraid she'd regret it. "I'm not entirely sure what he and I are, but . . ." She wet her lips. Adjusted the overhead air vent.

"But what?"

She huffed. "I think of him . . . a lot."

"You want to be with him."

"I can't. Won't. Not until my father's free."

"Does he know what you are?"

Narrowing her eyes in false bravado, she clearly resented him. Probably hated that he could read her so well, though he was a supposed stranger. "And *what* am I?"

"Easy," he murmured in warning.

And that moment, that simple word triggered something in her expression. She met his gaze, searching.

"In our professions, we hide a lot as we pursue normality," Tox said, trying to distract her. "Few can tolerate the secrecy, the silent answers to normal questions—*how was your day, what did you do?* The man who has your attention—"

"He knows," she snapped defensively. "You and I? We'll never have normal."

* * * *

**— RUSSELL ESTATE, NORTHERN VIRGINIA —**

Standing eye to eye with the niece she'd cradled in her arms fifteen years ago left Haven with an incredible sense of the lightning pace of life. "Happy Sour Fifteen."

Evie touched her shoulder, expression burdened with the memory of being shot with an arrow in London while she'd attended boarding school. The infamous Arrow & Flame Order had sought to teach Cole a lesson, using his niece to deliver the message loud and clear. Then nearly thirteen, Evie had a long recovery after the near-death experience that changed her.

Changed them all.

Now here they were a little more than two years later, celebrating her fifteenth birthday—which wasn't for another few weeks, but when your father was the president, sometimes events were bumped around to accommodate schedules. So it was party time.

"Well," Haven said, taking her niece's hand, "Evie Russell, daughter of the president and America's First Teen, it's time to show you and your guests the surprise."

"Surprise?" Evie had a pique of happiness in her tone as she trailed Haven past the adults, beyond the not-so-discreet Secret Service agents, and out onto the lawn.

Cole's parents had renovated the damaged outdoor patio area after the altercation with Alec King. She led Evie down the pebbled path and up onto the temporary stage that consumed the north lawn. Thick black curtains rustling beneath a late-fall breeze provided the perfect backdrop.

At the microphone, Haven smiled at her niece. "Ready?"

Evie's curiosity had blown into wide excitement. "Yes."

Their voices had the desired effect—Evie's friends from school were filtering down to the stage, staring up at her from the grassy knoll.

"Let me check something," Haven said conspiratorially. She hurried to the curtain and ducked her head through. The half dozen band members of Aiken Hearts stood to the far right side, talking. "Everyone ready?"

The lead singer looked up from a conversation and smiled. "Sure thing." The band took their respective positions, but the singer, Brad Aiken, ambled toward her with a grin.

"Give me a second to open it up." Haven let the curtain drop and walked across the stage to Evie. With each step, the lawn grew quieter. "Thank you, everyone, for coming out to celebrate the amazing beauty"—she took Evie's hand again—"who is my niece. And, Hot Shot, have I got a surprise for you." Smiling at the crowd again, she said, "Friends, give it up for Aiken Hearts!"

Screams rent the evening as the staccato intro of the drummer erupted. The curtains swung away, revealing the band, which launched into a rock song filled with shrieking electric guitars and thumping beats.

Haven slipped offstage as Brad took Evie's hand and sang the first song to her.

Satisfied, Haven made her way up to the terraced patio. Her parents and Cole's nodded their approval.

Turning, Haven smiled and looked out over the pulsing teens dancing, singing, and shouting to the songs pounding from the stage.

"Nicely done," Charlotte Russell said, coming alongside Haven, her gaze on the guests, too. "Any word from my son?"

Her heart tripped over that question. "Last I heard, he was okay." Not entirely true. There was that tinge in his words, the weariness, the longing to be with her again.

"If you're going to marry him—"

"If?" Haven laughed.

"—you'll have to learn to lie better than that, my dear."

"Why would I have to learn to lie?"

"People are nosy, and they'll push."

"Like you?"

"I'm the nosiest of them all." Charlotte laughed. "Especially with what I see in your eyes."

"And what do you see in her eyes, Charlotte?" her mother's patronizing tone intruded.

"Elation, Mom," Haven said quickly. "Elation that I pulled off this surprise, and none of you were the wiser!"

The party wore on with dinner, more sets by Aiken Hearts, and, of course, presents. During a particularly quiet moment, Haven drew Evie aside and handed her a box. "A small gift from me and your Uncle Cole. And your mom, I guess you could say."

Evie's eyes widened, and she plucked the ribbon off and opened the package to find a smaller velvet box. She popped the lid and gasped at the ruby and diamond ring.

"It belonged to your mom," Haven explained. "She gave it to me when I was your age, so I thought you should have it now."

Eyes glittering, Evie slid it onto her pointer finger and clutched her hand to her chest. Tears made her irises look like a chocolate fountain. She threw her arms around Haven. "Thank you! I have so few things of hers."

"Evie!" one of her friends called. "He's asking for the birthday girl again."

"Who?"

"Brad Aiken!"

With a giggle, Evie and her friend tore off across the lawn. Haven laughed, wishing for their enthusiasm, their energy. After the hours-long party, her energy was depleted. She went inside and lowered herself into a tufted arm chair and yawned.

Cool air swirled around her, warning that someone had sat nearby. She opened her eyes to find Galen watching her. "What?"

He glanced away. "I saw what you gave Evie." The planes of his face, so like Cole's and yet so different, tightened. "Do you know where Brooke got it?"

With a shrug, Haven wondered what was wrong. "She . . . no."

He nodded. Rubbed his jaw, then his knuckles. "Cole gave it to her. A promise ring."

Haven came up with a start. "What? She never—" Adrenaline shot through her. "She never wore it or told me."

"By the time he gave it to her, we'd . . ." He heaved a sigh. "After we eloped, she wanted you to have it because you liked him. I disagreed, but she said it was appropriate."

Should she feel guilty or happy? She worked through the confusion that engulfed her, thinking out loud. "It's still a piece of her."

"It is." He gave a nod, glancing at the drink he held. "And Evie should have anything that reminds her of Brooke."

"I'm . . . I'm sorry, Galen. I had no idea, no ill intentions."

Another nod. "I figured. You aren't the type to give backhanded gifts." He worked his knuckles again, sitting, watching his daughter. A weight seemed perched on his shoulders as the minutes ticked away.

"Is something wrong?" Haven ventured.

His blue eyes snapped to her. "No. No, I'm good." He rose and smiled, touching her shoulder. "Get some rest. You look tired."

Haven smirked. If he only knew. She laid a hand on her stomach. Leaned her head against the wing of the chair and closed her eyes, thinking of Cole. Thinking of what he'd say about this. About a baby. Of course, she couldn't tell anyone, because nobody knew the circumstances, and telling them could put Cole at risk.

"Sleeping again? The only time I was as tired as you have been lately," came her mother's singsong voice, "was with each pregnancy."

Haven's laughter exploded more forcefully than she meant. "Mom, you're being ridiculous." She hated deceiving them. Hated the hollowness in her words.

"Hopefully she won't empty her stomach every five minutes like I did with Cole." Charlotte sat beside Haven. "He was the worst of my pregnancies."

Heat clawed her cheeks. She needed to push their attention elsewhere. "You both should be out there with your granddaughter. And I wasn't asleep—I was here thinking about Cole, wishing he was here to wish his niece a happy birthday. It's the first one he could've been at, and he's not." Tears stung her eyes. Her heart writhed in her chest.

"Oh, honey, if you're pregnant," her mom said softly, "you don't have to hide it. I mean, sure, we'd have preferred you married fir—"

"Stop!" Haven pushed to her feet. She couldn't breathe. Couldn't fight the grief—she didn't want them to know. Not before Cole. It felt wrong. So very wrong. She had to get out of here. "Just stop."

She pivoted and raced down the hall, seeking solace. Refuge. She slipped into the library and flung the door closed behind her. Buried her face in her hands and sobbed.

Arms came around her—Mom. Though she stiffened at first, Haven clung to the perfumed blouse of her mother. "I'm sorry." She shuddered.

"Haven, sweetie," soothed Charlotte Russell's voice.

After allowing herself a few minutes' reprieve to release the agony she'd held within, Haven lifted her face and peered into her mom's eyes, then the blue irises that mirrored Cole's. "I just—I didn't—I wanted to tell him first."

Charlotte came closer and tucked Haven's hair behind her ear. "You can keep secrets, when—for the good of those not here—those secrets must not be spilled."

Her mother cupped her face. "But sometimes you have to find trustworthy friends so you don't crack under the strain of carrying those secrets."

Her mom was right. She needed to say it. "I don't know where Cole is. I don't know what he's doing, so I can't betray him in that respect. But I can tell you that before he left, he had months of"—she had to be careful here—"training. I spent those months with him."

Charlotte nodded, and her mom considered her warily.

"As his wife."

Both of them widened their eyes. Their lips parted.

The relief felt like a burst dam. "We married in Israel."

Her mother-in-law—it was so nice to finally own that name—trembled. "And now you're pregnant, and he's still on mission."

Tears ruptured the tight hold she'd had on them moments earlier. "He doesn't know. He can't know. It'd wreck his focus. But . . . I'm dying. Dying that I'm pregnant and he can't know. That if something happens to him . . ."

"He'd never know." Her mom sighed. "I think you should tell him, next time you talk."

"We don't really talk. Just in codes."

Charlotte raised an eyebrow. "Then code him in."

# 28

## — SAARC COMMAND BASE, VIRGINIA —

"How you holding up, Tzaddik?" Maangi eyed the enigma of a man.

"I have been better," Tzaddik mumbled, then grinned. "And I have been worse. Much worse." He inclined his head toward Thor. "And you?"

"Holding my own," Thor said. "Saline and Maangi's epic skills kept me alive. At least I'm on home turf and can see my kid born."

Ram stood over Tzaddik with a glower. "How'd you end up in the fortress?"

"You ask as if it were my doing, Mr. Khalon." Tzaddik's smile didn't reach his eyes.

"That'd be because you're good at getting yourself into fixes," Cell put in.

Laughter was the last thing Ram expected, but that was what Tzaddik did. "That I am, Mr. Purcell. What of your fearless leader, Mr. Russell? Where is he?"

"None of your concern." Ram lowered himself into a chair beside the mysterious man who seemed to know everything. "What do you know about the Adama Herev?"

Tzaddik's piercing gaze lasered in on Ram. "That it's missing and should remain so."

Ram's phone rang. One look at the caller ID pushed him away from the others. "Khalon."

"Good information came from the grain planted by your farmer," Omar reported.

"And the harvest?" Ram asked, skating a glance to the others. "Must be good for you to contact me here."

"A name you should look into quickly. I think there's a contract on her life. Sending you the encrypted file now. Good luck. Give Tzi—"

Ram ended the call, refusing to acknowledge the romance between his sister and the security chief. After reading the data, he drafted an email to SAARC and Iliescu with the information. His phone buzzed almost immediately, and this time, he received a file with mission parameters seconds before another call came through. He answered. "Sir."

"Raison is your next objective," Iliescu said.

"Roger that. And our ROE?"

"Raison alive. The others alive, if possible. But no matter what," Iliescu explained, "I want this woman alive and brought back here."

Ram did his best to stow the frustration coiling in the pit of his stomach. He had to get back to Russia, be there for Tox when he returned from London.

"There a problem?" Iliescu asked.

"What's the timeline?"

"The timeline is whatever it takes to get it done."

"With all due respect, sir, I have an asset in play. I'm needed there."

"Then get Raison back here—yesterday! Because your asset won't matter if we can't get ahead of the AFO and stop this."

"Ahead of them? We're so far behind, we can't see their taillights."

"You're wasting time and oxygen, Khalon. Get 'er done."

The line went dead, and Ram lowered the phone, scanning the team. They were all ready for this whole thing to be over. They'd been dragged from location to location over the last two years, an effort against an entity so large, they might as well be fighting the clouds.

Resignation darkened Thor's eyes as he sat at the command hub. "Where are they sending us?" He, more than the rest of them, had a bigger reason to get back—his expectant wife.

"France." Ram palmed the table. "Our objective is Grazia Raison, a French diplomat."

"French." Runt grunted. "They're coloring the map."

"Yes," Tzaddik chimed in. "The AFO wants the political landscape restructured so that they have control over most countries, and those they can't control, they do so through other means—bullying, coercion, or embargoes."

"What's with Tox?" Runt stood, arms folded. "Where is he and why isn't he here?"

"He's where he needs to be right now." Ram spotted Dr. Cathey being escorted into the building by a couple of guards. "Professor."

But the older man beelined for Tzaddik. "How are you? I heard what happened. How did they get you?"

"I am well, old friend. They ambushed me after our visit, but I am well now," Tzaddik said with a smile as he peeled himself off the cot.

"Our time is very short. The Adama Herev—"

Tzaddik slowed, his gaze hitting Ram again before returning to the professor. "What of it?"

"They have recovered a piece," Dr. Cathey said.

Tzaddik shook visibly. "No."

He lit on something beside Ram, who glanced at the floor. The wall? What? Only then did he see the reddish-brown bruise on his arm. He looked at Tzaddik again, only to have those unfathomable eyes come to his.

Anger sprouted through Ram's chest. Coiled around his lungs like a viper. Constricted.

"Tell me, please," Tzaddik implored, "that you have not done this."

"I haven't done anything!" Rage thickened Ram's veins.

"You know the price of reassembling the sword," Tzaddik said. "You know those with the strain will die! How could you—"

Ram grabbed the man by the shirt and hauled him up. Slammed him against the wall. "*I* haven't done anything. The sword has no power over the strain or me!"

"I was right," Dr. Cathey breathed, gaping.

The professor's pallor, the wildness in his aged eyes, froze Ram.

That and the way the men watched him. Like a lab rat. As if they'd tested him. As if he'd proven their theory.

"Do you sense it, Ram?" Tzaddik asked.

He peered down into strange gray eyes that seemed to probe the very hollows of his soul. What was Tzaddik asking?

"Do you sense the thirst of steel?"

Ram slammed his forearms against Tzaddik's chest, pinning him harder, then took a step back. Rattled by the rage inside him. "This is *not* the thirst of steel. It's the thirst"—he cast around for a substitute—"for justice."

"But you are unreasonably angry," Dr. Cathey said.

Ram glowered. "You haven't seen 'unreasonably angry' yet. What I have"—he held up his bruised arm—"is a disorder. Handled with medication. This isn't a curse tied to a sword. It's a blood disorder."

"Dude." Cell came to his side. "What's with the bruise? Why're they going ape?"

"It's nothing," Ram growled, irritated with himself for letting that slip.

"Then why *are* you so angry?" Thor asked.

"*Because.*" Ram steeled his fury. "False hope does no good. It drove my father crazy, and now it has my sister in danger. And all of us, if we cannot bring this war to an end." He took a measuring breath, then reconsidered his words. "No, not just the war. The Arrow & Flame."

The arrow symbol for their swift response to the Hebrews. The flame for the boiling of their blood. At least, that was what he'd guessed.

Dr. Cathey moved nearer. "It's coming to a head, is it not?"

Sitting, Ram threaded his fingers and bent forward, arms resting on his knees. "You are as feckless as those trying to reassemble the sword."

"Do not be quick to dismiss or mock," Tzaddik said. "What you suffer may well be disease-borne, but remember where it came from. On that battlefield, where Gulat sought to destroy the Hebrews, he was trapped by his own thirst for greed and power."

"I am trapped, but not by greed or power." Frustration squeezed

Ram's lungs. He hated what he'd had to fight all his life, what had too often left him weak. "All I want is to save my sister. Bring her back alive and in one piece. Get her away from him."

Dr. Cathey frowned, his head tilting in confusion. "Who?"

Ram started. Lowered his gaze. Gave the second answer on his tongue. "Nur."

Discerning eyes held his, and Ram stuffed back the memories, the nightmares. The truth of what he'd seen as a teen.

"What of your father?" Cathey asked.

"*What of him?*" There was no way the professor could know his father sat in the catacombs of a church in Russia, held by Nur Abidaoud. Or that Ram hated his father. And telling him anything would only further endanger Tzivia.

Tzaddik nodded. "Your answers grow more agitated and pronounced as we persist." Creased eyes considered him, leaking sympathy and perhaps even understanding. But it was the former that boiled Ram's blood.

"Hey," Runt said with a nod, "give it to us."

Concern carved through Maangi's expression. "We're your team. What's going on?"

"We got your six, man, whatever this is," Thor said.

With a sigh, Ram slumped. Might as well get it out there. "This stays here," he growled.

The team nodded.

He huffed. "It's called the Matin Strain."

"*Mateen?* Not Mattin, like Mattin Worldwide?" Thor asked.

"Same name—minus a *t*—but distorted over centuries." Ram hadn't told anyone about this. "The disorder mirrors muscular dystrophy and hemophilia. Without proper medication, the strain enables the slightest injury to put me in the hospital or leave me dead."

"So it's manageable," Maangi ventured warily.

"Injections every six weeks." Ram hated explaining this. "Yes, it's a disorder. A painful one. A torment I fight. Not because I am *cursed*." He glowered at Tzaddik. "Not because a supernatural God, who I *do* believe exists, sought to punish my father and his fathers before him. But because I have the same tainted blood as Matin, a

Nizari Ismaili said to have retaliated after losing his entire family to disease. Nothing more."

"Why didn't you tell us about this?" Cell asked.

"It's significant," Runt added.

Maangi agreed. "Especially for a medic to know. Is this in your records?"

Dr. Cathey came to his feet. "You must feel it, Ram. This—all of it—is connected. That you, one with the blood disorder, are searching for your sister. That your father is alive, and that Nur is involved in bringing the sword back together."

"My father has nothing to do with this!" Ram pinched the bridge of his nose. "Curse or no curse, the mission of this team remains the same: track down AFO operatives." He looked around at Wraith. "We're headed to France."

* * * *

**— NORTHERN VIRGINIA —**

"Dr. Cathey," Haven said into her phone, annoyed that she was having to leave a second voice mail. As if he didn't want to talk to her. "It's me, Haven, again. I need your help with an artifact. Please call me back." She left out mention of the bust. "It's important." What could she say to catch his attention? "Mr. Tzaddik has me looking for something. I think you can help." Would that be enough? "Okay. Bye."

With a sigh, she lifted the pages photocopied from the auction house records and stared at the bust. She had to admit there was a level of creepiness to this that she didn't want to entertain. In the sculpture, Elisabeth Linwood Russell wore her hair up in a traditional manner, curls framing her face. Head bowed, Elisabeth seemed to peer at her hands, held to her breast. Beneath the wrists and along her neck rested a tangle of scrolls. Haven squinted at the picture. It looked like . . . she wasn't sure, but it didn't seem to be made of marble.

VVolt ambled into the room. He pressed his shoulder and side against her leg, looking for some love. She trailed a hand over his dense fur, then set down the pages. "Hang on a minute, buddy." From the living room, she retrieved the journal and the photo album borrowed from Aunt Agatha. She returned to the kitchen island and flipped through the pages of the album. Found the tintype image of Edward with the bust. And stopped.

"Huh." She lifted the copied pages and held them beside the album photo. In the older picture of the bust, along with the intricate necklace, a diadem was set on the statue's head, dangling a tapered gem at the center of Elisabeth's forehead, beads delicately tracing the rolled hair along her crown.

Chiji wandered in and placed a mug in the sink.

"The bust," she mumbled, angling to show him as he came up alongside her. "Look. The diadem on her forehead in the picture Aunt Agatha had is missing from the auction house photo."

Chiji frowned, mirroring her own consternation. "Perhaps Dr. Cathey will know what happened."

"If he ever calls me back," she murmured just as her phone chirruped a reminder. She felt her heart catch: her doctor's appointment.

Chiji nodded. "I will pull the car around front."

She couldn't argue. Couldn't tell him she sort of dreaded this. Not the appointment, but not having Cole there. And not even having him know about the baby.

Twenty minutes later, they sat in the parking lot of a business complex. Haven squinted out the windshield at the multistoried building with its glass and cement façade. She sighed and slumped back against the leather seat of her crossover.

"You do not want to go in?" Chiji asked quietly, but his question was more a statement.

"If I go in there," Haven said, nodding to the building, "it gets logged into the system. If it gets logged, because I'm both the president's sister-in-law and Cole's . . ." She swallowed the words, remembering that she had never come clean with Chiji. Which felt like a betrayal. "It'll be in the system, which means *they* will know." She looked into his kind eyes and wished he was Cole.

"And you fear this?"

"I fear they'll get wind and tell him before I can. I fear . . ." She bunched her shoulders. "What if he never comes back?"

"He will." A ferocity laced Chiji's words. "Ndidi wanted a life with you. That is why he fights. That is why he will come back."

Haven peered at him. "You haven't asked about this."

Mischief sparked in his dark eyes. "Why ask what is plain? You have changed much since you returned."

"Returned?"

"From Israel. With him." He grinned. "I do not think you merely prayed at the wall. But I know your character. You are his. I have seen it in your eyes. I heard it in his when he talked to me about doing this thing for him. Now there is another of Ndidi's loved ones to protect. I will do my duty. Mine is not to question."

She sighed, dragging her gaze back to the building. "I don't mean to be secretive. I'm sorry if—"

"It is not a problem."

"He and I made a promise. Until he returns . . ."

"Let us do this thing, then," Chiji said, opening the door and unfolding his large frame from the car. He stalked around and had her door open before she could reach for the handle.

They entered the building and made their way to the third floor doctor's office. She signed in and waited for the official confirmation that she carried Cole's baby.

* * * *

**— HEATHROW AIRPORT, LONDON —**

Side by side with Abidaoud's goon, Tzivia walked the concourse toward the rental car area, hiking her backpack higher on her shoulders. The long-legged brute gave no care for how hard she had to work to keep up. But she didn't care either. Not about him. Her mind, her anger remained in Russia. On Abba. On the guys she'd killed. Mossad. That meant . . .

Omar.

How? How could he do this to her? Betray her? Send men after her? And oh, his anger when he discovered she'd killed his agents! It seemed for every ache she felt to be a good person, she dug another foot in the grave of the forsaken.

At the rental counter, Kazimir handed over a credit card. The woman behind the desk flirted with the crooked-nosed thug who had been sent to babysit Tzivia. As the woman started typing, laughing with Rybakov, Tzivia noticed two men speaking German next to her at the desk. One was filling out a form, the other eyeing travelers, both leaving a mobile phone on the counter unattended.

They should be more careful. Someone might nick it.

In a flash, she snagged the phone and murmured to Kazimir that she had business to tend to, indicating the restroom sign on the nearby wall. Dialing as soon as she was out of sight, she prayed her deduction—that German guys in business suits with smartphones at the London airport probably had international calling capability—was right.

When the line started ringing, she ducked into a stall and locked it.

"This is not a recognized number, please—"

Tzivia punched in the authorization code. A series of clicks preceded a male voice that said, "Hold please." She tucked herself farther back, keeping an eye on the sliver of a space between the door and the support.

"Tzivia?" Omar sounded worried—angry.

"That was you, wasn't it?"

He sighed. "I could do nothing—"

"You do *something*! Anything except send them after me."

"I did not send them. But Tzivia—you are no longer considered an ally. I warned you about pursuing the Adama Herev."

"*What*," she hissed into the phone, "am I supposed to do? Let my father die?"

"He left you—"

"He was *taken* from me."

"That is easier to believe, is it not?" Omar sounded smug and insensitive, but he gave back what she dished out by the truckload.

"They kept him to get the sword, Omar."

"You are not this stupid, Tzivia!" he barked. "*Think* about it—would they have kept him alive all this time? How long? How many years? And only now they order you to find it. And what progress, Tzi? You found the first piece weeks ago. You are on to the second, but still empty-handed."

He'd known. Mossad always knew. She touched her forehead. He was right—she wasn't this stupid, but she was getting lazy. Sloppy. "You're working against me. You want my father dead."

"I want *you* alive," Omar said, his voice thick with meaning, "and the only way I can do that is to protect you from yourself."

Possibilities exploded through her mind. Was he here? Were they following her even now, in the airport? Tracing this call?

Of course he was tracing it. As soon as she'd coded.

A chill seeped through her. "I thought . . ." Her throat tightened, remembering what they'd shared. The nights in his arms. Waking to his scruffy beard and rich eyes. And now, feeling the searing sting of betrayal.

It didn't matter what she thought. It didn't matter that she'd hoped for more with him. More life. More days. More happiness.

Because he'd made his choice.

So would she.

"Make sure I don't see you again. It won't end pretty."

"Tz—"

She slammed the phone against the tiled ledge of the stall, cracking it. She hit it again and again until the phone was in fragments. Like her heart. She let the pieces fall into the water and flushed.

# AND FROM THE BODY HEW'D THE GHASTLY HEAD

"It is for your own good, and for my own good, that it remain hidden," Matin insisted time and again.

For this reason, Thefarie agreed Giraude should remain. Doubts grew with each day that the Saracen knew the Adama Herev's true location. But in the barest thread of hope that he might know, the knights must have an asset near to recover it.

"You toy with me, Matin," Giraude said as the morning sun climbed high over the barren land. "With all of us." He thrust his jaw around the waking campsite. "You live here, abusing their hospitality, because they fear you have the sword."

"Fear?" Matin scoffed. "They hope! To them, it is power. To them, it is legitimacy of their beloved king."

Giraude lowered his gaze to his tin cup. They had forged the strangest of alliances and friendships since Matin saved his life that day in the tent. The Saracen had suffered setback after setback from his injuries, but Giraude oft wondered if he stole excuses to remain here—as had Giraude, because of Shatira, whom he had taken to wife.

"My people want that sword destroyed. If they learn what I know—"

"Why?" Giraude had not previously dared to ask. But it was done now. "Why do you hide it? If it is of benefit—"

Matin tucked his chin. "If I return without the sword, they will kill me."

"So take it to them."

A smirk slid into his features. "If I leave here with it"—he nodded to the Hebrews—"*they* will slaughter me."

"You mistake them." Giraude sipped the last of his wine. "These people are shepherds eking out a quiet life. That is all."

"King David was a shepherd."

Giraude laughed. "Aye, but once he became king, he sought rooftops and battlefields over tending sheep." He shook his head. "This life was too arduous for even him."

"Did you know," Matin said, gulping back his wine, which had been replenished from the skin he held, "that Solomon had nearly a thousand wives?"

"That's more trouble than I would entertain," Giraude replied.

"Just think," Matin continued, "some of these shepherds could have royal blood."

An odd thing to say.

"Giraude! It's happening!!"

He stood up from his spot near the fire, glancing over his shoulder at Devorah, Shatira's older sister, who bustled forward. His heart dropped into his stomach as he realized what she was saying. "*Now?*"

"She is with the women now. It shouldn't be long."

He couldn't move. Couldn't think. He had never been so nervous—not even when he had faced the great Saladin with his brother-knights. Giraude paced, having blistered his knees in prayer since learning Shatira carried his child. Times were cruel. Life out here in the desert was hard. He had seen one of her sisters buried not three months past, shortly after Purim. Both her and the stillborn boy.

It had nearly broken Shatira. Another reason Giraude remained, rather than uprooting her from her family. He would not shame her. Even if it meant his own shame in remaining with a shepherd healer instead of fighting the Saracens. Finding that sword.

The lusty cry of his progeny quenched the parched day.

With a breath of relief, Giraude hung his head as he and Yitshak waited outside the tent while the women assisted Shatira in bringing their child into the world.

It was strange, to dwell among the Hebrews. But the injury to his side . . .

Who did he jest? He stayed because of Shatira. And now the babe.

The firm thump of the tent flap drew his gaze up. A handmaiden stood there, smiling. "A son. Healthy." She held the flap open. "You can go in."

A shout arose among the men who had gathered, who then broke into song. Slumping in greater relief, Giraude could do nothing but thank his Lord Jesus for the double blessing of delivering his wife of the child and allowing them a healthy son.

Yitshak smiled.

"Come," Giraude said. "Meet your grandson!"

They both entered the tent and found Shatira resting on a pallet. The screaming babe was lifted from a basin of water and placed in swaddling cloths. Giraude went to his wife and knelt, kissed her sweaty temple. A handmaiden tucked the babe into Giraude's arms. Something in him awoke, something he had not realized existed until he stared into the round face of his son. Eyes crunched, hair jet black like his mother's, he seemed content to be held. To be adored.

"You must tell him," Shatira said.

Giraude tore his gaze from his son. "Tell who wh—"

But she was not looking at him. She was staring at her father. Hard. "Abba. He must know."

Alarm coiled through Giraude as he looked at the patriarch. "Tell me."

Yitshak glanced toward the tent opening. Then huddled closer to Giraude and his family. "Have you a name for the boy?"

"Abba!" Shatira said. "Now. Tell him, or I will."

"Be at peace, Shatira." Yitshak sighed, then met Giraude's gaze evenly, his eyes full of distress. "I am of David's blood."

Was there a meaning to be had? "I don't—"

Again, the older man looked to the tent opening and furrowed his brow. "The sword—if the Saracen learns we are—"

Giraude stood, understanding weighting his heart as he stared at the innocence of his son. Of what he and Shatira had produced.

"If they learn who we are, they will kill us all—especially your son!"

# 29

— NSA, MARYLAND —

Brazen wasn't a term Mercy usually applied to herself, but when it came to hacking or backdoor jumping . . . yeah, perf description.

At her desk, fingers on her keyboard and eyes on Ms. Takeri, who paced as she talked on the phone, Mercy was burrowing through the security walls into her boss's computer. She'd tried a few remote accesses to search for the file labeled *TAFF*-something that she'd seen for a nanosecond. It couldn't be a coincidence, the TAFFIP console having that weird glass plate and the centrifuge, then this.

Ms. Takeri hung up, grabbed her purse and jacket. There were twenty-three steps between her office and Mercy's desk, so she kept working. Right up until step twenty-one.

"Ready for tonight?" Mercy asked in a singsong voice as she opened another file for cover.

"Ugh," Ms. Takeri said, curling her lip. "You know I hate these things. I want you there."

"Of course," Mercy said. "I have a few things to finish, then I'll run home, change, and meet you at the club."

"You have the gifts ready?"

Mercy nodded. "Finished last night."

"Good," Takeri started away, then muttered something and spun around, returning to her office. With a flourish that would make any exhibitionist proud, she pulled her door closed and locked it.

And that, ladies and gentlemen, was Mercy's cue that her days here were numbered. Because Ms. Takeri had never locked her door before. Or shut it. That task had always been left to her faithful admin, Mercy Maddox.

*The clock strikes twelve, Mercirella.*

All the more reason to find that file and close up shop. But the deeper she dug, the deeper her frustration grew. There was no file labeled *TAFF*, not as a name, an extension, or a partial anything. Nothing hidden. Nothing erased.

*I'm kind of impressed.* She hadn't mis-seen that file. There was a reason three-letter agencies sought her help. It had been there. Ms. Takeri had seen Mercy accidentally open it, a glare of the white file flashing on the darkened screen. So what was in that file that set off Takeri's alarms?

It could be a thousand different things, but two were most likely. One, Takeri thought Mercy was a spy—surprise, not so dumb after all! Except she was dumb. Well, not in the strictest sense. She had managed to rise to the top tier of the National Security Agency, after all.

Or two, it meant that she didn't suspect *Mercy* but she worried about the file's contents being compromised. That was totally possible. Was it too much to hope Takeri wasn't worried about Mercy, just the file?

She eyed her boss's locked door again.

*Yep, too much to hope for.* Definitely time to base-jump from this ivory tower. After the event tonight, Mercy would walk away from the NSA.

Frustrated that the entire existence of the file was missing, Mercy left the so-called personal effects at her desk, knowing full well she'd never see them again, and walked out of the building.

She changed into something slinkily appropriate for tonight's dinner, grabbed the bin of goodie bags she'd assembled earlier, loaded them in her car, and headed to the bar. Good sense told her not to attend. To claim illness and let bygones be bygones, but there was this trickle of excitement that said tonight would be anything but boring. And maybe she had this thing about flirting with disaster. There was Ram, after all.

An hour into the event, Mercy was bored. She made her way to the DJ in the rear corner of the bar. "How much would it take to bribe you into something lively?"

His eyes sparked beneath a mop of shaggy brown hair. "A couple Gs."

Mercy scoffed. Then glanced around the room. "You realize who and what the people in this room are, right?"

He frowned.

"They work for a three-letter agency that knows how to make people disappear."

"Why do you think I said two grand? I break from this list they gave me, and it's my neck."

She smiled. "I made that list."

"*Your* funeral, then."

"Exactly, so change it up. I'll cover."

He shrugged and started working his system. A funky song radiated through the brick-walled club, eliciting a chorus of cheers from the crowd. And a scowl from Takeri, who stood talking to another woman.

Mercy slipped into the mob, relieved she wouldn't have to spend her last night with Takeri listening to put-me-out-of-my-misery music. At the bar, she ordered a Killer Whale, then settled into a corner booth. Her phone buzzed, and she eyed the secure message from Iliescu. He wanted to meet. She explained that wasn't possible, but he insisted on first thing in the morning. She texted.

No joy with the file. Vanished into electric air.

Interesting.

No, that was *fabulous*, because it meant the file had meaning. Takeri was somehow connected to the TAFFIP thing. Whatever it was. Mercy had to admit the genetic-based algorithm was sexy. Made her curious. Too many gray areas and unverified assumptions.

She scanned the pulsing atmosphere for her boss, taking in the brick walls, the iron-cord balcony rail and wood floors. Ultra modern. Ram's scene. Or it used to be when they'd . . . dated.

Wait. Awareness flared through her.

Takeri. Where—?

After tossing back the last of her drink, Mercy walked the club. Sure enough, her boss was MIA. Where had she gone? Mercy tapped into the security cameras via her phone but couldn't locate her anywhere. Her thumb slipped, jerking her to the alley feeds. She snorted. As if Takeri would be caught in a rank alley.

But as the screen returned to the interior shot, her mind registered something. She went back. Headlamps splashed light over the rear of the alley. No cars were visible, but the angle . . . Broad shoulders pressed into an alcove by the back door.

Takeri had posted a guard.

*What are you up to?*

Mercy worked her way out the front door, where the bouncer eyed her.

"Shouldn't you be with your boss?" he asked as she flashed him a smile.

"Needed air." She turned left instead of right, which would have taken her to the alley. No need to be obvious. Hustling down the opposite side of the building, she spied some apartments and jogged to the steel fire escape hugging the wall. Ditching her heels, she hauled herself up the ladder, then climbed three flights until she had a clear shot into the alley below and to the right.

Crouched in the corner, the iron biting into her bare feet, she drew out her phone and attached a small device to it, which effectively gave her a long-range lens. She peered through it, tightened up on the group meeting in the shadows. Two men with Takeri and her bodyguard, George.

Mercy tried to home in on the two men, but the image was grainy at best. She snapped a few shots for Iliescu, then decided to get closer. A risk, but if she didn't take it, this was over before she could get started.

She dropped to the ground, stuffed her heels into her skirt's waistband, and hustled down the back alley of the apartments. She hiked up onto a dumpster, pressed her belly to the nasty steel lid, and slunk forward.

Less than twenty yards separated her from the tête-à-tête, giving Mercy a perfect view of the two men. Her gut protested. Told her to get out of Dodge. But her training forced her to take pictures, stay where she was until she could safely exfil. Yet her mind screamed.

What was Takeri doing meeting with the White House chief of staff?

* * * *

**— FRENCH COUNTRYSIDE —**

They were clustered within a quarter-mile of each other, Thor on the rooftop of a home that seemed a retreat rather than a permanent residence, the others hidden in trees and shrubs on the steep hillside. They all looked down into the sprawling private compound that had a ten-thousand-square-foot home, pool, tennis courts, a building that seemed to be some type of office, two garages—one for cars, the other more mechanical in nature and complete with a hydraulic lift—and supposedly a secret bunker that held their objective, Grazia Raison.

"Sealed up tight," Cell muttered.

"Copy that," Ram said, noting guards posted every twenty feet. Towers built into the corners were outfitted with what looked like high-powered rifles and spotlights. These guys weren't messing around.

"Seems whoever owns this anticipated trouble," Runt said.

"Is our objective a prisoner or willingly hiding?" Thor asked.

"Hiding," Ram answered. "She probably won't want to come out, but we need to make her."

"Roger that," Runt said. "Let's get this party started."

Shouldering out of his ruck, Ram scanned the hillside, the slope, the ten-foot cement walls of the compound that went another two feet belowground. As if an approaching combatant would have time to blow the wall before having his gray matter splattered on the dirt.

He crouched and lifted the large spider-looking device from his ruck. Used his phone to activate it. "D-One coming online."

"Roger," Cell said. "Powering up D-Two now."

Using the paddle to control the expensive piece of technology, Ram made it hover at face level. "D-One ready to deploy."

"D-Two ready."

"Deploy the drones," Ram said, sending his into the air and watching the screen of the controller as he raised the drone a hundred feet, then sent it sailing above the countryside.

"Over vineyards," Cell reported. "Maybe we can pick up a case on the way out."

"Grab me some cabernet," Thor muttered.

"Prefer a good pinot noir myself."

"Clearing Blue Two," Ram said as his screen began to brighten. "Approaching compound in three . . . two . . . over the garage."

"D-Two clearing trees and nearing the compound in three . . . two . . . and we are sailing over the pool, where two—"

A flash of white exploded in the night sky.

Ram jerked his gaze to the compound in the distance. Saw smoke and fire trailing from the sky to the ground.

"Son of a—D-Two down!" Cell growled. "They shot my freakin' drone!"

Exposed. Ram tightened his focus. "Two, assume control of D-One." They were down a drone, which meant they needed more eyes on the ground.

"Assuming control," Thor muttered.

Ram slid the control pad into his ruck, lifted his M4A1, and started navigating down the hillside.

Shouts assailed the night.

"They know we're here," Thor subvocalized.

Ram paused, his keen gaze picking out Maangi making his way to him. "Have they spotted One yet?"

"Negative."

"Roger. Stay on course." Ram sorted the facts as he trekked the tricky terrain. There was only one grenade loaded into the drone, and it wasn't an explosive. That was what D-Two was supposed to do—create an infil/exfil point. "Three, you know what has to be done. Four, stay with Three. One on me." Two—Thor—would stay remote, watching through his scope to equalize the pressure a little once they breached the compound.

"Copy," Cell replied. "A little fireworks for our celebration tonight."

"Roger that, Actual," Runt reported. "En route. Twenty yards and closing."

At the base of the hill, Ram took a knee as Runt came up alongside him. They slid on their masks.

"Approaching the garage," Thor reported.

Gas mask on, straps tightened, Ram sprinted to the edge of the tree line.

". . . two . . . one."

Night turned to day. Light exploded. Shouts raised.

Ram and Runt sprinted for all they were worth toward the wall. They reached it seconds before it rained bullets. Plastered against the wall, trusting the line of sight would be obstructed until someone got to their exact location twenty feet above, Ram slapped a breaching charge to the wall. Runt did the same. They scurried in opposite directions and knelt, their backs to the detonations.

A concussive punch to the spine was followed by raining cement and bodies. Ram shoved upward, turning as he did, drew his weapon, and lunged into the gaping hole in the wall. Runt was on his six as they climbed over the debris and into the compound.

Light exploded across the compound, exposing their locations. Within seconds, the bomb detonation from the drone blurred the focus of the fighters inside. Yells mixed with cries as they pitched away from the fog filling the yard. They coughed. Gagged. Collapsed to their hands and knees, vomiting their guts into the night.

Seizing the initial confusion and sickness from the CS gas, Ram darted to the garage. To his left, he spotted Three and Four coming strong. Three scuttled to the garage door, now anchored shut, and strapped two blocks of C-4 to it. Hit a switch. Then sprinted away.

Ram and Runt pivoted away, swinging down to a crouch as the blast ricocheted through the night. Ram pushed to his feet, aiming straight for the new opening without doubt or hesitation. To his left, Runt slid to a knee, swung a launcher around, and aimed at the hole. With a *thwack*, the second CS cylinder rocketed into the garage.

Three seconds later, men spilled out like ants from a flood mound, emptying their guts. Those in the yard who'd recovered from the initial attack once more found themselves heaving.

The ground spit at them. Ram sighted the shooter, only to see him tumble from the wall.

"Shooter down," Thor intoned.

Ram pulled back and raced inside the garage. Someone loomed to the left, but he was too disoriented, gagging, coughing. Ram shoved him out the door and continued on. The map said the stairs were on the opposite side.

Weapon tucked tight against his shoulder, he slunk along the wall, sighting, breathing. His breath scraped the visor and echoed in his ears. Each puff exhausted yet determined.

"Stairs," Ram announced, angling carefully into the open.

A shape appeared. Plaster leapt off the wall beside him.

Ram ducked. Went to a knee. Peered over the lip of the stairwell. Sighted and fired.

The guard at the bottom of the wall, a dark blur against a haze of gray, crumpled to the ground. Ram hurtled down the stairs before more combatants could appear. A door to the right stood locked, secure. He drove his heel into it. Though the wood barrier bucked, it didn't surrender. He repeated the kick. The door sagged. A third one sent it pinwheeling away.

Bullets buzzed the air.

Spine against the wall, Ram drew back, waiting.

Runt was there, flashbang in hand. He gave a nod of readiness, then lobbed it into the room. They turned their heads and clamped their eyes shut. Waited for the detonation's searing light. Seizing the disorientation the explosion caused, they barreled into the room, weapons up, hearts jacked.

Three men were scrambling, fighting the eardrum-piercing effects of the flashbang.

Ram aimed at the first one, fired. The second. Fired as Runt neutralized the third.

Clapping hands on the person hovering in the corner, Ram verified the target. Compared the picture with the disheveled face. Her nose was bleeding and her eyes were wildly unfocused, but it was Grazia Raison. Ram hauled her out of the room.

She flailed in her confusion, not knowing where she was going or not going. But then she seemed to find her bearings. Realized what was happening and started screaming. Kicking.

That wouldn't work. Runt stepped in and coldcocked Raison, then threw her over his shoulder. They hurried back up the steps.

Cell and Maangi were topside, engaging the enemy. Picking off targets as they came through the door. Ram touched Cell's shoulder, and the men advanced, backs arced, weapons tightly pressed, toward the exit.

"Two, we're coming out," Ram subvocalized.

"Copy that," Thor responded.

Within seconds, the ground and walls shook. Ram shouldered under Runt to assist as they broke out into the dark night. Haze still drifted across the compound, the effect surreal with the stadium lights glaring harshly. They kept along the cement barrier, hustling to the exfil point.

"Actual, keep moving. They're like bees swarming from a hive," Thor warned.

"Copy." Ram signaled their group to the side wall instead of the eastern one intended for their entry and exit.

Crouching with his back to the wall and facing the opposition, Cell took up point at the hole. He laid down suppressive fire so Ram and Runt could clear it with their cargo. Chunks of wall spit and stabbed at them from the counter-fire.

"Augh!" Cell slammed back against the wall.

Ram registered the spray of blood, the grimace on his friend's face. Instinct had him grabbing Cell's vest straps. Hauling him through the opening, his body limp.

# 30

## — FRENCH COUNTRYSIDE —

Ram hooked Cell over his shoulder in a fireman carry and made for the trees. They hurried to the others clustered at the base of a gnarled, waxy-leafed tree. Ram's pulse thundered. Heavy breaths fogged the visor of his gas mask. But he didn't stop. Wouldn't. Not until they were clear. Not until they were barreling toward the extraction point so the chopper could ferry them to safety.

"Command," Ram huffed as he scaled the hill, his legs aching and threatening to disobey his order to continue, "en route with the package and one member down."

"Enemy's ticked," Thor muttered. "Don't stop. They're coming."

Pressing on was their only option. He glanced to his three, where Runt raced up the rugged terrain with the unconscious objective as if he carried a sack of potatoes. Did he have no limits?

Bark ruptured around them. Dirt erupted at their feet.

Ram pressed on, knowing any second could be his last. Then Cell was out of luck, too. He grunted, planting a boot and shoving upward. Though the burden of carrying his friend was great, the fear of dying here was greater. About to fire off a few rounds, he heard shots rattle the woods to his far right. Then his left.

Having deposited the target at the extraction point, Runt sprinted back to Ram and went to a knee, his weapon coming to bear.

"Wait," Ram hissed. "They're guessing. Shooting in the hope we'll return fire and betray our position." He nodded up the hill. "Light and fast."

Runt hesitated, then complied.

Maangi was already there, checking their objective, then turning to Cell on Ram's shoulders. "Breathing, but a bit shallow."

"He'll have to gut it up a little longer," Ram muttered. "Cell knows he can't die on a mission."

"You keep bouncing me . . . and I'll reconsider."

Ram snorted at the raspy, drained voice in his ear—Cell had come around. "Go back to sleep, slacker," he huffed.

Hot breath gusted out of Cell. "You should fatten . . . your shoulders. Make the ride more comfortable."

"Ride?" Ram scoffed as he climbed the rocky hillside. "How about the fall?" he asked, threatening to dump his cargo.

"Okay," Cell grunted, "but I'm filing a complaint . . . with . . . transportation authority."

* * * *

**— NORTHERN VIRGINIA —**

Haven grabbed her ringing phone, heart in her throat. Would she finally be able to tell Cole? But the identifier on the caller ID wasn't right. "Oh," she said, swiping the phone and swinging a raised eyebrow at Chiji as she answered. "Dr. Cathey!"

"Hello, dear. I'm sorry I missed your calls. It has been a bit busy."

"I understand," Haven said, "I'm snowed under with responsibilities, too. But look, Mr. Tzaddik put me onto something."

"Did he?" His tone seemed more pensive. "How can I help?"

"He asked me to work on Cole's genealogy while he's away, and I've discovered some very interesting things." Haven snagged the file from the coffee table and sat down on the sofa. She dragged a throw pillow onto her lap and opened the file. "I'm not sure if you want the entire story of how this came about—"

"I am in a bit of a hurry, unfortunately."

"Well, the short version, then. I discovered the Russells and Linwoods have been connected for a very long time." Haven glanced at the genealogy chart. "The most relevant time was in the early 1800s when Raphael Russell married Elisabeth Linwood. When she died, he had a marble bust made of her."

"Did he?"

Something about the way he asked that sent a trill of concern through Haven. He knew. "That bust ended up in the possession of a Linwood ancestor, but he sold it." Intentionally leaving a long pause confirmed her suspicion. "I did the research, found the auction site, and looked up the sale."

"Sorry, dear, but I need to go."

The dead tone of a severed connection rang in her ear. Haven stared at the phone, stunned.

Chiji moved around to the armchair in front of her and lowered himself to the edge of the cushion, threading his fingers.

"He hung up," she said, still surprised. "There was something in his voice . . . nervousness. Fear."

"This thing is important."

Haven nodded. "More than we realize."

* * * *

**— LONDON, ENGLAND —**

"You're sure he's not here?"

Tzivia glared over her shoulder as she fished in her crossbody bag. "You look worried, Kazimir."

With good reason. Sliding his gaze around the fifth-floor foyer that provided access to four flats, Tox cringed at the limited escape options. Correction: option. *One*. Down the stairs. That was it. The elevator was a great way to die in a steel coffin. There might be fire escapes if they could get into the flats . . .

She slid a key into the lock.

"He must trust you a lot," Tox noted.

Tzivia shrugged as she pushed into the flat, then strode quickly to a wall-mounted keypad. "It was about convenience—he often sent me to retrieve things he'd forgotten."

Tox closed the door, flipped the deadbolt, and let out a slow whistle as he took in the home.

"Nice, huh?" Tzivia shed her bag, dropping it on an armchair that sported hunting fabric. "And he could afford it, somehow. I was so annoyed that he lived on the other side of town and up five flights. But he insisted the stairs kept him healthy and the view happy. How that"—she waved a stiff hand at the curtained windows—"view keeps anyone happy is beyond me." She shrugged. "Whatever. His money and sanity, not mine."

From a safe distance, Tox eyed the window and balcony. A wrought-iron barrier protected the six-by-fifteen balcony overlooking a dirty alley that, to the right, led to more flats, and in the other direction, a somewhat-treed view of the city.

"On your tiptoes," Tzivia mused, pointing, "you can see the top of the Eye and the Thames."

At least he had his bearings. He tugged the curtains closed and turned to her. "What're we looking for?"

Eyebrow winged up, she moved away without answering.

Annoyance kept him in place as he once more assessed the flat. Expensive paper covered most walls. Surfaces not decorated in paper were painted a rich burgundy, making it feel cozy but also old. Like something from the turn of the century. Except for the divider separating the entry from the living room—an entire shelving unit at least twenty feet long with six additional shelving units jutting out. Like Cathey's own personal library within his home. Tox guessed going to the university took too much time.

In the living room, a leather sofa had been shoved back against an armchair and table to make room for a large oak desk that sat close to a fireplace. A gold filigree mirror hung above its mantel. Directly opposite, the kitchen.

Tox made his way there, surprised at the cramped, cluttered space. But the sink was clear. A small doorway next to the stove lured him through, where he found a long, narrow passage that ended with the front door on one side and a bedroom on the other.

"This is weird," Tzivia muttered from elsewhere in the flat.

Tox strode back through the kitchen and past a round dinette table to a short hall that provided access to a powder room on the left and—"Whoa." He stopped short, marveling at the three walls covered in floor-to-ceiling built-in bookcases. Though most of the shelves were stuffed with books, some held artifacts lit by lamps or domes. Thick, heavy velvet curtains restrained the light from violating the room's coziness.

"Yeah," Tzivia said, huffing as she planted her hands on her hips, glaring at the wall of shelving at the far end. "That's new, and I don't like it."

He tried not to snort at the absurd comment.

"It makes this room look smaller." She bunched her shoulders. "And it already felt cramped." Shoving back her thick black hair, Tzivia frowned.

"What's wrong?"

She slapped a hand at the offending shelves. "He's moved everything for these shelves, so the small shelf is gone and"—she swiveled her head, glancing about the library—"so is what I need."

"If you tell me," Tox said, "I might actually be able to help. Keeping secrets increases the chance we'll get caught." He walked the shelves. "Besides, I'm eventually going to see what it is once you locate it."

She huffed. "A picture—about five by seven. Gold frame."

"Thank you, Captain Obvious." He knew it was a picture. "Subject?"

"Dr. Cathey and . . . another man."

Her vault-like control with information was growing ridiculous. "*What* are you afraid I'm going to figure out?"

"Dr. Cathey is my friend."

He pivoted, surprised at her answer. At her defensiveness. The ache of truth that even though the professor was her friend, she was breaking into his flat. Going through his things. "This other man—"

"I don't know," she snapped.

The rug beneath his shoes rumpled. He eyed it, noting that the far end had been tucked under because the carpet was now too big for the room with the new shelving. Yet the rug was big . . . a lot bigger. Not just the twelve inches of the shelves. "How will your *friend* feel about you being here, rummaging through his things?"

"Just find the frame! We don't have time for an inquisition." She jerked away, bending to inspect a cluster of photographs on a lower shelf.

He stumbled again on the carpet. Why was it so much larger? He moved around a small table and lifted the carpet to reveal that the folded section continued all the way to the sofa. At least six feet. The rug was folded nearly in half. Straightening, he eyed the shelves again.

"What?"

His mind spun possibilities, but he wasn't ready just yet to betray his speculation. "Good craftsmanship," he muttered, deliberately running a hand along the inside of the shelves. Not even a forearm's length. "Now that I actually know what I'm looking for, I'll search the living room and kitchen."

She grinned. "He called that his alcove."

"Some alcove," Tox muttered as he crossed the room.

"Don't touch anything. He's a pack rat, but he's also obsessive about where things are."

"Order in chaos," Tox said with a nod.

Back in the living room, he made a quick scan for the frame, then slipped down the narrow hall spanning the length of the flat. He stopped halfway. Peering across the home to the foyer of the library where Tzivia was still searching, he lined up his shoulder with that wall. Eyes on it, he pivoted and faced the bedroom at the far end. He walked that way, counting steps. He nudged open the door and continued until a nightstand impeded his progress. Nearly thirty steps. Mentally, he jogged back to the library, remembering his steps in there. Fifteen, at best.

Tox went to the kitchen. Eyeballing the baseboards, he backstepped to the bedroom. He swung around the corner and strode to the closet. Inside, he reached through the wool suits to the back wall. Smooth. He tapped along its length. Solid. Not lightweight.

"Is that you?" Tzivia called from the library.

In the kitchen, he traced the wall—*alcove*. Could it be possible?

Tox's assessment jarred against his speculation. Cathey knew they were looking for the sword pieces.

Oak shelves gave way to a nook. It arched into the wall and held the statue of a woman. Classy little spot. But was it more? He eyed the molding trimming the arch. The baseboards! His heart punched his chest.

"*What* are you doing?" Tzivia's pitched voice interrupted his inspection.

Tox stepped back—and cracked his head against something. Rubbing his head, he scowled at the old carved clock hanging on the wall. He checked his timepiece against the hands of the clock. Stupid thing didn't even work.

"What?" she bit out.

"I think your good professor's alcove is more than an alcove."

Uncertainty forced her to consider the space. "I don't understand."

"In the library, I noticed the rug had been folded back."

"He's a miser."

"In a multimillion-dollar flat."

"Everything's expensive in London."

He'd concede that. "But it's not just a few inches. It's easily six to eight *feet*. Nearly half its length."

"So?"

"The shelves are only twelve inches deep."

Tzivia opened her mouth, objection poised on her features, but then her breath caught.

Tox pointed to a spot on the wall where the trim was different. "Slightly worn."

"Like it's been touched." She leaned in, eyeing the paneling. "Often."

"I think Dr. Cathey's alcove conceals a hidden room."

* * * *

Why hadn't Dr. Cathey told her about the secret room? Granted, it had been months since they'd spoken, but somehow a tremor of rejection raced through her. Maybe it was her guilty conscience feeling exposed—as if he'd known she would break in to find the photo. "It's not like he has great artifacts worth anything," she grumbled. "I mean, these tomes only have allure to him. So why a hidden room?"

"I really don't care why," Kazimir said, angling to the side as he ran one hand along the lower part of the trim and the other over the upper wood finial. "I just want to get in."

"I built it"—the professor's voice jerked them both around and yanked a gasp from Tzivia—"to keep nosy parkers like yourselves *out*!" His suddenly fierce gray eyes latched onto Tzivia, projecting anger and—worst of all—betrayal. "What are you doing here, Tzivia?"

"How did you get in without us hearing?" Kazimir asked, moving to check the door.

"You carelessly left it open," Dr. Cathey huffed as he pushed past her to the kitchen and lifted a kettle.

Kazimir stopped. Shot the professor a look, then Tzivia.

"I thought *you* locked it." She started when he pulled a weapon. Where had he gotten that?

"I did." He stalked forward, gun in his hands. The way he moved, that ready posture, reminded her of someone else. Of Tox with his height. Of Ram with his maneuvering. Hmm, maybe not—Ram was more intense. No, this man operated a lot like Tox, with calm focus and intent. Bouncing her gaze between him and the front door, she backed up to the professor, whom she'd need to protect if there was trouble.

"Why would you do this, Tzivia?" Dr. Cathey banged around the kitchen, opening cabinets, pulling open drawers.

A noose around her neck would have been less painful. "I thought you were with Wraith. I . . ." She swallowed her excuse.

"Why would you do this? Why would you be here? I trusted you!"

"It's not personal," she muttered, not wanting to face him. "Since you're assuming the worst of me—"

"I do not have to assume! You are here going through my things."

She pivoted. Glared. "Obviously it's not the first time you were worried about someone going through your things. Why did you build a secret room?"

He surged toward her. "Give up this quest, Tzivia. Do not search for the sword."

When she didn't respond, he shuffled from the far counter near the books to pick up a tin of his favorite loose-leaf tea. The lone light over a very small kitchen island provided little illumination. Dressed in a dark gray shirt with pale blue tie and black slacks, he seemed to blend with his dim surroundings.

"How do you know what I'm looking for?" she finally asked.

"Tzaddik knows more than you could imagine, and we feared this," he said gravely, disappointment carved in his aged features. "He said you would do this." His expression ached with betrayal. "We are friends. Tell me why you are here. What was so important you could not simply ask me?"

"Ask? When you're acting like this? Why else would I keep it from you? Look how you're behaving!"

"Me? You're the one shouting and not answering my questions."

She drew back, surprised at herself, at him.

Dr. Cathey murmured, shaking his head, and wheeled around to the stove again. "I thought you were smarter than this. That we were friends. I trusted you."

She'd never been especially good at friendships. Nor at making him proud. But in this moment, she realized just how far she'd strayed from the path she'd intended to walk. The one on which he'd believed her capable of traveling.

Guilt rolled over her shoulders and settled into her chest. "Good grief. I'm not stealing anything," she scoffed, but even that came out weak. "I just—" Forget subtlety. "There's a picture I need to see."

He slammed the kettle on the burner and faced her again. "A picture?"

"Small, gold frame." She nodded, glancing at Kazimir, who eased the door closed and flipped the locks. "You and another man."

Kazimir turned, sliding along the entrance hall toward the back bedroom. Something in his expression, around the scars from his accident, felt ominous. Did he suspect someone had gotten in?

"This is about the sword." Dr. Cathey gave a faint nod. Sagged. "He was right. Tzaddik told me . . ."

He knew. There was no pretense. So she might as well drop hers. "I just need it—actually, no." She tilted her head. "Just tell me who he is."

His face darkened. "First you break into my flat. Now you would have me put my friend in danger?" He gaped. "Who are you anymore, Tzivia?"

Deflecting the sharp insinuation, she jumped to the conclusion. "So he's a friend."

"Tzivia," he hissed, bushy eyebrows knotting beneath his glasses. "Do not persist on this path. You must abandon the search for the sword. It is not the answer you seek."

"It's exactly what I seek." Watching Kazimir clear a closet reminded her again of Tox.

"Because I love you as my own child, I will not do this. I must deny you—"

"You mean *defy* me. If you know I'm looking for the sword, do you know why?"

"It does not matter! The sword cannot be given to them, and I will not aid you in this deep betrayal." He pulled a mug down and set it on the counter. Then two more. "You may not have the thirst of steel like your brother, but you thirst all the same—for acceptance, approval. When what will fill you is only *Yahweh*."

There was a time she would've told him to shut up, save his religious platitudes, but she was tired . . . and he was right. She craved his acceptance.

"In each of us is a perfect God-sized hole that can only be filled with His love."

"Love." She snorted, but the hunger . . . the ache to be loved—she'd tasted that recently.

"What of Omar?"

She sniffed and shook her head. Omar. He'd accepted her, and though their relationship might be messed up in many ways, she never had to pretend with him. But this wasn't about her and Omar. It was about her and Abba. "You're getting off track," she mumbled.

"No," he said, snapping fisted hands toward the ground. "I am on the precise track I need to be on—to stop you."

"Please." She rubbed the middle of her forehead. "A name or the picture," she repeated, aching. Hating herself for putting a demand to the man who'd become like a father.

Steam spiraled from the mugs in which he'd poured the tea. "No matter how much you ask, I will not."

In that split second, she noted several things at once: a shadow peeling from the dark hall, a shout from Kazimir, and a dark arm sliding around Dr. Cathey.

*Crack!*

"No!" She lurched forward.

The arm hooked Dr. Cathey's neck. Pulled him back, up off his feet, toes scratching for purchase.

Mentally negotiating her options, she went with the most obvious—make the attacker talk as a distraction. "Let him go! What do you want?"

"Tell your goon to stand down," the man warned, weapon pressed to Dr. Cathey's temple, "or this will end in bloodshed."

Tzivia snapped her gaze to Kazimir, hunched by the wall, taking shots at another intruder. But something else triggered in her. "You don't want us dead, or you would've come in shooting. So what do you want?"

A warm presence pushed into her awareness, and Tzivia knew Kazimir had joined them. Somehow, she felt more confident with him there. Someone to convince her that holding her ground was the right thing to do. And yet the frantic eyes of Dr. Cathey and his arched back worried her.

"Smart man," the gunman said. "Now. The sword."

Tzivia blinked, stunned for a moment that they knew why she was here. Her mouth went dry. Nobody should know that. She and Kazimir had hopped on a plane within a day of her remembering the photo. No way would she cave to blackmail tactics, especially about that. "I have no sword."

His lip curled. "The *piece* of the sword, then. Hand it over." He tilted his head to the professor. "Or I end him."

She displayed her palms. Twitched when she noted Kazimir sliding to the left. "I don't have it."

"The sword!" the man bellowed, his face reddening even as his partner slid into view.

"You will never have it." Dr. Cathey struggled beneath the arm constricting his air, hard defiance making him tremble. "The Adama Herev belongs to history."

"Yeah?" the man challenged, his expression taut. "How about I make you history, old man?" He pushed the muzzle harder against Dr. Cathey's temple, forcing the professor sideways.

Tzivia fisted her hands. An island stood between her and them. She could pitch herself across it and maybe nail him with a round kick to the head. But would it be in time? He'd probably react before she was halfway there. So she needed to talk them to death, or at least to distraction, giving Kazimir time to get closer.

She wasn't going to fail now, not when she was so close to freeing her father. "The man I answer to would kill me if I gave it to you, so"—she shrugged—"I'll take my chances here."

"Nur Abidaoud is weak and faltering. Not worth his weight." The man glanced between her and Kazimir, who had reached the dining table. "Another step, Cowboy, and this one eats it."

Tzivia tensed.

The man met her gaze, and she knew she'd made a mistake. "A lesson, then."

As he stepped back and took aim at Dr. Cathey, Tzivia lunged. "No!"

The gun fired.

# 31

## — LONDON, ENGLAND —

Face contorted, Dr. Cathey howled in agony, buckling as he grabbed his leg. His cry of pain punched the air from Tzivia's lungs.

She cursed. Then started forward.

Kazimir stopped her with a hand. She flung off his touch, turning to the thug who once more had his gun pointed at Dr. Cathey's temple.

A vicious gleam in his eye, the man raised his eyebrows. "Maybe I'll take all four limbs before you cave."

"Release him," she spat. "He's nothing but an old man peddling religion."

"Oh, he's more than that—you have a soft spot for him, and he knows what's in the secret room." Another sickening grin as he flicked his gaze to Kazimir. "I heard that right, didn't I?"

"I will *not* give up my secrets," Dr. Cathey proclaimed defiantly. "You may not realize what I protect, but I do, and I never—"

"Quiet," Tzivia hissed. Though she tried to get a read on Kazimir's progress, she was distracted by the professor's bloodied fingers clamped over his wound.

"My life is *not* worth it," he gritted out.

It was the same thing her father had said. And if their lives weren't worth this, then whose was? As she stared at Dr. Cathey, an ache bloomed in her chest. She didn't want to fail him any more than she already had. On so many occasions. She needed this time to be different. She needed him to know—

Her gaze drifted to his, and her heart stuttered beneath another twinge of guilt.

"Look," she bit out, "I don't have it, so holding him does you no good. All I've been doing for months is chasing leads, one after another. I've only found one part of the sword, and Nur has it."

"But you are here for the second piece."

"I'm here for *information* about it," she corrected. "Big difference."

He considered her, then his expression cleared. "Another leg? Or an arm this time?"

Tzivia tensed.

"Call off your dog," he demanded.

So strange that his gaze never left hers, but he'd noted—had he known all along?—Kazimir's attempt to get close.

Frustration tightened her muscles. "Rybakov," Tzivia said, also not breaking the man's gaze. "How long do we play this game?"

"I don't care, as long as I get the sword."

Maybe their best chance was to cooperate. If he managed to get out of here alive, then she'd hunt him down. *If* he got away alive. Those were odds she liked. "Dr. Cathey," she said softly, noticing the captor gloating, "please tell us how to—"

"No!" the professor roared. He threw his head back, nailing the man in the nose.

A resounding crack sounded through the kitchen. The two men stumbled backward, colliding with the shelf of books. The second intruder scrambled away as books crashed to the floor and thumped heavily against Dr. Cathey and the attacker.

Kazimir slid in effortlessly, weapon raised, and fired twice at the guy sprinting for the hall. The first bullet chewed the wall. The next, muscle. An anguished grunt was all the guy gave as he vanished out of the flat.

Shoving Kazimir after the escapee, Tzivia dove forward. Reached for the two men wrangling on the ground. The attacker rose.

Tzivia leapt and palmed the small island, throwing herself around to drive a flying side kick into his back. The man whiplashed and slammed into the wall. He came up clumsily. She drove a knife-hand strike into his neck and sent him reeling. He pulled himself up against the wall and made for the door.

Tzivia sidestepped in the narrow passage and used a hook kick to nail him in the gut. Landing, she swung a left uppercut.

Floundering, he still had the gall to fight back. He rounded with a punch. She spun it, using his momentum against him to throw him into the plaster. His face hit hard. A picture dislodged, dropping and shattering glass all over the floor.

He drove his elbow into her side. Tzivia doubled, vision blurred from the pain of that perfectly placed strike. By the time her sight cleared, he had rounded the door. Vanished.

*Crack! Crack!*

The thud of a body hitting the floor reassured her.

A second later, Kazimir returned. "Let's go. More company coming. Get the professor."

She spun back. "Dr. Cathey!" She banked left into the kitchen and stopped short. Her breath seized. "No," she breathed.

She dropped to her knees where he lay on the floor, clutching his chest. A dark stain widened beneath his hands with each second.

"No," she said, more forcefully this time. "No, stay still." She whipped to Kazimir, feeling the drum of panic in her heart. "He took a bullet to the chest—it's bad!"

Kazimir flicked off the shrieking kettle, snatched a hand towel from the counter, and knelt by the professor. "Easy," he said quietly and stuffed the towel against the wound.

"Did it good . . . this time . . ." Dr. Cathey sucked in a hollow breath that sounded sticky.

Kazimir winced.

"Give . . . up," Dr. Cathey breathed, those gray eyes of his holding fast to hers.

"Yes, they gave up," she agreed.

His head shook. That smile wavered. "You," he gurgled. "Give up . . . sword."

Tears burned. "I can't. They have my father."

Another shake, this one half-broken. "Not . . . who . . ."

"The room," Kazimir said, trying to stem the flow of blood. "How do we get in?"

A distant look took possession of Dr. Cathey, sliding a peaceful smile onto lips that were pink against his gray beard. "Not . . . right . . . time."

He was bleeding. Too much. Stricken, she leaned forward. Closer. "Please," she cried, agony ripping the heat from her chest. "No!" She clapped her hands over Kazimir's. "Harder! You're not pressing hard enough."

"Tzi—"

"No!" she growled. "He'll make it. He's tough. Always has been." Both palms to the chest wound, she stared down at Dr. Cathey. "Dr. C, don't give up."

His eyelids shuttered closed.

"No!" Tzivia shouted. "No, you can't!"

Gray eyes came to hers in a flutter of surrealness. "So . . ." He smiled. His shaky fingers traced her cheek. "So . . . proud . . . love . . ."

Tears stung. Her throat felt thick, raw. "It's okay—we'll get you help."

"I go . . . the Father . . . waits . . ."

"Augh!" Tzivia screamed. "No no no. Please." She pushed hard, trying to stop the never-ending loss of blood.

His chest compressed, a wheeze rattling, then somehow gurgling back. Limp, he left his gray eyes locked on her.

"Dr. Cathey!" She froze, staring. Disbelieving.

"Tzivia." Kazimir touched her shoulder.

"No!" She slapped away his hand, pinning him with a glower. "He's going to live. He will."

"He won't. The bullet tore—"

"*He will!*" she screamed. Shoved him off her. Planted her hands on Dr. Cathey's chest again. Frantic. He couldn't leave her. Couldn't abandon her. Not like her father. "You have to stay!" she begged. "You promised!"

Hands clamped her shoulders. Hauled her backward.

A primal howl rent the apartment's stale air, and only as she was lifted off her feet did Tzivia realize the sound came from her, from the fissure within her that opened over a broken heart.

She glanced back at Dr. Cathey, where he lay. His gnarled but neat beard splotched with blood. Mouth open, eyes looking at the ceiling. Disbelief choked her.

Then she saw it. A glint of gold between two books.

"*Wait!*"

* * * *

**— LANGLEY, VIRGINIA —**

"You have a massive problem."

Mercy followed Deputy Director Iliescu into his office, where he tossed his pen on his desk, then skirted it to the high-backed leather chair. "I have more than one." The recessed lights and ambient glow from the blinded windows grabbed the silver strands in his dark hair.

"No, seriously. This is like Hulk smash."

"Mercy," he said with a sigh, "just the facts, not drama."

"Mr. Spy Boss," she said with a smirk, "these facts *are* drama. Nothing I'm adding or subtracting can change that."

"Is this about TAFFIP?"

She wrinkled her nose, confused. "No, I left that with you, as you instructed after my night of thrilling heroics." She waved dismissively. "Anyway, you'll never guess who I saw last night in the back alley of a club with Takeri."

He rubbed the back of his neck. "Out with it."

She plopped into the guest chair and sat forward. "The White House chief of staff."

Lowering his hand, Dru abandoned his ambivalence. Consternation filled his olive complexion and dark jawline. Warning nudged aside his anxiety. "Think carefully before you lob that accusation." He shifted, forearms on his desk. "That's the White House you're implicating."

"No accusation, Boss-man," she said without blinking. "I know what I saw, and"—she held up her phone, swiped it on, keyed in her code, then opened the photos—"boom! Proof. He was there with

Takeri. And if they're up to something legit, why are they meeting in a club alley, out of sight, and late at night?"

Iliescu leaned across his desk to see the screen better. He took the phone and dropped back against his chair. Cursed. Rubbed his temple, then cursed again. "Did they see you?"

"Not to my knowledge." She bounced her shoulders. "But it doesn't matter—I'm out of there. She got suspicious because I accidentally saw that file on her computer."

His eyebrow arched. "Accidentally."

"This time, total legit accident." Mercy flashed her palms. "A folder tumbled from my arms, hit her keyboard. Opened a file." She nodded to his computer. "It's in the email I sent you before."

"Haven't had time to read it all."

"Well, you should. Because I'm out with Takeri. We need to make Mercy have some horrible accident and die or something." She lifted a finger. "Maybe Clark can put in a call."

"Clark?" He scowled. "Your ferret?"

"Levi Wallace."

He grunted. "You are an expensive asset."

"All my dates say that. But you all know I'm worth it. Now. Back to Clar—Wallace. Maybe he could call the NSA and tell them I died some horrible de—no, that's a bad idea, since someone found the two of us messing with TAFFIP. And if Takeri is behind that, they'll put it together." She blinked. Looked at Dru. "So maybe someone else can tell them I'm dead." She pouted at the thought. "Sad. I really liked that name."

Her mind whirled through the implications that the president's right-hand man was connected to Takeri, who was connected to TAFFIP, which was connected—probably—to the slayings. "You think he's involved in the Soup Maker killings?"

Rubbing his jaw, Iliescu heaved a sigh. "Let's hold off on the leaping from tall buildings."

"But he was there—with Takeri."

"And you're blown as far as the NSA is concerned?"

He *would* come back to that. "I'm roughly 70 percent sure. Since I accidentally got into that file, she started locking her office. Lowered my IT privileges. Which tells me she probably has someone combing through my system as we speak."

"But they won't find anything," he said, more warning than question. "Right, Mercy? You know—"

The most reassurance she could give him was this: "They won't find anything conclusive."

"Conclusive."

"Boss-man, relax. You know me. I cover my trails. Hopefully my mouse-in-a-maze redirection virus, which will launch as soon as they breach the second wall of security—their security, not mine—can distract them. I wouldn't want to alert them by having personal software in there. Anyway, it'll send them on a wild geese chase."

"Goose chase."

She grinned. "Geese," she repeated with a giddy swell of pride. "More than one. In fact, dozens. They feed off each other. At least, a girl can hope."

"Hope?" he muttered. "That doesn't do us much good. It's the NSA, for cryin' out loud."

She poked a finger in the air. "Exactly." She scrunched her nose and shoulders. "Now, if we were talking about the NGA, then I'd be worried." The National Geospatial-Intelligence Agency scared her. Their ability to gather data, analyze it, and wreak havoc made the NSA look like kindergarten. They were the ones who found bin Laden. They were the ones who used drones to collect data, which they analyzed. Big Brother piggybacking cell phone calls? NGA. Agency able to determine, from a safe distance, the structure of buildings and objects? NGA. Agency with the most sophisticated facial-recognition software? Able to see through thick clouds—not even kidding—and leap to critical analysis? NGA. She shuddered.

"I have a lot of friends at the NSA who'd be offended by that."

"Probably." She couldn't help that they weren't smart enough to get where the goings were good. "What about TAFFIP? And Wallace?"

"Fine. Refused a leave of absence for psychological trauma."

Mercy nodded. "Tougher than I expected of the pretty boy."

Iliescu sent her a withering glare as he rifled through a stack of papers. He offered a folder to her. "What we have so far on TAFFIP."

Anticipation tingled as she opened it. Glanced at the heavily redacted file. "Cheaters," she mumbled, then turned a page. It was a diagram of a square—the glass plate—then a cross section of it. "I was right," she breathed.

"There are a dozen near-microscopic needles in the glass that pierce the skin and draw blood samples."

"So they *are* collecting DNA." Excitement rippled through her as she remembered all too well the night at the Manassas office, disassembling the system. "That's why they needed Makanda's program—to run analysis on the blood samples using that genetic algorithm." The next section of the file contained her official write-up about the coding, then a subsequent analysis. No doubt the CIA had taken her thoughts, run them against their own, then tested them before writing this up.

She skipped to the conclusion at the bottom of the second page. "'. . . seems apparent that despite claims to the contrary, Russia is complicit.'" She bounced a look at Dru, who watched her, thumb to his lips, then continued reading. "'. . . program is pervasively contaminated and therefore deemed a threat in light of the widespread implementation across government agencies.'"

She flapped the folder closed. "So they're being pulled offline?"

"Negative. Can't," he said with a huff. "Doing so would tip our hand. We were about to intervene."

"Until I dropped a truth bomb about the president's chief."

He nodded, then narrowed his eyes. "I need you out of sight for a while."

"Definitely—with NSA wondering and 'burying' me, we need time for people to forget me."

Another nod, this one distracted.

"Send me to Russia."

His withering glare turned sharp. "Russia?"

Despite his poker face, Mercy knew what she'd seen in that report. Some things blacked out. Others not. She had a quick mind, assembling the pieces. "What I found in TAFFIP's system suggests their hands aren't quite as clean as they claim—Mattin Worldwide is involved. I stayed up last night, comparing security protocols."

He nearly came out of his seat. "You what?"

"Easy, Boss-man. It's good. Nothing invasive. And I'm right—again," she said in singsong voice that betrayed her pride and pleasure. "Same protocols, which are like a signature. You get to know the coding, you get to know the coder."

He stared at her. "Why Russia?"

Though her pulse thudded against that question, against the reason he might be inquiring, she put her best foot forward. "Because that's where Mattin is, and I need to get onsite and into their systems to prove what we're already guessing."

Elbows on the arms of his chair, he gave her a disapproving look. "Any other reason?"

Mercy shook off the shudder tugging her muscles. "What else?"

He motioned to the door. "Close it."

Two possibilities loomed—she was about to get chewed out, or she was about to get her wish. After replanting herself in her seat, she crossed her legs. Folded her hands. Prepared for the worst.

"What happened with you and Khalon?"

Bomb out of left field.

Mercy swallowed. She could lie. She could hem. She could divert. But it would be no use. Dru Iliescu might let a lot of her personality slide with a smile, but there was a reason he sat in this office.

"It's not in any of your reports," he said, his tone anything but pleasant, "but how else would you have crossed paths with him unless it was under our purview?"

As she'd anticipated. *Out with it, Maddox.* "Our paths crossed during my time in Greece. Remember when that Special Forces team was tracking someone trying to release the identities of their operatives? Myself included?" She eyed him for some recognition, but he only gave her a blank stare. "Well, our paths . . . kept crossing. We"—*careful, tricky waters here*—"weren't exactly working *together*—"

"But you were sleeping together."

Her jaw dropped at the accusation. "I—*No.*" Although it had nearly happened.

"But things *were* intimate between you two."

"Intimacy implies sexual relations, and there weren't any."

"What I saw in that SAARC bunker looked a lot like unfinished business," he said pointedly, ignoring her attempt to be facetious. "And now you're asking me to send you to Russia. Where you somehow know he is."

She wet her lips, decided to push his attention to something less incriminating. "The report wasn't as redacted as you probably hoped," she said. "I put things together."

He cursed. "If I send you there and Ram finds out—there are things about that man you don't understand."

The fierceness in Dru's voice and eyes made her swallow. "Like what?" She scooted to the edge of her seat. "Because I got to know him pretty well. I knew about his vague connections to the Israelis and his citizenship with the U.S."

The deputy director sat in silence for several long, excruciating minutes that made Mercy wonder if she'd said too much, if she'd inadvertently and singlehandedly ruined her own career. She watched, searching for some clue to his thoughts. But it was like trying to read a book made of marble, the lettering hidden deep within the stone.

He huffed. "Do you know the name Tox Russell?"

"Sure," she said with a shrug. "Everyone does—he was on the news. Died in prison. Hero gone wrong."

"He didn't go wrong. He was set up. And he's alive, and that is who Ram is handling in Russia."

She blinked rapidly, her mind scrambling for purchase on this new information. "Doing what?"

"The operation isn't ours. Ram is clamped down on intel, but we have other assets feeding us information. Seems Tox is now personal bodyguard to Nur Abidaoud."

"CEO of Mattin. The man himself." Impressive navigation of tricky politics. "How'd he manage that?"

"Couple of lucky situations put him in the right place at the right time, and his instincts, which I trust over pretty much anyone else's, got him the rest of the way."

Though Tox's record spoke for itself, as did Dru's high praise, what made her heart pump hard was that Dru had brought this up. That he'd just handed her classified intel. She glanced at the folder.

*Above Top Secret*. "You're sending me," she said with entirely too much excitement.

"*If* I send you, it would be deep cover. It'll mean you can never cross paths with Ram Khalon."

"What?" She frowned. "Why not? He's ours."

"Because those Mossad connections you mentioned earlier?" His gaze pierced her with warning. "They aren't vague."

Her mind raced ahead to the obvious conclusion, but there was a piece of her that refused to move past his statement, that obstinately said she should've known. "What do you mean?"

"Come on, Mercy. It's obvious, isn't it?"

"He's Mossad." The words tasted like burnt popcorn.

"I'm not sure that's entirely accurate, but it might as well be."

"He contracts." She hated feeling guilty when it was Ram who'd had another layer of his oniony self peeled away. Then again, she'd never told him who she worked for. Besides, turnabout was fair play, wasn't it? "And his loyalty?"

"More than once he's sided with Israel over us. He's Mossad, Mercy. His loyalty, even to the detriment of his life, is to Israel." He pecked on his keyboard. "I'll get you read in on this, but what you need to understand right here, before we go any further, is that if Ram learns you're there, Mossad will know. And if they know—"

"No more Mercy."

# 32

## — OUTSIDE LONDON, ENGLAND —

Grief squeezed Tox's chest, strangling him. He wanted to curse the night, curse that his last memory of the professor was in death's embrace. He'd been good for Tzivia, good for them all. And now he'd fled to heaven. At least . . . at least in the end, he'd smiled.

A shrill whine strafed the air, drawing his gaze once more to the short airstrip. Red and blue lights popped to life, marking the runway.

Tox caught Tzivia's arm to guide her. She flinched. Flashed him a severe look but said nothing. In fact, she hadn't spoken in the three hours since they had fled more gunmen, leaving the professor's dead body behind.

"They're here," he muttered, nodding to where the jet's nose splashed light over the gray cement. "C'mon."

Hunch-running, they crossed the field toward the roar of the engine reversing to slow the jet. He watched it howl past, slowing unbelievably fast. The pilot used a jutting arm of the runway to maneuver a U-turn, then whined toward them. The side door slid open as they came even with it. The plane bounced to a stop, and an attendant in the hatch deployed the stairs.

Tox guided Tzivia up the metal steps. "Bathroom?"

The attendant's eyes were riveted to Tzivia, whose hands were coated in the professor's blood, as were his.

"Bathroom," he snapped.

"B-back. In the back." She pointed, her gestures jerky. "On the left, opposite the galley."

Tox stepped aside, allowing Tzivia ahead of him down the gangway past a section of seats arranged in foursomes, some in sets of two. Then two rows of five luxury seats on each side. A partition separated the seats from a long, narrow conference table with starship-looking chairs, a galley, and a bathroom.

The attendant stopped at the bathroom door, staring as if she didn't know what to do.

Punching open the door, Tox maneuvered past Tzivia. Slapped down the toilet seat and turned on the water. He backed out and nodded her inside.

Tzivia stood staring at the sink. Her expression seemed at least ten klicks away. In the flat. Tox nudged into the confined space, shut them in, and took her hand, gently placing it under the faucet.

When she made no effort to resist or assume control, he pumped soap into his palm and rubbed it over hers. Blood was the worst to wash off. You could scrub for hours and still find a speck under a nail or in a crease. In a way, it was good that it couldn't be easily removed—a poignant sign of what it meant: life.

He directed Tzivia onto the closed toilet seat and knelt, drying her hands, then looking into eyes that seemed as vacant as the professor's had been. A chill ran down his spine.

He focused on cleaning the blood from her face and neck. He hated even making the first wipe across her cheek, because he expected it would snap her back to the present. But when she just sat there, stone-faced, a bigger concern replaced his anxiety. Had she really cracked? He wanted to jar her out of it, but he'd give her space. They had the next two hours for introspection. Then they'd be on the ground and thrust before Nur, who would demand to know what she'd found.

Tox's gaze hit the pocket where she'd tucked the photograph after extracting it from the frame.

A rap at the door startled him. He tugged open the folding partition. The attendant handed him two T-shirts. "This is all I could find."

He thanked her, then waited for her to leave. He turned back to the woman who'd kicked life's butt and taken names. It bothered him to see her like this. "Tzivia."

She blinked but didn't otherwise respond.

He touched her shoulder. "Hey. Tzi."

Finally she snapped her gaze to his, exposing a hollowness that sent chills through him again. In her irises flared a fierce anger, drilling a deep chasm into her soul.

He pressed a black shirt into her hand. "Here. Change. Less than two hours before we're back with Nur."

She twitched, which was good. The name had been meant to jar her, remind her what she was fighting—and whom.

"You with me, Tzivia?"

Her left eye narrowed. "Who are you?"

He started at the question. Though he wanted to tell her everything, tell her she wasn't alone in mourning Dr. Cathey, a friend and ally, he couldn't. He wished she could know that he felt her pain. That he too grieved the professor, that she wasn't alone fighting the AFO.

But that was just it. She *wasn't* fighting. She was working with them. So telling her . . .

"Get changed." He sidestepped.

A vise tightened around his wrist. He glanced back into eyes red-rimmed with a mix of fury, anger, and fear. Her chest rose and fell beneath ragged breaths. He'd expected anger, but this was . . . fear. Panic.

"I'll be right outside." With that, he extricated himself and pulled the folding door closed. He glanced at the shirt he wore, stained with dirt and sweat. Blood. Splattered like bad spray paint. He tugged off his shirt and stuffed his arms into the clean one, though he'd have preferred to shower up before putting on clean clothes.

"Yes, sir. He's out," the attendant's voice drifted from the front. She sauntered toward him with a thick phone. "Mr. Abidaoud would like a word."

Why couldn't he give them time to recover? Tox took the phone with a nod. "Rybakov."

"That was quite a mess in London."

"Yes, sir."

"Amazing they found you there so quickly."

"Wondering about that myself, sir. Any ideas on how that happened?"

Nur scoffed. "Do you suggest me, Mr. Rybakov?"

"The trip was kept under wraps. Fast turnaround. How'd they know where we'd be and when? They also knew we were looking for the sword."

"That is what we should be discussing—that and your petulance."

"My questions aren't petulance. They're tactical. Because nobody should've known we were there," Tox said, trying to cool his anger, his protective furor over what had happened to his friend, Tzivia's mentor. "Now, either you sent someone to clean house, or you have a spy. Either way, I'm not real juiced about returning."

"Good thing you're on my plane and have no say."

"Good thing," Tox gritted out.

"My personal car will be waiting at the airstrip. It'll bring you and Ms. Khalon directly to me."

"Look, she's really rattled. I've never seen her like this."

"You've only known her a few weeks, Mr. Rybakov. What do you know of that spitfire?"

He nearly cursed at his slip. "That she's a lot more spit and less fire right now. You'll want to go easy on her. Give her room."

"What I'll want is to get what we were after." Silence gaped through the phone. "You overstep, Mr. Rybakov. Give care, or I'll need to introduce you to some humility."

The call ended, and Tox balled his fist. Leaned against the seat. Ground his molars and told himself to get a hold of the anger bubbling inside him, or he'd make more mistakes. This wasn't him talking. It was the adrenaline.

He wanted—needed—to hear Haven's voice. He slid into a seat and leaned his forehead on the back of the row in front. Let himself drift quickly and deeply to Israel, where they'd had moments he'd never thought possible. Marrying her. Loving her. Quiet moments. Intimate moments. It seemed those were a lifetime away now. She was a lifetime away.

He opened his eyes and gazed at the phone in his hand. He could call her. Just to hear her answer and say hello. The voice that had melted his reserve and spoken to something buried deep inside him.

The ache dug deep. Spread its desperation through his chest, down his arm. To his hands. He swept the keys. Pressed several in quick succession. The screen glowed green with the numbers, bright against the dim interior of the jet. His thumb hovered over TALK.

"What did he say?"

At the sound of Tzivia's voice to his right, Tox came to his feet and cleared the number. "Sorry?"

"You were talking to Nur," she said, her T-shirt crooked, hair disheveled. Her eyes were redder and the roots of her hair wet. She must have washed her face. Stepping closer, she motioned to the row, indicating he should let her in.

Tox allowed her to slip past.

She slumped into the chair. "What'd he want?" she repeated, though it still wasn't the Tzivia he knew.

He pocketed the phone. "Don't worry about him." He threaded his fingers. "How about you? Holding up?"

Her brown eyes met his, flecked with surprise. "You're not worried about angering Nur?"

"No."

She frowned. "Why not?"

"Because he's always angry."

A tremor of a smile met her lips. "And you? Don't you want to know?"

If he knew, then he could be bled for the intel. "Right now," he said, injecting his tone with as much authenticity as he could muster, "we have one-point"—he glanced at his watch—"two-five hours to just . . ." He couldn't say grieve without tipping his hand. "Process."

She pressed her head against the back of the seat with a scoff. "I'm not sure that's something I can do in that short amount of time."

"Then do what you can. Give yourself a breath while you can." He pressed his skull into the leather seat and adjusted his position. "Do what you need to, because once we're wheels down, you're on his turf and time." He looked at her. "I know the professor was important to you. I'm sorry."

She smiled wanly. "He was the only person who ever believed in me—really *believed* in me." Her eyes swam with unshed tears. "All the time. Never doubted. And when I got off track, he smacked me back into line, but lovingly." She pursed her lips. "And now, because of me," she said, her voice trembling, "he's dead."

"That's not fair."

"You're right—it's not. And I own that." Tears puddled in her eyes. "It's not fair that he's gone way before his time. It's not fair that he had a lot to give, and now he can't. Nobody new will discover the beauty of one of the most giving, passionate men ever."

"'The fear of death follows from the fear of life. A man who lives fully is prepared to die at any time.'" When Tzivia glanced at him with a frown, he shrugged. "Mark Twain—an American author—wrote that."

She frowned more. "Is that supposed to mean something?"

Tox shook his head. "It's just . . . I think"—*careful*, he warned himself, *play those cards close to your chest*—"he seemed the type of man ready for death." He nodded, thinking through his next words. "I've seen men die." That was true and could be said of more than just soldiers. "He wasn't panicked or afraid."

"He smiled," she said quietly. "He actually smiled as he died." She shook her head. "Which, in some ways, made it worse."

Tox frowned. "How?"

"Because," she said, scrunching her shoulders, "it was like he was glad to be free of me."

# 33

## — SAARC HEADQUARTERS, VIRGINIA —

"Anyone besides me not buying the whole 'on mission' thing with Tox?"

Tilting back in his squeaky office chair, Thor swiveled at the command hub to eyeball Leif, who stood with his arms folded. "Your attitude is jacked. Did you miss the whole black ops part of our jobs?"

Leif wasn't fazed. In fact, it fed him. "Tox has been gone upward of five months, maybe six, and nobody's worried." This was familiar to him. All too familiar. Nobody had been worried about his absence, assuming he'd been on mission.

"Whoa, no. Hold up." Cell didn't look away from his wall of monitors, the various glows highlighting his face and stubble. "Three months, maybe."

"Back up," Leif said.

"Dude," Cell scoffed. "Give it up. He was in training in Israel. Part of a joint terrorism task force effort. Remember?"

"That's what we were told, but none of us were involved." Leif lifted his eyebrows in emphasis. "Right?" He turned to Maangi, who'd said nothing but also wasn't arguing. "None of us were there."

Thor considered him for a long moment, and Leif hoped he was truly listening, but then the big guy started clapping. "Look here, boys. The SEAL has a brain of his own and tried to put it to work."

"Seems he got hurt in the process, too," Cell muttered, cradling his arm, which was in a sling from the France mission.

Frustration choked Leif. "What is it with you people?" he demanded. "Our team leader is MIA—"

"No." Thor dropped forward in the chair with a thud. Came to his feet. "I'm putting a stop to this right here. Right now. Tox is not MIA. He's on mission. And if it bothers you that you can't know what he's doing, then"—he pointed to the main bunker exit—"there's the door. Don't let it hit ya where the good Lord split ya."

"What if something's going on?" Leif challenged, his chest tightening at the possibility. He didn't want to sound like a freak, but—

"Yeah, Tox is doing his job, and we're"—Thor glanced around the team—"not. So let's remedy that."

A presence shifted beside them. Leif glanced at Maangi, who jutted his jaw toward the offices of Iliescu and Almstedt. "Look."

Stiff sounds buffered by bulletproof glass pulled their attention to where SAARC's supervisor argued with the CIA deputy director. Iliescu barked, hands a flurry of rage. He leaned toward Robbie, which revealed another woman standing behind him.

"What's Mercy doing here?" Cell mumbled.

"Rodriguez is teleconferencing," Thor said.

The comment pushed Leif's gaze to the wall monitor. Sure enough, the general was there, animated and shouting. What on earth . . . ?

The elevator dinged seconds before the doors slid open. An armed soldier entered with a large box.

Iliescu stomped out of the office. "Put it on the table there in the middle," he instructed the guard. Then he noticed the team. "Gather up!"

Almstedt and Mercy joined them at the command hub, the large wall-mounted monitor springing to life with Rodriguez's mug.

"Good news, bad news," the deputy director announced, glancing at Almstedt.

She accepted the silent baton and smoothed her suit jacket, looking a little worse for the wear, bags under eyes and strain in her lips. "I was informed a short while ago that Dr. Cathey has been killed—"

"Dude!" Cell growled. "We were just with him!" He spun away, motioning for everyone to leave him alone. He planted a hand on his head and walked the command module.

Leif stepped back, a hand over his mouth. Though Cathey wasn't one of their own, he was. He'd led them, educated them, journeyed with them. Leif hadn't known him as long as the others, but it was obvious the professor was a good man, albeit annoying sometimes. But his faith had been genuine. His wisdom profound. There was a gaping hole in the Wraith team now.

"What about Tzaddik?" Maangi asked. "Does he know about Cathey?" When Almstedt and Iliescu frowned, he went on. "They were friends. He should be told."

"*We* should tell him," Thor said. "Don't leave that to them. He's down in the bunker."

"Agreed," Cell said, snapping back. "We'll do it."

Almstedt nodded solemnly.

"How'd it happen?" Cell asked, his tone almost accusing. "How'd Cathey die?"

"It appears he was killed shortly after returning to London," Almstedt explained. "According to the intel we've pieced together, he could not have been in his flat more than a half hour before he was killed."

"Do we know who did this?" Thor asked

"AFO," Leif said with a shrug. It was really the only option.

"We don't know. Not at this time," Almstedt admitted, "but this is very fresh, and you can be assured that though Dr. Cathey was not officially a member of this team, he is considered a part. As such, we will deal swiftly with those responsible."

"What about the diplomat we extracted?" Leif asked.

"She's not talking just yet." Almstedt sighed. "We have people working her, but it's slowgoing."

Iliescu nodded. "When we have answers, you'll have them."

"And a mission to settle the score, right?" For Cell, it wasn't a question. If there was one thing Cell was serious about, it was team loyalty.

"It's murder," Robbie said plainly. "The perpetrator will be caught and brought to justice."

"I have a Glock named Justice I can introduce the perp to," Thor bit out.

"This is bunk," Cell objected, his face twisted with grief. "Who kills an old guy who needs a cane to get around and can't find the glasses on his head?"

The team had taken a lot of hits lately. Ram and Tox were busy elsewhere, and Cell got shot up in France. Then there were the ancillaries—Dr. Cathey and Tzaddik.

"What about the good news?" Leif asked.

Iliescu pointed to the box. "A few nights ago, Miss Maddox and Agent Wallace were attacked while they were looking into the TAFFIP lead."

Cell's head swiveled to Maddox. "You okay?"

She answered with a nod.

"The good news is in this box," the deputy director said. He touched Maddox's shoulder. "Why don't you take over from here? Then, you know where to go."

With another nod, this one to the deputy director, Maddox turned to the team and squared her shoulders. "Barc's gut instinct was right."

"Hooah!" Cell said loudly, arm in the air for victory.

"The TAFFIP system is not only sending data to the Russians, essentially handing over the identities of millions of Americans, but DNA samples *are* being collected."

"How?" Leif asked, jutting his jaw toward the box. "I mean, isn't the system just taking digital prints?"

"It's taking more than that." Mercy lifted something from the box and turned it. "This is the fingerprint plate." She passed it to Cell. "Touch only the sides of the glass."

"*Now* you tell me," he muttered, realigning his fingers to the sides.

"It looks simple." She shrugged. "A piece of glass."

"It's a bit dull," Leif said as he turned it, trying to catch the light to see abnormalities, but was surprised when it didn't reflect like normal. "Something's not . . . quite . . ."

"What you're noticing," Mercy said, extracting a page from a file, "is that the glass actually has near-microscopic needles embedded in its surface. They take blood samples and store them in a centrifuge to be collected later."

"Wait. What?" Cell frowned. "I mean, yeah—blame the Russians, but these are in our country. The code, the program I asked you to check out, is designed by them, but this—this machine is from our side. Who in our country is collecting samples for the Russians?"

Mercy nodded, her expression grave. "Exactly."

Someone cursed.

"No," Cell said. "This can't—" He huffed. "Are you telling me Americans are working with the Russians on this? We—we're killing our own?"

* * * *

**— MOSCOW, RUSSIA —**

Darkness settled heavily over Moscow, so much that even the lights seemed dull and mocking as the jet screeched down the tarmac. Tox glanced at Tzivia, hating that he couldn't reveal his identity, tell her she wasn't alone. They'd get through this. They'd get out of this. Of course, she would reply that she wasn't going anywhere until her father was free. But he'd make sure that happened. For Ram as much for her. They deserved to have their father back.

As the jet slowed and she had yet to stir from staring out the window, he leaned forward. "Tzivia."

She tore her gaze away.

"I'm with you."

She considered him, confused, then snapped her attention to the front of the plane.

The attendant strode toward them, her steps quick and clipped. "Miss Khalon?"

Tox rose to his feet.

"No," the attendant said. "Only her."

His gut twisted and knotted. Why only her? "She's my assignment. I have to guarantee her safe arrival back—"

"And you've done that. Mr. Abidaoud gave orders that Miss Khalon comes out alone." She motioned to Tzivia. "Ms. Khalon?"

"Not happening," Tox said, sliding between them.

A touch, light and gentle, on his side surprised him. He looked over his shoulder and found Tzivia scooting around him. "It's okay." She patted his arm. "I appreciate . . . everything."

Frustration balled his fists as she walked off the jet. When he started toward the door, a shape moved from behind a dividing wall. An armed guard. He gave Tox a slow warning shake of the head, palming the bulge of his weapon.

Tox sighed. Planted a hand on his belt. Eyed the open door that only gave a glimpse of the tarmac. Lights from a vehicle. Engine noise swallowed any conversation.

"Would you like a drink while you wait, Mr. Rybakov?" the attendant asked in a buttery-sweet voice.

He slid her a glower, then checked the door. Took another step forward. So did the guard. This was stupid! No, it was worse—Nur was separating them. Which meant he either knew Tzivia had found something, or he knew Kazimir Rybakov wasn't the same man he was six months ago.

No way he could know that.

The crack of gunfire outside jacked his pulse.

Tzivia! He surged forward. The guard came at him. Tox swung hard—and met air. The thug punched him in the stomach. Then the side. Rammed a hard left hook that spun Tox around. Right into the dividing wall. His vision blurred. An explosion of pain at the back of his head pitched him headlong into a chasm of darkness.

* * * *

Vision blurry, Tox waded out of the fog of confusion. Then his brain caught up. He whipped his head up—and growled at the hammering gong in his skull. He squinted around.

Alone.

He jerked his attention to the still-open door of the plane and the tarmac. A lone black sedan idled ten yards from the metal steps. Peeling himself off the floor, Tox groaned. He exited the jet and struggled to make sense of the stairs with his double vision. Approaching the sedan, he reached for his weapon, but the driver met his gaze and smiled. Kazimir's colleague Yefim. What was he doing as a driver?

Tox climbed into the passenger seat. "What—"

"Don't ask." Yefim huffed. "I should be at my daughter's recital, not driving your sorry carcass around."

Tox eyed him as they pulled away from the airstrip. "The woman—where'd they take her?"

"How should I know? I was just told to take a car and bring you back." Yefim eyed him warily. "Heard things went south in London."

Tox touched the back of his head again, and this time found the knot.

"It's on the news," Yefim said quietly.

That yanked Tox around. "What?"

"The doctor murdered in his apartment."

Heaving a sigh, Tox sloughed a hand over his face.

"Did you do it? Kill that old man?"

"*Nyet*." He shook his head, trying to avoid the memory of Dr. Cathey's awful, vacant stare.

Yefim seemed to relax, a small breathy laugh sifting the air. "Good."

Only then did Tox realize Yefim was nervous. "I had a job, and I tried to do it. That's all." The strain of speaking in Russian was almost more than he could tolerate after the last thirty hours.

"Tell that to him in the morning."

"Who?"

"Mr. Abidaoud. He wants you in his office first thing."

They glided along *ulitka Volkshana*, and the bright lights of the great white cathedral a few streets over caught his attention. "Here." He rapped the window. "Let me out."

Yefim gripped the wheel tighter. "I cannot. He said to bring you straight back."

As Tox watched the church slide away into the darkness, he marveled at how it felt like his soul did the same. Something had changed. He was worried.

They arrived at the tower, and Tox rode the elevator to the penthouse. He accessed the residence wing, not surprised to find it darkened and the staff bedded down for the night. He made his way to his room.

Voices carried from the den. A warm glow seeped from the room and danced down the marble floors, surging, retreating. Daring him to peek in at the secrets within. Who was he to argue? After a glance in both directions, Tox crept closer.

"What use was it? She returned empty-handed!"

Tox slowed. Stopped.

"He said she had it," Nur replied.

"Then one of them is lying. Use her, then get rid of her. She's too unpredictable!"

Anger spilled through Tox's carefully crafted identity. Who was so willing to throw away Tzivia's life?

"What of him?" Nur asked.

"Just a weakling thinking with his pants, not his head. Once she's gone, he'll probably be useful again. Keep him. But you need something over him. Does he have family?"

"Died in an accident that nearly took his life."

"Lover?"

Tox's heart spasmed.

"I doubt he has thought to entertain it."

"Get him entertained. You need something to hold over him. All men can be broken if you know their secrets, their longings."

Who the heck was talking to Nur like he was a dog to be commanded?

A phone rang, and Nur's voice changed. "I will be there." A second later, "Is Rybakov back?"

"Yes, sir," the guard said.

Startled at being named, Tox shifted to the center of the hall and stalked purposefully toward the kitchen.

"Rybakov!" Nur snapped.

Nerves jangling, Tox one-eightied and found the boss in the den's doorway. "Sir?"

"Where are you going?"

"Kitchen for ice." He pointed to the knot on his head.

"You were told to wait in the plane."

Tox nodded. "But then I heard a shot. And since I was responsible for Ms. Khalon's safety, I grew alarmed."

"There was no need for alarm. The scene was secure. It is always secure when I go somewhere." Nur threw his chin at Tox. "You are attracted to her."

"Too young and too mean," he countered.

The other man emerged, swinging in the opposite direction, a maneuver that kept his back to Tox as he exited the private residence. There was something oddly familiar to that walk. To the shape of the head.

"Come," Nur commanded as he spun and started down the hall.

"Sir?"

"We have a traitor to deal with, Mr. Rybakov."

# 34

**— MOSCOW, RUSSIA —**

*"Tzivia, you work too hard to convince yourself God doesn't exist."*

*He stood before her, smiling. His eyes full of life, laughter, depths, and mysteries. As she'd always known him.*

*"Joe?" she breathed, daring to use his first name.*

*"You've always protected those you love. Don't stop now." His eyes, corners weathered by years and age, held hers. Then, a flood rushed from him. A bloody, violent river. Washing over her. Sticky, Warm. Pulsating with his life and vitality.*

*Tzivia screamed. Threw herself backward.*

Her strangled cry pierced the darkness, snapping her awake. Panting, she propped herself up. Caught her breath. Told herself it wasn't real. *It wasn't real.*

But it was.

He was dead.

Because of her.

If she weren't in a strange place, she would collapse against the cold stone and sob. Instead, she grabbed the edges of her grief and folded them beneath her anger.

She squinted around the darkened room. *Where am I?* She'd been on the plane with Nur's man. Then she'd walked down the steps.

Men appeared at both sides. Her neck pinched. Her hand went to the spot where a tiny swollen knot lingered. After that, she didn't remember anything.

No . . . she had a vague, nuanced memory of . . . hands. Being touched.

*They searched me.*

She laughed, the sound cracking against her skull. She dropped back against the floor and groaned. She'd taken a chance on the plane, consumed by a keen sense when the attendant said she and Kazimir had to leave separately that Nur would take the photograph.

She couldn't let that happen. Not yet. It was the only clue she had to the next piece, and she wasn't going to lose the lone bargaining chip for her father's life. She'd outsmarted them. But the real question was—had *he* found it?

Blinding light stabbed through the room.

Sucking in a hard breath, Tzivia clamped her eyes shut, the negative image of what her eyes had captured in that instant burned into her corneas.

Bars. Separating her from another space. A rock—no! A body.

Tzivia squinted, surprised that the light wasn't as bright as she'd imagined. Slowly, her mind caught up with what she saw. What singed her conscience.

"No!" She scrabbled to the bars. "Abba! Abba!" Slammed herself against them. Shoved her arms through. Reached. Fingers grasping.

But he wasn't moving.

Was he breathing? She blinked back the blurry, aggravating tears as she strained to see. To watch his chest. Was it lifting? Rising? Falling? "Please, Abba!"

"You were told to find the sword, Tzivia," came a mechanical voice. "You failed."

Anger churned and writhed through her. "It's not my fault!" She would not tell the truth. She would not yield. Not after Dr. Cathey. But . . . but her father. "Abba!"

"He's dying. Just like the professor. How many more will die because of you?"

"It's been lost for centuries," she growled at the air, not sure where the camera hung. "How am I supposed to find the pieces, alone and without assistance?"

"Willpower! You want your father to live, don't you?"

Tzivia's gaze snapped to the still form. Then he wasn't dead.

"*Don't you?*"

"Yes," Tzivia hissed.

A spigot over her father opened and dumped water on him. Awakening, he hauled in a greedy breath, then gagged and choked, rolling onto his side.

Tzivia sagged against the bars, silent tears rolling down her cheeks as her father dragged himself from the spray of water. A strange muddle of dark brown ran in rivulets across the stone as he slumped even farther from her.

Face pressed to the cold iron, she stared at her father, his spine bent toward her, his face turned away. He was alive, and she had to keep him that way.

But give them the sword? Tzivia was no longer convinced Nur would free them.

Groaning rattled the floor behind her. She ignored it, not caring what was back there. Only what was in front. "Abba," she called quietly.

But he didn't respond. Had he fallen asleep again?

A gust of cold air traced her nape. Glancing over her shoulder, she found an open door. Light beckoned. But she turned back to her father and the slivers of brown taunted her. Something that wasn't quite right.

*Yeah, me.*

"Your father has two weeks left," the voice said. "I suggest you get started."

* * * *

Returning home to Haven seemed further and further away, especially as Nur's car stole through the night-darkened city on a traitor hunt. Exhaustion clung to every sinew in Tox's body. Assuming the life of Kazimir Rybakov required *being* that man. Thinking of himself not as Tox but as Kazimir, grieving husband and father. Recovering man. Bodyguard to one of the vilest men to ever exist. He could do it.

He'd done it for months. But there was an element of his own identity that seemed to fade with each day. A fragment of his willpower that broke off.

After the death of Dr. Cathey and the hollowing out of Tzivia, he struggled to remember why he was doing this. Dropping that grain had given him a name—he'd transmitted that to Ram while en route to London. But nothing else. Nothing about the sword. Was that diplomat an AFO member? For what good it did. He'd found nothing, save proof that Nur Abidaoud was evil personified and led the biggest organization.

And yet . . .

Tox pushed his gaze to the passing buildings. Nur led the AFO, right? But why was that man—the seemingly familiar one walking down the hall—telling Nur what to do?

"You are quiet."

Tox resisted the urge to twitch, to flinch. It was not merely a statement, but an inquiry into his state of mind. "Tired," he muttered as he turned to Nur and stifled a legitimate yawn. "Sorry."

"What happened in London?" Nur's gaze went dark. "Where did you go wrong?"

The tenuous thread on which Tox's life hung vibrated in warning. "Men got in, took Cathey hostage. I fought them, but . . ." He shook his head, hating the memory. Hating his failure. "I should've killed the gunman first. *That* was my mistake. He and Cathey wrestled. The gun went off."

"Did you not tell me the girl had a photograph?"

Tox nodded. Why was Nur asking this? Tzivia had snatched the photo from the frame. They'd fled with it.

"Then where is it?"

"I don't understand." Tox felt his pulse power down to a painfully slow pace. "She didn't have it?"

"Neither do I," Nur said. "I had her taken into custody as soon as she stepped off that plane. She was searched. Nothing. She had nothing on her person."

"How could that be? She had it in London." He felt like he was betraying her, saying this. "I saw it. Twice."

"Then she hid it." Nur looked out the window, his reflection painfully clear in the dark glass and etched with irritation. "I'm having the plane searched. Having her watched. We will find it."

"This makes no sense," Tox confessed. "She wanted to find that photo. She wants to save her father. Why would she change her mind now?"

Because of Cathey.

"That is what I intend to find out. You will stay near her, Mr. Rybakov," Nur growled. "We'll watch her closely."

"Understood." It was expected. There was no way he could contact Ram now. No way he could risk café meetings.

The car swung around a corner and glided along the thumping slats of a dock. Soon the repetitive noise gave way to crunching gravel, wobbling them back and forth as the armored SUV chewed its away over a sandy bank.

The river?

"Who's about to take the long walk?" he asked, praying it wasn't him. He wished for an M4 and tactical gear. For the familiarity of his team. Of knowing they covered his six.

"Have you heard of the Camarilla?"

Tox shook his head.

Nur spat a curse. "It is as nefarious as its definition—a group of people who advise rulers with a shared, typically nefarious, purpose. In this instance, they set themselves against me. To steal that which is not theirs," he said, his nostrils flaring as he stared forward.

Ahead, Tox eyed two parked vehicles and an arc of solemnly waiting men.

As their SUV lurched to a stop, Tox opened the door. Stepping out, he smoothed his jacket and slid his gaze over the six suits, expressions stark and cold. Tried to memorize faces in the predawn darkness, features harshly illuminated by headlamps. Though he felt the press of the Russian weapon in his side holster, he wanted his rifle. Tac vest. Ear comms. Eyes on that bridge spanning the area and pitching their location into relative anonymity and darkness.

Another man bled from the shadows with a weapon. One of Nur's men. He gave Tox a nod. Eyes roving the area, the shadows, the men, the vehicles, Tox kept pace and aware. As they neared the huddle, a shape shifted in a car.

Assessing the others, checking for weapon-betraying bulges and itchy trigger fingers, Tox had to make the call. Satisfied, he stepped aside, signaling the all clear.

Dirt crunched behind him as Nur emerged and stood to the side, buttoning his suit jacket. "Gentlemen," he greeted the waiting party, then started forward. "Where is Zakavij?"

A sharp whistle coupled with the jutting of a burly man's jaw pushed Tox's attention back to the vehicle where he'd seen the shape. A guard exited. Went to the trunk. Opened it. Hauled someone out. Dragged the battered, bloodied man toward the group.

The sick feeling Tox felt earlier intensified. Though he tried to tell himself to relax, to maintain his calm, the thought of what was about to happen made his gut roil. What would he do? What *could* he do? Saying anything, doing anything would expose him. Get him killed.

"So, Zakavij," Nur taunted, "you thought you could betray me. Work against me and do all this without being discovered."

"No, no! I swear it is not true. I"—he slapped his chest—"am being set up." Zakavij's accent indicated his Slavic heritage and his panic, words thickened with saliva and desperation.

Igor shifted forward, carrying something.

"Tell me who you are working with, and all this can go away," Nur said magnanimously.

"I know nothing. This is not—they are not—"

"The Camarilla, Zakavij. Name these traitors and buy your life."

The man's eyes widened. "Please, Mr. Abidaoud, this is all wrong. I am most loyal—"

"Yes, but not to me." Nur snapped a nod to Igor.

Something glinted in the night, grabbing the light of headlamps. Steel sang through the air. A meaty *thunk*. Then another.

Something wet and warm splatted Tox's cheek. He heard more than felt the splat in the seconds it took his brain to register what had happened. Igor wielded a sword. Had delivered the pleading man of his head. Tox told himself not to react, he'd seen plenty of horror in combat, but watching someone get beheaded . . .

Tox took a step back. Tightened the sweaty hold he had on his reaction.

Nur strode toward him. Gripped the back of his neck. "You look sick, Kazimir."

Sick? No. Angry? Yes. "Surprised."

"When I am betrayed," Nur said softly, lowly, lifting his black gaze to Tox and letting the words hang heavily before he finished, "I have swift vengeance."

*I am blown.*

He slapped Tox's cheek with a laugh. "Remember that, *da*?"

It was a warning. A threat that hung over him as they returned to headquarters.

Back at the penthouse, Tox shrugged out of his jacket and heard a crinkling. He patted the spot and felt something stiff. His mind leapfrogged over the events of the last twenty-eight hours and landed squarely on one possibility. The photo. The one missing from Tzivia.

If that was the case . . . Tox turned off the lights and moved through his quarters, sliding his hand into the right breast pocket of his coat. Felt the stiff corners of photo paper. The glossy face. How had he not noticed it before? But how had she gotten it into his jacket? He recalled her touching him in order to slide past . . .

Tzivia had used that moment to slip him the photo.

* * * *

Following Nur's lackey was probably the biggest mistake of Tzivia's life. But she trusted her instincts. They'd rarely let her down, but this . . . if she was wrong, it could get her killed. Yet it had taken her nearly two days to catch up with the thug on this muggy night.

He emerged from Mattin and stood out front, bouncing on his toes, scanning the street in the guise of warming up. *He's no average Joe.* This guy had training. She'd seen his skill in the fights at her apartment and Dr. Cath—the flat in London.

She closed off the grief that threatened to barrel over her.

Rybakov's gaze hit hers.

No, impossible. She was dressed in black and hidden in the predawn shadows. No way could he see her. But he sure seemed to stare hard. Crisply, he banked right and started jogging. He had a steady, determined gait.

She trailed him by a quarter mile, sticking to shadows, buildings, overhangs, and stoops to conceal her movements. Never once did he falter. Was he not paying attention?

But as he rounded a corner and the bright lights of the Cathedral of Christ the Savior came into view, her heart lurched.

No, not there. Nur's thugs guarded that place where, far below, her father was hovering near death. It amazed her that so much could go on beneath the church without the leadership knowing.

Her palms grew slick as he crossed the footbridge over the busy street traffic and entered the cathedral.

As she waited, Tzivia slipped beneath the overhang of a tree, then pulled herself up into its thick branches, watching.

What, was the guy religious? Dr. Cathey had been. He clung to his Scripture the way Tzivia did Krav Maga and weapons. And what good had it done him? *He's dead.* Suffered a death he didn't deserve. How was that right? How could God let that happen?

*He died for you.*

No, he died *because* of her.

As the minutes fell off her watch, she wondered if Kazimir had escaped out another entrance. Tzivia landed softly on the sidewalk and followed a couple traversing the footbridge. They went right, tracing the street, and Tzivia scurried up the church steps. She slipped inside, dropping into the darkness and mustiness of the cathedral.

A man moved away from her, his confident shadow stretched tall and broad.

Tzivia's heart spasmed, recognizing one of Nur's guards. She scurried along the foyer, using furniture to hide. His shadow receded along the far side and skimmed beneath the white arch over the altar. Frescoes covered the walls and ceilings, a glorious sight, if she were inspired by those things. She hurried to the center of the cathedral, then scanned it. A door to a smaller chapel beckoned.

Sure enough, Kazimir sat on a pew in the middle. What was he doing? Making peace with God? Asking forgiveness for not saving Dr.

Cathey? For killing him—because that was what they'd done, right? Killed Dr. Cathey by going to his flat to look for the photograph.

A strange feeling swept over her, and she glanced back toward the main altar. There she saw a larger-than-life mural of Christ. Something burned in her chest as she stared at the likeness of Jesus. The professor had so completely believed in Him.

She turned her gaze and guilt away. Checked on Kazimir. Her heart kick-started. Gone! She spotted him making his way out of the pew.

Tzivia slipped onto a pew and bowed her head. She made muttering noises, waiting for him to pass. A thud against the rear door preceded a hail of street noise. She lifted her head—caught the guard pacing Kazimir into the night.

*They're following him*. Why spy on Nur's own man?

If they were, were they doing the same to her?

An icy trill struck her spine. Shoulders hunched, she stood. Studied her feet as she exited the chapel through the rear door. Immediately sidestepped, plastering her shoulders against the stone church. Looked toward the footbridge with its lights and spied the repetitive bobbing of Kazimir jogging away from the church.

Her heart tripped. If she lost him . . .

Sidling up to the corner of the church, she peered around. Saw nobody else. She fell into a loping run, using every slick or mirrored surface to maintain a finger on her surroundings.

Kazimir made his way to the city's center, and she trailed, keeping enough distance that she didn't tip off his tail. Who was probably the worst in the history of tails. Unless this guy *wanted* to be observed.

The thought slowed her. Sent her down an alley, where she sprinted to catch up with the two on a parallel course. When she came up on the juncture, she waited for Kazimir to cross down the block.

In three . . . two . . .

He splashed a puddle, lamplight stroking his shoulders as the idiot jogged unaware.

She rushed to the next corner. In three . . . two . . . one . . .

Nothing.

She stared. Waited. Where had he gone? About to step out, she spied a lithe form gliding through the semidarkened shopping plaza.

He snagged something from the ground, then stumbled and caught himself on a planter. And then was moving again.

Picking up rocks? Realizing she was about to lose her vantage, she lurched down the next block and rushed up to the corner. Peered—

Weight slammed into her.

She yelped, but a hand clamped over her mouth.

"Why are you following me?" His words, husky and low, had nothing on the fierce glare in his eyes.

Kazimir! How had he—? His hand slid away, but his forearm thrust against her neck, forcing her chin up.

"They're following *you*," she warned.

"Seems to be a theme," he said in Russian, mouth curling in a sneer. "Why are *you*?"

She wet her lips, grateful when he eased the pressure on her throat. "The photograph."

"What about it?"

"I put it in your pocket." Why was he still frowning? Did he not know? Or worse—had he lost it?

"That was stupid."

Worry whooshed out. "Better than them finding it on me. Then I'd never get it solved, and they'd kill my father."

"So you plant it on me, endangering my life!"

She swallowed. "You had time to hide it. I didn't."

"Always looking out for number one." He sniffed. "You've already taken too long. They'll probably kill him anyway."

With a growl, she shoved Kazimir back. "Give me the picture!"

"Who is the man with the professor?"

The professor. He kept calling Dr. Cathey that. Most people referred to him as the doctor or Dr. Cathey. "Don't call him that. You didn't know him like that."

"Who's with him?"

"Give it to me, and I'll explain. Hurry, before Nur's thugs show up."

He angled in. "Trust me, Tzivia."

Whispers of the past trickled through her. She shivered, recalling another person who'd made that request. But something told her to trust him. Let him help. "Who . . . who are you?" This was insane.

This man *killed* for Nur. "No." She wouldn't trust him. "Never mind."

"Think!" he hissed, his breath stale. "Think about it, Tzivia. You know who I am. If you think, you know."

She shook her head. Wriggled free. Backstepped, surprised when he didn't fight to control her anymore.

"Time is running out—for you and your father," he said.

Did he actually care? How was that possible? "It's not the people. It's what's behind them."

"The sword?"

She sighed. "A piece of it."

He let his guard down.

Which left an opening. She hiked her leg, pivoted in midair, and threw a roundhouse kick to his head. It wasn't a lethal move, but it was focused. Perfectly aimed. Pitched his head into the brick wall.

She cringed at the crack of skull but took off running. She veered back to the plaza, sprinting through it, eyeing—on a hunch—the planter she'd seen him use for support. And slowed. There was a mark there.

Her heart shuddered.

Who was Kazimir Rybakov leaving a signal for?

# THE BLOOD IN GUSHING TORRENTS DRENCH'D THE PLAINS

"You are a true friend." Giraude clasped the forearm of Matin as dawn broke. "Thank you for easing my mind regarding Shatira and Avram."

"You have nothing more valuable, and here you trust them to my hands." Matin lowered his gaze. "It is a task I do not take lightly, to watch over them."

Giraude clapped a hand on his back. "Who would have thought a year ago that I would call a Nizari *friend*."

"Nor I a *Dawiyya*." Matin brandished a bright smile. "But here we stand."

With another firm clap on the man's shoulder, Giraude turned to

Shatira and six-month-old Avram. They had given him a Hebrew name, since he would always carry the Roussel surname. It was a good compromise.

Shatira met him with the babe and sad eyes. “Do not be long,” she insisted.

He pulled her to his chest and held tightly to both of them. Then he cupped his wife’s face. “You please me,” he said quietly, leaning in to kiss her. “Be strong, beloved.”

She clung to him, their son cradled on her hip. “For you. Hurry back.”

“Like the wind,” he promised, then pressed his lips to his son’s head.

“Before our next babe is born.”

Giraude started at her words. Stared into brown eyes that sparked with amusement. “What say you, Shatira?”

Smiling, she could not hide her blush.

“You are sure?”

“Quite,” she said around a smile.

He laughed, tugging her tight into his chest. Kissed her cheek. “I will be here for you. But this . . . this must be tended to. If Avram is to live in peace. If I am to—”

“Go.” She patted his chest. “We await your return.”

He threw himself up onto the destrier, glanced once more at his wife and son. A moment of panic struck him—what had he done? That babe so innocent despite the blood in his veins. The blood Saracens sought to wipe out.

He rode hard and fast with his brother-knights along the rocky terrain, barreling down on the band of Saracens.

# 35

## — MOSCOW, RUSSIA —

Returning to the Old City frayed his nerves. Ram stared at the bank of monitors, scanning and assessing, searching for Tox and Tzivia. He'd checked the planter outside the café before dinner but found nothing. Tox was late in reporting. The news of Dr. Cathey's death worried him. He needed to talk to Tox. Find out what had happened. Communication with him had been limited at best in the last few weeks. But the delay and the professor's death aroused alarm.

Mossad was breathing down Ram's neck. So was the CIA and DOD. They had nothing on his own roiling self-hatred for letting Tox do this. For not intervening, stopping things. He would never forgive himself if something happened to his friend. Ram had talked him into this. Activating Tox's embedded tracker would only alert Nur to the traitor in their midst, and it had been implanted as a last resort. He couldn't panic yet. Only four days had passed since Dr. Cathey died.

*C'mon, c'mon, c'mon. Where are you?*

Arms itching, he scratched and scanned. Scratched and recorded. Where was Tox? Why hadn't he contacted? He was nearly a week overdue. Was he in trouble?

Ram's email dinged, signaling a new message. Jerking his gaze to the right monitor, he noted the subject line: *He needs to know.*

Haven again. She knew better than this. No way would Ram deliver any personal intel to Tox right now. Distracting him could blow his cover. Yet when the email opened, his breath stalled. No text. Just an image. A grainy black-and-white sonogram photo that told him those months in Israel had grown more than a legend for an operative.

*Oh, Yahweh.*

He scrubbed the back of his head and groaned. Why couldn't a mission be simple? Get in. Do the job. Get out.

His phone buzzed. He saw the ID. Fisting a hand, he tucked aside his anger. Forced himself to answer. "Khalon."

"You have a problem," Omar growled.

*More than one problem*, he thought, his gaze hitting the emailed picture.

"Sending details now. Take care of it, or we will."

"Like you took care of London?" Ram barked. "What was that? You realize—"

"That wasn't us. He was dead when we got there."

"Then who? And why were you even there? Why were you following her?"

"You know the answer. What she's doing!"

"We have Tox—you put him there!"

"And he hasn't stopped her. Hasn't intervened as you said—"

"She went there for a clue. We had to know what it was."

"She had to be stopped."

Gut churning, Ram turned a slow circle, his mind tracing what that meant. Where that reasoning would lead. "Are you telling me—" He couldn't breathe. "*Tell me* you aren't going after her."

"The Valley of Elah is in two weeks," Omar said, his voice burdened and vehement. "If she found a clue in London, then we are too late. She's closer to assembling the Adama Herev."

"My father—"

"Don't forget the truth of him or complicate—"

"I *know* my father is in the catacombs. *That* is the only *truth* I have."

"How long will you lie to yourself? Think—*think*, Ram!" Omar growled. "If you don't convince her to give it to you, then we have no choice. You know I love Tzivia, but I can't stop this."

"You don't know what it means to love, Omar." Ram heaved a breath that felt as if a tank had parked on his chest.

"We're off track," Omar said quietly. "The problem is on your doorstep. Take care of it, or we will. And we can. There are plenty of assets there." Silence clung to the words. "Do you understand what I'm saying?"

Ram blinked. "Ye—" He took in a breath. Heard the warning. Heard what Omar could not say. Tzivia had Mossad agents close enough to kill her.

"Do you?"

"Yes," Ram ground out.

"Good."

When the call ended, Ram lowered his phone, mind warring. Omar was warning him. If an order was given . . . but one hadn't been given yet.

Because of Omar? Was he protecting her by slowing things down?

He had to contact Tox. But Tox hadn't made contact since before London. He'd been relocated to the penthouse residence, making it ten times more difficult to meet or communicate. No doubt Tox's phone was being monitored.

Frustration tightened Ram's shoulders and chest like a fiery band. He had to figure out how to warn Tox.

His system dinged the arrival of a new message, reminding him that Omar had warned of a problem. What else? Ram skidded the laptop toward himself and punched in his code. Opened the email. And froze at the image.

The front doors of Mattin Worldwide. Security camera capture of a woman approaching the front desk.

"No," he breathed. Clicked on it, enlarging it. Still disbelieving what he saw. No, not what—*who*. Bold as brass. Beautiful as ever. Trouble—as always.

* * * *

*Easy breezy, HackerGirl.*

Mercy sat at a monitor in the application center of Mattin's IT wing, going through myriad no-brainer tests designed to weed out the incompetent from the skilled and the skilled from the threats. Iliescu had done his part, securing the second-tier interview. Now the magic was up to her—and these manicured fingernails tap-tap-tapping on the keys. With a few intentional mistakes, a long pause here and there so she didn't do *too* well, she'd get the job.

And while the system she was operating right now shouldn't have access to the main hub, Mercy helped it along a little. Provided a pathway.

Shoes clicked closer, and she, with a few rapid-fire keystrokes, snapped the safewalls back to the doldrums. "Hmm," she said, frowning at the test.

"Impressive," intoned Pavel as he came alongside her. "Ah, the final tier always proves difficult."

Mercy sighed. "It is . . ." Acting confused always helped men grow overconfident. Miss obvious things. Like the fact that her left hand typed in her personal code for a subroutine that would spirit through the system, removing all traces of her roving access, while her right worked to finish the test.

And get it wrong.

"Oh," she said, deflating in her chair.

Pavel laughed. "Don't feel bad—most don't even get that far." His smile was genuine and showed interest. Which always worked in her favor.

"I'm mad I got the last one wrong. I don't—" She held up a finger. "Oh, I know what I did wrong. If I'd just—"

"Mr. Petryovich?"

Pavel turned to the door.

A dowdy woman in an expensive wool suit shot Mercy a dark look, then lifted her gaze to him. "A word, sir."

Touching Mercy's shoulder, Pavel apologized. "Sorry. This won't take but a minute." He pointed to the system. "Go ahead and log out. We have the record."

Alarm squeezed her confidence. "You don't need to download—"

He held up a finger. "Just a minute. I'll be back."

Oh snap. Her heart raced as she eyed the keyboard. The monitor. Iliescu had given her bad intel. This system shouldn't have mirroring capability. She glanced around, searching for a fountain. A bottle of water.

"Ms. Morozova?" he said, returning.

Snap snap snap. Last name. That wasn't good. She turned, lifting her purse as she came to her feet. "Yes? Did I do well?"

His expression fell. "I'm sorry, but it seems we've had a concern raised about your visa."

"What?" She frowned. "I don't have a visa. My father—"

"I'm sorry," he said, his expression tightening. "We have a strict policy. Any security concerns raised—"

"But I was cleared! Call them—"

"—means an automatic disqualification." He pointed to the woman who'd just ruined Mercy's day and mission. "If you'll follow Mrs. Gorsky, she'll take you to the consulate officer waiting for you."

Consulate officer? Mercy's spine exploded with heat. Were they kidding? "I—I don't understand," she said, her hands trembling. "This is a mistake. I haven't—"

Guards appeared at the door.

Mercy's heart thundered.

Petryovich took her by the arm and pulled her toward the security detail.

"This is a mistake," she objected. "I just need a job. Please! I've worked so hard to get here." They had no idea how hard—Iliescu had made her fly on Morozova's papers, which meant no first class or even business class. On a ten-hour flight!

Two guards cuffed and hauled her to the elevator. In the box, they punched the ground-floor button.

She wrested free to straighten her clothes and dignity. "This is a mistake," Mercy told the woman. "I came back when my father died. I need this job."

Mrs. Gorsky glowered and was the first one out of the elevator, as if she couldn't wait to be rid of the pestilence.

The guards had mastered the hovering thing all the way down the sterile white corridor, even though they allowed her to walk on her own. They urged her quite persuasively through double doors, beyond which the space widened into a steel and glass multistory waiting area.

"Mr. Kalev, thank you for notifying us," Mrs. Gorsky said as she stalked past Mercy to the waiting consular officer. "Here she is."

His back to Mercy and the guards, the man rose. Gave a nod. "I thank you for your patience and understanding. As I said, we are unsure of her intentions but felt it only fair to alert one of our country's most powerful influences."

"Of course," Mrs. Gorsky said, inclining her head all too graciously.

When the man turned, Mercy nearly choked at the green eyes that locked onto her. Though he wore an expensive suit and sleek wig, there was no denying the Bohemian gorgeousness that was Ram Khalon. What was he doing here? Iliescu would rake him over nuke-heated coals for this!

Fury collided with relief. "This is a mistake," she hissed at him.

"We will determine that, Ms. Morozova." He held out a hand.

Did his sexy-headed self really think she'd just give up?

Yes. Yes, he did. Because he knew—as did she—that she had no options. Not with two armed thugs and near-impenetrable security walls. The only way she was leaving this facility was with a police escort or with Ram.

She lifted her chin and swore on all the vices of every superhero she'd ever called him that he would pay.

"Thank you," Ram said in Russian and gave a half bow to the Mattin woman, then wagged his fingers at Mercy. "Come along, please."

Defiance had always been a skill she'd mastered. That and an iron will. Right now, she flung both at Ram. But quickly recognized the futility and danger. "This is a mistake. You will hear about this."

"I'm sure," Ram said as he produced plastic zip cuffs.

"Are you *kidding* me?"

"Sorry, it's necessary." Ram caught her upper arm. "Thank you, Mrs. Gorsky."

"Anytime," the frumpy woman said. "We are grateful for your timely visit."

Teeth grinding as Ram led her out into the afternoon, Mercy found herself willing the sun's rays to become lasers and bore holes through his thick head. "Release me at once," she hissed as they walked down the twenty-three steps to the parking lot.

"And risk my cover?"

"I will kill you for this."

He guided her to a black sedan and stuffed her into the rear passenger seat, then leaned across to buckle her in, his face within inches of hers. Handsome, rugged jaw.

"I could bite your ear," she said.

"Wouldn't be the first time." He backed away but paused. His green eyes swept her face and sent heat rushing into her cheeks. He reached toward her neck.

Mercy froze, her heart hammering.

He picked something from her shoulder—lint? A hair? Held it up and arched an eyebrow.

She had to angle away to look at it and her confidence evaporated beneath her very obvious stupidity. From the front console of the car, he lifted a bottled water, uncapped it, and dropped the tracking bug into it. Petryovich had planted it on her!

Mercy kicked the front seat with a barely held shriek as Ram climbed behind the steering wheel. After weaving quickly through the city, he swerved into a parking lot and eased the car next to a trash bin, where he pitched the water bottle. Then they were moving again.

"Do you have any idea what you just did?" she asked.

His gaze hit hers in the rearview mirror. "Do you?"

"The CIA sent me."

"I don't care if it was the president—which would be saying something."

"Dru is going to be livid."

"New boyfriend?"

"Try director of the CIA."

"*Deputy* director."

She growled again. Didn't anything get past all that fake hair? "Stupid wig."

Though she couldn't tell from the back, it seemed he was smiling by the way his cheek balled.

"You blew my cover," she said.

"No, *you* did that." Again, his gaze caught hers in the mirror. "Within minutes of entering Mattin Worldwide, you were ID'd and

I was notified. Lame cover. No disguise." He glared at her. "I taught you better."

"I had to get in, Ram. Now you've blown that chance."

"Better than you blowing my asset. We've been working on this for months. Things are too close, the op too tricky for you to screw it up."

They were on the south side of the city when he veered into a warehouse district and wound through the creepiest sections.

"Seriously, what are you? Penguin, holing up in the sewers?"

"They found me once. Won't risk it again," he vowed as he steered into a dank warehouse. She heard the garage door sliding closed as they slowed to a stop.

Darkness closed in, and she had to tell herself she was safe. Ignore the assailing memories. The all-too-real fear that slammed against her. Ram was there. It'd be okay.

"Lovely dark pit of despair you have here." She forced her voice to stay calm. *Breathe*. In. Out. In. Out. "Did you decorate it yourself?"

When a car door swung open, she expected the interior dome light to come on. But it didn't. Probably inoperable on purpose. Blackness snapped tight around her. Smothered her.

Her pulse spiked. Chest constricted. She closed her eyes. Listened in the darkness for the sound of Ram stalking around the vehicle to free her. But heard nothing.

Her heart thrashed. What if he left her here? What if he wanted to punish her for this perceived violation against his operation?

"Ram?" she said quietly. "Ram." A little more forceful. She whimpered. Choked back the terror. "*Ram!*"

The door opened.

Mercy dove to her right. Planted her feet on the ground. Shoved upward—right into the solid mass that was Ram.

"Easy." His hand came to her waist. Held her firm. "It's okay."

"That wasn't funny."

"Open your eyes."

Through her swimming panic, through her fear, she'd forgotten. A dim light glowed from the far right. She let out a shuddering breath as she visually latched onto it. "You're cruel."

"I had to set the alarm," he said quietly, steadying her. Watching her. "That's why it took me a minute."

"You could've wired it. You know how." She swallowed. Looked down.

He was still watching her, touching her. And that had to stop. He'd made his choice.

She shoved her hands up between them, displaying the cuffs.

Ram smirked, green eyes holding her hostage, as she heard the faint click of a folding knife. The steel blade dusted her arm before biting through the plastic. Freed, she rubbed her wrists and shot him daggers. Serr—

"Serrated daggers?"

She would not smile. Would not acknowledge how much he knew about her, knew her vow. She threw serrated daggers from her eyes. "I hate you."

That washed the arrogance from his stubbled jaw. A glimmer of something rippled across his features, and it clawed at her. Grief.

"You don't." Ram stepped back. "This way," he said, his voice hoarse as he turned toward the dull glow that caressed four steps to a doorway.

She followed him into a walled-off room where a bank of computers buzzed and hummed. A torn leather couch was stuffed into the corner with a table. The space had a lot of old and ton of musty, but not much light or new. "Wow, same decorator, huh?"

He headed to a dorm fridge and pulled out a bottled water. Handed it to her.

"You know, even Bruce's cave is better outfitted than this place." She took the water and opened it.

"When I have his billions, I might add curtains. Gold brocade."

Mercy smiled, a sudden ache flaring across her heart. She missed this—missed them. Him knowing what she didn't like—gold or brocade. Her taunting him. He watched as she took a swig of the water.

And she missed something else. She reached toward his face.

Ram caught her wrist, his eyes darkening.

"Easy, Gorgeous." She twitched so he'd release her arm. Then she slipped her thumbnail beneath the line of the wig and peeled it off. Tousled his curls. "Better. You and 'slick' don't go together."

Ram sidestepped her. Reminding her that he'd made a choice—he'd set her aside.

Seeking a distraction, she glanced at the monitors. And something caught her eye. Mercy sucked in a breath. "Ram." She couldn't take her gaze off the grainy image of a plaza. More specifically, a planter near a building's foundation. The camera was focused on it.

He came to her side. And cursed.

It was the same mark he'd taught her to use when they worked together. The mark that signaled an emergency.

"Who's in trouble?"

# 36

**— MOSCOW, RUSSIA —**

*Think, Ram. Think.*

Palms on the table, he stared at the mark. When had Tox left it? Ram had checked just before he got the call from Omar. The email. Augh! He pounded a fist on the table, rattling the systems. Mercy sucked in a breath and twitched. Making him all too aware of his anger.

"What's wrong?" she asked. "Who is it?"

Ram grabbed the car keys, then stopped. Looked at Mercy. He couldn't leave her here. Not with the equipment. She'd shred him. Ruin it. But he couldn't take her with him—she was exposed now. Tie her up?

Guilt suffused him. She had an unnatural fear of dark places because of him—because of that mission. The one that changed everything between them.

"Is it Tox?"

He snapped back to her. Surged into her personal space. "How do you know about him?"

"D-Dru." She stumbled back, tripping over a stack of boxes. She caught her balance. "Dru told me he was embedded. That you were working with him on a mission."

Ram erupted in a flurry of curses and rage. He couldn't see straight.

Couldn't think straight. "He had no business doing that!" Were they compromised? Was Tox? That could dissolve all their efforts in one fell swoop. Son of a gun. He lifted his eyebrows at her. "You going in there today could've ruined everything," he growled. "If they trace you back to—"

"They won't."

"The AFO's tendrils plague every country, infect every government. Even the Americans. *Especially* the Americans. They planted a bug that you missed, so don't underestimate them."

"Ram."

"Iliescu's going to screw it all up—get them killed. Then I'll kill him!"

"Ram!"

He jerked, startled by her yell. By the vibrating hum of his own shouts.

"What is with you?" Her amber eyes narrowed. "You're never unhinged."

He swallowed at her words. At the truth buried within them. "Unhinged?" He told himself to calm down. "You haven't seen unhinged."

"I have," she said quietly, ominously.

His mind ricocheted to the Greece mission. "How?" He paused at her haunted expression. "You were . . . in that box . . ."

A shaky nod. "I could see. There was a sliver of a space between the boards," she said with a hesitant nod. "I saw . . . everything."

He'd shown up for the drop, knowing she was hiding nearby with other members of their team. But when Ram saw the crates being buried, he quickly realized their man, Tommy, had betrayed them to the target. Burying the crates meant burying Mercy alive. He'd lost it.

"That wasn't me." Ram lowered his gaze, disappointed she'd seen that side of him. "I broke character."

"Then . . . why?"

He looked up at her. How could she ask that? "It was you."

"But I knew the risks, Ram. You *killed* Tommy. Your friend."

"He betrayed us! Compromised me, nearly killed you—"

"But you were better than what I saw. Why? Why go—"

"It was *you*!" he raged, his veins straining against the effort of making his point. "If I did nothing, you would've died. And he betrayed us—you. Put your life at risk."

Mercy drew up short. Studied him. Her chest rose and fell unevenly. "Then . . . why did you leave me?"

Ram deflated. Hung his head. "Doesn't matter—"

"It matters to me."

He scratched his head. Turned a circle. "I made a vow," he said miserably. "When my father vanished, I vowed to find out what happened to him. And the only way I could do that was by selling my soul to the Mossad. To Israel. I knew whatever my father was involved in, it was connected to our nation. Our people. If I . . . you . . ." He shook his head.

"So it wasn't me who drove you away."

He'd let her believe it was her fault. Let himself believe it. Anything to assuage the guilt. "No." He shrugged away the weight pressing down on him. "Look. That's . . . we have a mission. One I'm not going to screw up, because my friend's life is on the line. My sister's."

Mercy closed the distance between them. "Let me help."

Objection seared his tongue. "You—"

"I can use the comms to stay eyes-out as you go in." She nodded to the monitor. "I'll cover your six."

She always knew how to buy his agreement—keep it mission-oriented. But letting her in, opening that door again . . . there was too much happening. Too much with the operation. Too much with him. The last thing he wanted her seeing was the disorder eating him. The way the thirst of steel rummaged his veins for weakness.

Her plan made sense. But it scared him, too.

"Come on," she said with a grin. "My HackerGirl senses are tingling." Her expression seemed to clear, and she backed up a few taunting steps and touched a monitor. "Unless you want me to stay here and . . . babysit."

She was toying with him—knowing he'd never leave her alone with his computers. The things she could find and do left a bad taste in his mouth. "You need to change."

Her grin dulled the sun.

He pointed to a small room. "Extra clothes in there—they won't fit."

"They never did before." She took a skipping jump to hurry toward the room.

*This is stupid. She'll be your undoing. Like last time.*

At his bank of monitors, he wormed into the security footage until he found the moment Tox had marked the planter. Eyed the timestamp. Just before dawn. How had he missed this?

He had to get to the café. Park his butt there. Find out what was wrong. He—

"I thought you'd try to lock me in there."

Ram straightened, surprised yet not that she was at his side. Far too distracted by the last few distracting things, he turned to the most recent. "Would it have worked?"

Her left cheek twitched with the barest hint of a smile. "Not for long."

"Exactly." He shifted away. "Besides, I'm never again locking you anywhere." But that made sentimentality swell within him.

Her gaze rose to his head. "I'm glad you still wear it."

The beanie. He'd kept it when they went their separate ways, convinced she'd never see him using it. She'd made it, said crocheting relaxed her. But he'd grown so used to it, he hadn't given it a thought. A part of him said he'd messed up, showing her that it meant something to him, *she* meant something.

Her smile bloomed. "Good to know."

Oh, he missed her. Missed the way she called it like she saw it—but with flair. Toyed with his anger and invariably demolished it with logic or playfulness. That was what had created a lure to her that he hadn't been able to resist. In a world of deadly missions and dark souls, she was the laughter and balance that kept him this side of sane. Even now, just looking into her amber eyes, he felt the draw. An ache to once more experience the tangibility of what she embodied.

It was a cliché. *She* was a cliché, with her name that so perfectly spelled out what she possessed. It was a mercy to know her. To have her in his life. A respite from the intensity and driving compunction to prove himself.

Somehow, his hand hovered between them, fingers begging to trace the soft contours of her face. Eyes filled with relief and understanding, she caught his wrist. Brought his hand to her cheek, giving him what he himself refused—more Mercy. Her skin was still as silky as he remembered. He inched closer as she cupped his arm between her hands. Breathed her smile.

Like a waterfall that drowned the noise of the world, Mercy had silenced his every argument. As she always had. She went still.

Ram slipped his hand to her nape. Homed in on her lips as they parted.

"Are you sure?" Her whispered words skated along his jaw, slamming into his chest, his heart.

Reminding Ram he'd broken up with her. Reminding him that as long as Israel came first, a girlfriend was—at best—second.

"I'm crazy about you, Ram, but"—she wet her lips—"I can't do that again. I can't breathe life with you, then have you crater me again. It's not fair."

He nodded. Huffed at his own idiocy but also at his desperation not to be the guy who broke her heart twice. Not to be the guy who walked away. He wanted to stay. To kiss her until she forgot Banner and Clark. So she remembered only one hero—him.

"You're right," he said, backing up. "Won't happen again."

* * * *

Nerves frayed, Tox strode up the steps and into the glass-and-steel building. Made it through the security checkpoint with merely a nod from the team before he accessed the private elevator. Thirty seconds later, it delivered him to the penthouse.

"Did you hear about the security breach?"

Tox looked up from swiping his access card through the reader and frowned at Yefim. "What breach? Anything I need to alert Mr. Abidaoud about?"

"He's already aware," Yefim said.

"Guess I'm last to know." Tox waited. "That is, if you're going to tell me . . ."

"Some woman faked an interview for a systems analyst position. Everything went slick as snot until she showed up for the deprogramming test."

"Depro—"

"They sit her at a computer, and she has to deprogram it." Yefim shrugged his thick shoulders, making Tox note the imprint of a weapon holstered beneath his jacket. "She was in there working her fingers, fast and furious, when IT gets a call that someone is there to take her into custody."

"Custody?"

Yefim nodded. "Some embassy guy or something. It caused quite a stir. They've been testing that computer since she left."

Intriguing. Should he worry about this? The longer he lived and breathed Mattin Worldwide air, the more convinced Tox became that the AFO either never or rarely met together. Preventative measures. Which made it impossible to gather names and intel.

"Hey, you going up?" Yefim pushed out of his chair.

Where else would Kazimir be going?

"I'll come with you. I have business."

Yefim's unusual behavior unsettled Tox as they rode the private elevator. Nothing in particular had set off his internal alarms. Just . . . something about Yefim. About all of this—the security breach. Being escorted.

As he carded into the penthouse, Tox held the door. Allowed Yefim to take the lead, strategically placing him where Tox could see any sudden movements. Give him time to get his bearings. He tried to isolate what was off, what felt different, but everything seemed right. Fine.

Yet not.

When Yefim started for Nur's office door and lifted a fist to rap on it, Tox headed to the residence hall and aimed his card at the access reader.

"Rybakov!" Nur barked from his office, where Yefim was entering.

Tox stilled. With two long, measured breaths, he took a step back from the residence and looked over his shoulder at the office. Anything to keep his distance and hopefully buy a reprieve. Just long enough to figure out what was wrong and formulate an exit strategy.

But he couldn't see Nur. And he didn't dare holler his response. Reluctantly, he crossed the foyer. "Sir?"

"Come in," Nur insisted. "Close the door."

Shifting heavily into his Kazimir persona, Tox eyed Yefim. And the two other men in the room. He'd been right. Something was wrong.

He intentionally turned a slow circle to close the door so he could take in his surroundings. Determine his options. Exit strategies. He faced Nur and held one hand over the other as he stood at the ready. "Sir. How can I—"

"Where were you last night, Rybakov?"

"At the river, sir. With you. With—"

"After." Nur waved a hand, dismissing Tox's ready explanation. "We returned, but you went out afterward."

Aware the others had not moved or spoken, Tox managed a brief, disconcerted look. "I went to the cathedral."

Nur's eyes flashed. "You have never been a religious man."

"Nor am I now."

His employer gave a confused laugh. "Then why were you at the cathedral?"

"To think."

"Think?" Nur snarled. "About what?"

Doing his best to appear grieved, Tox lowered his gaze. "My family."

"Your family is *dead*," a man snapped from the corner.

Tox locked onto the shadowy figure. "In body, yes. But in memory"—he let the ache of missing Haven twist through his features—"they live. Some days more than others. Some days their absence is difficult."

Nur's expression had begun to morph from accusatory to questioning. A very necessary and big step if Tox was going to leave this office alive. The realization that he could be breathing his last stirred his survival instincts. Pushed him to be more assertive. "Am I on trial for visiting the cathedral?"

Nur punched to his feet. "You are on *trial* because you met privately with Tzivia Khalon."

"Not true," Tox countered.

"I was there," Yefim said, coming forward. Buttoning his jacket.

Pinning his gaze on the man who'd had to eat his own pride when Kazimir was promoted over him, Tox met his eyes. "Tell me where! *Where* did I meet her?"

"An alley. Just beyond the plaza down the road from the Kremlin,"

Yefim said, lifting his chin. "Saw the two of you back there. Real cozy."

Tox rolled a disgusted look to Nur, who was watching intently. "This—*this* is who you trust over me?" He glowered again at Yefim. "Did you also see me slam her against a wall? Did you see me demand to know why she was following me?"

"What I saw was a very good performance," Yefim said with a curled lip. "You lingered too long while holding her throat—she should have died with you holding her that long."

"Had I *strangled* her, then she could not secure the sword for Mr. Abidaoud, and I would have been standing here answering very different questions. If I was allowed to live at all."

Nur jutted his jaw at Tox. "And what was her answer? Why did she follow you?"

"She saw me as a soft target. Thought she could manipulate me to get her father released." It wasn't a whole lie.

"What did you tell her?" Nur asked.

"That I wasn't the answer to her problems." Again, not a lie.

Nur glanced to the right, where the two men waited. The shorter, grayer of the two shifted his gaze from Tox to Nur. "He's telling the truth."

A new wave of panic hit Tox. They had a "lie detector" assessing his responses the way Haven could.

"But he's also holding something back," the man added. "As I mentioned while watching him discuss the breach with Yefim."

*Watching me?* That entire conversation with Yefim had been staged. To test him. The sands of time on this mission weren't just falling. They were using jet propulsion.

Nur slid a narrowed gaze toward Tox. "Have you anything to tell me, Mr. Rybakov?"

Tox Russell wouldn't be threatened by this man. Instead, he would feed off the anger and accusations. But he wasn't Tox right now. He was Kazimir Rybakov. And that man would be panicked. Truth be told, there was more than a little of that coursing through Tox's veins. "About what, sir? That I'm supposedly hiding something? Or about the alley where I failed to kill your asset?"

"You're being sarcastic, Kazimir."

"Sorry, sir." He let his gaze drop a little. "I'm angry—angry that I stand accused when I have done no wrong." He remembered Haven's instructions in the past and shifted his feet. "I'm nervous, sir."

"Nervous?" That amused the power-hungry man.

"I've seen what you do to those who betray you, sir."

"*Have* you betrayed me?"

*Since I first entered this building.* "Only by thinking of my wife more than of being your security officer."

"There is more," the gray-haired man prompted.

"Shall we beat it out of you, Mr. Rybakov?" Nur stood, pushed back his chair, and came around the desk. "You are giving me half truths, according to Mr. Sergeyev."

Tox hesitated. Held his ground.

"If you do not answer, you convince me that I should have you punished or killed." The gleam in Nur's eyes warned Tox that he was on borrowed time right now.

He grasped at the one thing he was sure wouldn't go over well but might keep him alive. "I . . . I think you should release her father."

Face darkening, Nur edged closer. "You think I should. You *think*!" His nostrils flared as he squared his shoulders. "*I* do the thinking. You are a dog that does his master's bidding."

Tox yanked his gaze down.

"I have a meeting." With a flick of his hand, Nur stormed out.

That flick was not a dismissive one. It was an order. Given to the guards, to Yefim, who remained. The door closed.

Yefim came toward Tox and offered his hand. "Sorry, man. I have a job to do, too."

*Have a job to do.* Though he wanted to drive the man's nose through his gray matter, Tox reluctantly accepted the hand, convinced his apology was not legit. Sensing there was more to it. And the next second proved him right.

Yefim clamped Tox's hand. Yanked him forward. Another weight caught his left arm, constricted.

Tox twitched away. But the bigger man grabbed him. Jerked Tox's arm back and up, effectively forcing Tox to his knees. Awareness rushed through him: they were going to teach him a lesson.

Yefim drew back a fist and drove it at Tox. Again and again. Nailed his side. Pain exploded like white-hot fire. He howled, only to have what felt like a brick wall slam him into darkness.

# 37

**— MOSCOW, RUSSIA —**

It hurt to breathe, let alone move. Tox could only thank God that the surgical alterations couldn't fall off. After the beating Yefim and the other guy had delivered, it felt like at least half his face and guts were left on the office floor.

When he made his way back to his quarters and opened the door, he stilled, instincts buzzing. Something snagged his brain. The fringe of the carpet—on the far side where he hadn't walked. Though everything was in place, the room had been searched.

*They're looking for Tzi's picture.* His gaze skipped to the nightstand, and for a second, he feared they'd located it. But on the floor lay a book, a notepad, and a pen.

They hadn't found it.

Lungs afire, he stepped in and let the door close. Flipped the locks. Gratefully, the injuries gave him justification to move slowly. No doubt they were monitoring via the cameras that weren't as hidden as Nur thought.

With a groan and flare of fire through his side, he eased onto the edge of the bed, noting the messy, untucked corner. Hospital corners had been hammered into him in Basic. Tight creases. No wrinkles. And yet, here were wrinkles.

Tzivia had only found one piece of the sword, so it made sense that Nur was getting desperate. Making mistakes. He was already ruthless, but he'd become downright vicious.

Tox had to talk to Ram. Update him. But while he was monitored around the clock, there was no way. He could not afford to risk exposing himself or Ram. Unless he somehow threw off suspicion. Bought his way back into Nur's favor.

There was only one way he could do that.

Tox lifted the pen from his nightstand. Considered it heavily. If he did this . . . Tzivia might never forgive him.

* * * *

"Your assassins aren't very effective, Belda."

The woman, snow-white hair coiffed in a severe blunt style along her jaw, struck Nur with a hard look. "If we did not have interference from the authorities, like you promised, the list would be considerably shorter. But each day you add to it!"

"The list grows," Moriz said dully from his spot at the table, "because the system works. And starting with the Americans was smart—"

"Smart?" Belda bristled. "I warned you both we should start slow—"

"Slow isn't in the books," Nur hissed. "The Valley of Elah happens in less than two weeks."

"And we only have one part of the sword," Labaka said through the feed.

That was not entirely true, but Nur would allow them to believe it. "Labaka, you've earned my anger. I heard the Americans have your programmer," he said calmly, though he only felt rage.

"Makanda doesn't know what he was coding. Only that he was."

"Did he hear anything? See anything?"

"Nothing."

"You are too confident, my friend," Nur chided. "But because you were so clever, using that disgusting game to conceal the code's true purpose, I will forgive this mistake." His gaze slid to Belda. "I spoke with your sister."

Belda scoffed. "Zoryana is too caught up in her own pride. She should have killed them before they left her home."

"Who visited her and asked about the Adama Herev?" Nur asked.

"The man she knew, Dr. Cathey, is now dead in response." Belda shook her head. "But the woman and other male are unknown. We're working on it."

"Should we recall the assassins?" another voice asked. "The FBI agent is too close to the truth, and our agents failed to kill him. Now Grazia has been taken right out of her compound! They are brazen, so we must return the favor."

"Agreed. Can you find Grazia?" Nur asked.

Hesitation clogged the line. "I . . . don't know."

"Find her. We cannot afford for them to pry answers from her. She was always a little soft, I thought," Nur said, poison in his words.

"You think she's part of the Camarilla?"

"I never said such a thing," Nur said, glad the seed had been planted. "It would be a shame if she were, but we must be careful regardless."

"Understood," the voice said.

"On second thought, I want Grazia dead. They keep pushing and getting closer to the truth, to stopping us, and her knowledge could change everything," Nur said, annoyed.

Belda growled. "We should go after the head of that dragon."

"The Americans? Are you insane?" Moriz shouted.

Nur rubbed his forehead. Told himself to stay calm. "Moriz is right, Belda. If we go after them, we awaken the entire world to what has taken decades to build. This battle has been going on too long. We cannot have them preventing the reversal at Elah. Our ancestors have fought for centuries to make this day possible. It ends at Elah."

* * * *

Names. He had names. Leaning against the wall, the fiery pain in his ribs nearly unbearable, Tox pulled in greedy draughts of air. Months of work. All this time with Nur. Beaten and humiliated—punished. It had all netted him nothing but one name.

Until now. Dumb luck. He'd gone out for athletic tape for his ribs and ibuprofen . . . and returned to hear voices coming from the hall.

Belda. Moriz. Zor-something.

Go. Get them to Ram. How? He pushed off the wall.

"Rybakov."

Jerking at the call of his name shot daggers through his side and shoulder. He tensed, shuffling around to look beneath pain-hooded eyes at Yefim.

"What are you doing?" Yefim asked, sauntering menacingly toward him.

The talk with Ram would have to wait. First Tox had to buy himself more time. And there was only one way to do that—by betraying a friend.

"I need to talk with Mr. Abidaoud."

# 38

## — MOSCOW, RUSSIA —

Ram sat at the café, grateful the barista recognized him as a regular and kept his coffee coming through the two hours he waited, reading. Mercy sat across the aisle with a laptop, earbuds tucked in, cords straggling against her long hair. It was hard not to look at her. More than once he caught himself staring. Still annoyed that she'd told him to stand off. As if he'd enjoyed taunting her.

The thought jarred him. Was that what she thought?

It was stupid. The only way he could protect Israel and Mercy at the same time was to leave her in safety so he could do his job for his country. Were he to be honest, his efforts weren't wholly for Israel. Staying connected to the country had been a means to an end: to intercept news of his father.

Snapping taut the paper he held, Ram did the same with his attention, bringing it back to the reason his butt was sore. Waiting on Tox to show.

What was going on? Why hadn't Tox made contact? They had an agreement—even if he missed a rendezvous, Ram would wait. If he missed two, Ram would attempt to set eyes on Tox but not intervene unless absolutely warranted.

But for Tox to leave that mark, then never show . . .

Something was wrong.

Ram's phone buzzed in his pocket. His secure phone. Nerves twitching, he pulled it from his pocket. Eyed the screen. Though his heart thudded, he steeled his response. "Hello." Not a standard greeting for him, but in public, he couldn't afford to draw attention.

"I will keep this short since you are in a café," Omar's gruff voice announced.

Ram huffed. Struggled not to panic. Shoved aside the irrational anger that had been tumbling and roiling through him over the last few weeks. "What?"

"Your sister was seen two nights ago in an alley with your asset. He didn't seem happy to see her, but then, appearances are deceiving."

Tox was with Tzivia in public—two nights ago. That was when he'd left the mark. Internal claxons sounded as Ram wondered why they'd been out together, in an alley.

"We believe things are starting to collapse."

Ram swallowed, hiding it behind the white coffee mug and his silence. If Tox was seen with Tzivia in an alley, then yes. Things were bad. "Let me go to the cathedral."

"Negative. You do that, and our suspicions become reality."

"He's there."

"Your mission is not Yared. It's the AFO and their leaders. We need names, Ram."

"They do not meet on-site as believed."

"He is there. He can find out. We need them *now*."

Okay, that was obvious. So what wasn't obvious that had forced Omar to call? Ram tensed, waiting.

"We believe the pressure and the collapse is because of the Americans and their hunt for the AFO leaders. They need to back off. The stunt they pulled with your girlfriend—"

"She's not—"

"—was a very bad move. Things are exposed. Security is heightened."

"You gave them Grazia and Makanda. You put them on those scents to keep them busy. It's not their fault they're effective."

"Too effective. It was meant to distract, not complicate our efforts. Things are going south. Dr. Cathey's death was an aftershock we didn't need. We barely contained that, showing up after the Arrows."

Anger pulsed through Ram. This whole thing stank. Every aspect, every angle failed.

"What has Tox said? Why was he with her in the alley?" Omar asked.

Ram flinched. How was he supposed to answer that? If they knew he'd lost contact with Tox, they'd consider Tox a threat. They'd want him neutralized before he could do damage. Give names to the AFO.

"You've lost him," Omar accused.

"I'm waiting on him now."

"While you're waiting, tell the Americans to back off."

"I'm not sure they'll listen."

"They will if they want their man back alive."

* * * *

**— NORTHERN VIRGINIA —**

Haven studied the sonogram picture, staring at the black-and-white snapshot of their baby. Cole's baby. Inside her. It was still so surreal. And it was killing her not to be able to tell him.

With a sigh, she set the photo aside and tugged the journal closer. She was nearly done transcribing the Russell lineage. Working through the century-old writing, she kept coming back to the amazing fact that a Russell had married a Linwood before.

She turned the page, and her hand froze. The paper was different, as was the handwriting. It had been folded, and she carefully released the anchor that held the pages to the leather folio and drew out the odd page. Her heart skipped a beat. The handwriting was very different. Her eyes traced the slightly blurred ink to the bottom, where it was signed *Avram Roussel, 1750.*

The page opened with a short explanation: *What follows is the lineage of forebears as far as is known. This record is copied that my line and my father's might persist across time. It is a true and accurate account of those who have gone before me.*

Haven's gaze traveled the forty or so names listed. About halfway down, it started listing only the male names, no wives. She backtracked and stilled. "You're kidding."

*Devra Roussel m. Jorim Linwood.* Only one child was listed: Thefarie.

"But that can't be," she muttered.

"Ngozi?" Chiji said from the side chair where he was reading.

"Hmm?" *That can't be Tzaddik. Can it?*

"We have company."

Haven glanced at her guardian, but even as she did, she caught sight of a dark shape to her left. She whipped around and sucked in a breath at the sight of the Timeless One lowering himself into the other chair.

"Tzaddik." Shaking off the adrenaline surge wasn't easy, but she tried. "Interesting timing."

"The times are interesting," he replied. His gaze fell on the journal, but his grave expression returned.

Alarm shoved through Haven's veins. "Wh–what's wrong?"

"Grave news, I'm afraid," Tzaddik said. "Our friend Dr. Cathey is dead, killed by the rebel sect within the AFO, the Camarilla."

A wave of nausea swept her, chilling her. "Are you sure?"

Though he managed a smile, Tzaddik's graveness remained.

"I can't believe it." Haven cupped her head in her hands, bending forward. Feeling sick all over again. Not because of the pregnancy but over losing such a genuine man and the chance to find the bust.

"Have you found it?"

Annoyance cloyed with grief. "Found what? Dr. Cathey is dead. What does it matter—"

"It matters all the more. You said interesting timing. That could not be more true. The hour is upon us." Ferocity bled through Tzaddik's features.

She blinked, confused. "What hour?" She waved at the journal, notes, and printed genealogy charts. "You've had me chasing names."

"No, not names." He switched from the chair to the sofa beside Haven. Touched her arm. She half expected a jolt of electricity, but instead it was merely warm. Firm. She glanced at his large hand and imagined it wielding a sword in the 1200s, then sniffed a laugh.

"Have you found it?" he repeated.

Something about his insistence on that question made her not want to answer. Instead, she grabbed the odd page she'd just found and held it up. "Is this you?" she asked, pointing to the name. "It lists the child of Devra and Jorim as *Thefarie*."

Amusement creased his eyes. "It is not. The closer you return to the time of Giraude and Shatira, the more you will see the same names: Avram. Giraude. Shatira. Thefarie. It's important now, Haven, especially with Joseph dead—have you found it?"

"*Found what?* The irony that my line and Cole's crosses throughout history?"

A faint smile touched his beard. "No irony. The bond has always been strong. It does not surprise me that you continued to find each other through generations."

Haven put her feet on the floor and scooted to the edge of the cushion. "If that's not what I was supposed to find, then what? The bust?" She saw something flash through his eyes. "This is about the bust?"

He reached toward the table and retrieved Aunt Agatha's photo of the statue. Relief washed over him, lifting his shoulders and head, then lowering them. "You found it."

"No," Haven countered, "I found some pictures. I have no idea where it is. Dr. Cathey bought it in the late '70s from the Linwood estate. For the last several days, I've been trying to reach him to ask where it is, but now that he's—"

"Try his flat in London."

"How would you know that?"

Another maddening smile. "He is an old friend. We talked . . . often." Sadness touched his eyes, coloring them with the gray pallor of grief. "He hid much there."

"What's important about the bust?" Haven hated the question, because the piece had been a near obsession since she'd found out about it.

"Since Joseph's death, his flat has been secured as a crime scene," Tzaddik said, ignoring her question "You must talk with your government friends. You must go to his flat."

"I don't understand," Haven admitted. "You're timeless. You can go here, there. You show up in places without opening doors. Why can't you go to the bust? Why this chase you set me on?"

This time, the emotion that flashed through his face was stronger than sadness. "I cannot," he said. "The journey is not mine, and much has been hidden from me. His flat is a guess."

"But you just—" She waved a dismissive hand. "Why did Dr. Cathey buy it?"

"I told him to," Tzaddik said, then drew in a long breath and slowly let it out. "I suppose the history of the sword should be told. But not here. Let's contact your friends at SAARC. They will be needed for the Elah battle."

# 39

## — SAARC HEADQUARTERS, VIRGINIA —

"My name is Grazia Raison, and I am a member of the French Parliament."

Leif considered the woman, her gray-streaked hair cut short and neat around her face. Face weathered with age and worry. "Not to be disrespectful, but we had to drag you out of that compound."

"Yes," she said, eyes narrowed, "after punching me in the face."

"I hit you after you hit us. And you hitting us?" Leif sniffed. "Meant we came back with more holes in our bodies than already existed."

"Uh, yeah." Cell raised his good hand. "I did come back with extra holes."

Raison nodded, repentant. "I apologize for my part in the events at the compound. My resistance was vital to maintaining appearances."

Cell grunted. "I have your *appearances* in my gut," he said, pointing to the still-bandaged wound.

Her chin lifted. "It was necessary that the guards believed and security feeds showed that I was not a willing participant in what happened. If anyone suspected I was complicit," Raison said, "they would go after my family. My children—adults, but still my children."

"Wait." Leif eased forward, spidering his hand on the table, fingertips to the laminate. "Are you saying that you *wanted* to be extracted?"

"I *had* to be extracted," Raison said, her tone sharp, decisive.

Leif looked at Almstedt then Iliescu. "Did we get played? Ram gave us that name."

"It actually came from his asset," Almstedt said. "Ms. Raison, are you aware there was a kill order against you?"

The French woman flinched. Her eyes widened. "My family." Iliescu picked up the phone and started talking quietly, and that apparently gave the Frenchwoman the reassurance she needed. "I should not be surprised that Nur has done this. Being taken from the compound, I am now a liability to him."

"What am I missing?" Thor asked.

After watching Iliescu for a few seconds, Raison glanced at Almstedt, who gave her a nod.

"What's said in this room, gentlemen—as you know—doesn't leave it," Almstedt ordered.

The words were clearly for the diplomat, because everyone else here didn't exist, nor did this organization or bunker. It seemed to satisfy whatever lingering concern Raison had.

She adjusted her chair and took a sip of water. "My rise to power and the ensuing success . . ." Her attractive but aged face was taut with grief. "My path to Parliament was paved before I was old enough to drive. I inherited the position from my father through Nur Abidaoud and the Arrow & Flame Order."

The tension in the room ratcheted ten decibels, screaming the objection of every Wraith member.

Maangi and Thor looked at each other.

Cell snapped forward, his chair thudding hard against the table. "Sorry, but why are you still alive?" He scowled, then glanced at Iliescu. "Why is there not an extra hole in her head? She's an enemy."

"Mr. Purcell," Iliescu said, "tone down the rhetoric."

"No rhetoric," Cell bit out. "Our number one priority is hunting these people down. And she's right here. Still breathing."

"Have to admit," Maangi said slowly, "I'm with Cell on this one. Having one of the key people we're after, right here—"

"I am a double agent," Raison said, quickly and with plenty of stress.

Leif blinked. "A spy?"

"Convenient," Cell groused.

"Of a sort." She wagged her head. "I hold a key position within the Order, but a dozen years ago, I was recruited because of my . . . *concern* about certain endeavors the AFO was undertaking. I'm part of a group called the Camarilla. We are a handful working to overturn the Order. Return it to its roots."

"But isn't that still world domination?" Cell asked, extending a pen at her. "How is this any different?"

She lifted her hands. "What you need to understand is that within the AFO there are others like me, high in the Order but not loyal—at least, not the way most are loyal."

"And how is that?" Thor asked.

"Many blindly follow Nur and the Sovereign, regardless of what they do or what empty path they take the Order down."

"Sovereign?" Leif angled his head, frowning.

Thor sat forward. "Hold up. Almost two years ago, my team and I took out Kaine in London. He and Nur were the head."

"Actually," Cell corrected, "an *arrow* boiled Kaine out. Right in front of Tox and Ram."

"Two-headed serpent," Maangi added. "It was a two-headed serpent trying to restructure the political map. That's what we were told."

Raison nodded. "*Oui*, Kaine and Nur were the serpents." Her eyes pinched into a smile that gathered her wrinkles. "What do serpents do?"

"Strike," Cell said.

"Deceive." With an arched eyebrow, she inclined her head. "They were a distraction. The Order has always had serpents, designed to distract and deliberately draw attention so the true leader—the Sovereign—can operate unimpeded."

"True leader," Thor repeated. "Who would that be?"

"That is unknown," she said with a sigh, "except to Nur and Kaine."

"So, Nur." Cell grunted. "Since Kaine is dead."

"*Oui*. But again, the point is that you are not alone in your fight against what is happening. Nur and the Sovereign are off course, obsessed with this sword and its curse. But we, the Camarilla, are united with you."

"Camarilla." Leif stared at her with the distinct feeling that she wasn't telling them everything. He slid his gaze to Cell, who frowned.

Good, so it wasn't just him. But what were they missing?

"How many are in this Camarilla thing?" Thor asked. "Because if we're talking fifty or a hundred"—he glanced at the others—"maybe we have a shot."

"What? With *her*?" Cell choked out a laugh. "Are you kidding, man?"

"There are four," she said definitively.

The team dropped silent and stared at Raison.

"Four?" Cell repeated.

Lifting a hand, Leif sat back, crossing his boots at the ankle. He considered the other SAARC operators. This . . . *this* could work for them. "I have a question."

"*Oui*," Raison said.

"You said you were high up in this order."

She nodded.

"And you said there were others in the same position, both figuratively and literally. High position and in opposition." He tucked his chin, staring at her. "Right?"

She frowned—her confidence lessening. "Yes."

"But what you didn't say is why you'd come to us. If you're so high up in this *Order*, don't you have followers? Don't you have people to rally, those loyal to *you*?" Leif leaned forward and set both arms on the table, his hands animated. "What I'm not getting is why you'd risk exposing yourself, exposing the Order, which you've said you believe in." He scratched his jaw. "Unless you were in trouble. Unless you need us to do something you can't do."

Thor nodded. "Or won't do."

"Sacrifice American soldiers, they said," Cell muttered sarcastically. "It'll be easy, they said." He scowled at the team. "I'm not biting. You?"

"See?" Leif went on, ready to deliver his blow. "What I'm thinking is that you want us to stop this, stop Nur, so that you can find out who the Sovereign is and kill him—then take that power."

Her face went hard and cold, a new side of her emerging. "Eliminating Nur is in both of our best interests."

"Boom!" Cell said. "We kill him. We take the heat, the bullets. You take the power." He lifted his palms in a hands-off gesture. "Not touching this one."

Her face grew red. "There is so much more than that! The Camarilla is in danger because we have been feeding intelligence to our very adversaries. How do you think you found Didier Makanda?"

Leif glanced at Iliescu, whose expression remained impassive but hard as ordnance.

Slapping a hand on the table, Raison spat, "They have killed one of us already!"

"There." Thor snapped his fingers. "That's what this is all about. You do need us—for protection and to bring violence to Nur."

She bristled. "Does it not matter to you that if they assemble this sword, they will be unstoppable?"

"How does a sword make them unstoppable?"

"The sword is tied to a curse that has long afflicted the line of the mercenaries, which includes most among the Order, as well as the Niph'al, the assassins who devised the curse of the Adama Herev. This sword imprisoned our lines to small numbers. This sword—"

"No, no, no," Leif said calmly but forcefully. He motioned around the room. "What's happening here isn't about the sword. It's about you using a situation and us to your benefit."

"Since you will not listen, hear reason." Raison nodded to Iliescu.

With a long-suffering sigh, the deputy director lifted a remote. "We have footage—grainy, but at least we have it—of a killing we believe is connected to the murders here in the States," Iliescu said.

"So this one's not in the States," Leif noted. "Same assassin?"

"*Same?*" Raison scoffed, glancing at Almstedt. "There are countless assassins! They are the Nizari Ismailis, and more than anyone, they want the sword assembled and their bloodline cleansed."

"Why are they killing people, though?" Cell asked. "How does that put the sword back together?"

"It doesn't," Raison said. "It is precautionary in case the sword is not reassembled. Listen," she growled, "if you want allies, if you want hope of winning this war, protecting your country against Nur and the Sovereign, you *must* protect Lukas Gath. It will all come back to him, because he is rumored to have a piece of the sword, though none have ever seen him with it."

"Who's Gath?" Leif asked.

"Let's watch the video," Iliescu said, indicating the screen. "It'll give you eyes on some possible targets."

Lights in the command hub dimmed, and the silent video played out.

"This was taken by one of my people," Raison said. "It happened near the Yauza River. That's Nur getting out of the car."

"The stiffs waiting?" Maangi asked, indicating the seven men lined up, as if for the executioner.

"Nur's officers in Russia. Well, some of them," Raison explained.

A man was marched to the middle of the group and forced to his knees.

"That is Girts Zakavij," Raison said. "One of the Four."

Leif shifted noisily, craning for a better view. "Who's—"

The room fell silent when a glint flashed through the footage. In a blink, Nur was moving back to his car. And Girts Zakavij had been relieved of his head.

Cell cursed.

"Nur knows about the Camarilla." Accusation laced Raison's words, which she let hang in the air as she narrowed her gaze.

"Wait—you're blaming us?" Cell's voice pitched. "You serious? After we bail your sorry—"

"Cell," Iliescu said, holding up a hand. He then turned to Raison. "What are you suggesting, Grazia?"

She huffed. "I would think it's obvious. We have remained hidden for decades. Until . . ."

"Until we pulled Makanda out," Leif said.

"In doing so, it brought attention to the Camarilla, made Nur more suspicious. Now that I am gone, it's clear he knows we are working against him." She nodded to the screen. "That would not have happened without someone feeding him intelligence."

Leif rolled his gaze to Thor. "You saying we have a mole?"

"Worse than a mole," Raison said. "An agent of the Arrow & Flame embedded in the American government."

# 40

**— MOSCOW, RUSSIA —**

"Is it him?"

At the voice crackling through the phone, Ram came up out of his chair, heart crashing against his ribs. "Tzivia?" Mind exploding with impossibilities, he tried to harness them. "What—How—"

"*Is it him?*" she demanded, each word ground between her teeth and apparent anger.

Lifting his head from the disbelief that weighted it, he stared across the room at Mercy, who slowly rose from the rickety chair she'd been perched on, eyes rife with the same surprise that smothered him. "You know better," he chided his sister. She'd pegged Tox.

"Than to ask? Or better than to think he would be here, that you would do this—with him. With *our friend*!"

"Why are you calling?" It was not merely to lecture him, to chastise him for allowing Tox into this game she'd started when she leapt off the cliff of reason. He pushed his gaze from Mercy as she drew closer, his mind bouncing between the two women.

"You are going to do me a favor," Tzivia said.

Anger sweltered through his muscles at what he heard in her voice. This was not a request. "You threaten him?" When Mercy came close, Ram reached for her without thinking. "'Our friend,' as you called him. You would use him—"

"*Who* is using him?" Tzivia hissed. "*Who* is putting him in harm's way? You are! He's an idiot to think he won't be found out. They will kill him!"

"That man felt it was worth the risk to help you. Save you."

"I do not need saving! Already one of my friends is dead." Grief burgeoned through her words. Dr. Cathey. "Is that worth the cost of you sending them after me?"

"Yes, Tzivia. They both feel you are worth it." Ram knew she had never seen herself as worth anything, all because their father had vanished. "I do, too, but Dr. Cathey—for you, he would have gone to the ends of the earth. You know that's true. And you didn't even attend his memorial after leaving him to die."

"And what did *your* friend do but *watch* him die! He is useless if he can't even save an old man."

"Isn't the same true of you, then? You have skills," he shouted, extricating himself from Mercy and going to the far side of the room. "I trained you! Give it up. Give up this foolish quest for the—"

"Foolish? *You* suffer the curse of the Adama Herev. I saw all those times you gave yourself injections, the ones you hid from everyone. But I saw," she said, her voice raw. "All those bruises when there shouldn't have been any. The time as a teen you missed an injection and ended up in the hospital—"

"This is not about me," he spat.

"It is! And Father, and every other innocent suffering beneath the weight of the curse. Especially Father—he's alive, *Ach*."

Her use of the Hebrew word for brother twisted a knot in his gut.

"Abba is alive! I have seen him." Tzivia sounded like she was five years old again. "So, no. I will not stop. Not until I have freed him."

"At what cost, Tzi? Dr. Cathey is *dead*. How many more must die?"

"Shut up," she ground out. "Our friend has the photograph. Find out where it is and who is in it."

So that was her favor—make him unearth the clue and give it to her. "No."

"Do this, or I will expose him."

Ram stilled. Felt the cold wash of dread in his veins. "Tzivia—"

"You have connections and access. Find out—"

"No."

"Just tell me who is in the photograph—you've seen it before. It was in Dr. Cathey's office. On his mantel. For years."

His mind jogged through the dusty halls of his memory. He'd been in that flat a few times, but hadn't paid a lot of attention. Yet . . . somehow it was familiar. Somehow it loomed before his mental eye.

"Stop this, and nobody else will die."

"Except Abba!"

Ram flinched, realizing Mercy was once more at his side. Touching his arm.

"Two men in the picture," Tzivia insisted. "Dr. Cathey and someone else. I just need his name."

"No, Tziv—"

"I'll call you in two hours. Tell me his name, or I go to Nur."

When the line went dead, Ram roared. Reared and slammed the phone against the table. Again and again, rage bleeding through his restraint. Palms on the table, he clenched his eyes, breathing hard.

Cool hands touched his back.

What had happened to the sister he loved, the brat who'd annoyed the tar out of him but always somehow also made him proud? How could he keep Nur from winning and still survive this blasted curse and keep Tzivia and Abba alive?

No, he didn't care about Abba. He was a traitor. Tzivia had gone over the edge, but so had he. The entirety of life seemed to be imploding.

Soft, teasing fingers traced the arch of his back.

Annoyed, Ram straightened, shifted away from Mercy's touch. He looked at the broken phone. The cuts he'd inflicted on himself.

Mercy pried away the phone and blotted his cuts with a paper towel. She'd probably lecture him. Or tell him he'd done the right thing with his sister. But so help him, if she did—

"That burst of anger was nothing." Auburn hair hung in her face as she dabbed an antiseptic wipe along his palm. "Banner has you beat by a mile. You'll have to try harder if you want to win my affection."

He blew through the laugh that dared him to shed this dark mood. Instead, he noticed things he shouldn't. Like the dusting of freckles along her nose and cheeks that taunted him. Lips perpetually pink. Soft. He remembered how they tasted. How she tasted. How she felt in his arms. The way life fell away and it was just them. He ached for that. To have all this insanity gone and—

Ram drew his hand back. "Thanks."

His mind suddenly pitched to an image. Taking a photo years back with Tzivia in Dr. C's office. Could . . . was it possible they'd captured the professor's photo in the background?

He dug into his personal computer and skimmed through the gallery. Finally, he found the one he was thinking of from a Christmas event. Him and Tzi. Tox. He opened it. Maximized it. Zoomed. Breath trapped in his throat, he stared. Squinted past their likenesses to the framed photo on the mantel behind them. He muttered an oath.

"What?"

He tapped the screen. "That's the picture my sister is after."

Mercy learned forward, her hair spilling over her shoulder and whispering against his cheek. "Who's in it?"

"Dr. Cathey and one of my father's oldest friends, Lukas Gath." Settling into his chair and mindless of the cuts on his hand, he typed the name into the system and pulled up a number. He dialed using the sat phone.

"Hello?"

"*Shalom*," Ram greeted.

"*Gut Shabbes*, Ram," Lukas said with a smile in his voice. "It has been too long."

"Indeed," Ram replied. "You know why I'm calling?"

"With Joseph dead, I suspected it might be coming."

"My sister has a photograph, Lukas. Of you and the professor."

Silence ensued, then was punctuated by a sigh.

"Do you know why she thinks it's important? Why she's after you?"

"It is not me she is after. It is the scrollwork."

"Scrollwork."

"You have the photograph?"

Ram's gaze hit the computer screen again. "No, just a grainy picture of a picture. I can't make out much."

"Ah," Lukas said as he cleared his throat. "The photo was taken in my study. Behind us is a display made for the scrollwork of the Adama Herev."

Shock rolled through Ram. "Lukas, you're in danger. If—*when* she figures out who you are and what you have, she's coming. I do not believe she intends you harm, but she is blinded by this pursuit. And there are others. They'll be coming, too."

Another long sigh. "It has been coming for centuries, Ram. Neither you nor I can stop this. Not even the Camarilla, who are vastly more effective."

"I fear for them. I have a report that one is dead. If they reach you—"

"'He was very thirsty, he cried out to the Lord, "You have given your servant this great victory. Must I now die of thirst and fall into the hands of the uncircumcised?"'"

Ram hesitated. "Sorry?"

"That was Judges 15:18. 'Thirst, like newly-born infants, for pure milk for the soul, that by it you may grow up to salvation' First Peter 2:2."

Awareness swelled inside Ram of something bigger than himself. Something powerful. Something that quenched the anger flowing through him.

Lukas continued. "'Jesus answered and said unto her, Every one that drinketh of this water shall thirst again: but whosoever drinketh of the water that I shall give him shall never thirst; but the water that I shall give him shall become in him a well of water springing up unto eternal life.'"

"Lukas, this makes—"

"No sense?" He laughed. "Good. It should not—until the time is right. What many see as a curse is merely the drive for survival. I have suffered it for decades. So did your father, as you well know."

Lukas was talking in circles.

"The rage you feel is righteous. It is not a curse, but a force. A fire to rise against the tide of evil. Its time has come. Fear not the thirst of steel, Ram."

The admonishment cut the breath from him. As if Lukas had ripped open Ram's heart and read his soul between the blood and guts. The rage. The anger. "It's not a curse." He wasn't sure who he was trying to convince—himself or Lukas.

"Only if you let it be."

"The sword—"

The line went dead.

* * * *

Options had run out.

Tox held the photo, wishing he had a choice. Another choice. Any choice other than this one. *God, help me.* He needed Chiji's wisdom. Haven's reassurance. He'd never felt so despicable as right now. But he'd also never felt so depleted of options and hope.

Nur was growing suspicious. And though Tox had figured out that Nur wasn't the top dog—or that he perhaps shared the position with that other man—he'd been able to do nothing with that information since they'd sequestered him. A smart move for a man with enemies and great power, but a disaster for a covert operative needing to communicate with his handler.

If he did this, the hint he'd given Tzivia about his identity could be his end, especially if she'd put it together. Because if she believed it, Tzivia would use it as leverage with Nur. With the recent security breaches, Nur would give no berth to possible leaks or moles. He'd act swiftly and violently.

Which meant Tox would never again see Haven.

Yet he wasn't ready for the AFO to find another piece of the sword.

He bent forward, elbows on his knees, head cradled in his hands. Eyes closed, he prayed God would give him wisdom. Show him what to do. How to handle this. How to get back home.

An idea struck him. He tugged out the photo and scratched his thumb over the face of Dr. Cathey's friend.

Someone knocked on his door. Maybe Nur would hear him now.

Tox straightened, wincing at his bruised ribs as he scrolled the picture back up and returned it to the pen. Simmering in disbelief that he'd ever violate Tzivia's trust, he reminded himself that he was here to help her. Help the cause against the sword. But the pen felt like the dagger with which Brutus had betrayed Caesar.

He opened the door.

Yefim stood there with an expression that said Tox had taken too long to answer. "Nur wants you."

With a nod, Tox grabbed his keys and phone from the counter. A few deft swipes of the screen, and he joined Yefim, who led him out of the residence wing and through the foyer.

Realizing they were heading not to the office but to the conference room, Tox palmed his phone. Manipulated the buttons as Ram had taught him so it would start recording. Because he was really losing hope of getting out alive. Entering the conference room solidified that belief.

Around the black, glossy table were ten individuals, all of whom had mastered the glare of dominance and disgust. These were the people whose names he needed for his mission to end.

Nur watched Tox, his expression one of practiced disinterest, but behind those brown eyes lingered the anger of a man betrayed. "Kazimir, an accusation has been brought against you."

"Again?" Tox didn't mean to be belligerent, but it seemed the best defense for now. Where he expected chuckles or bemusement, he only found more disinterest.

Nur flicked his fingers, which sent Yefim to a small forechamber. When he reappeared, he wrangled someone before the great table.

Tzivia. She looked . . . crazed. The woman Tox had dated a couple of times was gone. In her place, this wild, frantic being. Hair normally in a ponytail or curled around her neck lay frizzy and unkempt. She glowered at him.

"What we have here, ladies and gentlemen," Nur said morosely, "are two failures. You recognize Tzivia Khalon, the one who feigned great love for her father." He scoffed. "It was a game. She has toyed with us—"

"Not true," she growled. "I have done everyth—"

"And this man I trusted as my personal guard, yet who was caught meeting with her privately." With a dramatic sigh and hum, Nur reclined in his chair. "What am I to believe but that they are conspiring against me?"

"Lovers?" a man suggested.

"How droll," a woman replied.

Tox said nothing. Seeing Tzivia broke his inclination to follow through with his plan. She was desperate to save her father. He'd do the same if they had Haven.

"I have something to say that will convince you I am determined to save my father's life," Tzivia said.

"Really?" Nur's thick eyebrow arched. "Go ahead—amuse us."

"This man is not who he says he is," Tzivia said, her words fast, frantic.

Though alarm and panic warred within, Tox forced himself to remain calm. To not give in to his thundering heart. His mind screamed to get out before they killed him.

Nur considered Tox before turning to Tzivia again. "Then who is he? A spy? A rogue operative?"

She licked her lips, deftly avoiding Tox's gaze. "He's a man I've worked with before, an American."

This time both of Nur's eyebrows rose. He frowned. Scowled at Tox.

Tox remained calm, realizing Tzivia had chosen the wrong tactic. What she failed to understand was that Nur had met and dined with Kazimir Rybakov before Tox assumed his identity and appearance.

"American." Nur's gaze proved penetrating, and Tox struggled not to shift beneath it. "What do you say about this, Mr. Rybakov?"

"I must apologize to the young woman," Tox said softly.

"Apologize?" a rotund woman barked. "What for?"

"She approached me in the alley a few nights ago, desperate for help. She said she'd planted a photograph on me."

Tzivia gasped.

"I didn't believe her." He shrugged. "I had no photograph—had last seen it when she was in London, as I told you, sir. Besides, it angered me that she followed me through the city and cornered me. Though I am now a widower, I still love my wife very much. It was inappropriate for her to approach me."

Nur was on his feet. Face dark and eyes narrowed, he strode to Tox. "This photograph—you found it?"

"I did." Tox lifted his phone from his pocket, then the pen. He looked at it hesitantly.

"You protect her?" the rotund woman scoffed.

Tox looked at her, playing his part. "Having lost my wife, I understand the rage that drives her to protect family." Rotating his phone, he sighed, then placed it in his pocket. Twisted open the cavity of the pen. Withdrew the photograph.

"No!" Tzivia screamed, lunging.

Taking the picture, Nur's eyes widened—barely. But then his left one twitched. "Why did you not give this to me immediately upon discovering it?"

Tox lowered his gaze, but only a little. "It was a mistake. I . . ." He huffed. "I worried for her, so I thought to help her."

"You were drawn in by her? Perhaps thought to—"

"Stop the needless suffering of an old man."

"Her father."

"Again"—he lifted his shoulder in a shrug—"a mistake."

"What about her accusation that you're an American operative?"

Tox stifled a smile and a laugh. "She wants her father. She herself has said she will do whatever it takes to free him. To her, I am a stranger—so there is no loss to her if I am killed."

"Mmm," Nur said with a nod.

"He's American," she growled. "His name is Tox Russell."

Nur's gaze snapped to Tox. Studied him with a keen understanding, a knowing. Brown eyes assessing, measuring. Concern laced the irises and creased his brow. His lips thinned, slightly narrowing his left eye again.

Tox grew worried Nur would see past the reconstructed nose, the widened jaw and darkened pigment. What would he do if the bluff was called? If anyone thought to run DNA on him?

"No defense?" Nur asked him.

Tox managed to look surprised. "I didn't think that accusation needed one," he said more calmly than he felt.

"What you fail to understand, Ms. Khalon," Nur said, "is that I am well aware of Mr. Russell. I know him—the blow he dealt my organization eighteen months ago when he killed my colleague and friend will never be forgotten." He tapped Tox's chest with the pen. "This man is all wrong. Face is wrong. Eyes are wrong. Height is wrong."

"He had surgery."

Someone belted out a laugh.

"To be fair," Tox said, touching the scars on his face, "I have had surgery, but . . . well, they did the best they could after the accident."

"He is right," Nur said to Tzivia with a laugh. "You will do anything to save your father." But his gaze drifted back to Tox, assessing once more. Wondering. And that—that was more dangerous than knowing. "The picture is scratched, making it impossible to tell who this is."

Tox's only chance of salvaging his betrayal. "Perhaps someone could reconstruct it," he suggested, knowing that would take time.

"Perhaps." As Nur rounded the table, he handed the photograph to Igor. "Have that looked into."

"I will kill you," Tzivia hissed between gritted teeth, straining against Yefim's hold. "If my father dies—"

"It is your own doing!" Nur injected. "Had you delivered the photograph when you arrived, we could have already determined who is in the picture and be well near the end, if not finished. But here we are—because of *you*."

"Tell him," Tox said, watching her. Challenging her. Game time was over. "About the picture. What you said to me."

Tzivia paled visibly. Her confidence and anger faltered. She shook her head at him.

"Tell me what?" Nur circled the black table with casual confidence. Fingertips on its surface, he waited to assume his chair.

Tzivia wrestled Yefim's grip, kicking. "How could you—"

The split second between her words and her fluid motion that leveled Yefim and had her throwing herself at Tox registered just in time for him to block the punch she threw. Catch the right hook. Which he shoved down and twisted behind her back as he simultaneously palmed her nape and forcefully pinned her to the ground.

Knee planted between her shoulder blades, Tox cursed himself. He'd pushed her. Though he'd had no choice, he wasn't proud. Having to defend himself, doing what it took to stay alive, had come at her expense. But this was a dangerous game. She'd been willing to expose him, which in turn would expose Haven. He couldn't—*wouldn't*—allow that. Ever.

"I thought you wanted your father safe," Tox hissed.

"Again you withhold things from me?" Nur said. "And you want me to believe Kazimir is the enemy?"

"You have no ide—"

"Tell me now, or your father breathes no more!"

Tzivia sucked in a breath. Flared her nostrils. Swallowed. "It's not the man," she muttered, her face pressed against the industrial gray carpet. "The scrollwork of the sword is in that picture."

# 41

— MOSCOW, RUSSIA —

He'd changed. Not simply in the way most people changed between years, but in a massive King Kong leap from one point to another. Especially since that call last night from his sister.

Mercy's heart squeezed tight as Ram grabbed his keys and phone. "You waited four hours for him yesterday," she said quietly.

Hazel-green irises hit her. "We had an arrangement—days missed equals another opportunity. I will wait again today. And tomorrow. However long it takes." He started for the door.

"He's in *trouble*," she said with a growl. "Why are you not doing more?"

"This isn't about you or what happened in Greece," he snapped, his face crimson, eyes ablaze. "This is about Tox. This mission is like walking a live wire! Espionage is not a hurried profession. You wait. And while you wait, you plan. I've never known a more capable operator than Tox. He will come when he can. And I will be there."

"What if he's being held or tortured? If it were me—"

"Augh!" Ram slammed both hands on the table. "This isn't about you!"

This moment, his anger, his railing, put her in mind of Bruce when he hulked out, channeling pure rage. And unlike the last time, unlike when she'd let Ram send her away, unlike her former simpering self, she would be there for him. She would be his Betty.

"Ram," she said even more quietly and stepped closer. When he swung around, she smiled. "He's lucky to have a friend like you."

His gaze met hers warily.

She focused on the golden glint that reminded her of honey. "He trusts you. Or he wouldn't have done this." She drew in a breath. "I should know that. I'll help. However I can. Do whatever I can."

"Just—" He clamped down on the rest of those words, then slumped marginally. "We have to watch for him in the feeds."

She nodded, surprised he'd leave her with his computers but relieved at the apparent trust he offered. "I can do that."

For several long seconds, he stayed there. "He didn't want to do this," he muttered. "He'd finally found a girl who loved him. They started a life together—she's pregnant now. He doesn't know. And if he doesn't come home . . ."

A new ache blossomed in her chest. She'd wanted that dream with Ram. Thought they'd have it. But she had to go slow, or he'd shut her out. Ship her off. Again.

Mercy framed his face with her hands. "He will. Because you'll bring him home." She knew that firsthand. "You always do." Brushing aside the dark, curly hair that fell across his brow, she couldn't help notice his reaction.

He came closer. His breathing went a little shallow. "Mercy . . ."

She stilled, lowering her hand as their eyes locked.

"You remember, don't you—"

"Yes."

"That Betty was poisoned by Banner's enemy. She died."

Confusion pulverized her hope. "Technically, she was cryogeni—"

He pressed a kiss to her lips. A fast one. Not for romance, for silence. "I'm not going to let you die because of me."

With that, he strode from the warehouse.

*Curse that man!*

He knew better—knew she wasn't the type to sit and be submissive and compliant. She had too many skills, too much fire in her blood. Okay, so she wasn't exactly Tzivia with her mad Krav Maga skills, or Black Widow with her complicated Russian background and training. But she was HackerGirl, and there weren't many places she couldn't go, thanks to the massively invasive World Wide Web and governments using naïve citizens' addiction to social media to spy. It gave her a peek into practically every kitchen, corporation, and restaurant across the globe.

She slid a sly glance at Ram's bank of computers. He really shouldn't have left her alone. Naïve citizen, indeed.

With a decent amount of glee, she tucked herself at his station. The screen twitched. Blanked out. It flickered once more, then a video played. Ram, shaking a finger. "Sorry, HackerGirl. Not this time."

Annoyance flared. "Challenge on." She bristled, eyes on the screen, fingers flying over the keys. First she disabled the internal camera, which she figured was tied to a program that threw up that video. In three . . . two . . . one, she bypassed it.

Mercy clicked her tongue. "Silly Mossad agent." Thinking he could outwit her.

Her phone rang. Absently, she glanced at the screen, thinking to ignore it. But she froze at the caller ID: *Answer Me.*

"Wha . . . ?" She reached for her phone, confused. Concerned. A little scared.

Then a bigger part of her rebelled at the command. With a sniff, she went back to work on his system. She planted a backdoor access program to save time on her next venture. With his tight-lipped way of working this mission, she was going to need that.

A few more minutes and she'd wormed into his surveillance package. Breath stolen at all the feeds, she sat back, staring, sorting. A cathedral. Outside the Kremlin. An office—she leaned in and snorted—Mattin Worldwide's lobby. How had he hidden that? And where? Several more cameras monitored the plaza where Tox had left the death mark, as she'd always called it, because to her it meant if she didn't get help, she'd be dead.

It must be killing Ram not to go in after Tox with guns blazing. There was too much at risk, she realized. His sister. His father. The AFO. Tox. "The fate of the world," she mused. "Just another day in the life of gorgeous Ram Khalon."

The screen to her left blipped. She ignored it, pulling up the plaza feeds and watching, waiting for Ram to show.

Scrolling text on the lefthand screen caught her attention. Another message: *No Mercy.*

"Pfft." She powered it off. "That's what you get for forgetting the comma, genius." The other monitor caught her attention.

Under the watchful eye of the camera, Ram strode past the fountain and into the small coffee shop. As always. Predictable—him with the coffee and that shop. She hoped his time wasn't wasted, that Tox would show and prove he was okay. Having his friend MIA bothered Ram a lot.

Sitting there, she noticed his inbox. Curiosity had always been a curse. Her middle name might as well have been Alice. But she shouldn't explore.

*Respect Ram*, she told herself. But her fingers had a mind of their own.

"No," she breathed. *Show him some respect.*

The left monitor blipped again. More words. This time, haunting ones.

*Our Silly Mossad Agent Shouldn't Have Trusted You.*

Her breath caught in her throat. Having her own muttered words spelled out there made her heart thud like a perfectly placed drone strike. Her mind registered too late that it wasn't Ram talking to her. In the feed, he hadn't been on his phone. So he probably hadn't sent the earlier message either.

Someone had gained access to his computer. Someone who wasn't her.

Remnants of the Greece mission came tumbling back like a hurricane. Ram. Ram was in trouble! *She* was in trouble. This location wasn't secure. She had to warn Ram.

*Get out. Get out before they catch you again. Bury you. Like last time.*

Things gathered, Mercy sprinted from the warehouse. Chin tucked, she scurried away. Headed into the city, warning and fear like fire in her chest.

A new panic thrummed through her veins. They'd seen *her*. Which meant they knew her identity. She moved fast as possible without actually running to reach the plaza so Ram could allay her fears. Reassure her she hadn't just destroyed her legacy, her ability as a covert operative.

"No," she snarled. She was not starting over again. She was not running. This—this was what superheroes did, right? Faced enemies. Faced terrors. Fought evil and tyranny.

*Call Iliescu.*

She should. It made sense to do that. A good operative would.

But not until she talked to Ram. There had to be an explanation for why the Mossad spied on their own operative. Because that was who'd sent that message, right? They'd called him "our Mossad agent." Would they do that—spy on him?

Of course they would. Just like the U.S. government spied on its own to protect its own. But Ram . . . he would've told her, wouldn't he?

*Maybe that's why he said not to mess with the system.*

Her steps slowed as the truth dawned. He *had* known. Ram, more than anyone else, knew the MO of the Mossad. Israel always faced real and catastrophic threats from its neighboring countries. It was surrounded by enemies. It wasn't a matter of trusting their agents but protecting their country.

She rounded the corner and scanned the plaza with its red cobbled courtyard, benches, and fountain, surrounded by multistory buildings that were older than her twenty-six years.

As she approached, Mercy had the paralyzing feeling that she was overreacting. That when she ran frantically up to Ram—and exposed him, which would go over real well—he'd chew her up. Spit her out.

Clutching her jacket collar to her throat, she paused and stared across the plaza at the café. Remembering the camera feeds, she glanced up. Which she shouldn't have done. Never acknowledge the invisible watching eyes. It tipped your hand. Revealed you knew they were there, when normal people were too oblivious, noses stuck in smartphones that were recording their facial expressions. She shuddered.

The café door swung open. Ram strode out.

Mercy blinked. *Already?* He'd only been there an hour. Hope leapt inside her. Tox must have contacted him! She surged forward, lifting a hand.

His gaze connected. Flashed with warning. He started away from her.

What? She stopped. What was he doing?

He tripped. Went to a knee.

She snorted. Clumsy oa—

Three men converged on him. Grabbed his arms. Hoisted him to his feet.

Somewhere in her numbed shock, she heard tires peal. A woman screamed as the trio dragged Ram toward a van that lurched to a stop. He hadn't tripped! He'd been shot with a drug dart!

Mercy gasped. Pushed forward, a scream lodged in her throat. But instinct, training, shoved her backward. Into the shadows of a shop. Brick digging into her shoulder blades.

*Phone. Get your phone.*

Stricken, she fumbled in her pocket, watching. She snapped a picture as the van sped by. It felt like she stood in stricken terror for hours. But when she finally hauled herself out of the adrenaline-induced reaction, she thumbed her phone. Dialed Iliescu.

Her phone beeped. No signal.

She tried again. Same. They must have jammed the cameras to shield the kidnapping.

A huddle of teens were laughing and talking, drawing her attention. One held a phone, and the others were gaping at it. Covering their mouths in bemusement. Pointing.

They'd seen it. Recorded Ram's kidnapping.

*I need that phone.*

Running straight out, knowing if anyone saw her, captured her likeness, she'd be as good as dead, Mercy barreled right into the teens, locked on one thing: the phone. The collision flicked the device out of the girl's hand. Mercy, still running, followed its trajectory and leapt at it.

Her finger grazed it. Shot it sideways into the street.

A delivery truck barreled past, its wheels flattening the phone with a sickening crunch.

"No!" she screamed, whipping her gaze back in the direction of the van. But it was out of sight. Ram was out of sight.

A flurry of Russian curses and shouts lobbed at her. Having their attention and anger aimed at her ignited a sea of panic. Escaping, Mercy zigzagged, across the street, avoiding camera angles. Hopping from one shadow to the next. Using cars to hide in places that would have exposed her. She checked her phone for a signal. Nothing.

She jogged on, legs aching. Lungs burning. About to surrender to the shadows and terror of seeing Ram kidnapped, she glanced around—and her gaze locked on the cathedral.

There was a camera there. Ram had the feed to it.

Which meant Mossad did, too.

* * * *

**— SAARC HEADQUARTERS, VIRGINIA —**

Haven could not shake the dread filling her as she sat at the black laminate conference table with Robbie, General Rodriguez, Iliescu, Tzaddik, and Chiji. She couldn't explain or shake the feeling, but somehow, being here without Cole—was that it?—an ominous haze shrouded her mind. Though SAARC had allowed the meeting, something hung in the air that they hadn't shared. Instead, they'd ushered her and Chiji into the room and asked them to wait.

Merry chatter carried through the hub as Cell, Thor, Runt, and Maangi sauntered in. They shared a look and hesitated in the doorway.

"Have a seat," Iliescu said, rubbing his jaw.

"This feels like a whole lotta messed up," Cell muttered as the men sat down.

Iliescu nodded. "Okay, let's get started. First—I'll be reading all of you in on a situation and black-ops mission." Steel glinted in his gaze as he met Haven's eyes, then Tzaddik's and Chiji's. "But what I say does not leave this room. Am I clear?"

Haven nodded, glancing at Tzaddik.

"Especially you," Iliescu said to the Timeless One. "Hear me?"

"I understand perfectly, Deputy Director. This is not my first battle or war-room conference."

Iliescu huffed, lifted his reading glasses, and flipped open a manila folder, from which he started reading. "Yesterday at 1657 hours Moscow time, Ram Khalon was forcibly removed from a plaza two blocks from the Kremlin." He dropped the folder and peered at them over his glasses. "At this time, details are slim, and there is no demand for ransom. In fact, there has been no communication with his captors."

Cell turned over a hand. "Then how do we know he was taken?"

Lips tight, Iliescu cocked his head. "Because Mercy Maddox witnessed the incident."

"What was he doing that he'd drawn enough attention to get nabbed?" Runt asked.

"Wait," Cell objected. "Why is Mercy over there?"

Iliescu considered each of them, but lingered on Haven, where his expression softened, and she knew things were about to be laid on the table.

"Oh man," Cell moaned. "This is about Tox."

As if someone had cranked the heat in the room, temperatures rose. Attitudes flailed.

"Hold up," Runt said. "You've been telling us—"

Iliescu raised a hand. "Six months ago, Ram made a request of the Agency at the behest of the Mossad for an operation that required a detailed, immersive mission. The intel provided all but guaranteed inroads to the upper echelon of the Arrow & Flame Order—names, connections, ranks." His face bore the weight of his unspoken words. "Things we had not been able to secure despite nearly a decade and a dedicated task force."

It hadn't been an easy decision for Cole—or her. Haven lowered her head, staring at her lap.

"So Ram went deep cover?" Maangi asked, his brow knotted.

"Negative," Runt said, eyeing Haven. "Tox." When she looked at him, he gave a grim, apologetic nod. "Tox went deep cover."

"Correct. After reconstructive surgery and an intensive months-long language-immersion program, Tox entered the very bowels of hell—Mattin Worldwide. A man in their security detail had a fatal accident, but with the cooperation of the Mossad and a few other international agencies which shall remain unnamed, we concealed his death. Altered Tox to look like this man, and sent him to work with scars."

"Dude, that *worked*?"

"Better than we hoped," Iliescu admitted. "A couple of months ago, Tox was promoted to personal head of security for Nur. The intel about Grazia Raison came from him."

Haven startled at that tidbit. It terrified her that Cole was so close to that man.

Someone hissed a curse.

"If it was so effective," Runt said with methodical precision, "why are you telling us now?"

"Several reasons." Iliescu swiped a hand over his upper lip. "As mentioned, Ram has gone missing. We aren't sure if that's Mossad's doing or Nur's people. We assume the latter. Mercy Maddox went over to integrate into Mattin," Iliescu explained. "We had her cover, and she got in without difficulty. But"—he shook his head—"Mossad identified her. Ordered Ram to yank her. From there, it's gone downhill."

Stomach squirming, Haven wrung her hands, desperate to hear good news. "What about Cole?"

It was the obvious question, and by the expression on the deputy director's face, one he'd hoped she wouldn't ask. "Unknown at this time." He started to look at her, then retracted his gaze. "He has not made contact in a couple of weeks. We have assets trying to get eyes on him, but as you can imagine, things are helter-skelter there."

"You have sent a lot of good people into the heart of the lion's den," Tzaddik said.

"We have," Rodriguez agreed. "It's what we do to protect the innocent."

"Your willingness to allow us"—Haven glanced at Chiji and Tzaddik—"to be here, then to read us in, makes sense now. But I think you all should know something that may help motivate you beyond the norm." She folded her hands on the table. Drew in a breath and let it out slowly. "I went with Cole to Israel, where he did his training, went through his surgeries. But we weren't going to be there and live contrary to our beliefs, so we married."

"Dude. I didn't get to be best man," Cell teased.

"Or worst," Thor threw in with a smile.

This team was as much a part of Cole as she and VVolt were. She appreciated their acceptance. "I stayed until it was time for him to deploy. I didn't know where, but I knew there would be little-to-no contact until he returned months later." Why was she so nervous to admit this? In a way, she felt like a teen who'd skipped classes. "I wanted him to know first, but . . . I'm pregnant." She cast a glance about the room, still jittery. "Cole doesn't know about the baby." Her chin trembled. "I want my child—*our* child to know his father."

"Don't worry," Thor said with a fierce nod that bespoke his allegiance to Cole. "We'll get him back."

"Agreed. In light of that, you should all see this." Iliescu nodded to the wall monitor, but then hesitated and considered Tzaddik. "You were good friends with Cathey."

"I was," Tzaddik said.

"Will this be too hard for you to see?"

"I have seen more deaths in my lifetime than you could imagine, Deputy Director." Tzaddik motioned to the wall. "Please go on."

Iliescu nodded. "This video footage was taken from security cameras in Dr. Cathey's place."

"We know who killed him?" Thor asked, fingertips pressed together.

"Negative. Watch."

Haven hugged herself as the grainy feed splashed over the screen. A man and woman entered the flat, their backs to the camera. The woman turned to the man, who hung near the door.

"Tzivia," Cell muttered.

Haven's heart ricocheted through her chest—that was Cole. She tried to steel her reaction, because she didn't know if saying anything would expose or compromise him. Her gaze skidded into Iliescu's, which held question, uncertainty. But then understanding slid through his expression, confirming the man on the video was Cole.

Tzivia and Cole walked the flat, rummaging through it. Iliescu fast-forwarded to when Dr. Cathey appeared.

"He's not happy she's there," Maangi noted.

"It's not every day you find a friend breaking into your home," Tzaddik noted.

Two more men showed up. Shots were fired, the muzzle flash painting streaks of white across the screen. Haven cupped a hand over her mouth, tears blurring her vision. Around her shoulders came strength in the form of a reassuring touch from Chiji. She steeled herself, locked onto Cole. Her pulse danced a wild cadence, frantic that she might actually see him killed. It was horrendous to see the sweet, godly Dr. Cathey die.

"Male number one has military experience," Runt noted.

Male number one. Cole. Haven swallowed.

Thor nodded. "Yeah, but it's more than that." He squinted. Frowned. And looked to be on the edge of epiphany.

Cell leaned forward, eyes wide. "Hold up!"

"The guy—that's Tox?" Thor pointed to the feed, looking at Haven, then the deputy director.

Iliescu clenched his jaw. "It seems Nur assigned him to monitor Tzivia, which worked in our favor."

"I can't believe Tox let the professor get popped," Cell muttered.

Maangi slapped the back of Cell's head.

"Ow! Hey, what—" His gaze hit Haven. "Oh. I'm sorry. I didn't—"

"I'm sure he did everything in his power to stop it," she said.

"He was in the hall taking care of the second tango when Dr. Cathey ate lead," Runt added.

"I know Cole respected and admired Dr. Cathey. I'm sure the professor's death weighs heavily on him," she said, her voice cracking. "I also know it probably tears at him that he couldn't prevent it."

"I ought to strangle you," Thor growled at Cell, "inflicting angst on Tox's *pregnant wife*."

"Tox'll take care of the punk when he gets back," Maangi added.

The elevator door dinged, and a man in slacks and button-down shirt jogged toward the deputy director. "Sir. I was told to bring this to you immediately."

Iliescu took a file and flipped it open. His gaze darted back and forth over whatever lay within, then he huffed a laugh. "Mercy . . ."

Cell grinned. "What'd she find?"

"Apparently, the virus she planted in Mattin's system went active, allowing her a back door." He strode to a computer, typed, then looked at the screen. "She found this photograph scanned into their system." He cocked his head. "It may be the very one Tzivia broke into Cathey's apartment for."

"You mean the one that got Dr. Cathey killed," Cell said. "Call it like it is. She got her own mentor killed."

Arms folded, Iliescu considered them. "Moving on to item three for this briefing. Wallace has made a significant discovery. The team knows this already, but for your benefit, Ms. Cortes—Mrs. Russell, I'll repeat that with the help of Ms. Maddox, Agent Wallace discovered TAFFIP *was* collecting DNA. The two were attacked one night while working on the systems," Iliescu recounted. "One suspect was killed, two escaped, another captured and bled for intel. He's loyal to his cause, but he's also scared spitless, which will crack him eventually. However, analysts have finally determined that people with certain markers in their DNA are the ones being targeted by the AFO."

"Markers?" Runt asked. "And by targeted, you mean being boiled alive."

Iliescu ignored him. "Analysis is still preliminary, but the markers are connected to nationality."

"Race?" Haven breathed, startled.

Another nod from Iliescu. "In particular, Jews. Wallace confirmed those already killed with these arrows are all Jewish."

"Wait, you mean this is like advanced Hitler stuff?" Cell said with a snort. "Isn't that a little . . ."

"Evil?" Tzaddik supplied.

"I was going to say *Hollywood*. Or maybe *conspiracy theory*," Cell said.

"Wait." Runt ran a hand over his mouth, thinking. "I'm not seeing the connection between the Soup Maker and Goliath's sword."

"Yeah," Cell said. "Y'all did say it was his, right? Like, medieval?"

"Correct—Iron Age," Tzaddik pronounced firmly, his gray eyes sparking. "The Niph'al crafted the sword, gifted it to Gulat. The then-shepherd boy David kept the sword."

"The sword vanishes from the Bible," Chiji noted. "It is last recorded that the priest took and wrapped it, keeping it behind the ephod."

"You are right. First Samuel mentions that. And yes, it was there," Tzaddik agreed, "for a time."

He was so maddening! Despite his older, handsome features, there was a ferocity about him that dared anyone to challenge him. "You know what happened to it," Haven noted.

"What I know is that it has been fought over for centuries. Then, in the time of the brother-knights, the Adama Herev was dismantled into three pieces and sent across the world to keep it from being destroyed or used again." Tzaddik roughed his hands together. "The Nizari Ismaili—Nur—would have this sword reassembled in the hopes of finding a cure."

"Okay," Runt said, expression heavy with the revelations tossed out in this meeting—and Haven could relate. "You dropped the bombs on us. What are we going to do about it?"

"Act," Iliescu said definitively. "We're mobilizing Wraith."

"Hooah!" Cell barked.

"Acting on the intel provided by Raison, we're putting together a snatch-and-grab mission for Lukas Gath. You'll head to Lakenheath, then deploy from there. Also, you're escorting the civvies," he said, nodding to Haven, Chiji, and Tzaddik, "to Cathey's London flat so they can hunt down an artifact."

"Ladies," Thor grumbled, "Wraith is on the hunt!"

# 42

## — OUTSIDE MADONA, LATVIA —

*Thwump-thwump-thwump.*

The rotor noise grated on Tzivia's nerves as she sat across from the traitor. It would be easier to call him Kazimir. To believe him a stranger. The wound would not have gone so deep then.

But it was Tox. A friend. A man she considered like a brother. Or *was* he really Cole Russell? He'd never outright said he was.

His basic frame—shoulders, torso, neck, and head shape—seemed right. But the nose. The eyes. The fact that he'd turned on her. Tox would *never* have done that.

No way this could be Tox.

*Everyone betrays me in the end*. She had always felt a casual comfortableness around Tox. It was why she'd tried dating him. But he was too loyal to his codes and honor for her tastes. She needed someone who responded. As Omar had. The ache worsened, knowing that each day that went by increased the likelihood of never seeing him again.

She pushed her gaze to the pretty Latvian landscape of rolling hills, rivers, and glass-like lakes. Tranquil, unlike her thoughts about Tox. She hated him for the many wrongs he'd done her, but the betrayals flew both ways in these muddled skies. If it was him. She wasn't completely sure.

"Radio jamming," the pilot called through the comms. "Going to have to set down well outside the compound."

Tzivia perked up, sliding closer to the jump seat where Nur's soldiers straddled steel and thin air. The location was supposed to be simple, innocuous. But now that they were here, they saw a thick wall surrounding a small wood-frame home.

"Smart," someone said in Russian. "Boulders and vegetation on the wall disguised it from satellite imaging, made it look like the rest of the area."

"Anyone been out here?" Kazimir asked. "Actually put boots on ground?"

"Negative," Igor replied. "This location wasn't in our files. Lukas has always been secretive."

"So this could be a trap," Kazimir suggested.

Igor snorted. "He doesn't even know we're coming."

Right. A chopper barreling at a compound an hour outside any city, and the owner didn't hear or see it? The descent unsettled something in Tzivia's stomach—and not her food. A general unease slithered over her, eyeing the walled-in compound protecting what seemed to be a nondescript home. A very ordinary, small home at that.

The helo touched down a mile outside the compound, forcing them to hoof it the rest of the way to the iron front gate.

"Need to blast it?" someone asked.

"Why?" Kazimir nodded to it. "It's not locked." His gaze swung to Igor, then Tzivia. "I think he wants us to come in. Which probably means it's a trap."

"He is an old man. Probably forgot to lock it," Yefim said.

"If you believe that," Kazimir said, "you go through first."

Tzivia strode toward the home, away from the men, caring about only one thing: getting that scrollwork. Maybe that was why this guy had walled in his one-story home. Fifty paces separated the gate from the first step of the screened-in front porch.

"Hey, *ostanovis*!" Igor barked.

No, she wasn't stopping. Wouldn't stop till this was over and she had won her father's freedom.

When a hand clamped down on her shoulder, Tzivia spun. Drove a fist at Igor's face, which he narrowly avoided—but only because she pulled it. "Go in, or I will," she hissed at him.

Eyes sparking, he snapped a gloved hand forward. "Alexei, Lyosha. Check it out."

Murmurs of complaint rose, but the two men moved forward, weapons warily held up, unsure they'd need them but too scared not to have them ready. As they pushed past it, the iron gate squawked, the noise echoing across the valley, which was hemmed in on all sides by hill or mountain. *Protected*, Tzivia thought.

"Watch for mines," Yefim warned.

"Right," Kazimir muttered as he joined Tzivia, "because Gath wants to blow himself up each time he returns home." He pointed to the hard-packed ruts in the ground that stopped at the porch. "The only tracks are those." He motioned right and left. "No others. Safe to say he isn't blowing up his guests."

Good enough. Tzivia stalked toward the house, unyielding, despite warnings from Igor. To her right, she felt a presence. Knew it was Kazimir. Tox. She needed to call it like it was. She half expected him to say something, apologize for passing her off as crazy in front of the AFO. But no. He just kept walking. Just stayed close.

Less than a dozen paces separated them from the wooden steps to the screened-in porch. Instinctively, Tzivia stopped—and so did Kazimir. Tox. Toximir.

"He's not going to kill us," he muttered.

"How do you know?"

"He's had ten minutes to do it and hasn't. He wants us in there." He indicated the house. "Let's find out why." Stalking forward, he scanned the jamb, probably to insure there weren't any wires that would send them sailing into the afterlife. He opened the screen door, his boots thudding heavily on the boards as he went for the half-glass door that led into the house.

Tzivia waited just inside the porch. Pulse thrumming. It felt wrong. And yet right. "What if he's not alive?"

Tox glanced over his shoulder. "Then I guess he won't answer."

"No. I meant—" She huffed, eyeing the others who skirted the house and cleared it, some going to the rear, but most circling back to the front. "Never mind."

Toximir rapped on the door. "Mr. Gath?"

Creaking ensued and sent shivers up her spine, and the door squeaked open in a way straight out of a horror movie. Tox stepped back, his posture taut and confident. Fingers twitching, probably for a weapon. The stunt Tzivia had pulled in Moscow had weakened his credibility with Nur, and the decision had been made for only Igor's team to have weapons. She was finding it difficult to feel sorry.

"Rybakov, *ostanovis*," Igor called, his boots pounding up the steps. He squeezed past Tzivia with five of his men.

Toximir allowed the others to take point, annoyance playing across his scarred face. And there—right there, she saw Tox. Yet *Tox* wasn't scarred. Regardless, this man was used to leading, not being a lackey. And she hated him for it. Hated him for turning on her.

"You okay?" His voice was quiet as he drew alongside her.

Spearing him with an angry glare did little to loosen the knot of tension in her chest as Igor pushed open the door. "Fine," she bit out, following the others.

She stepped into the dim setting. A living area. Very well kept, but simple. Small. Classical music drifted down a hall on her left.

Yefim and Igor headed that way.

Tzivia stiffened as the notes registered. "Oh no," she choked out. "Chopin's 'Funeral March.'"

# 43

## — OUTSIDE MADONA, LATVIA —

Something in the air shifted. A scent or texture—something.

Tox hesitated. Noted several things in that split second. The inches-thick jambs boxing in the small hall on two sides—one that led to the living room, the other to a back room. The different creaks of the floor as they walked side by side. Yefim's steps were heavy, pounding. His steps, which should be the same, came more as a groan. Which meant the subfloor was different. The smell here in the passage—clear, cool, and not like the musty space when they'd entered. Grunts in the yard, which sounded too much like men getting taken out. The first hint of confusion in the rear room. And last, the *click-whoosh*.

Lunging, he simultaneously snagged the KA-BAR from Igor's belt and snapped around. Grabbed Tzivia. Hauled her against the wall seconds before steel doors slammed down on both sides, trapping them alone in the minipassage. Powder room on the left. Wall on the right.

"What the heck?" Tzivia breathed, shoving him back.

From the other side of the steel came distant shouts as the team banged on the barrier. The floor shifted. Vibrated.

Then lowered.

Tzivia threw her hands out for balance as they descended. "It was a trap."

"Think I might've said that." Not quite convinced they were in danger, though this situation sucked, Tox tried not to cringe at the light falling away into darkness and a cool, sterilized breeze wafting across his face. He hit the shoulder lamp on his tac vest.

Light bloomed down a lonely, dark corridor. "Crap," he said, his mind vaulting back to the tunnel that had nearly buried him alive.

"Always tunnels," Tzivia mumbled, her voice shaky. She had also been nearly buried alive in an explosion at an excavation.

Tox grunted. "Let's just hope we don't find Tzaddik at the end of this one."

* * * *

**— MOSCOW, RUSSIA —**

Darkness pervaded his vision as Ram woke. He blinked, trying to clear the black from his eyes, but nothing changed. *Where am I?* His head felt like a two-ton boulder, aching and swimming as if he were underwater.

Memories crashed through him of sitting in the café. Noticing a man hovering at the door. Skating his gaze to the plaza, where four more men in black suits waited, all with military bearing. Knowing he'd been blown. Knowing if he stayed, the chances increased that Mercy would show. He wasn't going to put her in danger again, so he'd walked out. Sensed the trail he'd picked up, like the wake of a motorboat. Felt the prick in his neck.

Why was he abducted? Where was he? He pushed off the ground and straightened—and his head collided with something, pain exploding through his skull. He ducked, realizing he'd hit a wall. He palmed it, panicking when he found it cold and damp. Were they holding him in the same place they held his father? Below the cathedral?

Steps crunched closer and closer, though he could see nothing. A scraping, then the sound of scratching stone sliding closer. "Eat," a disembodied voice demanded. The steps receded.

"What do you want with me?" Ram called, his voice bouncing back, taunting.

Darkness held him hostage.

* * * *

— OUTSIDE MADONA, LATVIA —

Light fractured the dark tunnel, and Toximir advanced, the glint of metal paralleling his forearm.

"Where'd you get that?" Tzivia asked, hunkering behind him as they moved.

"Igor loaned it to me," he said.

She huffed. "Why couldn't you snag something useful, like the Kalashnikov?"

"Because they're crap," he muttered.

She breathed a laugh around the thick tension as they advanced slowly, a step at a time, the shoulder lamp only giving a peek at the next five feet. Over his shoulder, she saw a looming wall. "Uh . . ."

He shouldered left—more darkness.

"I really hate this," she whispered. "And you."

"You said that once."

"Nine-hundred-ninety-nine to go."

He sidestepped forward. A subtle click stopped them. *Whoosh!*

Light flooded the tunnel as the wall to their left leapt aside. They both whipped toward it, wincing at the searing flash.

Tzivia lifted her arm to shield her eyes. "Wha—"

"Welcome, Mr. Russell and Ms. Khalon. Please, come in."

# 44

## — OUTSIDE MADONA, LATVIA —

Firming his grip on the knife, Tox crossed the threshold, disbelieving what lay past it. Immaculate and modern, a large living area with television and computer monitors blurred into a monochromatic palette of whites and grays. The entire length of the far east wall boasted tall kitchen cabinets and an industrial stove. Several doors banked off the main area, which stood empty and sterile.

"What the—"

Tox swung a hand to stop Tzivia, but the emergence of a man with a beard, wearing a brown tunic and a smile, stilled him. He hefted the knife again.

"I am not your enemy, Mr. Russell." The man pointed to the ceiling. "The men up there are. But you know that, don't you? The changes to your appearance haven't dulled your instincts."

"So it *is* you."

Ignoring Tzivia's hissed words, Tox studied the man. "Are you Lukas Gath?" This man knew too much, and that could be the death of them.

Their host smiled, held out his hands. "You came for Lukas Gath, right?"

Tzivia stepped past Tox.

"Wait," Tox snapped, but she pressed forward.

"You know why we're here," she said, glancing around the living arrangements.

Something akin to grief filled Lukas Gath's bearded face. In another time and place, he'd be likened to a gypsy or flower child. There was an ethereal quality to him, a way he moved, that was unsettling.

"Give it to us," she demanded.

"My child," Gath said as a whistle screeched from the kitchen—a teakettle. "The last time I spoke to your father, he mentioned your . . . impetuous nature." A weak smile twitched his dark beard. "He was proud, yet concerned for your future." He glided to the stove, where he lifted the kettle. Poured steaming water into a mug, which he lifted, along with his eyebrows, to Tox. "And you, Mr. Russell."

Tox snorted. "You knew my father?"

"No," Gath said, blowing across the cup. "Your girlfriend."

"Haven?" Tzivia's voice squeaked.

"No, not his wife," Gath laughed. "His girlfriend—once, a long time ago."

"Brooke," Tox breathed.

Gath's thick, dark eyebrows pushed up beneath his shaggy, shoulder-length hair. "Mm, quite."

"Wait—what?" Tzivia snapped around to Tox with wide, shocked eyes. "*Wife?* You married Haven?"

Strangely disoriented by this man, Tox shifted his weight and swallowed. There was something . . . familiar. Like that tenuous, just out of reach déjà vu that plagued him sometimes. "What about Brooke?"

"No," Gath said, moving to the white sofa, where he sat on the low seating.

"No?" Tox thumbed the tactile grip of the knife, frowning.

Gath slurped his tea noisily. "No, that's not our purpose, talking about Brooke, though she is not what you thought, and I would have you own that knowledge. Brooke was many things, but a traitor she was not. She was a good woman, fighting for those she loved and making sacrifices none would understand. Well, not any of you." He lifted a finger. "Our purpose here is you and your forebears, Mr. Russell."

"Actually, I think our purpose is the scrollwork," Tzivia growled.

"Wait," Tox said, slicing a hand at Tzivia. "You can't expect me to leave what you said about Brooke at that. Not after . . ."

Gath's gaze softened marginally and he nodded. "It is a burden you need not bear. You are not responsible for her death. Look elsewhere for someone whose shoulders carry that guilt." He lifted his palms. "I can say no m—"

"You have the scrollwork of the Adama Herev," Tzivia said, surging forward. "You knew my father, and you need to help me save him."

His sharp eyes locked onto Tzivia.

Unsettled by the eerie sense he'd seen those eyes before—or that look, or whatever—Tox didn't like it. "Why'd you bring us down here? I'd ask how"—he let his gaze trace the ceiling, noticing joists and hinges in odd places—"but I have a feeling you'll be as cryptic about that as you are about Brooke and everything else."

"Quite right, Mr. Russell," Gath said, coming to his feet.

Tzivia's ire flared. "The sword—"

Gath flung a searing glare that silenced and pushed her back a step. Then she finally seemed to understand what Tox had as soon as they entered the underground complex. Their host wasn't just an AFO asset. He wasn't just a traitor. He was far . . . more.

He languidly approached.

Everything in Tox constricted, itching to pull away. But no. This . . . this was what Gath wanted. *Me*. But why?

Placid, sanguine eyes held his. Gath reached out a lanky hand and grasped Tox's shoulder. Brutal and ironlike, the grip sunk into his flesh. Something spiked through Tox, and he went still.

Eyes crinkling beneath an aged smile, Gath said, "He would be proud."

"Who?"

"Giraude."

Drawing back did nothing to help Tox put distance between that name and this moment. "What . . . ?"

"You have searched, have you not? Tzaddik told you to, yes?"

"Haven has," Tox admitted, confused. "But how—"

Understanding rippled through Gath's expression. "You haven't found it. You haven't found the connection between you, the sword, Giraude . . ."

"I'm not sure what I'm looking for."

"When you find it, you'll know."

"Sorry, but we're here for the sword," Tzivia bit out. "The men upstairs will bring your house down if you don't—"

Gath spun. "A threat, Ms. Khalon?" He surged toward her. "You dare threaten me in my own home?"

"N-no," she said, leaning away. "I only—"

Something in Tox reared up, not liking the way Gath confronted her, but he held the instinct, the urge to defend her.

Gath's expression enlivened. "Those men can do nothing to me. Bring my house down?" He scoffed. "I think not. In fact, I would venture that they are fleeing the grounds even as we speak."

Those words held too much meaning to be frivolous. Tox tensed. "What'd you do to them?"

"Perhaps you should return to the elevator and find out."

"The sword," Tzivia persisted, her defiance rising. "I saw the bronze scrollwork in a picture of you and Dr. Cathey."

"You are thick, aren't you?" Gath snorted at her. "It's not here, child. Run and play your war games. The sword will not be known"—his gaze swung to Tox—"until the time is right."

At those familiar, haunting words, Tox stilled. They'd been among the last words Dr. Cathey had spoken. Being with this man was as bad, if not worse, than Tzaddik. "We should go."

"Hm, it might be too late for the elevator." Gath moved to the wall and swiped a palm over it. A panel receded. He punched a keypad. "Go!"

The floor vibrating under his feet, Tox heard something behind him and pivoted. A wall had vanished, and in its place, a new opening gaped. A new tunnel. He started for it with Tzivia.

"At the right time."

* * * *

**— MOSCOW, RUSSIA —**

Weakness saturated his limbs. Muscles stiff and painful, Ram grimaced as he rolled onto his back. Stared at the nothingness that ate his vision. Why did he hurt so much? He'd had his last infusion less than a week ago. He shouldn't be in pain.

*Maybe I'm growing immune.*

It happened to some who battled the strain, their body developing an immunity to the steroids and clotting agents. But advancements in medicine had nearly eliminated that possibility. This shouldn't be . . .

He had to get his mind on Tzivia. On the battle for the sword. Had to stop her. He didn't want his father to die, but neither was he convinced that his father was worth anyone dying for. It was awful, but he couldn't let go of the one suspicion that had haunted him for years. One overheard conversation before his father walked out into the night.

Cranking echoed through the chamber.

Dim light greedily strangled the shadows. It stretched, strained to reach him, and ushered in three men.

"What do you want with me?" Ram growled, dragging himself—so weak—against the wall behind him. Propped himself up. "What'd you do to me?"

"Nothing," came the monotone voice of Nur Abidaoud.

"You," Ram growled and lunged to his feet, tripping. This . . . this was wrong. Why was he off balance?

"You know the incubation time for the strain, yes?"

Ram leaned heavily on the wall. Looked at the men wearily. Of course he knew its incubation period. His biceps ached. Pressing his thumb into the muscle felt good in a raw, agonizing way. Like a chiropractor's adjustment.

"If you don't have the infusions regularly, you grow weak." Nur angled his head. "I would not press too hard, Ram. You would not want that to bruise."

Ram stilled. He'd had his infusion. "I'll be fine."

"Will you?" Nur swept back his slick hair. "Oh, that's right. You believe that because you recently gave yourself the regular infusion. The one you keep in that safe in the black—no, navy blue pouch."

How did he know that? Nobody knew. Ram had hidden it. But panic squirmed through him at the insinuation. "What'd you do?"

"Me?" Nur scoffed. "I did nothing." He laughed. "Igor, on the other hand, might have exchanged your infusion vials for"—he shrugged—"simple saline?"

No. Ram struggled to breathe. "That's not—"

"Possible?" Nur jutted his jaw toward Ram. "Your arm is already bruising."

Though he didn't want to play into the man's hand, Ram glanced down. His gut tightened when he saw blood had risen to the epidermis where he'd pressed his thumb. Thought of the weakness he felt. The bruising Mercy had noticed. He was in trouble.

"It's a painful way to go, Ram." Nur paced, rubbing a finger below his lower lip. "I've seen grown men shriek like newborn babes as their insides hemorrhaged. A brutal, excruciating way to die, drowning in your own blood because your body no longer has the ability to clot, to heal itself."

This couldn't be happening. Panic swirled through Ram and he slowly—carefully—lowered himself to the ground.

Nur narrowed his eyes, and his lips thinned. "You've been trying to stop your sister from saving not only your father but thousands of men who, without the cure the sword will bring, live in fear every day that their bodies might reject the infusion or simply stop working. Our line nearly died out thousands of years ago, Ram. The curse has plagued us—"

"It's not a *curse*."

"Are you sure? Shall we test your theory?" Nur lifted a finger.

The mountain of flesh behind him came forward and unlocked the cage. The look on his face betrayed his intent, his orders.

Ram knew what was coming and staggered back to his feet. He thought about throwing himself at the burly man, but the weakness, the trembling muscles warned he'd only injure himself. "Nur." He tried to sound strong. Threatening. "Don't do this."

"Those very words are the ones I would have you hear yourself, Ram." Nur nodded to the mountain. "I fear you will not abandon this path against the sword. I take no pleasure in doing this to you. It's a slow, cruel death."

A meaty fist drove into Ram's gut. He doubled. Panic exploded through him, imagining the veins in his stomach breaking and seeping blood into his system.

When the mountain reared back, Ram hurled himself into the man's gut. It knocked the man back a step, but that was it.

Fists pummeled Ram's sides and ribs. He cried out, his knees buckling at the pain. He thought to fight. Knife-hand to the throat. To the groin. But his limbs hung defiant. Exhausted. With each blow, he lost another measure of hope. Of strength.

The fist reared back again.

"Not the head," Nur commanded.

A left hook nailed Ram's right abdomen.

"Augh!" White-hot pain ruptured his ability to think, to stand. He fell against the wall. Slid to his knees. To his hip. Tasted blood.

When the mountain retreated, Ram wanted to lunge at the gate. Instead, he was owned by a failing body.

Blood trickled down his temple as the man faded to shadow. Closed the iron gate. Locked it.

"Remember this pain," Nur said. "Thousands will have this fate if you forget the way, if you abandon your kin. The Nizari Ismailis will defeat the curse. We will break the curse, but the only way is with the sword. You will understand."

Darkness swallowed Ram once more, clamping him into its oppressive embrace until all he heard was the hollow knock of death.

# THE SOUL FOUND PASSAGE THROUGH THE SPOUTING VEINS

"Brother—behind you!"

Giraude rounded in time to see a Saracen barreling toward him from the side. Searing steel sang through the air, slicing as Giraude parried and blocked. His blade connected hard with the man's gut. Though exhaustion rimmed his eyes and blood coated his clothes, the Saracen persisted.

Yet Giraude persisted more. His wife and child made him unrelenting, forced him to remember what he fought for. Who he must return to. It surprised him that he had left those he most loved under the protection of a man he once called enemy. The journey had taught him to weigh not the skin, not the oath one took, but the heart one possessed.

The savage Saracen shouted to his god and once more tried to sever Giraude's life. Their swords clanged hard. Giraude swung up and around, breaking the man's grip. The Saracen's long blade flew from his hand and thudded to the earth behind him.

Face twisted with fury, the Saracen screamed and produced a dagger. That would be his end. Not the blade, but the anger. He was a fool to come at Giraude in this set of mind. And against a man whose strength was not the sword but strategy.

The blade drove forward. Another foolish maneuver.

Giraude caught the Saracen's wrist. Snapped his other hand against the man's throat, then gripped his nape. Drove him down and around, dropping him to his knees, all the while still holding his dagger hand. With an arm stretched up along his spine, the Saracen howled in pain.

Giraude freed him of the dagger.

"You are a fool." Spittle foamed at the corners of his mouth and black beard.

"Am I?" Giraude firmed his hold on the man's dagger.

"You think he is your friend." He laughed. Dark. Maniacal. "He is your enemy. Even now he rapes and murders your wife."

The words dug through the haze of adrenaline and rage. Giraude slowed. Froze. Matin. With a swipe of the blade, Giraude delivered the Saracen of his life. He spun. Raced for his destrier, panic driving him back to the tribe. Back to Shatira.

"Brother!" he shouted as he mounted. "They are in danger!"

Thefarie yanked around. Eyes ablaze. White mantle splotched with the blood of their enemies. "Go!"

The hours-long ride seemed to take days. Giraude stopped only to water his horse before barreling on. Ameus rode with him, his own silence mirroring Giraude's rage.

Shatira. No. No, it could not happen.

Matin would not. He had lived with them. Laughed with them. Protected them. Killed the Saracen who tried to steal Giraude's life.

As daylight surrendered to the specter of night, smoke billowed in the distance. Giraude drew up his mount, heart in his throat.

The three oaks. Bright with fire and smoke.

"No," he whispered, disbelieving. Horrified. "No!" He drove his heels into his mount and tore across the half league to the encampment.

Bodies lay strewn on the ground like trash tossed aside. Giraude navigated the dead, noting too well the Saracens moving through the tents, still murdering. Screams spiraled through the smoke-laden sky. Tents whooshed to the ground, surrendering to the flames and stirring dust and ash.

Giraude rode hard to his tent. His destrier shifted sideways as he launched from the saddle to the ground. He landed hard but came up running. "Shatira!"

"She's not there!"

Pivoting, Giraude caught sight of Yitshak propped against a tree, badly wounded. Bleeding heavily. His hooded eyes held Giraude's.

"*Where?*" Giraude demanded. "Where is my wife?"

"South!" Yitshak growled, pointing in the direction of the holy city. "She fled."

"Avr—"

"She has him. But"—blood spurted between Yitshak's lips as he coughed—"Matin has gone after her."

"I—I will return for you."

Giraude took to his mount, angry he could not stay with his father-in-law, see to his wounds or see him into the arms of God. He rode with the fury of a sandstorm, barreling down on the man he saw in the distance.

Matin kept a steady pace, not riding as if his life depended on it. A mistake that promised Giraude a blood price. Beyond Matin in the haze of the early evening, Shatira ran. Her dress and head covering fluttered. Her small frame making quick work of her trek to safety. But she was not quick enough. The Saracen would catch her. Take her. Kill her.

Giraude spurred his destrier. Heavy snorts huffed in time with the hooves of the mighty beast as he gained on the Saracen. "Traitor!" he roared.

For the first time, Matin glanced back. Slowed. Then his horse reared and shot forward.

No. Giraude could not let him run her down like a wounded animal. He would not.

Matin raised a bow and arrow.

Giraude's breath caught, staggered through his lungs as he looked at his wife. At the woman he loved. "*No!*"

The arrow flew with intent and accuracy. True and fast. Straight into Shatira's back. She jolted forward. Toppled to the ground.

Howling, Giraude rammed his boots into the destrier's flanks. The beast screamed and vaulted forward.

Matin continued toward Shatira, raising yet another arrow. Would he kill her a second time? But then Giraude saw movement. A small mound.

"Avram," he breathed, the pounding of hooves matching his heartbeat. Wailing, his son pushed off the ground to sit beside his dead mother. Confused. Terrified. The sound proved an anchor to Giraude's soul.

Matin closed in.

Giraude was not near enough to reach him. He had but a blade. So with all the rage and strength his Lord had given him, he sent his sword spiraling tip over hilt at the Saracen.

Steel found its target with a meaty thud. Flipped the Saracen from the horse. Pinned him to the earth into which he had spilled blood.

Though the sword hit Matin, it had yet to stop him. The Saracen reached for a dagger. Hefted it.

Giraude barreled past him. Swung down and snatched his shrieking son from the ground. Startled and terrified, Avram flung out his arms, his screams suspended for a terrified moment. Then he let loose with more outrage. Giraude clutched him to his chest.

Ameus thundered up to him.

"Take him," Giraude said, handing Avram to his brother-knight. "Get him to safety. They will kill him if he's found."

"Matin has the Adama Herev."

Giraude met his brother-knight's gaze, then spun, panic writhing through his chest. He pivoted and saw Matin hoist a blade and struggle to his feet.

"Go!" Ameus ordered.

Drawing out his dagger and shiv, Giraude dismounted. He sprinted toward the Saracen. Knocked him to the ground.

Matin lost his grip. The cursed sword flipped out of reach.

"Betrayer!" Giraude cried. "I called you friend."

Propped up, Matin sneered. "Then you are a bigger fool than I believed." He spit a stream of blood to the side. "I had but to wait for you to leave. It was too easy."

"So easy you failed." Giraude tightened his hand around the dagger's hilt, anxious to drive it into the Saracen. "Why?" He had only to make the man work hard to stay alive, an effort that would bleed him out.

White teeth stained red, Matin struggled. He glanced to the side. At the sword.

"Do not!" Giraude warned.

But the Saracen lunged.

So did Giraude. Instinct wielded his knife at the enemy's outstretched arm. The collision of steel and bone resonated through the blade.

With a scream of pain, Matin threw himself back. Cradled his arm to his chest. Growled at Giraude.

"*Why?*" Giraude demanded again.

"Because you are *Dawiyya*. She of Daoud—I needed her blood to free my people from the curse!"

"That will never happen."

"She is dead and her father with her. Their line is—"

"My son is not, and he carries her blood."

Disgust writhed through Matin. "I will find him. And I will kill him," he growled. "I will—"

Rage found release as Giraude fell on the Saracen with his blade.

Fire exploded through his gut. He realized, too late, that the Saracen had produced a second dagger. Shoved it through the side of Giraude's armor and into his flesh. Straight up. Into his lungs.

He pulled in a searing breath. Giraude would not die with this man alive. Shiv in hand, he drove it into Matin's neck.

They slumped in mutual defeat, and Giraude pulled in a ragged breath. Grabbed the Saracen's tunic. Shook him. "*You were my friend!*"

Matin blinked. Then blinked no more as he fell back against the earth. Lifeless eyes stared at the moon.

Arms weak from blood loss, Giraude fought to push himself up. Instead, he collapsed. Propped on an elbow, he looked toward his beloved. Staggered to his feet. Stumbled. Tripped. Pushed himself to Shatira. Dropped at her side. Pulled her into his arms.

"Shatira," he choked, tears and the approach of death stinging. "Forgive me." He placed a hand on her womb, where another child had begun and died. Head on her breast, he battled for air. It would be over soon. He would . . . "I'm coming, my love."

He breathed—tried to. There was naught but pain. He lay beside her but could not bring himself to lay his head down and welcome the coldness. The emptiness.

"Giraude!"

He lifted his eyes. "The sword," he choked out, pointing.

Ameus charged across the field and seized the Adama Herev. At last they could put an end to this cursed weapon.

The babe was still in Ameus's arms. Dark hair. Blue eyes. Confused. Distraught. Strong.

*Avram, my son, I would like to have known you.*

# 45

**— MOSCOW, RUSSIA —**

Mercy could endure a lot, but not being alone. Maybe it was seeing Ram snatched in broad daylight that wore on her. Or the fear that those who'd taken him would come for her next.

She glanced at the doors. Visually traced the locks. Deadbolted. Windows—secured. Roof vents. Then back to the system monitor that had no cameras. No way to communicate haunting messages like his computers—whose pieces lay spread across the floor. She was using a rudimentary system that would block most hacks but also limited her capabilities. Which might be what was driving her nuts.

Car doors thudding outside stabbed her awareness. Mercy slapped the laptop shut. Hugging it to her chest, she stood, wishing she could see through steel walls. With a pounding heart, she abandoned the laptop and scurried up to the wall by the door and slammed her back against it. Ear to the wall, she listened over her staccato heartbeat.

The alarm would go off. They'd run in fear.

*Bang! Bang! Bang!*

Each pound on the door struck Mercy's courage. Then—unbelievably—the locks disengaged. What? She stepped back as the door flung open. Three men carted in another and deposited him on the bed she'd just vacated in the corner.

Stunned, she stood there, staring. Gaping.

"What is this?" a burly man growled, bending over the disassembled computers. "No wonder we're blind. Where is she?" He straightened and looked around, his gaze colliding with hers. Anger shot through his features. "You did this?"

"If you had a name, I might consider answering that."

"Mercy Maddox."

She smirked around her hammering pulse. "I think that's *my* name. Did you need to borrow it?" God help her, but men like this brought out the worst in her.

He huffed. Stalked toward her. Thrust something at her.

She yelped, catching it, only then registering whom they had laid on the bed. "Ram!"

His face was swollen and bruised. Limbs coated with black and blue marks.

The bearded, dark-eyed man pointed at the padded black case he'd tossed at her. "He needs infusions every two hours, starting at"—he looked at his watch—"1400."

"What'd you do to him?" she railed, lunging. "Why? How dare you—"

He shoved her back. Pinned her to the wall. "*I* didn't do this. We lost two men getting Ram out."

Her mind whirred. The only people who could get Ram out who weren't Americans were the Mossad. This had to be Omar Kastan. "Why? Why'd they take him?"

Omar checked over his shoulder, watching Ram. "The wrong people wanted to make a point to him." He sneered, his breath hot against her face. He snagged the pouch from her hands. Held it in her face, shaking it so she heard the tinkling of glass. "One vial. Every two hours."

She scowled. "I'm not giving him anything you—"

"You don't—he dies." His dark eyes narrowed. "And that will be on you, and I will be angry. And *you* will pay." Heated anger shadowed his features. "Got me?"

"You can't expect me to just stick a needle in his neck and inject him with something—"

"Not his neck. His thigh." He released her with a shove that bounced her head off the wall. "Every two hours, or his death is on your head, and we all come after you."

With his threat hanging in the stale air, Omar and his men stalked out of the small warehouse, leaving Mercy with an unconscious Ram and a pouch. She opened it—syringes and vials. She held up one of the vials and eyed the milky white solution it contained.

A moan lured her attention away. "Ram?" She went to his side, only then seeing the extent of his injuries. What had the AFO done? Beat him all day long? It seemed every inch of him was covered in bruises and cuts. Reddish-purple bruises. Near-black welts.

A strangled yelp writhed in her throat and pushed Mercy to her knees, grieved. Worried. She laid a hand over his, squeezing.

He moaned again, and his head rolled toward her.

"Ram? Can you hear me?"

Drawing in a breath, he seemed to hear, though he didn't open his eyes. A minute snuck by before he shifted a leg. Clenched his eyes in pain. Stiffened. Pulled his hand from her touch and pressed it to a spot above his right pelvis.

"Ram, can you hear me?" she repeated. "Please—if you can—"

"Yeah," he moaned, not opening his eyes. "Tox."

Beat to a pulp, and he asked about Tox. "Don't worry about him. You have to get better."

"I'll b—" He shuddered through a breath. ". . . okay."

Time fell off the clock, and his body pulled him back into unconsciousness to help him recuperate.

Mercy stood and retrieved her phone. First, she set reminders for the injections, and then she called the deputy director.

* * * *

## — LAKENHEATH AFB, SUFFOLK, ENGLAND —

Two days after the briefing, Wraith gathered in the hangar at Lakenheath, awaiting instructions. Leif stretched out his legs and leaned back against his rucksack. He glanced around at Wraith and the civvies, all chilling.

"I thought we were doing something," Cell complained.

"Besides getting R&R in a different country," Thor threw in.

Maangi shifted his hat over his eyes. "Might as well catch some Z's while we can."

Geared up for the last eighteen hours, they still had no "Go" order.

This was a solid team. Leif appreciated their resolve and determination. The grit they operated with. Also the camaraderie that cemented who they were as a team. It reminded him of days long gone.

Haven and Chiji were sitting in the only chairs left. She heaved a sigh. "We could've already gone in and been back," she said. "Not that I'm anxious to root around in his home. It feels wrong."

"But it is necessary," Chiji said. "If only to rule out whether or not the bust is there."

"Or if it's a *bust*," Cell mumbled from where he lay on a folding table, boots on the edge. He rolled his head to look at them. "What's so important about it anyway?"

"We're not sure," Haven admitted. "Just that it needs to be found."

"Gather up, ladies," the stern voice of General Rodriguez reverberated through the hangar amid the screech of an F-15E landing.

"What's the holdup, General?" Leif rolled off the wall and sauntered over.

"There's activity in the area—right on top of our objective."

"An attack?"

"That was our initial assessment, but there's been no indication of weapons' fire or explosions—until we attempted to send a drone. They took it down, so whatever's happening up there, they don't want anyone seeing."

"Which means it's probably not good," Leif said.

The general nodded. "So we're putting you into this mountain range that circles the dwelling." He held out a sheet of paper with a satellite photo. "We'll drop you on this side, and you'll scale into position. Get eyes on what's going on."

"Kind of interesting that someone else shows up on a guy with AFO connections purported to be a turncoat." Runt glanced at the image. "Think the AFO took out the drone?"

"No way to know," Rodriguez said. "AFO don't wear a uniform or stick to one nationality. But"—he nodded—"that's our guess at this time."

"ROE?" Thor asked, taking the picture.

"For now, no body count. Get eyes on that place and tell us what's happening."

# 46

### — OUTSIDE MADONA, LATVIA —

"Albatross, Wraith in position," Thor subvocalized as he nestled between rocks and thick-bladed grass on the mountain overlooking a large valley where a lone compound existed in peace. Until today.

"Copy, Wraith," the droning voice of Rodriguez replied. "Stay low and recon."

"Roger," Thor answered.

Leif used binoculars to peer down at the valley floor, where two large vehicles huddled near a chopper. A foot-thick wall enclosed the home, but in the space between it and the house stood a group of people. He homed in on the man who stood about six feet and adjusted the nocs for clarity and grunted. "That's some nose job."

"Unbelievable," muttered Cell from his left, long-range nocs pressed to his face. "This is some kinda messed up, seeing Tox all beak-nosed and crap."

"How long have y'all known Tox?" Leif asked.

"Dude, I don't like your tone."

"Easy, Three," Thor muttered. "It was just a question."

"That wasn't a question," Cell argued. "He's looking through nocs and sees Actual embedded with the enemy and gets to wondering if it's legit. If he's been turned."

"I've seen bigger men turned faster." Leif didn't like the way the enemy combatants were grouping up on Tox. No trust there.

"Well, that's Actual, so you better shut your pie hole, because that man? They don't make soldiers like him any—whoa! Hold up. There's hottie."

Tzivia Khalon emerged from the house, dragging a hand over her mouth and then up over her head and ponytail. Silence clapped through the crisp afternoon as the team monitored the action below.

"Albatross, confirm visual on Secondary Objective," Thor radioed the plane circling at thirty-something thousand feet above them.

Tzivia joined Tox, but by the way the small army circled them . . . "Seems things aren't going so well for Actual," Leif said.

"Roger that," Maangi said. "Unfriendlies seem worried."

"They should be," Cell growled. "Actual will gut them!"

"Wraith, we count eleven tangos on property," Rodriguez said through the comms, "but thermals show another nine to your eleven."

Eleven? Only mountains there. Leif swung his nocs that direction and scanned the vegetation for disparity, movement. A swath of black glared back at him. Whoever was holed up, they weren't even trying to hide, using black gear. Brazen. "This is Wraith One, confirm visual on unidentifieds." He visually trekked their gear, weapons, and shoulders for insignia, but like Wraith, they wore none. "Negative on ID." They did, however, wear ferocity and intent. They weren't here to monitor.

"Guess these guys to be black ops," Maangi said. "Middle Eastern."

"No," Leif said quietly. "Israeli special operators."

"How would you know that?" Cell growled.

"I know," Leif insisted, lowering the binoculars and meeting Cell's gaze. "I think they're here for the same reason we are."

"Should we attempt to communicate with Actual?" Thor asked into the comms.

"Might compromise our position," Leif said.

"Agreed," Maangi said. "Can't without giving ourselves away."

"Dude." Cell snorted. "I thought that was the point of coming—giving away, ya know . . . bullets. Wounds. Holes in the head." He shrugged. "I mean, let's not be stingy."

* * * *

"Look," Tox bit out in Russian to the armed men pressing in on him, "how many times do you want me to repeat this?"

"As many times as it takes for me to believe it." Igor glowered at him. "You seriously expect me to take that report to Nur?"

Tox shrugged. "I'll take it myself."

"Your funeral," someone taunted.

"Give it to me again," Igor demanded.

Tox sighed. Looked at Tzivia. "Lukas Gath lives in a bunker below-ground. He intentionally separated us from you so we could talk privately."

"And he gave you no information about the sword?"

"None," Tzivia said, frustration coating her words. "He was . . . infuriating!"

Glad she had answered, Tox looked at the tunnel they'd exited when leaving the bunker. Yefim and the others had searched it but only found a twenty-square-foot area. No opening to a living area like Tox and Tzivia described. Baffled, they'd started a perimeter search for another way into the underground compound, but after two hours had found nothing.

A piercing glare hit his eye, and Tox angled away from the source, blinking.

"Mr. Abidaoud will think you had something to do with this, that you wanted or helped this to happen." Igor stepped into Tox's personal space. "You knew Gath would bring up those walls."

"If I recall, you insisted on taking lead," Tox countered.

The light again stabbed his vision. Annoyed, Tox shifted. What was that? He peered past his upheld hand, glancing around the walled compound. But it had vanished.

"So you know nothing," Igor spat. "We came out here for nothing. No sword. No information."

On the contrary—they had information, but Tox wasn't sure what it meant. "Gath said the piece wasn't here."

"And you believed him?" Igor sneered. "You simpleton! He told you that so you'd leave."

Yefim returned from his search, shaking his head with a dour expression. "Nothing."

"Inside," Igor barked. "Find the mechanism and get us down there."

"Again?" Tzivia complained. "We searched for the last hour!"

"And we'll search for another, unless *you* want to explain about this. Mr. Abidaoud's already prepared to separate that pretty head from your body."

Light like a laser blinded Tox again. He grunted and looked away, shielding his eyes, but first he took a second to register the location. High. Past the compound. He pushed his attention in the general direction of the source. The mountains? He'd expected it to be a windshield or metal reflection, but up there?

Another flare flickered from the mountain at his two o'clock.

*What the . . . ?*

"Move!" Yefim shoved Tox, spinning him toward the house.

*Someone's in the hills.* On that ridge overlooking the valley. Who? Who was up there? Someone who wanted him to notice them. But didn't shoot at him.

Mossad. Or Wraith. Dare he hope?

"Kazimir?" Tzivia's voice was soft, pliant. "You okay?"

"Fine." he said, guiding her to the front door. A prismed glare struck the wood. Stepping aside, he let Yefim take the lead, using the moment to press three fingers against the door, then two. Hoping the guys saw. Hoping they understood his signal.

# 47

— OUTSIDE MADONA, LATVIA —

"Was that a hand signal?" Cell said with a laugh. "Did the chief just give us a hand signal?"

Thor nodded. "He wants us to hold position, stay out of sight."

"In other words," Maangi said, "probably no more mirror glares."

"What about our eleven o'clock?" Leif asked. "Any movement there? I can't find them." Why hadn't someone watched the Israelis?

Thor shifted his gaze in that direction. Sighed. "Nothing we can do. They're too far away."

Leif grunted. "Let's hope it stays that way, or we have a boatload of trouble on our hands."

* * * *

— MOSCOW, RUSSIA —

"I don't think I can take it anymore," Mercy said into the phone.

Recovery had been surprisingly quick since Mossad had delivered Ram. But she feared he was running mostly on pure willpower. He could walk, though he moved like an elephant trying to navigate Red Square when it was crowded. And yet still he sat at the café, staring at the fountain. Sipping water or a latte or nothing. Just sat. For hours.

And that took every vestige of strength. Were it not for the injections, it would've been too much.

Mercy had harped about how he needed to rest, but he'd argued, said what he needed was to find Tox.

"Well, I need you to put aside your feelings for Ram," Iliescu said. "There's a very big game happening Thursday, and our team is already out there, so we need him in the game."

"I hear you, but he's not the same."

"We just need him there. He'll figure it out."

"I'm not sure, Dru."

"He will. Just—"

Keys jiggled in the lock.

"Gotta go." Mercy ended the call and turned.

Stiffly, he entered the warehouse, left arm tight against his side. He'd favored that since returning from wherever it was Mossad found him.

She didn't dare ask if Tox had shown because his dejected demeanor answered that. But she was desperate to talk to him. To hear his voice. To cheer him up. She hated it. Hated not knowing. Hated his ambivalence about his condition. Coming to her feet as he stepped in, Mercy also hated how he acted like she didn't exist. Granted, he'd done that for years—but they hadn't been in the same room.

Wind gusted in and shoved his hair into his face.

"You could use a haircut," she said all-too-cheerily, thumbs hooked in her back pockets.

Ram strode to his computer, which he'd ordered her to reassemble. He pecked on the keyboard, shedding his coat with one hand, which elicited a few painful grunts.

"Still henpecking, huh?" she said, forcing a laugh.

He snatched off his beanie and pitched it toward the bed, but it landed on the floor.

She stared at it, realizing how much everything about them mirrored that tossed-aside beanie. She picked it up and rubbed it between her fingers, glad to have him back, safe. Yet she didn't like the Ram who'd returned. He was different. Broody. A thousand times more introspective than the man she'd fallen in love with.

*What do I do? How do I pull him back?*

"Mercy." Her name was a warm whisper that skated along her neck.

She snapped her head up to find Ram at her side. Close. Very, very close. There was a look in his eyes. She stilled when his hand came to the small of her back, sending darts of fire up her spine and coiling around her heart.

"I need your help."

"Okay," she said. At least, she thought she did. She wasn't sure, because he didn't move, and neither did she. It worried her. That different something was even more different right now. It confused her. Scared her.

"I need you to give me a haircut."

Mercy blinked. Laughed. Then she paused. "Seriously?"

A tremor of a smile tugged his lips. Then he took the beanie from her. "You're good with scissors."

"I'm good with coding and keyboards. Maybe with a crochet hook, but I'm not a stylist."

"Please."

No. No, he was too . . . soft. Too nice. Too— *This isn't right!* It was like he was someone else. Or someone had taken over his body.

He trudged to a box, set aside the beanie. He paused, fingers on the crocheted piece, eyeing it. Then he turned back to the box and dug inside it, metal banging against metal as he did. He returned with a pair of scissors. Handed them to her.

This made abso-freakin'-lutely no sense. "And I'm not supposed to stab these through your heart?"

"Preferably not," he said with a wry smile.

Staring at the stainless-steel shears, she let her thoughts ricochet through potential purposes. Why would he ask her to do this? Sure, he needed the cut, but in his appearance, he'd always been a bit conservative with a side of Bohemian. It was that quiet, irrepressible spirit that was a perfect counter to her borderline eccentric one.

"One condition," Mercy said, having no idea why she was even agreeing. "Tell me what they did to you."

He lowered his gaze. Caught her hand and tugged her toward the folding chair, where he sat.

Standing over him, she realized he hadn't agreed to her condition. Then again, he hadn't argued either. "I think they usually cut *wet* hair."

Holding his side, he pushed to his feet, strode to the bathroom, and shed his shirt, then dunked his head in the sink. It took everything in Mercy not to rail at the map of bruises laid out across his olive skin, racing up his spine and side. They weren't angry red but had aged to a purplish blue. Some a sick green. It turned her stomach.

*Just look at the muscles, not the bruises.*

"Like that would help," she muttered under her breath. She'd always been weak when it came to Banner's corded muscles. Ram wasn't bulked up, but he was sculpted.

Curly, dripping hair hung around his face and shoulders as he resumed his seat, showing off not only his toned pecs but also the mural of tissue damage.

*Hair, Mercy, hair.* She cleared her throat. "How short?"

"Very." He gave a firm nod. Touched his temple. "As close as you can get it. A little longer on the top, maybe."

"Remember?" she said, pointing to herself. "Not a stylist." She looked at his wavy-curly hair. She'd always liked his hair. "You sure?"

Another firm nod.

With a breath for courage, she slid her fingers into his hair and aimed the scissors. She tried not to cry or realize how close she had to lean in to be an accomplice to this crime. "Start talking," she said, far too aware of his proximity, "or I leave you with half a head of hair."

With a *shink* of the blades, the first section fell away. She watched it, feeling like it was a piece of him, not just his hair.

"They taught me a lesson," he said quietly.

She swallowed, surprised that he was actually telling her. "What lesson?"

"You know the strain." Was his voice husky?

Another section cut. She shook her head, forcing herself to keep cutting. "I can't believe I'm doing this," she whispered, avoiding his beautiful eyes as she angled the scissors.

"I feel free already." He held her gaze, mere inches from his, capturing her attention for a few long seconds. "Keep going."

She diverted her gaze back to his hair, noting how dark the strands were against her pale skin. "You, too."

"The bruises might seem like I was beaten for days. I wasn't. Only at the end. It's the Matin Strain. It's a terrible curse."

She hesitated, scissors half through a chunk of hair. "You don't believe that—you always told me it was a disorder."

"And yet," he said with a sigh, "I have the strain. A *curse* that, when not managed through drugs, will leave me vulnerable to hemorrhaging. Painful damage to my tissues. My blood unable to clot."

"And the vials Omar gave me help, right?"

"Yes."

"You told me about the strain, but you would never say more than that." She shook out her hand, flicking off the black hair. "How long have you had it?"

"All my life," he said quietly. "It's ancient. It is said the Nizari Ismailis have sought a cure since the days of King David, when it was placed on our line. A way to free us, to make it possible for us to have children without the strain. For centuries, our line dwindled until the early 1900s, when the infusions were designed. The strain so similarly parallels hemophilia that scientists within the Order applied the advancements in medicine to our cause. It worked. Very well. We've grown in number in the last century, but the battle is every day. Every injection."

"But you take the infusions. How—"

"They switched my vials."

Mercy paused, looking at him. Her heart thudded, realizing there was something . . . not right. Something missing in this story he told. "Why would they do that?"

"*. . . they wanted to make a point to him,*" Omar had said.

"To weaken me, to make me feel the full effects of the strain, remind me why I should not be fighting against them but with them."

As his words settled in, so did a virulent dread. Mercy drew back. Considered his marred stomach and side. Then his eyes.

Startled by what she saw there, she had an epiphany about what was missing from his words, from this story. Hatred. Anger. Why wasn't he angry about what they'd done to him?

"You done?" he asked.

She twitched and snipped off a few more spots, not thrilled with her handiwork. "It's not far from a hackjob, so if you hate it, blame yourself." She tossed the scissors on the table. "But you don't look like a shaggy dog anymore."

He ran a hand over his head. "Better." He nodded. "Thanks."

"Ram," she said, pulling in a breath as he came to his feet and stood practically nose to nose with her. She traced his ridged brow. The sparked eyes. The olive complexion and stubble. "What happened?"

"I just told you."

"No," she whispered. "You—"

His arm slid around her waist and tugged her close.

Sucking in a breath, Mercy tensed, despite the fiery sensations of her betraying body. "Ra—" She choked on his name, so pleased at his touch, so scared at what she guessed of his plan.

"It's okay," he whispered, angling closer.

It was? She looked at him, startled to find his gaze on her mouth. She couldn't breathe. Couldn't understand what was happening. "You're different."

He smirked. "What you always wanted."

"No, this is—"

He caught her mouth with his and pulled her against his chest. Splinters of attraction slipped past her concern. Melted her ability to wonder about his urgency. His hands slid up her back, crushing her against himself. The warmth of his skin on hers. His touch. His strength.

The kiss went from zero to sixty in a second flat. Mercy curled into him, savoring it. Savoring him. He deepened the kiss, nudging her backward.

Passion alive, arms around his neck, Mercy had the distinct awareness of him aiming her toward the bed. Her heart thudded wildly. Panic and excitement beat against each other as he lowered her to the mattress. Caught her hand. Extended it over her head.

"Ram," she murmured, hating herself for not stopping him. For wanting this, liking that he was stretched over her. He kissed her neck and the line of her throat up to her ear, tickling and teasing. He'd never been willing to go here before. That he was now—

*Clink.*

Ram slowed the kiss. Brought his hands to her sides. He lifted his mouth from hers.

Her brain emerged from the dense fog—alerted her to the pressure around her wrist.

He pushed off her, his knee digging into the mattress. Met her gaze with a smoldering one. His face was flushed. His lips red. He kissed her again, this one long and slow. Kissed her jaw. "Sorry, Mercy," he said, his breath hot against her ear, sending electricity through her. "I have to do this." And he stood.

Blinking, swallowing, feeling the rawness of her lips, she looked at him.

He grabbed a shirt. Threaded his arms through it, determination carved into his rugged features.

"What . . . ?" Mercy sat up—but her arm yanked backward. She cried out and glanced at the metal pipe that ran down the wall behind the mattress. Found her wrist handcuffed to it. She yanked at it. "Ram. What?" She whipped back around to find him lifting a bag and his jacket. "Ram!"

Head down, he strode out of the warehouse. Out of her view. Her life.

Again.

# 48

## — OUTSIDE MADONA, LATVIA —

Tzivia could not tell what had happened, but when Tox stepped through the door, he had a confidence that hadn't been there a moment ago. Nerves frayed, she considered those inside the home. Igor was still huddled with Yefim and another man, their Russian flying so fast, she barely caught a few words. But what she heard made her worry.

Towering beside her, Tox watched as well.

She skated her gaze to the other soldiers. "They want to blow it," she mumbled.

"Let them."

She snapped her eyes to his.

His expression hardened. "Where does my help come from?"

She scowled. That . . . was a Bible verse, right? Hadn't Dr. Cathey said it dozens of times? But how did it end? Where does my help come from? It comes from . . . the hills. Hills? What?

*No, who.*

Through the sheer curtains and past the cement wall, she eyed the sloping ridgeline. The spine was hidden because of the home's limited view. Was someone up there? Who?

Who else would bolster Tox's confidence? His team.

"No," she hissed.

He frowned.

"If they screw this up and my father dies—"

"Your father isn't who he says he is," Tox growled.

Confusion raked her. "What do you mean?"

Tox glanced around. "It's taken too long, Tzivia. If they haven't killed him already, then—"

"He's been beaten and tortured!"

"And yet no broken bones, no internal bleeding."

"What are you saying? That he's doing this to himself? To me?" She shoved him backward with a growl. "How dare you!"

Tox stumbled, whacking his head on a clock that hung on the wall. He grimaced and cupped his head. Scowling at it, he stilled. Straightened.

"What're you doing?" She eyed the carved wooden clock with a great bird atop it. Inside, barely visible, the figures of a man and maiden— "The clock." There'd been one—

"What about it?" barked Igor as he stomped toward them.

Tox shifted behind the man and gave the slightest shake of his head.

"I—nothing," she said. "I just noticed it has the wrong time."

Igor growled. "Find the opening, or your father dies!"

Tzivia had grown numb to their threats, but it still made her pulse race. A little. "If Abidaoud kills my father, I stop looking. Will he risk that?"

"We are two days from Elah," Igor said with a shrug. "I think it's too late already." He put the phone to his ear, then tensed as the person on the other end answered. Soon, he nodded. "Nothing." His gaze struck Tzivia.

A bolt of adrenaline erased her numbness. Tzivia lifted her chin, unable to breathe.

"I think we have trouble," Tox said in a calm but clear voice.

Igor turned as shots erupted outside. Amid the chaos that arose in the house, men darting to the windows to steal glances outside, Tzivia noticed one thing: Tox. He hadn't been taken off guard. Hadn't been surprised.

He'd anticipated it.

* * * *

It wasn't that he'd anticipated. He'd just *known*. Crazy, but when you've been in combat and seen evil work its wiles in men, a soldier had a sense for things.

Okay, that and the Morse code sent via light flashes that warned of a rogue element. That *element* must've seen their communication and chosen to engage. When he saw the first of Nur's perimeter guards eat lead, Tox knew.

He shifted to Tzivia, her gaze skipping around the room and landing on his with panic. "Tzi—"

"No!" She gripped his forearm and held tight, terror rimming her brown eyes. "Wraith can't do this. My fa—"

"Not my guys," he whispered, pulling her aside and positioning himself to face the door. He monitored the entrance. Waiting, expecting bullets to pepper the wall so sunlight could poke into the room.

"What trouble?" Yefim asked, glancing back at them with suspicion.

"You idiot," Igor called. "Get away from the—"

*Crack!*

The curtain fluttered. Yefim stumbled back.

In the split second the man had been shot, Tox spun toward Tzivia, feeling the splat of warm blood as he did. He curled around her, pushing her to the floor in a crouch.

"Shooter on the ridge!" someone shouted outside.

Tox didn't know who was firing, but they weren't his guys. And that worried him, because he could be a target just like the rest. "Stay down," he hissed into her ear, checking his six. Twelve. Then the door.

Hands pawed at him. "Get up, you dog! This is your doing."

Tox was thrown forward by a forceful shove. Two guards leapt in, wrangling his arms. "What're you doing?" he demanded. "There's a sniper—"

"Yes," Igor growled. "And you're going to be my shield getting out of here."

Planting his foot, Tox wheeled. Drove his elbow back.

A rifle butt flew at his head. Nailed his temple. The explosion of pain slowed his thinking, muddied his response. Made him stumble.

"Wait," he groused, holding a hand to his temple. "I—I don't know who's shooting. If they—"

"Either way," Igor said, "I don't lose. If they're not yours, you die first. If they are, they let you live."

"You don't want to do that," Tzivia said. "You need To—Kazimir alive."

"Do we?" Igor mused, arching an eyebrow. "Why's that?"

In that second, Tox knew what she was going to do. "No." His heart thudded. "Tzivia."

"He knows where the sword piece is."

"I don't," he growled, wondering if there was any piece of Tzivia Khalon left that had a conscience.

"The clock!" she said quickly.

Igor hesitated. Looked at the elaborate timepiece on the wall. "What about it?"

"There's one just like in Dr. Cathey's house."

"So?"

"I . . . I don't know," Tzivia conceded, then indicated Tox. "But he does."

"Shooting stopped," one of the guards called. "Incoming chopper!"

When Igor's phone dinged, he glanced at the screen. Grunted. "The boss is here."

Nur. This just couldn't get any worse. Tox glowered at Tzivia, before he was shoved toward the door, his back needled with a muzzle.

"Let's go." Igor guided him out the porch, then down the steps, all while making good on his promise to use Tox as a shield.

Dirt and rocks crunched beneath his boots as they forced him into the fading afternoon light. A weight knocked into him—Tzivia. She'd been pushed. Caught his arm for balance.

"I'm surprised you haven't killed one of them yet," Tox gritted.

"I'd love to, but they have my father."

But did they?

A chopper swung in across the skyline, racing fast and hard ahead of another slower, larger helicopter. The distinctive coaxial rotor system helped Tox identify the first bird as the Kamov Ka-50 "Black Shark."

The single-seater Russian attack chopper swooped across the valley floor, a comparatively quiet bird compared to the Mil Mi-8 bringing up the rear.

*Oh no. No no no.*

Tox stopped. Didn't care about the crack against his skull. Locked onto that helo. Prayed that what he expected to happen wouldn't. *God, please—*

The Black Shark fired a cannon at the mountain where Wraith had been holed up. Another quickly followed. Then another.

Frozen in horror, Tox could do nothing in the several heartbeats that crashed against his ribs as the incendiary rounds pummeled the mountain. The very spot from which the mirrored messages had been telegraphed. The same spot where Wraith lay in wait.

*Boom!*

He sucked in a breath as fire and black smoke shot into the sky.

*Boom! Boom!*

His knees buckled as the green hillside became an inferno. "No," he whispered. No way could anyone survive that.

Exultant shouts went up from Nur's men. Tox stared hard, begging for a glint. A glimmer. Any sign that his men hadn't just been blown up. His limbs took on the weight of those lives, the hopes, the dreams, the loves, the losses. He couldn't move. Couldn't think. Couldn't—

They'd moved. They'd seen the chopper and taken off running. Right?

*Please. God.*

Those were the best men he'd ever known. Men in love with their lives as protectors of innocents, of their families.

Cell. Thor. Runt. Maangi.

He was going to be sick.

"Kazimir!" Tzivia pointed to something.

He shifted, glanced back—wind and dust swirled in a vortex of agitated elements stirred up by the landing Russian Mi-8. Dirt peppered his eyes and face. He turned to shield himself—

A fist came at him.

He tensed but had no time to protect his face. The punch landed. Connected. Spun him to the side. His legs, still heavy with the adrenaline of watching his team die, went rubbery. He landed on a knee. Touched the ground to catch himself. It took only a second to clear his head. Let the deaths of his men be the ignition source.

Grief-fueled anger shoved him upward. Awareness flared—five muzzles aimed at him. He stifled his response. Lifted his hands. Eyes connected with the man who had punched him.

Nur Abidaoud wiped his bloody hand with a cloth. "You have a hard head, Mr. Rybakov." His expression morphed to a sneer. "Or should I say, Mr. Russell?"

# 49

## — OUTSIDE MADONA, LATVIA —

"Did you seriously think we didn't know?" Nur complained.

After months of mission success and with the end in sight, Tox had failed two days before the final confrontation. His gaze hit the still-burning mountain, praying his ineptitude hadn't cost his men their lives.

"You are both fools to think we would be so easily cowed by your machinations," Nur said.

"I told you he wasn't Rybakov," Tzivia growled, "but you wouldn't listen!"

"It's interesting how flimsy loyalty is to Americans."

"Just as flimsy as those working for you," Tox said, but the shame was his own. He had tried to work the deals to keep them both protected, provide just enough information to throw off suspicion but not endanger either of them.

"What was your goal?" Nur asked with a smirk. "To kill me?" He shook his head. "No, had that been your objective, you would've tried long before now."

Tox shifted his gaze to the Mi-8, where a man hopped out and yanked another, older man out of the bird. The second man stumbled, collapsing to his knees. He cried out. With a fierce scowl, the first hauled him up, spinning him around.

Tox tensed. Yared Khalon.

With a primal cry, Tzivia surged toward her father.

"*Nyet*," a guard snapped, jerking her back.

But Tox saw something he wasn't sure how to translate. How to read. The man dragging Mr. Khalon forward had lost his vigor, his ferocity.

Tzivia came off her feet, writhing for her father. "Abba!"

Nur nodded, pleased with this display. "I thought it good to remind you what you are fighting for."

"It's a ruse, Tzivia," Tox said. "Your father's not a captive."

Wearing a smile that made even Tox's stomach squeeze, Nur turned to Yefim, who handed him a gun. With a flourish, Nur turned and fired. Right at Mr. Khalon. Watching the old man wail and drop, cradling his leg, Tox flinched.

In a rage, Tzivia jerked so violently she freed herself. "Augh!" she screamed, pitching herself at Nur.

Four guards tackled her.

Nur made a show of checking the magazine. "Ah, plenty more. Shall I aim a little higher this time?" He pointed the gun at Khalon's temple.

Holding his thigh, the older man stilled.

Tzivia sobbed, nearly bent in half, calling for her abba. Over and over.

Nur's finger twitched in the trigger well.

"London," Tox heard himself saying. He blinked and met Nur's cutting gaze. "We need to go back to London for the next piece."

Nur glided closer. "And how do you know this?"

"I don't," Tox admitted, eyeing Khalon's grip on his injury. His expression. Had he made a mistake? "But if anyone else has a better guess . . ."

"She betrayed you! Why help her?" Nur asked.

"I'm not," Tox said coolly. "I'm helping myself. Buying time."

"Then why would I let you go?"

"Because you want the sword and can't afford not to take the risk, especially with Elah in two days."

"My men go with you."

"I wouldn't expect anything else."

* * * *

**— LONDON, ENGLAND —**

"He's dead."

Directly in front of Dr. Cathey's upscale flat sat a police car with an officer inside. He wasn't moving.

"You sure?" Even as Haven glanced up at the red brick building, then back at the car with the dead officer, she couldn't shake a sense of dread. She looked at Tzaddik in the driver's seat, then back to Chiji. "Why would they kill him?"

"So he can't interfere." Tzaddik's tone turned icy. His suddenly dark eyes scanned the street.

"Interfere with what?" Though Haven saw nothing, chills still skittered up her spine and swirled through her, a potent concoction of fear and foreboding.

Tzaddik pushed open the door, forcing Haven to do the same. As they stepped onto the sidewalk, he hesitated.

"What?" she asked.

"You still have the photo?"

She lifted the copy from her pocket, and her gaze once more hit the likeness of Elisabeth Linwood Russell.

"The ampoule," Tzaddik breathed. "Where is the ampoule?"

Haven looked at him, then the picture. "The what?"

"Adorning her hair"—he traced the crown of the statue's head—"resting at the center of her forehead was a bejeweled ampoule. It's not in the picture."

"What do you mean, an ampoule?" she asked as Chiji joined them.

He radiated urgency and panic. Which was alarming. He'd never been so ardent. "You have another photo, do you not?"

Haven frowned, digging into her tote. But the answer to her question dawned on her. "You knew—you knew what we needed." It made her a little light-headed, her mind unable to reconcile this timeless being before her.

He snatched the picture from Aunt Agatha's album from her.

"Here! The ampoule." He tapped the gem hanging at the center of

Lady Elisa's forehead. "We must have the ampoule before the great battle."

Haven studied the droplet-shaped piece fashioned out of what looked like bronze.

Wait. How could she know that? The photo was an old tintype, black and white. Why did she think it was bronze? A hand flashed before her mind's eyes, holding the ampoule. A laugh. Haven hauled in a breath. "No wonder . . ."

"What is it?"

She looked at Tzaddik. "I think my great-aunt has the ampoule—she wears it as a necklace." But they were in London. Aunt Agatha was in Virginia. "The battle is tomorrow. Do we even have time to fly there and back?"

"I can go."

Haven opened her mouth to question him but remembered his uncanny ability to appear places.

He nodded to the building. "Go on in. Secure the bust. You will be safe."

"I—" Haven peered up at the building, the second floor. Safe. With the enemy who had killed the police officer up there? "I have to question your definition of *safe*."

Tzaddik touched her shoulder, then nodded to Chiji. "Stay close to her." He turned and started walking down the street in the opposite direction.

A real fear wormed through her that if she took her eyes off him, he'd vanish. So she stared, long and hard, until her eyes dried and forced her to blink. And he was gone.

"That is so crazy," she mumbled, shaking her head. She turned to Chiji. "Ready?"

He looked at the doors. "I do not like this place, Ngozi."

"I don't either. But . . . we have a mission," she said with a huff and started up the half dozen steps to the entrance. Steps. Always steps. She sighed and climbed. The knob twisted without complaint, and she pushed it open. Another flight of stairs waited there, and around it, four doors.

"Second floor," Chiji said, pointing up.

She allowed herself a small groan as they climbed the steps carefully, quietly. Her heart hammered as she listened, all too aware that things were off already. At the landing, they hesitated. Glanced at each of the four doors spread around the staircase, just like the lower level.

"There, Ngozi," Chiji said, rising to the last step and moving in front of her. The door he indicated stood ajar. "I do not like this."

"Haven."

She pivoted at the new voice, stunned to see who was walking stiffly toward her. "Ram! What are you doing here?" Relief choked off the anxiety that had made her limbs feel leaden.

"I would ask the same of you," he said with a nod of acknowledgement to Chiji.

"A clue to the sword—at least, I think," she said as she took a step forward. "I'm not sure what it is exactly, but Tzaddik sent me here to find this bust." She produced the picture from her pocket.

Something in his expression changed. "I've seen it." He pointed to the apartment. "It's in the alcove. Come in. I'll show you."

"Wait." Haven hated the tremor in her breathing, the strange, sudden feeling that doused her in unease. The way he wouldn't look at her. "Why—why are you here, Ram?"

He turned, and in his gaze glowed an angry flame. "Inside, Haven. Now."

* * * *

A great precipice hung before him. If Tox did this, if he'd figured out the clues given by Gath and the professor, he'd find the sword piece. A victory for Tzivia. A defeat for most of the world. But if he didn't, Yared Khalon died.

Or would he?

*When the time is right . . .*

Dr. Cathey had tried to utter that with his dying breaths. Then Lukas Gath repeated it before everything went haywire. And now, as Tox stared at the ornately carved clock, he couldn't help but condemn himself for not connecting it sooner.

The clock wasn't set to the correct time.

*When the time is right.*

It couldn't be that simple, could it? He glanced at Tzivia, her wide, expressive eyes begging. Pleading. Full of desperation and hope. To limit exposure, only the two of them had come up. "If we do this," he said, "you know what happens."

Belligerence brightened her face. "Yes." She glowered. "My father is free."

"You know better than that, Tzi. I'm not sure he's a hostage."

She blinked. Frowned. "You saw the beatings, the bruises."

"Easily done with makeup. Why are his bones not broken, his will? Why does he walk without complication?"

"Did you miss the part when Nur shot him?"

"Flesh wound. If the bullet had gone through, there would've been a lot more blood and piercing screams. Trust me," he snapped. "I know."

She shoved her hands into her hair and gripped her head. "Stop." But confusion played havoc with her tight scowl. "Just—we have to do this." She sounded weary, less convinced. "Do it," she said. "Please. We're out of time."

"Nur knows who I am, Tzi. If he knows that, what else does he know?"

"He doesn't care about anything but the sword," she bit out.

Tox had reservations about her father, but no proof. Nothing definitive. What if he'd read it wrong and Yared Khalon was truly innocent? And killed because of Tox's mistake? Clenching his jaw, he huffed and strode to the clock, recalling the knot it had given him on the back of his head.

"So," she muttered, eyeing the timepiece, "what will it take to get you to reveal the secret?" She glanced at Tox over her shoulder. "Do you even know how to fix a clock?"

"No." Muscles tight with apprehension, he aimed a finger toward the white hour hand.

"Then how do you know we're supposed to do this?"

"I don't."

She caught his hand, eyes bulging. "You're *guessing*?"

"It's what I do best." He traced the sides of the clock, nerves buzzing. If this thing had a trigger, if it was wired to blow in the event of failed protocols, would he blast them into the afterlife?

*Don't think about it. Think about Haven. Getting home to her.*

Igor appeared behind them with an irritated huff. "Get on with it."

"I rush this, we could all be mopped up," Tox said, looking at the three new men in the room. Once they backed off, he dug his fingers along the back of the clock but felt no wires. No intricate connections. Shoulder pressed to the wall, he leaned his head in, feeling the scrape of plaster along the side of his face.

"What—" Thankfully, Tzivia swallowed her question.

But he felt her presence close. Felt her hovering. Even felt her tension thicken the air to the consistency of dirty oil. They were all impatient to get this done. Tox was impatient to get home to his wife.

Between the clock and the wall, he barely spied the nail that held it up.

"You think it's rigged?"

"Has to be," he muttered, and then he saw it. The wires feeding along the nail from the back of the clock into the wall. Way more wiring than a cuckoo clock needed. He hefted it forward a fraction.

"Wait!" Tzivia hissed as she caught his arm.

Holding the clock, Tox slowly slid his gaze to her. Telegraphing his annoyance at her jostling of his arm.

She wet her lips. Gulped. "Listen." Though they were practically toe to toe, she leaned closer. "Look, you know"—her voice was barely a whisper, hard to hear, especially over the thundering of his own heart—"how you want to get back to Haven?"

"Yes, which is why pulling my arm while I'm holding a possible det cord is a bad idea."

Her fingers eased off, but her intensity did not. "I want to get back to Omar."

Surprise darted through him. "What about your father?"

Conflict clouded her features. "I . . ." So his queries earlier had aroused the doubt that had lain quietly beneath her steel surface. "Of course—but . . ." She shook her head. "I've never—Omar gets me. I need to fix things. I need him to know."

Strong, confident Tzivia struggling with her emotions. As always. But new-to-her emotions. Ones she probably hated having.

Tox nodded. "I hear you."

She stepped off.

He set the clock back on the wall, then swung around to the front. Stared at the Germanic design. *When the time is right . . .* The clock read 2:24. Tox checked his watch. 9:52.

So did he wait till 2:24? Or did he set it to 9:52?

They didn't have time to sit around for four and a half hours. Besides, if that was the case, whatever the mechanism unlocked or set off would happen twice a day. Didn't make sense.

*So change it.*

But Cathey had never been one to conform to norms. And if he was supposed to wait, changing the time could kill them.

Tzivia had gone strangely quiet. While he appreciated the solitude to focus, it also somehow weighted the moment. He rubbed his jaw. *So move the clock hands.*

"Just do it."

Again he slid his gaze to her. "Do what?"

"Whatever you decided right there—I saw it in your face." Her eyes were alive, bright. "You felt it was right."

He arched his eyebrow, dragged his focus back to the clock. He lifted his finger to the delicate hands and manually forced the hour hand around. As he neared the precise moment, he twitched his wrist to verify the time.

*Shunk!*

A strong vibration thudded beneath their feet.

"What'd you do?" Igor demanded.

Popped and released, a full doorframe presented itself where there had last been a panel break.

"What is that?" Igor pressed forward, but Tox held out a hand.

"Unless you know where all the trip wires and triggers are, I'd stay back." He didn't really expect any, but he wanted them at a distance.

Tzivia sucked in a breath and darted past him. She dug her nails into the door to pry it open. It came out an inch. Then another. And another.

Tox stepped over to assist with the seemingly endlessly thick door. He braced with his feet and pulled the heavy steel. Igor and one of his men moved in to help, but there wasn't enough room for all of them.

"Good grief," Tzivia muttered with a grunt. "I knew he was anal about security, but this is obscene!"

There came a *pop* as the door's seal broke. "There." Tox glanced along the edge of it to where a sliver of space provided the first peek into the hidden room. "A little more," he said, and they gave another pull.

The hinge flew loose.

The room before them was exactly the size Tox had expected. Yet with the floor-to-ceiling shelving and glass cases stuffed into it, it felt much smaller. Crowded. So much that standing shoulder to shoulder with Tzivia, he could reach most of the shelves. This wasn't crowded—it was suffocating. Like a tunnel.

Tzivia whistled. "He was holding out on me," she said with a breathy laugh. "He never fully trusted me." Those words were less lighthearted, more filled with sadness, grief.

Picking up a well-aged tome, Tox glanced at the spine, but the lettering—once probably gilt—had worn off. "I don't think it was a matter of trust."

Using her fingers as well as her eyes, Tzivia traced the shelves. "Yeah? Then what?"

Tox returned to the book in his hands. "A mission—he felt he had a mission, like Tzaddik, to protect humanity from itself."

Tzivia eyed him and shook her head. "You always were a little too deep for me."

"I thought you were going to say dense."

"Didn't I?" she teased, then nodded to the shelves. "I see a ton of books, but where's the sword?"

As her words met his ears, Tox spied a tome on the shelf. *A Wrinkle in Time.*

Time. *Right time.*

He tugged the book out. The clap of wood on wood sounded behind them.

Tzivia flinched. "What did you—*Oh!*"

Tox turned and found the wall of books behind them had slid aside. In place of the shelves, a light flickered to life. There, beneath that dull glow and cradled in glass, waited the scrollwork.

"There you are," Tzivia said, then hesitated.

"What?" Tox asked, his momentary relief vanishing at her confusion.

"The scroll—it's only half." She muttered an oath and shoved her hair back from her face.

Half? How was that possible?

Tzivia reached into the box. A faint red hue struck her hand.

*Rigged!* Tox's gut seized. "Wait!"

As her fingers closed around the hilt, a buzz sounded. The foot-thick steel door started swinging shut. It would lock them in!

"The door!" Tox shoved the wooden stand stacked with books forward, sending it sprawling into the door's path. "Go!"

The wooden stand creaked. Popped. Snapped. Tzivia threw herself through the ever-narrowing space. Tox couldn't wait for her to clear the space or he'd be trapped. He flung himself out after her. Shoulder ramming into her back. Colliding, they both went down.

His leg caught on something. Pulled. He landed hard, flipping around to see a steel rod had torn through his pant leg and anchored him in the door's path. Struggling would do no good.

"Tox!" Tzivia shouted, grabbing his shoulders and pulling.

He kicked. Stamped his right leg against the wall. Shoved hard with the left.

Steel scored his calf. Blood flowed. Material and muscle ripped. Only a few inches remained.

He was not going to lose his leg. Couldn't. Wouldn't.

Again, he kicked. More material gave.

Hands hooked under his arms. Caught his shoulders. Hauled him backward. His pants tore free, and he flopped. Landed again on Tzivia. Heard her nervous, breathy laugh as he rolled to the side and dropped onto his back. With a relieved exhale, he stared up at the ceiling. It felt like he'd scraped a year or two off his life.

A shadow dropped over them.

Tox jerked upward—so did Tzivia.

Three muzzles pressed them back down. The crowd parted, and Ram appeared in the apartment entrance.

Tox leapt to his feet, ignoring the sting of objection from his calf—especially when he saw whose arm Ram held in a tight grip. "Haven!" He rushed toward her.

Igor and his men intercepted Tox, barricading him from his wife. Behind them, forced into a chair and hands cuffed behind his back, Chiji sat glowering, blood sliding down his temple.

"Sorry," Igor sneered. "You're not getting any of that just yet."

Scowling, Tox looked at Ram. And it finally hit his brain that his friend held a gun.

Held a gun on Haven.

Ram's hair was shorter. His temper hotter, by the hard expression glinting in his eyes. "What're you doing?" Tox growled.

Betrayal.

No. It couldn't be. Not Ram.

But it was.

"What's wrong with you?" Fury erupted in Tox, his mind refusing to accept what he saw. Rejecting the reality that Ram was leveling a weapon at Haven. "Let her go!"

Tzivia sucked in a breath. "Ram! What are you doing?"

"Ram," Tox said in a low, warning tone. "Don't."

But Ram stood steadfast on the wrong side of Tox's anger. On the wrong side of honor and integrity. "Sorry," he said without regret. "It has to be done."

Tox threw himself at the line of men. "Ram!" he roared.

"Cole, no!"

"Ndidi!"

Red. He saw red. Rage. Violence. Whatever it took to protect Haven. Hands clawed and pawed at him, restraining him.

"Stand down," Ram said, tugging Haven back.

"Cole!" Haven cried. "Cole, stop. I'm okay. I'm okay."

His gaze struck hers, and it felt like a cool breeze washed over him. He slowed from the fight, stopped throwing punches. Fell into her reassurance. She gave a small nod.

Reluctantly, he pulled up. Locked gazes with Ram once more. Allowed the guards to shove him against the counter. Secure his hands. All while visually warning Ram that he was making a big mistake.

"The bust," Ram growled to the side, to Haven. "Did you get the bust?"

"What bust?" Tzivia asked, coming around Tox.

"A statue," Haven said. "Of a woman."

"It's in the library," Ram said.

Tzivia nodded, confusion in her gaze as she eyed her brother. "Yeah, I saw it when we were here last. Why do you want it?"

"Tzaddik said it's related to the sword somehow," Haven said, bouncing her gaze to Tox.

Rage vibrated through Tox's veins, and it took everything in him not to launch himself over the counter and take a chunk out of Ram's hide. And yet a large part of him sagged at this turn of events. How? Why? Had Ram been doing the AFO's work all this time? The thought sickened him.

"Igor, bring the bust."

The new voice snapped the AFO guards to attention, sent Igor hurrying to the library, and drew Ram around. The voice also jolted Tox. He'd heard it before—in the penthouse.

"Abba!" Tzivia gasped. Then froze. And Tox saw what she saw. No bruises. No swelling. No limp. Yared Khalon was in the pink of health.

"Stand down, Tzivia," Ram said, his expression hard and impassive. He turned the gun toward Tzivia. "I do not want to do this—"

"She's your sister," Tox growled, straining against his captors.

The barrel canted toward him. Ram lifted his chin. "Don't give me a reason."

Balling his fists did little to help Tox restrain his rage.

Stepping closer, dragging Haven with him, Ram tightened his lips. As if begging for a reason to shoot.

Nur followed Yared Khalon into the room and jutted his jaw at Tzivia. "Do you have the piece?"

She glowered but held up the scrollwork. "It's only half."

Face reddening, Nur shot a frightened look at Yared. "We have no time to find another half, sir."

Sir? So Nur *wasn't* the head of the AFO. Yared Khalon was. Tox had seen him, seen Yared walking the penthouse when they were in Moscow but hadn't recognized him. Something familiar had sparked, but Tox had been too slow to put the pieces together.

"Where is it?" Yared demanded of Tzivia, surging forward.

"How would I know? I'm only the daughter you abandoned. The one you manipulated and used to get what you wanted."

"What we *needed*! You do not understand—"

"You're right! I don't understand!" With that, Tzivia unleashed her skills. Hooking her leg, she caught and yanked the nearest thug's calf out from under him. Pitched him forward. Her hand shoved hard, nailing his head against the wall.

*Crack!*

"Tzivia!"

Wide eyes flared with anger as she pivoted to Ram. "You are my brother!"

"You didn't care about that when you set off in search of our father against my advice. When you forced me to pull Tox into this. When you dragged *me* into it." His jaw muscle twitched. "Now—*now* you'll play your part. You'll free our father and me from this curse." He pivoted to the rear hall. "Igor! Where is the bust?"

# 50

**— LONDON, ENGLAND —**

After a cursory look toward Cole in the hopes of once more reassuring him—though it tore her heart out to see him writhing internally over not being able to stop this madness, not being able to protect her—Haven turned when the man emerged from the library.

The great bust of Elisabeth Russell seemed to float in his hands. She was a grand work of art, so lifelike. So much larger than Haven expected—nearly in proportion with a real person. And despite being carved of stone, Elisabeth's features were elegant and beautiful. Haven's gaze naturally fell on the empty space at Lady Elisa's forehead where the piece was missing.

"Why do you need this?" Nur demanded.

Haven hesitated. Fearful that mentioning Tzaddik might inflame things, she kept to facts, not names. "I am not entirely sure. Just that it's tied to the sword somehow." Which, now that she thought about it, seemed ridiculous.

"Ngozi," Chiji said calmly from the chair he was cuffed to. He nodded to Tzivia.

Haven glanced toward the other woman, confused.

"What?" Tzivia shrugged, lifting her hands. "I don't know anything about that statue, except the professor has had it since before I met him."

But Haven's gaze seized on the metal in Tzivia's hand. "What are you holding?" She drew the picture from her pocket.

"Actually, that belongs to me," Tzivia's father said.

"Wait." Haven stepped forward without thinking about the repercussions.

Two men slammed into her. She stumbled and hit the wall.

"Leave her!" Ram shouted. "She's pregnant!"

Startled at the pronouncement, Haven stilled, then came to her feet with the rough aid of the goons. She glanced at Cole. Saw the shock in his expression, the way he seemed to move in slow motion. Grieved that this was how he'd found out, she gave him a sad smile. "We couldn't reach you. I wanted to tell you, but . . ."

A thousand emotions roiled through Cole's normally stoic features. Surprise. Joy. Shock. Fear. Then anger, no doubt over their predicament.

"So," Ram barked, "now you know what you risk, Tox. Your wife and your child." He stalked closer, indicating the bust. "What is this?"

Once the men let her go and stepped away, Haven straightened. She traced the indentations around the neck of the bust and then, bolstered that she might finally understand why Tzaddik had sent her here, she turned to Tzivia. "Can I see that?" When the woman hesitated, Haven added, "Just for a moment."

Tzivia glanced at her father.

Yared Khalon considered Haven for several long seconds. Then he nodded sharply.

With quick strides, Tzivia crossed the room and handed off the scrollwork. "Careful with it. Centuries depend on it."

"So it seems," Haven said quietly as she accepted it. Surprised at how lightweight it was, she bent toward the bust. While she wasn't sure what would happen, especially with the ampoule still missing, Haven knew she needed to return the piece to Elisabeth.

"Who is the bust of?" Tzivia asked.

"Elisabeth Linwood Russell," Haven said, still a bit surprised by the legacy staring back at her. She set the scrollwork around Lady Elisa's neck, right into the grooves near the shoulders. It fit perfectly.

Nothing happened, so she drew back her hands. Stared at it.

"Is it supposed to do something?" Tzivia asked.

"I don't know," Haven muttered. Had she set it right? She glanced at the place where the ampoule should rest. There was a slight indentation, but it wasn't like the spots for the scrollwork. "Maybe . . ." With her fingertips, she pressed the indentation.

*Schink.*

At the heavy sound that cracked through the bust, Haven snatched her hands away and drew back. She searched the marble for a crack or opening.

Tzivia glanced at her. "I don't—"

"The back," Igor noted.

They shifted around and saw a small panel had opened. Haven widened her eyes as Tzivia drew out the other half of the metal scrollwork. She removed the piece around the neck, which snapped the panel closed, and held the two pieces together.

"I will take those," Yared Khalon said. "They must be returned to the Adama Herev."

"But this isn't the whole thing," Tzivia said. "I found one half of the blade, and this scrollwork. Half the blade—"

Yared's brows drew down toward his nose as he homed in on the scrollwork. He took it in hand, then flashed a furious glower at Haven. "*Where* is the ampoule?"

Most lies were borne of truth and therefore seemed more believable. Haven's only reassurance that she might get away with this. "I don't know."

"But you know of it?" Yared edged into her personal space with a show of contempt to exert his power.

"I do," Haven admitted, the journal burning a hole in her pocket.

"How?"

Her gaze drifted on its own to Cole, pulling her pulse into a faster rate, especially when he gave her a nod. Which she knew was only in the hopes of securing her safety. And their child's. Yet Tzaddik had entrusted this task to her, even though he knew what lay before them.

*"Mrs. Russell?"*

Though Yared hissed that name, and though it was the first time she'd heard it spoken directly to her since Israel, when Cole said it as they stood on a hill overlooking the Sea of Galilee, it did not have the desired effect of weakening her. "Tzaddik told me." In a way it was true.

A storm rolled through Yared's face, darkening his eyes.

"You know him," Haven noted and took courage when he did not answer. Whether it was the mere mention of Tzaddik's name or something else, she wasn't sure. "Then you know I am not lying."

He whirled, stalking toward the door. "Bring them all!"

Cole, somehow freed, came to her in three long strides. Hauled her into his arms. Held her tight. Kissed the top of her head. And Haven wondered if they would survive.

"Are you sure?" Nur asked, glancing at Haven, then Cole. "They—"

With a stab of his hand, Yared curled his lip and pronounced, "More sacrifices at Elah!"

* * * *

**— VALLEY OF ELAH —**

"Am I to believe you have suddenly changed sides?"

Ram betrayed no emotion, a skill he had mastered since the night his father walked out of the house. Out of their lives. "I do not care what you believe." They had beaten him to force his awareness to their plight. "Would you like to beat me again?"

His father sneered, staring at the sword pieces laid out on a table. "More than you know."

What had Ram done to earn such seething hatred? Granted, he felt the same raw energy toward the man whose seed had given him life, but that was where the connection stopped.

"Yared," Nur said, shifting on the seat brought in to make their tent accommodations more comfortable. "The ampoule. Without it—"

"Cease!" His father flashed Ram a look of fury and disgust. "This woman—your friend's wife—can you convince her to turn over the ampoule?"

Ram frowned. "I don't think she knows where it is." Besides, talking to Haven meant facing Tox again.

"She's but a skilled liar—as your mother was!"

The words struck below the belt. "Do not speak of her," Ram bit out.

Igor and his guards shifted at the way Ram spoke to their leader.

But Ram didn't care. This man was his father, and a coward. "You left her with no job and two children!"

"I left her with her lies. She made out fine for decades with them," his father spat. "Don't think I will feel sorry for that witch!"

Heat shot through Ram's chest. "What did she ever do to you? She was the kindest, most loving—"

"She *lied*," his father said, dragging out the last word. "Tricked me. De—"

"You are *weak*!" Ram spat. "She was the best of women. You drove her to the grave early with your selfishness and abandonment! I knew—*knew* you weren't dead. I heard that call. Heard you say it was worth the cost."

The words were meant to anger his father, but for some reason, Yared seemed to gloat. "It took her too long to die!"

Fists balled, Ram lunged at his father.

Nur stepped in, flanked by Igor and two guards, to protect their leader.

"I hope you die on that battlefield," Ram growled and pivoted toward the tent entrance.

"I am willing to die, as long as your friend's blood is spilled as well!"

* * * *

In a tent with a cage divided into four cells, Tox drew Haven into his arms, mind spinning at all she'd shared about the bust, his genealogy, and their interlinked lines throughout history. About their child.

"Hard to believe Linwoods and Russells married before us."

"It's just a sign that God intended us to be together from the start—well, once you were no longer blinded by Brooke and noticed me."

"Hey," he whispered, "who did I marry? And who is pregnant with my baby?" He shared a look with Chiji, who'd watched after her. Though Tox wanted to berate his friend for letting her go to London, he couldn't. Haven had a mind of her own. A strong one. And she was here. It had been too long since he'd held her. Too long since he'd smelled the scent that was uniquely hers. He pressed his face into the crook of her neck and breathed deeply.

Haven laughed. "You okay?"

"Yeah, but no." He snorted. "We're in a terrible situation, but all I can think is that I can't believe you're pregnant."

"You've said that a few times." She laughed again, clinging to him.

His hand rested on her belly, and he was amazed at how it was already rounding. "How far along?"

"Coming up on five months," she said with a sigh.

"Do you know the sex?"

"No. It was cruel enough not to have you there when I took the test. I wasn't going to learn that without you."

He brushed the frazzled strands of hair away from her face, staring into the eyes that had become a haven to him, just like her name. "I won't let anything happen to you," he vowed.

"I believe you," she said quietly. "But I can't see how we get out of this—the cage or the situation. They're planning a slaughter."

"We are not alone," Chiji said. "Remember that the odds were stacked against a shepherd boy as well. Yet God provided the means to slay the enemy."

"I'll take any means He's willing to supply," Cole said.

Worry did not look good on Haven, and he hated it. Especially knowing that his child grew inside her. It was a terrifying, wonderful thought. There was so much more to protect now. Such fragility in his rough, bloodied hands.

She peered up at him. "I wasn't entirely honest with Mr. Khalon."

"Good." He'd seen her expression, seen that she was hiding something. "What do you know?"

"Tzaddik went for the ampoule. I don't know what it is or when he's coming back, but both he and Yared are concerned about it." She rubbed her lower back. "Do you know why it's important?"

"I do."

Tox spun at the voice, his mind a blur of rage and disbelief as he stared down the man he'd considered closer than a brother "What're you doing? Why?" he snapped. "You're better than this."

Ram looked at Haven. "Where is Tzaddik?"

"He's not a person like us. He goes where he wills or God wills." Haven took Tox's hand as he drew her to himself.

Ram scratched at his beard. "Okay, let me rephrase—where is the ampoule he went after? I saw him on the street outside the flat. You said something to him, and he left quickly. What did you say?"

"Which question do I answer first?" Haven asked, her defiance beautiful but dangerous.

"None," Tox said, tucking her behind him. "You're not using her like you have me."

Something twisted through Ram's features that couldn't be read. He slid his hands into his pockets and inched closer. "You must know that this"—he glanced over his shoulder, out the tent flap, into the creeping dawn—"cannot be stopped."

"Whatever that ampoule is—"

"It's the blood of Gulat," said a deep, resonating voice that drew them all around.

Tzaddik stood in the tent entrance with Tzivia. And yet, it wasn't Tzaddik. This man radiated something . . . otherworldly. Confidence. Authority. Righteous anger. His clothes were not modern, like Tzaddik had worn. Instead he wore the distinctive white mantle with the Templar cross and a wide leather belt, from which dangled a sword and dagger.

Tzivia stood to the side and folded her arms, clearly not happy to be here. No—not happy to be near her brother.

"Thefarie," Haven whispered.

"I asked Miss Khalon to join us. She must hear my words as well." The warrior inclined his head to her, but focused on Ram. "When David killed Gulat in this valley centuries ago, the Adama Herev drank the mercenary blood that spilled into the blood groove and gathered in a thin ampoule. Without it, the sword is nothing but hammered steel." He stepped farther into the tent, his presence consuming. "It is the ampoule that the Nizari Ismailis and their Order have sought—and sought to cleanse."

"Cleanse?" Haven asked, frowning.

"Blood for blood," Thefarie said, nodding to Tox. "It is a grievous parallel that the sword comes yet again between friends, seeks to divide and kill." His eyes, leaden with a painful truth, shifted from Tox to Ram, then back. "It was Ram's ancestor who killed my friend and brother-knight, Giraude, all because Matin yielded to the thirst of steel. Giraude's wife was slaughtered, even as she carried his second son."

Tox drew up, heat blazing down his neck and spine at the thought of Haven pregnant. Instinct thrummed. Anger boiled.

A sharp intake of breath came from Tzivia as she stared at Haven.

"Our brother-knight Ameus was there on that plain. He saved the child who would continue Giraude's line." He looked at Tox. "Your line. Ameus delivered the Adama Herev back to Shatira's father. Once Yitshak healed from his wounds, he sought a blacksmith, who sectioned the sword. He hid the pieces well and was slaughtered by the Nizari for what they viewed as destruction of the sacred sword."

Ram shifted. "This is insane."

Thefarie's razor-sharp gaze struck him. "Has your father explained why he left your mother and you two as children?"

A ripple of confusion worked through Ram's hard features as he and Tzivia shared a long look. "Yared said she lied to him."

Thefarie inclined his head. "Granted. Your mother, Nadine, was not of Nizari blood as she claimed, and the evidence she produced of her lineage was fabricated by a century-old sect, the Camarilla, that has hoped to thwart the AFO."

Ram shook his head. "My mom was just a teacher."

"Your mother was one of the most intelligent women to cross my path," Thefarie said. "Shrewd and perceptive, she was quickly chosen when the sisters presented their candidates."

"Candidates?" Tzivia scowled.

"For what?" Ram asked.

"To infiltrate the AFO—even now, there are more than a hundred spread throughout the structure of the Order. Though the plan bordered on ludicrous," Thefarie said, looking a bit sheepish, "we knew regardless of the Adama Herev's recovery, it was imperative to disrupt the Nizari Ismaili bloodline. For centuries, they have clung to maintaining a pure lineage, but in doing so, they unwittingly strengthened the disease, the thirst."

Tension had rolled out of Ram's shoulders. He gave a slight shake of his head. "I . . ." He cleared his throat. "What is your point?"

"Once your mother realized Yared was a clear contender for Sovereign of the AFO, she targeted him. Married him. Bore his children."

"Sovereign?"

Tox twitched, watching as Ram connected the same dots he had. It was obvious, but hearing it, saying it, was a whole new level of real.

Ram scowled, lifting his palms in a shrug. "I know who my mom was—who gave birth to me."

"You were raised among the Israelis and in the Hebrew faith—"

"I know how I was raised," Ram growled.

Thefarie held up a hand. "It was all done to protect your father's position and his influence in the Israeli community, give him a good name and reputation, so he would be trusted."

Apprehension held Tox still, not wanting to set off Ram, whose fists were white-knuckled and his lips tight beneath his beard. Though Ram had betrayed him, though he'd held a gun on Haven and threatened her life, he was still Tox's friend. He yearned for Ram to find his way through this dark hour.

Tzivia shifted forward, disconcerted. "What're you saying?"

The Timeless One held Ram's gaze for a long time. "You know the truth. Somehow you knew."

"What truth?" Tzivia asked.

Ram lifted his chin, glowering at Thefarie. "We are of Nizari blood."

"But you aren't—not pure anyway," Thefarie said with a sad smile. "Your mother concealed the truth of her heritage to marry your father, to position herself." He glanced to Tox again before redirecting to Ram. "Your mother was pure Hebrew."

Ram had gone deathly still.

Was he angry? Daring Tzaddik to say the wrong thing so he could lash out? But Tox didn't see any anger. No . . . he saw nothing. Ram was like stone, holding it all back. If that internal dam broke, what would happen?

"Neither of you are pure Nizari. Add to that your mother's connection to his enemy—*that* is why your father abandoned your family. That is why you clung to the church, to the *yarmulke*." Thefarie's tone grew grave, burdened. "Yared had already assumed leadership of the AFO before he moved your family to America, an endeavor designed to hide his identity from the enemies of the AFO. Once he learned of Nadine's betrayal . . ."

"He faked his death. Left," Ram mumbled. "So he could assume full control. Rule."

Sovereign. The thought still rattled Tox, though it was logical, considering the facts.

Thefarie inclined his head. "You've lived to honor your mother and defy your father. Continue that now, Ram. Defy him. Defy what they ask of you."

Ram took a step back. Shifted on his feet. "Did he kill her?"

"No. She had a guardian to protect her."

"Who?" Ram and Tzivia asked at the same time.

For the first time, Thefarie hesitated. Dropped his gaze from Ram, then dragged it to Tox. With a soft exhale, he glanced over his shoulder toward the tent entrance. "Ameus."

A large shape spilled inside. Of the same age and dress as Thefarie, the man moved a little less nimbly. Bearded, he had a familiarity about him.

Tox jolted with recognition. "No!"

With a strangled cry, Ram leaped away, flinging out his hands as if to find balance. "You—you're dead!"

# 51

## — VALLEY OF ELAH —

Tzivia's knees buckled as she recognized his eyes. "No!" she cried out, her words strangled. "I saw you die. You—right in my arms!" Tears blurred her vision as the man came toward her. She scrambled back. "Stay away!"

But he reached for her, caught her shoulder, and held her steady. Cupped her face. "I am sorry."

"Doctor—" The name caught in her throat. Sanity forbid her from speaking it. But was that his name? Who was he? "You're . . ." Had he tricked her all this time? "How—?"

"When Nadine died," Thefarie said, coming up behind the resurrected Dr. Cathey, "Ameus took on a new protectorship—you, Tzivia. But with your rather strong beliefs against our Lord Jesus and God the Father, it was more natural for you to come to know a bumbling archaeologist. Ameus did quite well."

"It was not far from the truth," Ameus rumbled, years gone from his once aged face.

"Your voice is different—your face!" Tzivia shook her head, as if this insanity might break loose and fall away. She held her stomach. "I think I'm going to be sick."

"Forgive us," Thefarie said. "It is hard to hear, hard to see the truth, when it is so contrary to the laws of the world you live in, the readily erected walls of rejection to the power of God and the spirit realm."

"Why are you telling us this?" Ram asked, his words grating with anger.

Tzivia frowned but could muster no response. Her mind had drowned in this impossibility. Of seeing her mentor alive—yet . . . not. He was so changed. She gripped her temples. It made no sense!

"Brothers," a voice called from outside. "The hour is upon us." Another man peeked into the tent, and Ram hauled in a breath.

"Lukas!" Tox gasped, staggering.

Thefarie rumbled a laugh. "To me, he is Sir Raoul Asanes."

"That is the name I have borne longest," Lukas Gath said with amusement. "Alas, reunions are grand but inconsequential. We must to war."

Disbelief still strangling her, Tzivia again found herself studying Dr.—"Ameus."

His gray eyes came to hers once more. The eyebrows were still thick, but not crazy anymore. The age in his cheeks had lessened, but experience scratched lines around his still-kind eyes. "I beg your mercy, Tzivia. We could not reveal ourselves as such, especially not after what happened, but the hour is dark, and war is before us."

"It's cheating," she finally managed, "to pitch faith when you are . . . whatever you are."

"Not cheating," he said with a rueful smile, "when you wholly believe what you speak."

"Why tell us? We don't benefit from your secrets," Ram protested.

Thefarie went to him and held up the ampoule. "No, but this—"

"No!" Tox lunged forward. "Don't let him have that. He'll give it to them. Then it's over."

However, Thefarie never wavered. "Before you stands a decision."

With ire, Ram wrapped his fingers around the ampoule, but Thefarie did not release it.

"Your mother sacrificed her entire life, her chance at true love, at wealth and happiness, to end this thirst. To free you—her son. Will you now continue her work? Or will you destroy it?"

Ram tugged the ampoule free and stepped back, glancing at Tzivia, who shook her head imploringly. He then shifted to Tox, and guilt flickered through his eyes. Without a word, he pivoted and strode out of the tent.

"Ram!" Tox shook the bars of his cage.

Thefarie palmed his chest. "Let him go to his end."

"No!" Tox barked. "I'm his friend. I won't let him go without a fight. I'm not—"

Voices outside drew their attention. Tzivia watched in broken disgust as Ram handed the ampoule to their father, who patted his shoulder and smiled, proud.

In stunned grief, Tzivia felt a chill and turned. "Why did—"

The brother-knights were gone.

Her father motioned for her to join them outside the tent on the plain. Teeth grinding, heart crushed, she gave Tox an apologetic look, then complied.

The lush valley spread before them in a long, narrowing swath rent in two by the road to Gath, home of the ancient Philistines and the giant Goliath. A small brook interrupted the rich green landscape, which had been freshly mowed to accommodate the reenactment. Ram and her father talked quietly.

How could Ram even talk to him after Tzaddik's explanation and Dr. Cathey's return from the grave? The betrayal by her father—and Ram! Both of her family members. It gutted her. Made her own actions seem that much more abhorrent, made her wish she'd chosen a better path.

Just as Tox had tried to tell her, Abba was not injured, save the flesh wound to his leg. Her brother and father were so alike in posture, in build. In intensity. Abba motioned over the field, giving instructions, which her piece-of-crap brother made swift strides to carry out.

Her father trudged toward her. "You are displeased."

She snorted. "Try disgusted. Ashamed. Even *shamed*."

His gaze traveled up the hillside a little more, to the hundreds gathered around small campfires. The Hebrew contingent of the reenactment.

Abba stood before her. "I am proud of you, Tzivia. You accomplished what no man has in centuries."

"You're missing the third piece," she pointed out, taking too much pleasure in that unintended victory.

His lips lifted in a grin. "The third piece has always been in the possession of the Order."

Her hope died. "So it's true. You're their leader, the Sovereign."

Pleased, he pivoted and motioned to the valley below. "It will happen tonight, Tzivia. The two factions already fill the valley. The battle will rage, but this year"—he drew in a long breath and slowly let it out—"it will be different." He nodded, eyes squinting at an imagined victory. "Tonight, the curse will be broken."

"Ram said there was no curse."

"Desperate men cling to idealism when it suits them. Your brother was desperate to be free. I know what it is to hope and then have that hope crushed. He is the same. As have been all men in our line for centuries."

"Why me? Why did you make me hunt down the pieces?" It sounded petulant, even childish, but Tzivia had to know. She had to quash this ache that had bloomed upon his betrayal. "You . . . you lied to me. Made me believe you were dying, that they were hurting you. That Nur shot you. Why could you not trust me?"

She thought of Dr. Cathey. Trust with him had been implicit. And yet, here with her own father, she couldn't find a grain of it.

"Was there another way to convince you?" His smile was hollow, his words emptier. "Besides, you are my daughter, and I wanted you—"

"Under your control?" She began plotting how to free Tox, Haven, and Chiji. She might have broken their trust in smaller ways over the last few months, but she would not shatter it as Ram had. One Khalon had to be worth their salt.

That hollow smile again. "With your skills in archaeology and the connections you developed through the years, I knew you'd find the sword with just a little motivation to look outside yourself."

"*Look outside myself?*" Her pulse shrieked in her ears. "I walked away from *everything* to find you. To save *you*!"

"And in the end," he said, unaffected by her anger, "you have. Good girl."

Anger thrummed through her veins, begging for freedom. "And Mom?"

He frowned. "What do you mean?"

"You abandoned her! And us! Because what? She wasn't *pure*?"

His expression went hard, feral. "How do you know that? Who told you this?"

"So it's true." Air—she couldn't breathe. Her lungs ached with restrained sobs. "She worked herself to death after you vanished."

"We cannot allow the line of David to thrive when we struggle."

"Are you even hearing yourself? Do you even care about me?"

"Of course, I do. Nobody could've gotten the sword but you."

"Is that all I was to you, a means to that stupid sword?"

"Enough." He rose to his feet. "Make your decision, Tzivia. Or you will bleed on this field, too."

* * * *

Wraith.

Tox struggled to keep his head up, but with Haven here—plus one—and Chiji . . . he could not focus on loss. But his brothers-in-arms were probably dead. And who had been on the other range, attacking Igor's men?

Then there was Ram.

Tox had never seen his friend like this. Never imagined he, of all people, would betray him. Grief had tossed a frag grenade into their relationship. Blinded him. Deafened him. How had he missed it? This had to be a ploy on Ram's part to get in, find the plans, and wreck them.

Right. It was. Had to be.

*God, please let it be.*

"You okay?" Haven lay curled on her side nearby.

He'd forgotten—missed—how she could read him so well. On his back, arms beneath his head, he stared up at the tent ceiling. "Thinking about Ram."

"Thinking what?"

"I can't accept he's gone to the dark side."

"Good."

He snapped his gaze to her, desperately hoping her deception skills said it *was* a ploy. "Did you see something?"

"I saw a lot of conflict in Ram, but I think we all saw that." She sighed. "No, I said that because you wouldn't be Cole Russell if you easily accepted a friend's betrayal."

Shouts rang through the afternoon. A din, chants by hundreds. He listened but couldn't make out the words, which were in another language.

"It has begun."

Tox glanced to where Yared Khalon again stood inside the tent. As Yared sauntered around the interior, Tox came to his feet and pulled Haven to himself.

Yared smiled through the bars. "Hear it? They are beginning the chant of the infamous Battle of Elah. One we will take part in. One you can no longer stop." He was infuriatingly assured.

"How'd you turn Ram? What price?" Tox asked.

"A little lesson in the ways of pain corrected his thinking."

"So you tortured him." Tox snorted. Gave a disgusted shake of his head, reassured by the vast difference between Ram and Yared. "Your son is a better man than you."

"I hope so. My son will take my place when I am gone. He will rule."

"No," Tox said. "Ram has no desire for that kind of power—he never even wanted to be promoted to team leader." He scowled. "Do you even know your son? Do you know he owns an art studio?"

"It was a front," Yared hissed. "Of course I know!"

"It was his outlet," Tox said. "What about the woman he loves?"

"He has no wife."

"I did not say wife. I'm referring to the woman he abandoned to protect Israel—interestingly enough, the country that you'll decimate on this field."

"It is the right of the Nizari to be free and take back centuries of what you have stolen from us."

"Stolen from you?" Again, Tox snorted. "You tried to enslave them, and it backfired! At what cost will you continue this madness?"

"Did anyone care when it was us who lost? Who were ruined with this curse?" Yared sniffed. "No, you rejoiced."

"What d'you mean, 'you'?" But Tox knew. Recalled what Haven had told him. What Thefarie said of the ampoule.

"Do you not know your genealogy, Mr. Russell? You are descended from King David. You carry the blood that will free us."

He didn't like the sound of that. "You have the ampoule. You don't need me."

"The ampoule is the beginning. You are the end." Yared snickered, his words holding a double meaning.

"What? You're going to sacrifice me?" What flashed in the older man's eyes coursed a new dread through Tox. "No. I'm not participating in this. You can—"

"I think you will." Yared motioned to someone standing just inside the tent, and Tox noted Igor training an M4 on Haven.

"No!" Tox barked. "You—" He stopped short when Ram entered.

His friend strode to the cage door and unlocked it. Motioned Tox out.

"I'm not leaving her," Tox growled.

Haven swung panicked eyes to him. Considering the man with the M4, Tox flexed his fists. Unflexed. Flexed.

"Now, Mr. Russell," Yared commanded, "before Igor gets trigger happy. He's not very patient, nor am I."

Tox turned to her. "It'll be okay." But he couldn't inject much confidence into words whose truth died on his lips. "Sorry," he said, giving her a kiss and praying it wasn't a good-bye kiss. Stiff and furious, he flicked daggers at Ram as he walked out of the tent. "I'll kill you if anything happens to her," he hissed.

"Very good," Yared murmured, pleased with himself and his plan, as iron clanged shut behind Tox. He shifted back to her.

Haven looked stricken. Alone. She gripped the bars, and he clamped a hand over hers, to reassure them both. This wasn't over. This wasn't their end.

"Now, would you like to reconsider your refusal to help?"

Baited, Tox tensed. Knew he'd do whatever it took to keep her alive. Seeing Chiji move behind Haven gave Tox the smallest hope that she'd be okay.

"Well?" Yared prompted.

"You don't want help," he growled. "You want me dead."

"You dead. Her alive." Yared pursed his lips and shrugged. "Quite a bargain, I think."

Not answering, unable to, Tox walled up the anger-fed grief that churned and writhed through him as he turned his gaze on Ram the Betrayer.

Yared's sick laugh played through the heavy air. "Your little world has been so disrupted, Mr. Russell. Tell me, do you know what happened to your girlfriend, to Brooke?"

The words drew Tox up sharp. His gaze bounced to Haven, who'd gone still, pale.

"You see how vast our organization is, ever-reaching."

"And yet you couldn't find the sword without tormenting your own daughter." Tox shouldn't anger the guy holding his wife, but the words escaped before he could stop them.

"What you call torment, I call motivation. So did a certain friend of the Russell family."

Tox waited, tensed. Ram had his life upended by incredible revelations that morning, and he guessed turnabout was fair play.

"When your brother's wife was given information about our highest operative in your country, we were forced to silence her."

Confusion pummeled Tox. "I killed her."

"To be precise, no. You did not. But when one has people in all the right organizations, anything can be made to look true." Yared grinned, a sickening sight, and wiped a finger along the side of his mouth. "You see, you took the shot that killed al-Homsi—also intel fed to your superiors by our asset. But another sniper took care of the president-elect's wife. We could not allow her to expose our asset. He is such a delicious plant. Controlling the president. Influencing policy. But lest he become a target of suspicion, he helped the president's brother. Arranged a special deal."

Drowning in the tangled revelations, Tox felt sick. The deal he'd taken had been to help him. "To get me out of the way."

"What better way?" Yared scoffed. "You were so ready to leave, to hide your head in shame for killing your first love. It was even easier than he expected."

Only one name came to mind, one person who had so much influence with Tox's brother, with DOD officials.

"Barry Attaway."

# 52

## — VALLEY OF ELAH —

Drums beat the steady cadence of war.

"Finally," Igor muttered, a dark gleam in his eyes. Her father had ordered the buffoon to stand guard and keep her out of the way.

Arms folded, Tzivia watched as the "armies" drew into formation in preparation for the mock battle. Feeling powerless, she eyed those who'd donned mantles and long tunics for the reenactment. Familiarity wreathed several faces. She twitched, recognizing a couple of the people she'd worked a dig with. *Hebrew*, she thought.

Well, of course. They were in Israel.

But then she noticed their hands. They weren't simply holding swords. The blades were tied to their hands.

Tzivia straightened, pacing the length of the hill, verifying what she'd detected. This didn't make sense. Why were they . . . ? Her gaze skipped across the road to the Philistine ranks and then hit the generator used for lighting and equipment. Its large tanker sat close by. Too close.

"Hey," Igor growled. "What are you doing?"

"Nothing." But something . . .

He smirked. "Are you impressed? You brought the sword together, and now he will start first with punishing their line."

There was only one explanation for that vicious drive—the thirst of steel. Had it so wholly controlled her father? But it was scientific, right? From the strain. It drove men to the brink of madness. And this was truly madness. "He's insane to want to kill everyone."

"Not everyone. Just the blasted Niph'al and the Israelites," Igor said with a nod. "He has it planned."

Understanding dawned—these people weren't actors. They were prisoners. Horrified, she realized the AFO had rounded up their enemy, brought them to this field, and . . .

Tzivia followed Igor's gaze and saw a long, thin band of men forming at the edge of the road. They shifted their stance and lifted—

"No!" She sucked in a breath as she saw the crossbows the first line held. In the early light of dawn, the arrows glittered silver beneath the sun's first kiss. "Dear God, help!"

She had never cried out to God before, but the plea was desperate and earnest now. It wasn't possible to argue against His existence any longer when she'd stood face-to-face with Dr. Cathey reborn. Ameus.

*Do something!* She lurched forward, only to be yanked back by Igor.

"Stay—"

Tzivia caught her balance. Planted her left foot. With a solid side kick, she drove her right heel into his face as she heard the command from downhill to nock arrows.

Igor stumbled, spun. But came up, weapon with him.

"Mark!"

Her ears rang with the next command to the archers. Tzivia landed with her right foot. Hopped, swinging her left around and nailing Igor's head again with a hook kick.

Shouts and shots peppered the morning.

"Draw!"

She ducked, aware others were coming to Igor's aid, but she had to alert someone. Do something. They couldn't kill those—

"Loose!"

Tzivia swung around, breath trapped in her throat as she stared out at the battlefield.

Startlingly blue phosphorous arrows sailed into the predawn skies. Screams and shrieks gave chase to daylight, vanishing beneath the thick cloak of death. Dusk hovered over the rich, green valley, ready to bring the dawn of David's era to rest along the brook. The same brook from which the shepherd David had chosen five smooth stones.

Tzivia crumbled to her knees, stricken. Mortified.

Mute with horror, she watched the people as another wave of arrows struck. Some tried to flee but only crumbled to the ground, writhing. Their screams raked her soul.

* * * *

Cuffed and chained to a cement block east of the battleground, Tox stood helplessly as arrows whistled through the brightening sky. Unable to breathe, realizing hundreds of innocents would die, he yanked against the chains. "Augh! No!"

Futility coursed through him.

Shouts went up, snapping his attention to the field.

A shock went through him as Thefarie, Ameus, and Raoul appeared in the midst of the Israelis, weapons raised. With a thunderous bellow, they wielded their swords, deflected arrows. Some strikes activated the arrow tips and released glittering blue phosphorous across the field. The acidic properties hissed and sizzled on the forced combatants, but it was a far less tragedy than what Yared intended.

Ram broke from a small band of AFO operatives and climbed the hill to their group.

"Stop this," Tox begged, still attempting to break the chains and free himself. "It's murder!"

With furtive words to a soldier on Tox's right, Ram eyed the macabre scene without an ounce of emotion.

"This isn't you!" Tox growled at him. "Where is your conscience? You're a soldier—do something. Protect the weak!"

Ram's green eyes flashed. "Who defines that? Who determines this one is weak, that one strong? Is it muscles or the heart or—"

"When did you become double-minded? You're a warrior. It's in your blood—"

"The *strain* is in my blood!" Ram indicated over his shoulder with a nod. "As it is in each Nizari gathered. A cruel and debilitating curse."

"And you would not will that pain on anyone, yet you stand by while they kill people with those arrows, a similarly cruel death."

"It's much quicker than what I'll suffer."

"You cannot—this—what happened to you?" This was not the same man he'd called friend and brother. And it awakened a new fear in him for Haven. "I swear on every holy thing that if anything happens to Haven . . ." Tox trembled at the thought, out of both horror and fury. "You were my *friend*."

Ram drifted closer, taking in the scene. "It had to end."

"Our friendship or—"

Gunfire strafed the air, and jerked Tox around.

"Sir," someone barked to Ram, "they're in the valley."

Ram pivoted and stared down over the landscape. Tiny bursts of light betrayed the gunfire.

"Ram!" Yared Khalon shouted over the din. "Bring him. It's time!"

A spark came from another location to Tox's eleven. Then another to his nine. The rain of arrows slowed, and Tox realized someone was killing the archers.

His heart tripped at the thought. "Coordinated," he muttered, even as Ram unlocked the chain anchor and drew Tox down into the valley.

The guard with Ram collapsed to the ground, dead, exit wound at the front of his head. Shocked, Tox glanced from the body to Ram, then over his shoulder. Scanned the blue-black shadows not yet exposed by dawn.

Hope breathed. They were alive!

*Wraith*.

* * * *

They'd snuck into position hours ago after barely evading the attack that wiped away the face of the mountain in Latvia. It had been close. Too close. But they were alive. That was what mattered.

Leif had been through a lot of things, but this took the cake *and* the ice cream. He trained his sights on Tox and Ram. "Eyes on Blue One," he subvocalized from behind a barrier on the hillside. The first shot fired had exposed their position, so they'd deliberately targeted the security around the tents, where their people were being held, then focused on liberating Tox.

"Copy that, Wraith One. Stay eyes-out and keep him alive," Rodriguez ordered from the bird, thirty-three thousand feet up.

"Roger that." Maintaining cover kept Leif's head and life intact. To his three, Maangi chambered another round, sighted an archer, then released another kill shot.

"They're making it easy," Thor muttered about the archers.

"Open season on AFO operators," Leif agreed. Each time an arrow launched, it left a trail that pointed right back to its shooter. He scanned the field again, verified Tox was still only with Ram, then checked the battle. Saw a shadow looming ahead. Zigzag movement. He muttered an oath.

He eased back the trigger. The sonic boom thudded against his chest, the stock smacking his shoulder. The person who'd been trying to gain their position tumbled back down the hillside.

"Archer down," Cell called, spotting for Maangi and Leif.

"Wraith, you have active shooters looking for you," General Rodriguez said. "Stay low and eyes-out."

"A little late," Leif said, targeting another encroaching figure, "but thanks." *Boom!*

"Dudes," Cell grunted through the comms, "what's Ram doing with Tox?"

Silence dropped as they all swung their attention there.

"What the fluff?" Cell growled. "Is Ram . . . did he switch sides?"

"No way," Maangi said. "He's loyal."

"Yeah, but to who?" Leif asked, noting Ram wasn't just *with* Tox, he was steering him. "That's a problem." He tightened up his scope, following as Ram delivered Tox into the middle of the chaos. Right to Nur Abidaoud. "Command . . . ?"

"You have targets, Wraith. Take care of them."

Leif hesitated. If he took a shot and missed . . . *Then don't miss.* Another round. "One less AFO."

Realigning his sights and targeting another archer, he noticed something in the background. He shifted his sight marginally. Fifty yards past the archers stood a huddle of people who were joined by Ram and Tox. At the center of the chaos, Nur and another guy.

Was he reading this right? It seemed Abidaoud looked to the shorter guy for direction. They drew Tox to the center, and as if on cue, crowds filled in around them, leaving an open swath in the middle. Ram broke from the group and positioned himself a few yards in front of Tox.

"Command, you seeing this?" Nausea swirled in Leif's gut. "This looks like a battle of champions."

* * * *

"You like quotes, do you not, Mr. Russell?" Nur asked, smirking. "How about, 'the tree of liberty must be refreshed from time to time with the blood of patriots and tyrants'?"

*This* wasn't what Thomas Jefferson had meant. Grinding his teeth, Tox forced his gaze to Nur. "'I would prefer even to fail with honor than to win by cheating.'"

Confused glances bounced among the group around him.

"Sophocles," Tox said. "Want me to explain what honor means?"

Nur laughed, but Ram's father motioned to someone. "Zoryana, Barry, the weapons please."

Tox startled at the last name. Then he saw the squirrelly form of Barry Attaway stalk forward with a long, thin wooden box in his arms. "You—"

"Tox." Barry curled his lip. "It's so good not to have to pretend anymore that I like you or your brother."

"Feeling's mutual," Tox snarled. "Then again, I never did *pretend* to like you. I knew what you were when you bought my silence."

"Much easier than I'd expected."

"What about Brooke? How can you justify killing her?"

"It was me or her."

"You selfish—" His fist was faster than his words. It connected violently with Barry's nose.

"Augh!" The traitor staggered, cupping his spurting nose.

Guards hauled Tox back a few steps, but he felt the immense pleasure of that punch. Of seeing Barry bleed. "That won't be the only blood you spill before this is over, Barry."

"Get on with it," Yared snapped.

Rage tremored through Tox as the sniveling Barry presented Ram with the box.

The woman Zoryana came to Tox and held out a similar box, then lifted the lid. A sword stretched elegantly along a satin premolded form. His gaze hit Ram, who drew out a reassembled Adama Herev.

Holy crap. Dueling? They intended a duel for Tox and his best friend. To fight Ram. "Are you kidding me? We're soldiers, not knights!"

"Both are warriors, and this day and method are critical to the liberation of our bloodline," Yared said.

"I'm not doing this. *We're* not doing this." Tox glanced at Ram, who rolled his shoulders, readying himself. Hot dread exploded through Tox's veins. "Ram." He tried to shove away the fear. "Don't do this. Please."

Ram simply stepped away from Attaway and shifted to the side, swiping the sword through the air. It seared and screamed with his swift moves. When had he learned swordplay?

"I will not fight you," Tox said, refusing to accept his friend was so far gone. Refusing to believe his brother-in-arms would cut him down.

"Then you will die," Yared Khalon pronounced. "Which serves all of us quite well."

Tox's gaze caught on the scrollwork that wrapped Ram's fingers and knuckles. He saw the ampoule. "Thefarie trusted you to do the right thing."

Finally, Ram met his gaze.

"Brother . . ." Tox said, unable to think of anything that would convince him. Anything that would be more than delay tactics. He would delay until eternity if possible.

"Champions, take your mark!"

# 53

— VALLEY OF ELAH —

Distraction killed. And this time, Tzivia really hoped it did. The entirety of the valley's participants—those who were still alive and not engaged in combat—stood around Ram and Tox. She could do nothing for them. But maybe she could help Haven and the others.

Slipping out of the crowd, she skirted the perimeter, then darted past the enormous generator truck that fueled the thousand-watt lights shining on the battle of champions. After one more glance at the two men who were her brothers, she took off again—and her foot slipped. With a strangled yelp, she caught herself on the large steel bumper of the truck, only to note a smell emanating around her.

She took a step—*squish*! She lifted her foot, then put it back down in another sluice of sodden earth. Sniffing.

Her gaze jumped to the large tanker, traced its rounded hull, and froze. A hole from a bullet gaped in its side. Petroleum slushed onto the ground, saturating the earth.

Panic welled. She stood in a sea of gasoline on a field where AFO archers were loosing phosphorous arrows.

*I'll go up in a ball of fiery glory.*

No. Not if she could help it. Careful of her steps, Tzivia moved as fast as possible without slipping. She grew more confident when she no longer heard the squish of her steps. Halfway up the hill, she started running, eyes on the tent where Haven and Chiji were held.

A dozen paces, and she'd clear it. Getting caught put them in danger. And Tox would never forgive her. Of course, none of them would anyway. She'd abandoned them, lied to them—all for a father who had not fled for his life but for his own selfish gain. So he could slaughter people.

*And I helped him reassemble the sword.*

Shaking her head, Tzivia aimed for the tent opening.

A large shape blurred to her left. She planted a foot, ready to spar.

*Thud!* He landed at her feet a second before she registered the splat of warmth across her face.

Someone had shot him.

*Don't look a gift horse in the mouth!* She darted into the tent.

Haven turned, and her eyes widened.

Chiji loomed faithfully beside his charge. "Behind you," he warned.

But Tzivia had felt the guard. She stepped back, skimmed a glance, and drove her elbow into his face. The *crack* resounded through the tent, but she wouldn't trust that to stop him. She pivoted and threw a hard right at his face.

He caught it, but she flipped his grip. Violently, she twisted his arm behind him, around, and up his spine. Another *crack*, this one of tendon and bone separating, made him howl. In control of him, she slammed a palm heel strike into his face. He dropped backward, unconscious. Maybe dead.

Quickly, she searched for the keys to the cage and yanked them off his belt loop, tearing it. At the cage, she rammed the key into the slot. Tzivia flung open the gate and stepped back. Her periphery warned her of another guard.

Launching into a jump-spin hook kick, she saw the face too late and let out a strangled cry.

The man ducked.

She landed awkwardly, sucking in a breath.

"Lamb," he said.

"Omar!" Not caring about the emotional display, Tzivia threw herself at him. Tightened her arms around his neck, strangling him.

Wanting to get as close as possible, but it wasn't enough. "I'm sorry. I'm sorry. I'm so sorry."

His burly arms encircled her frame. "You are well." His voice rumbled through his chest and hers. "That is what matters."

"You came for me."

"Of course." He held her at arm's length. "We must go. Our teams are nearby. Come."

Making sure Haven and Chiji were with them, Tzivia followed him into the shadows. They trod across the ridge, scurrying behind tents and vehicles, to make their way to the southern edge of the valley.

Haven drew in a sharp breath.

Tzivia glanced back. Saw Haven's stricken expression, her gaze glued to something in the distance. There could be only one thing that caught her attention so wholly. "We have to go," Tzivia urged.

"Cole," Haven choked out.

Head down, shoulders sagging, Chiji wrapped an arm around her. "Ngozi, you must get—"

A guard fell upon them. Even as Chiji shoved Haven toward Tzivia with an order to go, he hefted a stick—Where had he gotten that?—and cracked it against the skull of the guard. The man stumbled but raised a weapon.

Elegant and lethal, Chiji was a flurry of strikes and moves, steadily, ferociously advancing. Several cracks—bones? hits?—sounded, but he never slowed. Not until the man lay in a heap.

Only when fierce, intense eyes met hers did Tzivia realize she hadn't moved. "You have to teach me that," she breathed.

"Someday." Chiji moved determinedly toward Haven and guided her away.

Omar loped across the field and delivered them safely to where his men and Wraith were protected but engaged—at a distance—against AFO fighters.

"Look," one of the guys said, pointing to the field. "Who are they?"

At the sight, a swell of pride bloomed in Tzivia.

Dr. Cathey—Ameus—fought with his brother-knights, protecting the remnant of the Israelis, who were fleeing the battlefield. Their white mantles were mottled with blood, their faces carved with ferocity as they drove toward the battle of champions.

* * * *

"Ram," Tox said miserably, deflecting yet another strike. "Stop," he hissed.

Thrusting, Ram drew in close. "I am no Gulat," he whispered.

Tox frowned, glancing at his eyes, trying to read—was Ram telling him something?

The Adama Herev sliced through the space between them. Tox leapt away, arching his spine to avoid the tip of the ancient sword.

*He's just distracting me. Focus.*

Sword in both hands, he assumed a sparring stance. He had no idea if this was right, if this was how swordsmen readied themselves, but it centered him. Helped him focus.

With fluid grace, Ram advanced. Attacked. "No Brutus."

Tox parried, ignoring the words. Watching the steel.

"No Benedict." Ram's breath was as hot and searing as the blade, which trailed a fiery line across Tox's side, from near his belly button to just below his arm.

"Augh!" Tox hissed, holding the worst of the cut, blood trickling over his fingers. For one who said he wasn't a betrayer, Ram was excelling at it. What was he doing, then?

"C'mon!" Ram growled. "Lift your sword, coward. Strike!"

"That's right," Yared shouted. "There is no honor in killing a weakling, but it can free us all the same."

Something shifted in Ram's gaze. Gritting through the pain helped Tox study his friend. Think through his words. No—names. They were all na—

Ram lunged.

Tox yanked up his sword. Steel clanged. Sang as they scraped lengths.

Ram elbowed Tox in the back. Made him stumble, nearly falling to his knees. He came up, his gaze dragging along the crowd, which now included Thefarie and his brother-knights. All three nodded as they moved. Spread out. What were they doing?

Again, Ram came at him. Deflecting the blade, Tox launched into his friend's gut. Felt the swords rattle loose and fall to the ground. Hand-to-hand combat was his preferred method. He threw a punch. Nailed a right hook in Ram's side.

His friend howled.

The primal sound pitched Tox back, as he realized what he'd done. Who he'd struck. No. No, he wasn't doing this. He stepped away and reached for his sword. He took another step back. "No more, Ram. I won't—"

"No!" howled someone from the side.

Tox jerked his gaze to the source—Yared. His face a fright, eyes wide. Mouth agape. Shaking his head. What—?

Ram leapt to his feet with his sword. Glanced at the blade. And a strange, surreal smile broke through his tortured expression.

Tox lifted his sword in both hands, all too aware he was weak. Bleeding. Injured. His grip slipping because of the blood.

"You know me," Ram said with a greedy gleam. He eyed Tox's sword.

Something happened right there. Tox wasn't sure what—but then he was. In the heartbeat in which his brain registered that he'd accidentally picked up the wrong sword, that he now held the Adama Herev, he heard Ram's howl.

His friend threw himself forward.

Instinct tensed Tox's grip. He realized Ram's sword was uplifted. His abdomen exposed. Screams tore through the crowd.

Ram drove himself at Tox.

Straight into the ancient blade. Bone grated against steel, flesh surrendering.

A gurgling breath reached Tox's ears as Ram jerked back violently, freeing himself. Then he stumbled forward and slumped against Tox, shoulders colliding. Blood slipped down his lip. A fountain of sticky warmth soaked into Tox. "No!"

Weary, relieved eyes met Tox's. "Forgive me," Ram breathed, "brother."

"Ram," Tox choked, peripherally aware that chaos had broken out around him. "Medic!" he screamed, catching Ram. Supporting him. More blood spilled over his hand—his friend's blood. Ram had driven his body onto the blade. Why? Why would he do this? "No. No no no."

A roar came from behind—Yared. "No! You fool, Ram. You've re-cursed us for another thousand years." Blazing eyes turned to Tox. "Kill Russell!"

Nur charged them.

In a lethal blur, Thefarie manifested. With screaming steel, he delivered a deadly blow, severing Nur from this life.

"I could not," Ram said with a staggered, weak breath that drew Tox's gaze back to his friend, "let him win. Could not . . . betray."

Thefarie turned and touched Ram's shoulder. "Well done." He retrieved the Adama Herev, glanced at Tox with an apologetic expression, then strode away.

*Boom! Boom!*

Tox shifted, clutching at Ram, who sagged further against him. "Help!" He glanced back, startled to see the generator tanker engulfed in fire, pitching flames twenty or more feet in the air.

There he saw the outline of Thefarie. Striding purposely, AFO operators chasing him, straight into the raging inferno with the Adama Herev.

Maangi sprinted toward Tox with two others. They took Ram and laid him on his side. Tox staggered back, hands covered in blood, in death. He dropped to a knee, unable to bear the burden. Unable to forgive himself. Unable to believe. Ram was dying. Would die. He could not survive that wound.

On all fours, Tox moved to his friend. Touched his head. "Why?" he cried miserably.

Ram brought heavy eyes to his. "It had to end."

He heard a strangled cry and realized it was his. Shaking his head from side to side, fighting the sqaull of grief, Tox dropped to his elbows. Tears blurred his vision. Angrily he growled at them, because they blocked his sight of his friend. "Brother," he choked out.

"'I will not fail . . .'" Ram coughed.

Strangling the tears did no good. They poured out, hot and angry. Tox picked up the line of the Special Forces creed Ram had begun.

"'Those with whom I serve. I will not bring shame upon myself or Special Forces.'"

Wincing at the pain and blood pulsing from him, Ram gave a strange smile. "No . . . shame . . ." His gaze grew distant. Empty.

"Ram!" Tox shouted. "Ram, no! Stay with me!"

One of the medics with Maangi cursed. Shook his head. The three of them shifted on their haunches, fists to their mouths, as if they could not fight the terror of seeing a brother die on the battlefield.

A cry of rage went up.

Tox looked up, seeing two things at once—Maangi's holstered Glock, and Yared Khalon rushing them with a dagger. Tox came to his feet, snatched the Glock, and brought the weapon to bear. Fired twice into the chest of the man who, by using him as a pawn, had murdered his own son.

Yared stumbled, shocked. Slumped to the ground and breathed his last. Near him lay Nur Abidaoud, a gaping hole in his chest. He lay strewn over the bodies of Barry Attaway and the woman, Zoryana. Most of those who had stood with Yared and Nur now slept eternally with them, the work of the brother-knights.

"You wanted freedom from that curse?" Tox growled. "Done."

# 54

— ISRAEL —

This was not how he'd imagined the battle ending.

Bent forward in a metal folding chair, Tox stared at the ground hours later. Though he'd scrubbed his hands, he still saw the blood. Saw Ram's life spilling out before him. He sat in a field command tent with Rodriguez, Wraith, and Israeli intelligence. Haven and Chiji flanked him but afforded him the space to work through this. It would take months, if not years, but right now he felt ready to lose it.

"Tox," Rodriguez said from a table where the Israelis were huddled over some military-grade laptops. "I think you'll want to see this."

He didn't. Not really. He didn't want to see anything except Ram's face again. Still, he dragged himself to his feet and crossed the tent. Let his gaze hit the screen. Black and white. Satellite imaging.

"What is that?" Runt asked.

"Inbound missile camera."

"Target?" Tox heard himself ask.

"Mattin Worldwide," Rodriguez said. "With Mercy's code and virus, working in conjunction with Wallace, we determined the code they used to track down their victims originated there."

Tox lifted his head and drew in a breath, watching as the target grew in size and shape as the missile closed in.

"Late at night," Rodriguez added. "Limited casualties, but enough damage that whatever he had developed will be lost."

Omar Kastan turned to Tox. "Nur was stupid enough to keep almost everything in one location. But they had some other sites, and our teams are hitting them now. The AFO no longer exists after this morning."

Tox met the Mossad agent's dark eyes. "Thank you."

"It wasn't just for you. He was one of my men, too." Omar looked over Tox's shoulder. "And I had hoped he'd be my brother."

Tzivia slipped through the crowd and tucked herself against the Mossad director's side.

Turning away from the screen, from the sea of death, Tox saw Haven. Took her into his arms. Held her. Closed his eyes and this book on the war against the AFO.

# EPILOGUE

**— OUTSIDE JERUSALEM —**

Tzivia stared out the window, the sunrise now and forever a reminder of the moment her brother sacrificed his life. She wrapped her arms around herself, throat raw as fresh memories sailed over her. Watching her brother die, even from a distance, and seeing him struggle for breath, to assure Tox that he hadn't betrayed them—it had nearly killed her.

Though she was still alive, she was determined to make sure the Tzivia who'd played a hand in that fateful battle was no longer the Tzivia living and breathing today.

"Breakfast is ready," Omar called from behind her.

She pivoted and smiled, shaking her head at the sight of him. Bare-chested but wearing an apron, he held two plates of shakshuka.

Tzivia teared up, biting back tears. It was Ram's favorite.

He slid one toward her.

Wiping away the tear, she accepted it. "Delicious."

"Me or the food?"

Smiling at him, she folded herself onto a chair and left him wondering. Lifting a fork, she looked at the plate. And froze. "What is that?"

Omar sat down with his food and shrugged. "A ring."

"I know it's a ring, but—"

"I didn't want you to forget the vows we took."

"How would I forget?"

"You can be pretty forgetful. Like that time you forgot to tell me where you were going and ended up in Moscow." He winked and stabbed his fork into the eggs.

"I was so selfish."

"Yes, you were," he said with a rumble of laughter. He set aside the fork and plucked the ring from the bread twist he'd threaded through it. "But I love you, Tzivia. And I do see the change. Just make sure you are true to yourself." He held her hand and slid on the ring. "Now you're mine."

"I'm sorry, I didn't see a certificate of ownership."

"Sure you did," Omar said, stuffing shakshuka into his mouth. "It's called a marriage license!"

* * * *

**— A MONTH LATER**
**— NORTHERN VIRGINIA —**

The surgical scars to reverse Tox's transformation were healing, but the loss of Ram never would. The pain might lessen, but he prayed it never faded. They'd buried Ram in Israel, and shortly after, Tzivia and Omar made things official. Other wounds were more tender. But he and Haven were putting that behind them. All of it. The sword. The crown. The *miktereths*. The team.

Having stepped down as team commander, he was determined to focus on building a life and family with Haven. First step was this house. He stood in the empty living room, looking around.

Domesticated. He grunted. *Never thought it would happen.*

"What is the point of saying between eight and two," Haven growled as she stomped across the wood floors with VVolt's nails clicking behind her, "if they show up at *four*?"

He smiled, taking in her round belly, her beauty. "To rile you."

She stopped and gaped at him. "And the point of that?"

"So I could see how beautiful you are when you're ticked."

"Well, you're about to get a full dose if you don't stop getting so excited over my anger."

Three long strides carried him to her. He caught her shoulders. Pulled her back against his chest, then slid his hands around her belly, feeling the swell of life there. Kissed her temple. Her cheek. That spot that drove her crazy below her ear.

"No," she said with a giggle, "you aren't getting away with that this time."

"This isn't about you," he said, coming around in front of her and dropping to a knee. He cupped the baby bump and kissed it. "I need to talk to my son."

"If it's your daughter in there, you just ticked her off, too."

He grinned up at Haven. Marveling. Amazed. As he came to his feet, he cradled her face in his hands. "If it's a boy, I think we should name him Ram."

Emotion danced through her eyes. "Absolutely. How about Charlotte Elisabeth if it's a girl?"

"I have one Charlotte in my life, and she's plenty."

Haven laughed.

Tox sighed. "I still can't believe—"

The doorbell rang.

"About time," Haven said, pulling away and stalking to the door. She flung it open and stopped short.

"Surprise!" a chorus of voices sang out as bodies, one after another, flooded into their mostly empty home.

Thor and Maangi brought in folding tables and chairs. Thor's wife, Steffani, pushed a stroller that carried not only their newborn daughter, Justice, but several bags of food in the bottom. Toting a drink cooler, Runt sauntered in with a grin. Behind him, Cell led a demure Mercy Maddox, who'd lost a lot of her spunk and spitfire since Ram's death.

"Hope you don't mind me crashing this," she said around a wan smile.

"Can't crash somewhere you belong." Tox squeezed her shoulders. "You doing okay?"

"No." She nodded, then shook her head. "He's not . . . I can't . . ."

Tox nodded. "Yeah."

"This party starting or what?" Maangi asked.

Tox scowled. "What party?"

"A party," Maangi said, "for your birthday, which we never got to celebrate."

"And a reception," Tzivia said, coming in after the others and giving Tox a playful slap, "for the wedding we never got to attend."

"And a gender reveal," Haven announced.

The voices died down.

Tox thought his heart did, too. "You know?"

"Of course not," Haven said with a mischievous grin. "I told you we'd do it together, so"—she motioned to the team—"we're doing it together." She held up a finger. "Wait right there."

"You know, it's a good thing you married her, or I would have," Cell said.

"You want to be punched?" Tox lifted an eyebrow.

"Not today, thank you. I have a date."

"You mean, you brought a friend along for a bash at your team leader's house," Mercy corrected.

"Yeah, that. Look at the food!"

The doorbell rang again, and Tox considered his team. Heart full, he answered the door and laughed. "I should've known she was up to something." He pulled his mom into a hug and shook his father's hand. Welcoming the Linwoods was a little more awkward but still genuine. "Come in."

"I just want to know what my grandchild is," his mom said as she stepped into the empty living room and peered across it. "Oh, a baby!" She was there in a second, asking to hold baby Justice.

His father met Chiji at the door, and the two fell into tense dialogue.

"Here we are," Haven said as she hoisted up some colorful papier-mâché thing. "Okay, outside. The gift-shop lady said this would make a mess. So we're not doing this in my new home." She waved everyone out and stood on the freshly sodded grass.

Tox finally got a good look at the object she held. "Is that a grenade?"

"Appropriate, don't you think, considering the bomb dropped on you about this baby?" Haven grinned, rubbing her belly. She handed the grenade to him. "You have the honors."

"What do I do with it?" he asked, turning it over. "There's no pin."

Haven laughed. "You slam it on the ground." She eyed her mom. "Videoing?"

"Of course," Mrs. Linwood said.

Tox had to admit he liked this. Liked her in their home. Liked his friends gathered. His parents. With a shrug, he raised the paper grenade above his head. Glanced at Haven and slammed it to the ground.

Blue powder puffed into the air, filtering across the small lawn with vigor.

Tox shoved both fists in the air. "Yes! A son!"

# ACKNOWLEDGMENTS

Of course, many thanks to the real Dr. Joseph Cathey, who allowed me to use his identity in the creation of the fictional Dr. Cathey. Thanks, Joe, for your inspiration, long chats, and brainstorming. You have an incredible mind and heart!

Special thanks also to Ian McNear and Elizabeth Maddrey, PhD, for your technical help with coding and its intricacies to make the fictional *Blood Genesis* game legit.

Thank you to my Rapid-Fire Task Force, a team of amazing readers and reviewers, who have been a tremendous help to me: Rel Mollet, Emilie Hendryx, Mikal Hermanns, Heather Lammers, Jamie Lapeyrolerie, Lydia Mazei, Brittany McEuen, Elizabeth Olmedo, Sarah Penner, and Steffani Webb.

And 100,000 thank-yous to my publishing team at Bethany House. My editors, Dave Long and Jessica Barnes, who have been so amazing in helping hone this story into the incredible read that you are holding today—even inspiring me to kill off one character and save another (plotting murders by moonlight . . .). And the marketing and publicity team, who are ever-gracious and so wise in this quickly changing environment. I'm so grateful for each of you!

**Ronie Kendig** is a bestselling, award-winning author of over twenty novels. She grew up an Army brat, and now she and her hunky hero are adventuring on the East Coast with their grown children and a retired military working dog, VVolt N629. Ronie's degree in psychology has helped her pen novels with intense, raw characters. Visit Ronie online at www.roniekendig.com.

# Sign Up for Ronie's Newsletter!

Keep up to date with Ronie's new book releases and events by signing up for her email list at roniekendig.com.

# More from Ronie Kendig!

When an archaeological dig unleashes an ancient virus, paramilitary operative "Tox" Russell is forced back into action. With the help of archaeologist Tzivia Khalon and FBI agent Kasey Cortes, Tox races to stop a pandemic, even as a secret society counters his every move.

*Conspiracy of Silence*
The Tox Files #1

# You May Also Enjoy . . .

Private Investigator Kate Maxwell never stopped loving Luke Gallagher after he disappeared. Now he's back, and together they must unravel a twisting thread of secrets, lies, and betrayal while on the brink of a biological disaster that will shake America to its core. Will they and their love survive, or will Luke and Kate become the terrorist's next target?

*Dead Drift* by Dani Pettrey
Chesapeake Valor #4
danipettrey.com

Annalise knows painful memories hover beneath the pleasant façade of Gossamer Grove. But she is shocked when she inherits documents that reveal mysterious murders from a century ago. In this dual-time romantic suspense novel, two women, separated by a hundred years, must uncover the secrets within the borders of their town before it's too late.

*The Reckoning at Gossamer Pond* by Jaime Jo Wright
jaimewrightbooks.com

U.S. Marshal Casey Quinn is tasked with escorting a reporter to testify before a grand jury regarding a missing environmentalist. At first, the assignment seems routine. But when it becomes dangerously clear that there's more to the story than anyone knows, Casey and two other marshals—one a man from her past—will have to do whatever it takes to survive.

*Blind Betrayal* by Nancy Mehl
Defenders of Justice #3
nancymehl.com

BethanyHouse